D1382126

TRUST

TRUST

RITA DALLAS

Matador
Unit E2 Airfield Business Park,
Harrison Road, Market Harborough,
Leicestershire. LE16 7UL
Tel: 0116 279 2299
Email: books@troubador.co.uk
Web: www.troubador.co.uk/matador
Twitter: @matadorbooks

ISBN 978 1 80313 296 9

British Library Cataloguing in Publication Data.
A catalogue record for this book is available from the British Library.

Printed and bound in Great Britain by 4edge Limited
Typeset in 11pt Adobe Garamond Pro by Troubador Publishing Ltd, Leicester, UK

Matador is an imprint of Troubador Publishing Ltd

For
Sarah and Kate
Juliette and Olivia
with love

CHICKSANDS PRIORY, BEDFORDSHIRE

1649

I run my fingers along the back of a sheep. Coat intact, haunches untouched. The dog has fared less well – the proud face slashed in three places, one watchful eye torn and hanging. In the background, two lovers running towards the river have been neatly and cleanly separated with a single sweep of a sword.

When we were children, Robin and I would stand in front of this tapestry and invent stories. The central figure was of great interest then. We would argue over gender. I was sure it was a shepherdess. Robin insisted the muscular legs beneath flowing skirts were those of a man, as confirmed by the likeness to our brother Henry. Now, except for a hand still clutching a staff, the figure no longer exists.

We wander silently through the house. The withdrawing room, once infused with my mother's delicate perfume, bears traces of coarse army tobacco. The hallways, where our dead brothers once ran barefoot and hopscotched on the black and white tiles, now carry the dents and scuff marks of heavy boots and muskets.

The door to my chamber is jammed shut. Robin puts his shoulder to it. Except for the bed, the room has been stripped of furnishing. My *escritoire* and rocker, gone. My little French virginals, a gift from my father, gone. No trace of my paintings and trinkets. A sampler in green and black thread that I'd worked as a child has been torn from the wall and lies dirty and discarded in a corner.

I cannot cry. Save for a tight knot of anger, I am numb. "All will be well, you know," Robin says. We lean against each other. In the space of a day, we've both grown older.

BOOK ONE
COURTSHIP

CHELSEA AND
THE ISLE OF WIGHT

1648

Yesterday, the river flooded. I watched this from the bedroom window of my aunt's house in Chelsea. And even as water gushed through the garden and towards Aunt Gargrave's door, I managed to stand my ground. Watching a great river burst its banks is a humbling experience. And for those of us daunted by the elements, it takes courage. Also, patience. You may wait for hours as the water gradually seeps into the fields, lapping through the reeds, testing its strength before receding back into an angry, restless flow. Then, just as you are about to turn away, thankful that, after all, nature is no stronger than man, it happens. With one mighty roar, the river is over its boundaries, sweeping up all that stands in its way – claiming the fields and beyond.

I thought, this at least is a God-given calamity and not one we've wrought on ourselves. And for a moment I prayed God might send this great river sweeping through our entire ruined land, cleansing and replenishing it. This morning, the water has subsided, leaving in its wake a thick coat of mud and stinking debris.

I've been awake since 5 am, clad in my travelling gown, my mantle packed within the hour, even though we don't leave until noon. In truth, I slept little last night, my mind wound as tightly as the clock on the dresser. It's not the journey that plays on me. I've been to and fro St Malo many times. But this is a particular day. Today is the twenty-first anniversary of my birth.

From the floors below, I can hear the house stirring. Aunt Gargrave's high, girlish voice drifts up from the kitchens, calling instructions to one of the maids. Even though reduced to just two wenches, my aunt runs her kitchens with all the gusto of a general commanding the King's own army. As I step into the hallway, the smell of freshly baked bread pervades. Exotic perfumes may connect me to my mother – I've only to sense the aroma of lavender and orange water to be transported back to the time she was considered a beauty: reddish brown hair that naturally curled; soft, sparkling eyes; a wide smile – but I will always associate her sister with the comforting smell of warm bread.

As I pass, I see the door to my mother's chamber is open and I can hear her painful, laboured breathing. I know from her persistent coughing in the night, she did not enjoy a peaceful sleep. The room is still in darkness – and I am full of guilt for the relief I feel.

Down in the kitchens, all is activity. Though first to rise, I am obviously last to descend. My aunt, pristine in morning gown and cap, is conducting the transference of bread from oven to table. Even though this is a daily ritual, both wenches are nervous as they lift the heavy tray of steaming loaves onto racks and across to the table to cool. One has a limp, and her sister bears most of the load. Things are not made easier by my aunt's scolding. "Not so close to the table edge. Do you want the dogs to get them? It will be a sorry day for you if they do!"

Jane is also abroad, leaning her weight against a trunk, breathless and laughing as Noah struggles to close it. And my brother Robin, sitting by the hearth, conducts his own campaign. "You will need to sit on the thing, Jane, whilst Noah fastens it. Why on earth must we carry so much?" Robin himself is engaged in nothing more strenuous than cradling a mug of ale, one of his treasured pamphlets across his knee. My brother has the largest collection of political pamphlets of any I know – but I've yet to see him read one through. I fear for all his enthusiasm, Robin lacks patience for such an exercise.

Aunt Gargrave's greeting is terse: "An ill day for a journey, Dorothy." She thinks the road from here to Yarmouth may well be unpassable. And there are more evils than mud to grieve my aunt. Less than a week ago, not a mile from her door, two men dragged from their carriage. The coachman slaughtered – his throat cut; the horses bolted; the coach overturned into a ditch. "Noah, be sure to watch the trunks at the posting stations." It is plain from the stiffening of Noah's bent shoulders that he is offended by this implied neglect of duty. Aunt Gargrave sees it too. "I only mention it since they say Cromwell's men be still desperate for anything that might be melted."

Robin says in that case we'd best keep Jane well hid. "She'd make a tasty morsel once melted."

Aunt Gargrave ignores this, and Jane pretends to. Though by the colour in her cheeks, I see she's still not used to my brother's bantering. I shall speak to him. Having finally got the first trunk to close, Jane concentrates on her careful folding. Breeches, two undershirts, one doublet, four tins of baccy. She thinks my father could have got the last with ease at St Malo. I tell her he finds French baccy too strong. "You'd not begrudge him his taste of England, Jane?" Jane earnestly declares she'd walk the whole of England and France too, to bring that good man his wishes. And with pain in my heart, I glimpse my father as he once was – gigantic and joyful, waiting to greet us at the port in Guernsey. I am resolute, though: for this one day I'll not dwell on the past.

Noah must open the trunk again, and with only the merest sigh, does so. "The yellow gown, Dorothy." Aunt Gargrave takes it out and holds it against me. "Not your just fit, but it might suffice. It will do well when you dine with the Dingleys. Robin, be sure to send your card soon as you fetch up in Newport." Robin glances at me and shrugs – a gesture not lost on our aunt. "Come now," she says, "you've surely heard me speak of the Dingleys?" It seems they are relatives, albeit not close. "I have made enquiries and they are well set on the Isle of Wight, with a deal of land and influence. They would think it ill indeed if you failed to call." And she adds, as if an afterthought: "Methinks there are two sons and a daughter." I daren't look at Robin for fear we both laugh. But at this moment, when nothing may ever again be as it was, I've a sudden rush of feeling for this small, determined woman who has seen so much to dispirit her, yet continues to bake her bread – and would grasp our lives and knead them into a whole again. The yellow gown is carefully folded back into the trunk.

" I will wear it to the Dingleys'," I promise. We make both trunks ready, and after much heaving, drag them into the hall.

When the bread is finally cool, it is set with some cheese and leftover ham and we make a good meal. My birthday is toasted with a flask of ale brought in from the yard by Noah. "Now, Noah," my aunt tells him, "you must eat with the rest of us. I would not have you grow faint on the road." And Noah heaves his creaking bones down on the bench next to me. But I cannot persuade him to take more than a few morsels of ham. Noah is stubborn as a mule. He has served our family since before I was born, and despite his advanced age and our altered circumstances, he prefers to stand and serve rather than sit and eat.

My aunt's words remind Jane of her own tendency for faintness on the road, and she bids me be sure to keep the Sal Volatile close by. I wonder again that such a sturdy island girl, one who has no trouble keeping upright on the deck of a heaving boat, and despite the lashing waves, will deftly net the most slippery creature in God's ocean, can be brought to straits by the rocking of a coach.

"'Tis said a great number of pigs in the field were swept away." Aunt Gargrave's mind is full of yesterday's flood. "What a squealing they must have made." It seems the herdsmen waded in after them, and did manage to cling onto a few slippery bodies and take them to higher ground. It's not hard to imagine the thoughts of those men: just one more misfortune in the face of all lately endured.

My aunt has more news. "'Tis said folk in Putney village had to climb from their windows, so high was the tide."

Jane, with her warm heart for God's creatures, is more concerned with the fate of the pigs: "'Tis a shame pigs can't swim, else the poor pink things might have saved themselves by climbing back through them windows."

And Robin declares Jane better than any church minister when it comes to solving God-given problems. "Think, Jane, the good people of Putney could be eating roast pork from now till Yuletide!" Despite herself, Jane is the one who laughs most.

When the bread is removed and a big bowl of apples and sweetmeats set before us, Aunt Gargrave turns her attention to my brother, pointing out, with her customary bluntness, the weight of responsibility he is about to assume. "Now, Robin, you are in full charge and on no account must there be... adventures." She says this last quietly but with emphasis. And Robin, feigning bewildered innocence, kicks my foot beneath the table.

"Don't fret, Aunt. I am your man. The girls shan't take one step lest I am at their side. I am seriously considering locking them in a room on the Isle of Wight till the boat sets sail for France." He takes a bite of his apple. "Except of course when we sup with... what was their name again?"

Our aunt is not to be diverted. "I am not one bit at ease with this arrangement, and if times did not demand it, I would never sanction such an outing. As it must be, you, Robin are charged with the absolute well-being of your sister and her companion until they are safe with your father at St Malo. And I will have your word, sir, there shall be no foolhardiness."

This is the first time any of us have ventured abroad without the watchful eye of a weighty relative. I look across at Jane, *my companion,* as Aunt Gargrave is pleased to call her. Plump and pretty, Jane is more in need of a chaperone than most. And Robin is close to my heart, but even I recognise his headstrong nature. This journey, I think, will be in my keeping. Though perhaps I do Jane a disservice. When she first came to us at St Malo, she travelled alone at night on the boat from Guernsey. Later, she told how she'd refused all pleas to go below and had stood on the deck the entire journey, even though the wind whipped her and tore the pins from her hair. *I was determined to get that first glimpse of France, and woe betide any that tried to stop me.* Would that I had such strong spirit. As it is, the minute I set foot on a boat I am anxious to scuttle below, where with a deal of ale I am sometimes able to calm my irrational fears.

The meal over, Robin announces he must make a short outing. This does not sit well with our party. Aunt Gargrave reminds him the coach must leave on time if we are to reach Yarmouth before dark. Before she can finish her long list of likely mishaps, Robin is out the door. With only the slightest narrowing of her eyes and barely a pause, my aunt turns to Jane. "Cromwell's men be no respecter of women." Two, it seems, were taken from their coach at Richmond and not been seen since. This, I think, is the moment to absent myself and bid farewell to my mother.

The curtains of her chamber are drawn back and I see she is awake, her face as pale as the pillow she rests against. I sit beside her, and taking her hand, place it next to my cheek. My mother runs her finger soft along the side of my face. She says my countenance is always sad. She says the air in St Malo is almost as pure as at home. But in truth there's no salt in the air at Chicksands, and the breezes are less rough. I cannot tell her how I long for home. None of us have set foot in Chicksands for nigh on two years. It's something we seldom mention. To do so might let loose a flood more powerful than any the great river could unleash.

Dearest, sweetest mother. You are so weak. Promise me, faithfully, to gather your strength. Robin and I will go to our father, but I fear we shall not meet his needs.

I say none of this. What I say is: "I am glad to leave you so improved. Father will be awaiting this news. Now, you must rest and ready yourself, for you will soon make this same journey." It's the first time, as I recall, I have deliberately spoke false to my mother.

When my father, as the King's Governor for the Isle of Guernsey, was forced to hold siege in Castle Cornet for five long years – every one of them paid for by himself – my mother never wavered. She pleaded at Court; begged from relatives and friends; sold the last of her plate. The money never reached the island. My mother's strength has always been for her family. Once she saw events were beyond her, so the blood thinned in her veins. My father wrote to her: '*The men and I now have nothing to eat save one biscuit a day and porridge at night*'. Even when he was safe at her side in St Malo, my mother couldn't forget those desperate words. For days, she lay listless in her chamber. When we finally brought her back to England, she could barely walk.

Now, exhausted, she closes her eyes. "The box, Dorothy. On the table next to me. It was always my intention to give it you on this day." I take the small velvet box and bend to kiss my mother. She puts her mouth close to my ear. "I have lived to see it is impossible to believe people worse than they really are. And so will you." Despite myself, I pull away.

The baggage is checked and accounted for and safely aboard. There is no sign of Robin. Noah is up on post and Jane and I already seated when he finally comes running across the fields and flings himself in beside us. I lean out of the coach and reaching for Aunt Gargrave's hand, reassure her all will be well. She is still chiding as we pull away, her words lost on the wind and rain.

"Where were you?" I ask Robin. As he tells it, he's been saving the King. "No doubt in one of your taverns." I know there is impatience in my voice. And Robin counters those are the only places he can find sober debate.

"I could not stand Aunt Gargrave's prattle one more moment." I say it must be hard to engage in sober debate given the quantity of ale flowing. And I'm startled by the look of anger Robin casts me. "How could that old woman talk of revelry on the Isle of Wight, when it's at that very place His Majesty is so cruelly incarcerated?" I feel my weariness return. I cannot, for the moment, have one of those conversations Robin so favours, where I play adversary even though we are in agreement. I try to find a comfortable position in which to rest my head. As I raise my hand to make a pillow of my hood, I realise I am still clasping the little velvet box. I open it carefully and taking out the delicate miniature inside, find myself gazing on a dark-eyed woman clad in strange apparel. What little can be seen of her hair is also dark, and escaping at the sides from an intricate lace head covering pulled low over her brow. It appears to be tied at the back, with the ends gathered and bunched about her shoulders. Her gown is of grey lace, with a motif of huge black flowers and fashioned in a style I can't place. Everything about her, from the direct challenge of her eyes to her single adornment – a long jet necklace, caught at the throat and then hanging low over her bosom – is foreign to me. I put the miniature back in its box and close my eyes.

Who would have guessed Jane Wright from Guernsey would be attending a grand supper such as even the house in Chelsea couldn't match? I pride myself as a person of sense, but as soon as I stepped into the Dingleys' dining hall, all lit by so many candles, I was a child at the fair. And there's those at home would doubt their eyes to see me at this table, all fine in Miss Dorothy's yellow gown and with my wild hair tamed and curled. I'm happy to stay close by my lady, though. I'm glad enough to study how a gentlewoman conducts herself amid such grandeur. There's plate so fine at this table, candle holders too, that would make Lady Gargrave gasp. I've already lost count of the platters of food, one with a boar's head so large it took four wenches to bear it in. And with so much to taste and see and hear, my head is giddy as the Queen's fool. I can do nothing but stare at the finery of the guests. Especially the ladies, who sport every kind of new fashion, including fans that fold, which I've never before seen – even in London. I wonder with so much snapping and twirling how they manage to eat.

Across from me, Robin is engaged in close discussion with a woman who eats little but is a fair expert with *her* fan, which she keeps close to her face. From what I can see of those dark eyes and fair skin, many might deem her a beauty. Though when she finally lowers that novelty, I see she's not as fair as her preening would suggest. I'm also quick to note that she's disquieted, either from Robin's jesting or from some blunt words he's uttered. And I'm just set thinking how contrary Robin oft is, and how he's almost bound to rub people badly, when he catches my glance and raises one eyebrow in that saucy way he has. I shan't give him the satisfaction. I turn my head and straightway meet the gaze of an old gentleman with ear trumpet seated to my right. When he enquires the pleasure, I have my practised words ready. "My name is Jane Wright. I am seventeen years old…" I get no further when he lowers his earpiece, turns away and talks to someone else. I'm supposing it's my island brogue.

Still, I'm glad to see my good lady less reserved than usual in company and enjoying conversation with the tall gentleman seated on her other hand. In truth, there's so much lively talk at this table, my ears are off in all directions. And not one word, as I can hear, of the Harshness of the Times, or Oliver Cromwell's Torturers, or the King's Just Cause. Then, just as I'm thinking that, after all, things might be right with this world, I hear Miss Dorothy's neighbour make such a forward and ungentlemanly remark, it fair takes my breath. First, I hear him ask if she likes cherries, and that he's thinking of growing them in England. Straight – as always – Miss Dorothy replies she understands cherries need constant sun, and trying to grow them in our own intemperate climes oft results in sour imitation. I'm just set wondering at the dull conversation gentlefolk indulge in whilst eating their way through magnificent wild boar and drinking the deepest ruby wine, when I hear said gentleman say, quite clearly, "Your lips were made to eat them."

Your lips were made to eat cherries!

I feel my whole face redden. I stare at the scrap of meat on my plate. I daresn't look up. For one long moment, Miss Dorothy is silent. Shocked, I'm supposing, by such a crude remark that even the lads on dockside in Guernsey would be slow to utter in fine company. And then my lady laughs. Something she seldom does. As for me, I'm all confusion. And I'm not much eased to hear her declare cherries should always be eaten in private: "since they tend to play havoc with the senses." And that sets both laughing. Later, I hear the gentleman ask: "Are you the only one here wearing blue?"

And my lady replies: "I am the only one obeying the rules."

And I can make no sense at all of this, since there's no shortage of blue finery at the Dingleys' table. But by now the sweetmeats and fruit are being passed, the most foreign and exotic I ever saw. And I'm so busy choosing and tasting, I pay no more heed to the odd and unseemly remarks rich folk care to make at supper.

Yet again, it seems we must wait on Robin. All made ready to set sail from Newport. Myself and Noah tidy with trunks at dockside, when my lady decides she must off and find her brother. Though Noah doesn't say so, I know by his stony face that like me, he's not best pleased. I wonder again how one person can so disrupt the easy harmony of any given day. I've oft heard my lady say – and with some admiration – that Robin dances to his own music. For myself, I think it better to keep time with others than to strike out and irritate all.

I'm so busy forming some choice words in my mind to deliver to Robin, I fail to notice the three gentlemen approaching. It's only when their glum faces are up close and they're demanding our names that I sense trouble brewing. And there surely is. It seems one of our party was observed using a diamond ring to scratch some low message on a window of the Rose and Crown, which we lately left. Course, I know it's down to Robin. With time to idle, he's sure to use it ill. Now, quick as a flash, we are to be hauled before the Governor! And I know by the rough way Noah and I are bundled back into town and into a big, draughty room, that we are in a pretty pickle.

Miss Dorothy and Robin are already summoned and waiting. I daresn't look at my lady. As for Robin, well, I'm glad to note he's at least pale, and with none of his usual jollity.

"My name is Jane Wright. I am seventeen years old. I was born on the Isle of Guernsey where my father helped Sir Peter Osborne hold Castle Cornet for the King."

An unhappy chance indeed to be using my practised words.

"You must address me as 'Your Honour', Mistress Wright."

"Yes, sir – Your Honour." I've never been before a magistrate. God's will my father shan't hear one word of this.

"Thank you, Mistress Wright." My heart is beating so hard and fast and loud in my ears, I fear the whole room must hear. But I think mine is not the only heart doing its hammer dance. Miss Dorothy is deathly pale and I note her shaky hands. And I know by the small, red patch, where Robin has been scratching his neck, that he too is uneasy – and so should be, since 'tis all down to him. But with arms folded and feet astride, I fear the justice might take this for arrogance.

My heart remains a leap when this justice ask Noah his age. I've often been on the sharp end of Noah's tongue when it comes to prying questions. Still, I'm truly surprised when after some deliberation, Noah admits to fifty-five – younger by far than both my grandfathers. I'm set back too, to hear him declare "widower" when asked his status. Though what matters this to the justice, I can't fathom. Noah is so worn and woven into this family, it's scarce possible to give him a life apart. I look at his big, square face, half covered in grey whiskers, and with eyes so puffy and small, it's hard to tell their colour. Try as I may, I cannot imagine Noah being loved by a woman. Then Noah, nervous no doubt from the grilling, runs his tongue over his lips, which I see are full and red beneath his beard. And just for a moment I can picture that other man. When our inquisition is done, Noah looks fit to drop. I reach out to steady his elbow, but he's his usual testy self and pushes my hand away with such force. Yet again, I chide myself for not learning to conduct things less awkward with folk.

Having bid his man write our every word in a hefty ledger, this justice is in a hurry to be gone. He declares we must wait on the Governor's pleasure, then sweeps out the room with his man scuttling behind and the door banged after them.

It seems we've lost our capacity for speech. The only sounds being Miss Dorothy's shoes as she walks to and fro the wooden floor, and Noah clearing his throat every few seconds. Robin keeps himself apart – over at the window looking down across the port. No doubt watching as our boat sets sail for France.

And so, we wait. And all because of that boy's mischief. For that's what Robin is – a great boy. He has a child's mind, as this latest misadventure is proof. Even though he is five years my senior, I know myself to be Robin's elder – not just in ways of deporting myself, so's not to be thought a fool, but knowing in these bad times, when not to speak too plain, and when, indeed, not to speak at all. And certainly not to write – scratch – shameful words in a public place. A sorry end indeed to our stay in Newport. And I'm glad none at home can see me now, a prisoner waiting to be sentenced. There's some might say it were just reward for getting above my station, for there are those in Guernsey who've never wholly favoured my opportunities.

I'm worrying these thoughts in my head when in comes a group of men. And even though he's shorter than the rest, it's easy to know the Governor by his proud walk and haughty look, and by the way the others pander to him. One man, though, keeps himself apart. And I'm surprised to see that same forward gentleman we met at the Dingleys, whose name I now know to be Mr Temple, and who has lately, and I do believe unbidden, attached himself to our party. Seems, like us, he's destined for France – and from what I've gleaned, a jolly year or two idling in foreign parts. He goes straight to my lady and stands close by her.

And stand we do, even though we've been doing so this past hour. The Governor and his cronies sit, though. Making themselves comfortable around the table and all the time ignoring us and talking amongst themselves. With no boat to catch, they're not to be hurried.

Finally, the Governor looks at us long and cold, before taking up a paper and reading out the words Robin writ. And I know by the gravity of his voice, the Governor has not took kindly to them. "*And Hammon was hanged upon the gallows he'd prepared for Mordecai.* Will it please you to explain yourselves?"

And Robin says, a little too blunt to my mind: "Why, as must be plain to all, it can be found in the scriptures."

I am quick to see this is not the answer the Governor would have. He fixes Robin with a gull's eye and says, "I take it, sir, it is you, then, who committed this act of vandal and slander?"

And of a sudden, I'm reminded of the Governor's name: *Hammond.* But before I can put this together with what Robin writ, cool as you like, Miss Dorothy steps forward and says, before any can interrupt, that it was herself that writ those hasty words, which she now knows "through Your Honour's gentle chiding," to be wholly offending and misjudged. And she drops a deep curtsy. "I hope Your Honour will look kindly on a foolish woman." And this voice don't sound one bit like my good lady, for she too is oft wont to speak too warm for gentlefolks' liking. Indeed, I've sometimes thought this a family trait. But her silky words do seem to have stopped these gloomy proceedings. The Governor looks intently on Miss Dorothy, then goes into a huddle with his minions.

We're all, it seems, at a loss. Robin, shamefaced – no doubt from letting his sister step up for him – stares at his boots. And none looks more astonished at this turn of events than our new acquaintance. Indeed, Mr Temple displays none of the arrogance I witnessed at the Dingleys'. No. He appears quite agitated. He puts his hand out towards my lady, and for one terrible moment I think he's about to clamp it over her mouth, no doubt to stop the flow of incriminating words. But he brings that hand back smartly, and, as if he would prevent it doing mischief, sticks it inside his waistkit. Despite the chill in this room, Mr Temple's brow is damp, and a drop of sweat trickles down from where his hair curls about his face. For no good reason, and despite the seriousness of this moment, I find myself dwelling on that thick, unruly mane, which I do believe may be his own.

Robin and I stand forward on the deck, quiet as we watch Newport and its governor become a speck on the horizon. "Well," I finally say, "that's a nice kettle of fish you cooked us in, and one that almost cost us our journey." I tell Robin 'twas lucky those gentlemen hadn't forgot their chivalry.

"Jane," he says, and I note the strain in his voice, "when for days we've been forced to gaze on Carisbrooke Castle – the very place His Majesty is so cruelly detained – how can you chide me for making my stand against such injury?"

I tell Robin straight those words he writ served only to deface an inn and insult a governor, and did not in the least honour His Majesty. "Well, Jane," says Robin, "I must surely chide you for not knowing your scriptures." And he recites the whole passage: *And Hammon was hanged on the gallows he prepared for Mordecai – and thus was the King avenged.*

So that's how I come to know what a serious business this could have been. And one that might have ended with us chained at the bottom of a boat and sent back to face Cromwell's men, themselves fair craftsmen when it comes to preparing gallows. And I'm struck again by that quick wit that saved us.

Seems I'm not the only one impressed by a certain gentlewoman. Mr Temple, if you please, has determined to accompany us to St Malo. And though this is very irregular, none seem to object. I do wonder what Lady Gargrave would say. Nothing is known of this gentleman beyond his being a relation of the Dingley family. My own view, given his demeanour at their table, is not favourable.

"Penny for them, Jane." I'd like to tell Robin my thoughts are worth more, but he's already preparing to go below. "I'm not one for watching wind and rain do battle," he says. "No doubt you'll be happy to stay atop, Jane, and get that first glimpse of France you're so fond of." Robin is once again smiling and jousting, and even though I find him wrong-headed, I'm glad to see him back to himself.

As for me, I'm happy enough to be up here alone. The sea's been my companion since my father took me out in a boat when I was so small, I'd needs to be astride his shoulders so's not to be blown away. He taught me to catch eel and sardine and to bag a good net of sprats for supper. Sometimes, he'd moor the boat on a small island and we'd cook fish on the beach and eat together, just the two of us. If any were to ask what I miss most of my old life, I'd be bound to say the sea – and my father. But not much else.

The waters are calmer now, and there's a peep of orange coming over the horizon. Most likely it will be fair when we wash up in St Malo. I'm no longer the only one up here on deck. Just goes to show what an odd day this is to see Miss Dorothy atop too. It's the first time I've known her not closeted the entire voyage. And though she clings tight to Mr Temple's arm, I do believe she's enjoying the feel and taste of sea breeze. As for Mr Temple, he sticks that close to her, I'm minded of them barnacles we'd find on the beach at home, and sometimes would attach themselves to any exposed part of us. I'm bound to admit, though, seen in profile, taller by at least a head than my lady, and with black moustache and that thick hair blowing, Mr Temple do appear exceeding fair. I have always favoured a tall man.

But then I think again on those barnacles, and how, if we were not quick to dislodge them, they would suck and sting at us.

ST MALO

I've made this journey often enough, but never before have I stood on the deck of a boat and watched dawn break. The sea is calm and I've a strong arm to support me. But despite the beauty of this moment, the urge to shut my eyes and imagine myself on land is strong. Mr Temple arranges my shawl more closely around my shoulders. His fingers brush my neck. "I think the sea is not your friend," he says. "I promise you shan't be washed away." He draws me nearer to his side. "You have nothing to fear."

And what of the creatures, Mr Temple? The ones that dwell beneath that calm surface?

Where does it come from, this dread? When I was a child, my brothers would swim in the pond behind the cattle barns at Chicksands. Once, I stood in the shadows and watched as they shed their garments and swam naked. I still recall my fascination and fear as my brother Henry dived beneath the water. When he remained there, I had to place my hand over my mouth to stop from crying out. By the time he emerged, his sixteen-year-old body glistening and triumphant, my terror was such I could scarcely breathe. Was that when it began?

Or was it that summer at the spa in Epsom? The waters were cloudy, and when my mother bade me drink, I saw there was sediment at the bottom of the stone tankard. As I drank, a woman waiting mentioned prisoners being let out to drink there, some with lesions on their mouths. I remember thrusting the tankard at my mother and turning towards a clump of bushes, where for several moments I retched.

I've had this dread of water for as long as I can remember. And to this day I've tried to avoid outings that include it. But God has seen fit in these troubled times to test that resolve. And here I am, once again a voyager, and – to Jane's wonder, I see – atop a boat, my arm in that of a man I scarce know, shivering with cold as the coastline of St Malo slowly emerges. Heaven knows what my aunt would make of this arrangement. Or what my father will say when he is introduced to this stranger who is to be his guest. Robin's impetuous invitation and Mr Temple's eager acceptance is, to say the least, irregular.

From this vantage, the house where my father dwells cannot be seen. It is hidden by the thick stone wall of the town. It is in every way a French house. When I first saw it, I wondered aloud at the high ceilings and huge windows opening onto the gardens; the light, elegant furniture, all carefully placed. And I marvelled silently at the chill in the air. The rooms boast few paintings, and those that hang show animals or views of the town. Like the house itself, they are impersonal. Nothing is worn and warm to the touch as at Chicksands, where, if I were blind, I would recognise every table and chair, every seam in every tapestry.

Mr Temple bends towards me: "You may open your eyes, Miss Osborne. We have reached our destination. France makes ready to welcome you."

My father rose late this morning. He sits alone, as if in state, at a table that would hold a great many more. If I were not in my father's house, I would wonder at this sunken figure toying with the smallest portion of food. But then this is not my father's house. We dwell in St Malo through the kindness of strangers.

I sit beside him. I wonder if any of the garments we have brought will fit this man. "The sun is shining, Father. Shall we walk a little?" He looks at me with such weary eyes. I take the hand beside his plate, and opening it carefully, finger by finger, lay it flat against my own. "Or we might take the carriage into town – or inspect those grand houses being built along the shore."

My father is scornful. "And with what currency, Dorothy? Gains made from robbing our ships and other mischief at sea. The Corsairs believe their trumpeting houses shall make gentlemen of them." He tells me he has no wish to indulge such fantasies. "You will see for yourself how they roam the streets of St Malo, insulting any who by birthright be not French. These are no friends of England, Dorothy." I don't doubt this house and all in it – the very table at which we sit – may well be the property of one such swaggering French buccaneer.

We walk in the gardens. I've always considered my father taller than any man I know. So it gives me pause to note my head is now almost level with his. There is, too, a hesitation in his step, as if for fear of letting his foot fall too firmly lest the ground beneath prove treacherous.

The gardens are a feast of colour and texture after last night's rainfall. Our elusive landlord may well be a brigand, but he is one who respects nature. There are no formal flowerbeds but an abundance of roses and foxgloves, camellia and anemones, growing in clusters amongst the fruit and sycamore. A wood, rather than a garden. I draw my father's attention to a half-finished nest, abandoned in the thickest part of the ivy that covers the wall. The fate of a diligent wren, perhaps, too absorbed in its careful construction to notice the swooping magpie. "What think you, Father?"

My father, once an expert of all things natural, shows little interest. His mind is elsewhere. He turns his gaunt face to me and asks the question that haunts him: "How does Castle Cornet?"

How does Castle Cornet? Dead, Father. Dead on the field of battle. "Much as you left it, Father. Your little garrison has still not surrendered to Parliament."

"But the men, Dorothy – are they kindly disposed to me now?" My father is still unable to extract this particular arrow that twists and pierces him. He suddenly stops in his tracks, as if trying to infuse some order into a flood of painful memories.

When he was finally forced to abandon Castle Cornet, my father had received no supplies for months, either of victuals or armaments. Driven almost to starvation, the men were close to mutiny. In desperation, my father wrote to the King. My mother carried the letter to His Majesty's makeshift court at Oxford. Some of the words are still written on my heart.

May it please your Most Sacred Majesty... I should not assume the boldness to offer this into your Royal Hand had I known who else to address myself. The extremities in which I foresee we may shortly be reduced... for unless we can be furnished with a speedy and complete supply... it will go very difficult, if not impossible, to relieve this castle.

My mother was sure the King would respond. *Once he is aware of your plight, His Majesty will surely provide.* The King did not provide. It's uncertain the letter ever reached that Royal Hand. Instead, my father received an edict from one of the Queen's courtiers. He was to leave Castle Cornet immediately. By then, Cromwell had snatched Chicksands. Exile, it seemed, was my father's only choice. This house at St Malo was put at our disposal. We may never know who stepped forward in our hour of need.

There's a sudden coolness in the air as the sun disappears and the morning darkens. The wind, never far from these shores, is whipping about our clothes. As we walk back to the house, I prepare myself for more talk of that isolated and unhappy garrison. But my father's next question is wholly unexpected. "What think you of Robin's new friend?" For a second, I'm not sure to whom he refers. "I am uneasy to see Robin still making such hasty attachments," he says. "What think you then of this Mr Temple, Dorothy?"

I answer carefully. "Mr Temple is surely a gentleman and showed us great kindness on the Isle of Wight." I don't, of course, mention the circumstances in which we found ourselves on that island.

"The Temple family has many branches, Dorothy, but I believe William Temple's father to be one who put finger to wind and went with Parliament. I think that as evil a choice as a man might make."

"I do not think Robin regards him as a friend," is all I can manage.

"Then why is he here?"

Jane and I exchange glances. There's been a transformation. My father is wearing the jacket we brought from England, and even though it is too large for him, he bears it with dignity. There are many candles lit, and Noah has fetched some good French wine from the cellars. My father says: "I cannot speak for the food we are about to eat, Mr Temple, but I do have confidence in the wine. Since we are on French soil, we can be sure of good vintage."

Potage de poisson is served, followed by quail and a delicate dish of chickpeas, all at my father's bidding. For the first time since we arrived, he is talkative, even animated. Though not when it comes to Chicksands. Mr Temple asks where in Bedfordshire our estate lies.

"We have no estate, Mr Temple." It's Robin who answers. "Our property was snatched these two years. We have rumours of Cromwell's men finding a haven there between looting and killing." Robin adds that were it possible, he would take up arms and drive a sword through the very soul of Cromwell's army. And when I think of those men tramping through our home; handling our possessions; defiling, perhaps destroying, our little chapel, I have a great impulse to do the same.

Mr Temple voices sympathy. Seated next to my father, he is solicitous, offering his congratulations on everything, from the subtleness of the dishes and the bouquet of the wine to the cleverness of our parents in producing such exemplary offspring. "I swear, Sir Peter, I've seen nothing more noble and courageous than Miss Osborne stepping up to the Governor at Newport and saving the day. Things could have gone very badly had she not shown such foresight." I look across at Robin, who is scratching his neck with an urgency destined to draw blood. Next to him, Jane is the colour of an over-ripe plum. None of us look at my father. We wait for the angry questioning to begin.

My father frowns, and for a moment seems to be mulling over Mr Temple's unmeasured words. Then he asks: "What is your connection with the Dingley family, sir?" Mr Temple replies it is a tenuous one, Mrs Dingley being a distant relative of his late mother. In the silence that follows, I realise there will be no more questions concerning Newport. Why am I disquieted? Is it my father's indifference to our late travails, or Mr Temple's lack of sensitivity in mentioning them?

Sensing the tension of the moment, Mr Temple feels the need to relieve it. His chosen method is to wade in deeper, telling the table at large how he himself spoke to the Governor privately, asking him to pay no heed to a young man's foolish prank. "But I do believe without Miss Osborne's confession, our little party might have been set to join the King at Carisbrooke."

Jane gives her nervous laugh. As for my father, he stares blankly at our guest, and I see that Mr Temple is about to explain himself further. Before he can stumble on, I say: "Is it so, Mr Temple, that whilst staying at Newport you had the pleasure of an audience with the King?" And Mr Temple acknowledges it to be so. My father is immediately alert.

"And how did you find His Most Sacred Majesty?"

In his frank way, Mr Temple says he found the King of commonplace appearance and air. "As like Tom or Dick as ever I saw anybody in my life."

For a moment, there's silence, as we all try to swallow these words. None has more trouble digesting them than my father, who struggles to his feet.

"I demand to know, sir, if you are set to insult the King, who this family hold in great honour and esteem."

Mr Temple's reply is reasonable and not in the least heated. He stands committed to the King... "But the King is a man, like any other, and not a god to be worshipped and sacrificed to."

My father is not to be placated. "Do you think then, sir, it is right to detain the monarch in conditions no better than a prison?"

And in that same even tone, Mr Temple replies he saw so sign of a prison in the King's surroundings. "Indeed, when I met with His Majesty, he was engaged in a game of Boules in the castle grounds." And since none speak, Mr Temple adds that he himself deplores this battle that has almost destroyed our country, and with such fatal consequences. "How much blood has been drawn from our honest subjects? How ravaged and defaced is our little island?"

My father bangs his fist down on the table, bringing Noah hurrying from the kitchens. "Good God, sir. This family has seen more than its share of sacrifice. I have lost two sons to battle and there've been times when I knew not where my wife and children were, or whether they were living or dead. But are we to cower and cringe whilst England is destroyed? The usurper and his vermin must be faced down, and His Majesty returned to his people, however much sacrifice is needed."

Noah steps forward, ready to help my father back into his chair. But it's Robin who saves the day. Adjusting his cravat about his unsightly neck and raising his goblet, he proposes a toast. "To his most revered majesty, King Charles. May he be speedily restored to his rightful ordinance." And I see by Robin's face that despite his passionate allegiance to king and cause, he does not wholly disapprove of Mr Temple's discourse. A sentiment I admit to sharing.

I am on my way to my father's chamber when Mr Temple catches me. "I must apologise for my rash talk at supper," he says. "I merely wished to make clear my view that this war, pitching brother against brother, has wrought nought but destruction. And when the cards are counted, I fear there shall be no winners. All will have lost. But it seems I have offended your father. Will you forgive me – and agree to take a turn in the gardens?"

I tell Mr Temple that although I understand – and share – his disquiet at this war, he had indeed spoken rashly, and on more than one subject. "I would not ask you be less than honest, sir, but when you are at my father's table, I think it only right you should temper your conversation to honour a man who these past five years has been ready to lay down his life for his sovereign, and as a result has lost everything." I am about to add I think the garden a dreary prospect at this hour. Instead, I ask him to wait whilst I fetch my shawl. Mr Temple announces he too has something to fetch.

We choose a bench close to the wall, where the moon is at its brightest, and Mr Temple hands me a manuscript, roughly bound and written in a strong, sure hand. "I think you are someone well familiar with books and reading, Miss Osborne. May I ask your advice on this paltry effort of mine, dashed off in the past few days? It's a translation from the French, during which I took liberties to change the story the better to my liking. If you find it worthy of your attention, I should be greatly honoured."

"I am a great reader when I am able, Mr Temple. But far from accomplished enough to judge another's work. If you promise to bear that in mind..." In truth, I'm completely taken aback. We sit side by side in awkward silence. Finally, I point out the sad little nest amid the ivy. Mr Temple says it's not rare for a male to drop his guard in hazardous circumstances.

"Don't you agree, Miss Osborne? If your theory is right, and it's a wren, then I believe it is the male that builds the nest. And chance is his mind was full of the female and her needs, and his joy of winning her after so many futile flights. He did not sense what a dangerous game he was involved in until it was too late. What think you, Miss Osborne, of these dangerous games that are the undoing of many a poor male?"

He turns towards me, and I feel, and keenly, the barely contained surge of energy this man always seems to exude. In the moonlight, I note the strength of his jaw; the shape of his brows – thick and dark, but orderly; the curve of his mouth. I reply that I believe any game that pitches passion above reason should be avoided.

"Ah, I see you're a pragmatist," he says. "You prefer to dwell in your head rather than your heart."

The moon disappears behind a cloud. I can no longer see his face. "I give heart and reason equal measure, Mr Temple. But if you are asking what I value most in others, I would have to say friendship. It's hard to love where you cannot like."

"But to like *and* love, Miss Osborne – that, I think, equals the perfect friendship. And one in which both parties may embark with trust on the risky road to passion."

We part in the hallway. Mr Temple gives the knee in formal fashion. Then, leaning towards me, whispers: "It's true – your lips are made for cherries."

What am I to make of this man? I fear I was too free with him at the Dingleys'. But does he imagine a little forward banter at supper gives him the right to sport with me in this fashion? I'm determined to dismiss his words for what they most certainly are: the conceit of a young cavalier used to confusing silly, gullible girls. As I make my way to my father's chamber, I'm set thinking of all I might have said in response.

My father's candle is still burning. He is in his nightshirt, seated at the bureau, quill in hand. "I am writing a full account of the castle siege," he tells me. "One I can present to His Majesty should he require it."

"It's late, Father. Shall I summon Noah to help you to bed?" My father ignores me and continues to write. To distract him, I search in my gown and place on the desk the little miniature I've been meaning to show him. "Do you know this woman, Father?"

My father glances at it. "Bess Neville, though it flatters her."

"Is this woman a relative of ours?"

"Elizabeth Neville was your mother's mother, Dorothy. Your grandmother."

I stare at the miniature for the hundredth time before stating the obvious. "But this woman is surely foreign."

"So goes the story." My father is impatient. "Now, please allow me to continue. It is important to make this ready for when His Majesty may have need of it."

I can just remember the wizened old woman who was my grandmother and whom I met only twice. I recall a cold, cloudy eye and a sharp tongue, and hiding behind my mother's skirts to avoid both. Try as I may, I cannot marry that image with the dazzling creature in the miniature.

My head is too full for sleep. I lay awake and ponder the evening's events. In particular, I think about this man who has come into our lives. In truth, at one year younger than myself, more boy than man. But despite his youth and reckless talk, I sense in Mr Temple a core of honesty and purpose lacking in most young men of my acquaintance.

Your lips were made for cherries. What an absurd remark.

Sir

With reference to the essay you kindly bade me read. Let me straightway say you have an excellent script, and I think your style has much grace. But in truth – and I think you wish me to be truthful – I find your hero weak, and too overcome with sentiment. I believe there's a deal of difference between the romantic and the sentimental. One being uplifting, the other cloying. I confess I'm less surprised than your hero at the indifference of his mistress to one so given to flurries of fine words and bouts of self-pity. I think this might have played better in the French. An Englishwoman of such character as you create would surely not be satisfied with a suitor who stays abed writing tedious prose instead of telling her what the future might hold with a man whose devotion would allow him to climb mountains. If your essay is truly to please, I fear you needs think again on your hero.

Your Humble Servant

D.O.

Madam

My grateful thanks for your valued thoughts on my small literary efforts. I see, Miss Osborne, you are hard to please. What you dismiss in my hero as mere sentimentality, I had hoped to convey as the purest emotions of his heart. Alas, it seems I must begin again and strive to put new words to paper that you may understand the depth of my hero's sentiments towards this seemingly immovable woman for whom he would climb any mountain, however perilous.

Your Obedient Servant

W.T.

A request! After more than two weeks in your father's house and in your company, I do not consider it inappropriate to ask if you might use my given name in place of your usual address – which is surely formal for persons who, if I dare venture, seem set to become friends.

Mr Temple bids the coachman stop at the gateway to the town. "Shall we walk a little?" He helps me from the coach and offers his arm. I'm unused to this freedom and its exhilarating effect. Still, I wonder my father raises no objections to these early-morning excursions. For as long as I can remember, I've been aware of the protection my father wishes me. To find it so completely removed is unsettling.

The air is full of fish and pungent cheeses. St Malo is preparing for the day. In the square at the front of the church, tradespeople lay out their wares. Mr Temple points to a young girl bearing a basket of herring on her head, weaving her way between stalls. He remarks it is the length of her neck that allows her to keep such perfect balance. "She is so young and slight, she may crumble beneath her load," I say. Mr Temple replies Breton girls are strong of body. "I see, sir, you are an expert in such matters." This remark is said in jest, but looking up, I note Mr Temple has reddened. It pleases me to know I've found a way of confusing this man. In all earnestness, he directs my eye to a group of young children.

"Look, that girl – no more than five or six – can already bear her brother on her back. No doubt she's been doing the same with a sack of apples or firewood since she could walk. These girls are not bred to be creatures of leisure, Miss Osborne." I wonder if this is a rebuke. As if to reassure me, he reaches across and touches my fingers, tucked beneath his arm. "Your hands are cold. Let's take this alley. With luck, we'll find an inn where we may warm ourselves."

It is not yet ten o'clock, but the coffee house is full. And with the exception of the serving wenches, I'm the only woman present. If this were London, I would almost certainly be turned away at the door. As it is, I receive more than my share of stares. I wonder again at this man who has seen fit to bring me here. But now that I am come, it takes but a moment to see the attraction. The room is full of busyness. Men sit in groups talking animatedly over steaming tankards. Others pore over books or sit hunched at backgammon. The air is thick with voices and the stench of clay pipes. I have entered another world – and it is a million miles from the world of women. We find a place in the corner next to the hearth. Mr Temple moves the bench so I may sit. "You are unfamiliar with these new establishments, Miss Osborne?"

"And I hope my reputation shall survive."

"You surprise me," he says. "I took you for an independent spirit. From your comments on my essay, I imagined you sympathetic towards a woman who is entirely her own mistress."

As so often with this gentleman, there is a gleam to his eyes. I reply I'm a firm believer that women, and men too, should follow independence of thought. "But I would never want to expose myself to the world's scorn."

"If you are unwilling to risk the disdain of others over a path or principle you feel to be true, Miss Osborne, how then are you to keep to it? Beware, lest your philosophy lead to a life of dullness with a safe dolt of a fellow at your side."

I am about to challenge these words when we're interrupted by the arrival of a serving wench. Her sleeves rolled to the elbows, she sets down two tankards of thick, dark liquid. The fine, fair hair on her arms glistens in a sudden splash of sunlight from the window above. I note the appraisal in Mr Temple's eyes and remember his remark about Breton girls. The drink tastes acrid and bitter.

Mr Temple returns to his subject. Leaning towards me and keeping his voice low, he asks what sort of man I envisage passing my life with. "Or would you leave the choice entirely with your father?"

"I would never agree to be what others think I should be, Mr Temple. My father has always sought my opinions in all matters. But I would not marry without his blessing. I've oft seen the folly of giddy people who marry without thought of reputation and family obligation and live to repent it."

"Then we are indeed different, Miss Osborne. In all honesty, I believe it more important to follow one's own heart and conscience than that of the world."

As our eyes meet, I wonder where exactly you find the true person – in the eyes or in the voice. In Mr Temple, both are distinctive. "And if you *were* persuaded to follow your heart, Miss Osborne? You've still not told me what manner of man you would favour."

I tell him there are a great many ingredients must go into making me happy in a husband. "I would not, for instance, want to be tied to a town gallant who pays court to all the women he sees, thinks they believe him, and laughs and is laughed at equally."

Mr Temple seems to find this amusing. "Then you would rather have a country bumpkin who knows not the difference between a woman and a sheep?"

With some heat, I defend myself. "It would depend on the character of the man. I would never be content with one who thinks of nothing but his dogs and hawks and is fonder of both than he could ever be of his wife." And I add I'd never take someone who was a fool or ill-natured or proud.

Mr Temple is obviously enjoying this cut and thrust. "I see you do, after all, have strong opinions, Miss Osborne. But what of love? Where does love enter into all these weighty requirements?"

I say, and forcefully: "We must love each other as much as we are both capable of loving. And I must be sure I will always have a place in his heart."

He leans across and takes my hand in both of his. "I suspect you already have a place in a great many hearts. I needn't tell you how firmly you are set in mine. No doubt you've already found that out – by being there." It's my turn to redden. I've no idea how to answer. Is this more sporting or a declaration? My hand still in his, I stumble out some words as to the lateness of the hour.

Walking to the carriage, Mr Temple shifts back into teasing mode, telling me he intends to make me smile more. "It has become my mission in life. Else I fear the only husband you will find is a weeping widower whose countenance is as sad as yours so often is." And he draws my arm through his. "We shall have no more formality. From this moment, you shall be Dorothy and I William – else I promise only silence when you address me."

It seems I am involved in a game. And if I am to keep my composure, it is important to retain the upper hand. But I fear I am in danger of relinquishing it. Soon, I may have no cards at all. Mr Temple – William – looks set to hold them all.

I'm drawing back the shutters in Miss Dorothy's chamber and she not yet risen, when, intent on giving that name another airing, she asks: "Is Mr Temple abroad yet?" To my mind, she's dwelling on a certain gentleman a deal more than is proper.

I reply, formal as you like, "I believe Mr Temple and Robin rode out afore the hens rose." This news is not warmly greeted. My lady, suddenly tetchy, bids me stop my busyness.

"You are not a household wench, Jane. There are those of my father can attend such chores." I say nothing, for I've learnt silence is always best when Miss Dorothy is out of humour. Neither of us speak till she's seated at her dressing table and I'm fashioning her hair. I must admit to enjoying this particular task. As my lady has oft told me, I'm better at coaxing a curl than any she knows. And Miss Dorothy is not of great vanity. No, when it comes to her person, the least fuss the better. As usual, my labours are quick to earn gratitude – and a change of temper. "What think you of Mr Temple, Jane?"

Sensing the import of a careful answer, I bide my time, testing the curling irons for heat and placing them back amongst the embers of the hearth. "I think Mr Temple a very pretty gentleman." Of the many things I could say of that person, this, I think, is least likely to offend. It proves so. My lady, all cheerful now, dwells lightly and with some wit on the many aspects of Mr Temple's appearance, from the flamboyance of his cravats to the unkemptness of his hair.

"That hair would be more appreciated if he were a woman. As it is, he doesn't deserve it since he takes so little care of it." She adds that seeing he is not unhandsome, Mr Temple is at least not taken by vanity. "You'd not credit, Jane, how many men of my acquaintance have succumbed to that, and with much less reason."

For all his forward ways, Mr Temple does seem to have a careless disregard for his own handsomeness. And I must admit, that gentleman has a way with him. "When he puts himself to it, there's no doubting Mr Temple can charm the birds," I say.

My lady laughs. "You are right. I fear we are all in danger of being charmed out of our senses! But William is a good man, is he not?" I'm shocked by this sudden free use of Mr Temple's given name. Robin's been all 'William this and William that' for days, having gone from frosty to friendship in a blink. But my lady is usually more caring of propriety. "This past week," she says, "William has been as solicitous towards my father as he would be to his own."

"He's no doubt glad enough of Sir Peter's hospitality, my lady." What's running through my head is said gentleman is nicely settled, thank you, and with no sign of moving on. She's then enquiring where Robin and Mr Temple have gone on such an early rise. "I believe they were set to ride over to St Servan," I tell her. I don't mention Noah's look of disapproval when he told me this. At any given moment and without warning, Noah is apt to disapprove of almost everything. Without words, of course, so's a person has to guess the reason for his huffiness.

"Did you know, Jane, William's mother died when he was but ten years? Since then, he's taken responsibility for the whole family, including the rearing up of his young sister."

"That do seem a Christian thing," I say. I'm thinking of my own mother, who died when I was born, leaving me no younger sister to love and care for. And it does so irk me that Miss Dorothy insists on ignoring the niceties. I've noted familiarity is oft commonplace amongst gentry. I was reared more cautious. I'd no more address a body I scarce know by their given name than shed my robes in a public place (though to my shame I've oft done just that – when sound asleep and dreaming!)

My lady says: "It's true, of course, he can be headstrong." Seems we're to talk of nothing but Mr Temple this entire day. "But it's rare to find maturity in such a young man, is it not, Jane?" And as we muse on this, I'd wager we are both thinking on Robin.

We are in the gardens when we hear the horses. "I believe they are returned, Jane. Go and tell them where we may be found." My lady has persuaded me to a game of shuttlecock. Pushed me to it, in truth, for being a proper bungler at the sport, I would rather not. And as usual, she's beating me too soundly for anyone's enjoyment, so I'm glad of a diversion.

But it's not Robin and Mr Temple in the courtyard. No, it's a fair-haired, unfamiliar gentleman alighting from a grayling. Were it not for his stoop, I believe he would be taller even than Mr Temple – and he's so thin and of such pallor, I'm thinking he might keel over. Noah, instructing the groom where to house the horses, is obviously well acquainted with this party. "We were not expecting you, sir, but I'm right glad to see you." And I'm just set thinking these are a fine flurry of words for Noah, when he turns to me and adds, "Go and tell Miss Dorothy her brother Mr Henry has come."

This supper is not the cheeriest I've attended. There's no doubt Sir Peter is overjoyed by the coming of this son. He's brought out some good ruby wine to celebrate. But the mood is dull as a sermon. Robin and Mr Temple have still not returned and my lady isn't at ease – her eyes constantly flying to the door. I'm supposing she fears an accident. For my part, I think it's more likely they've been waylaid by revelry and are even now face down upon the floor of some inn.

Our new arrival is preoccupied too, but with matters weightier than the mischief of young men. "There's talk in London of bringing His Majesty to trial." And no doubt noting our startled faces, Mr Henry tempers his words. "For myself, I'm sure this is merely the prattle of the times. There are wild rumours flying at every corner. No one truly believes such an outrage possible."

"But even to talk of such a thing!" Sir Peter's face has lost all colour. "If this is a sign of the times," he says, "they are not times I wish to live in."

His son assures him there's no Englishman alive who would not agree. "Such evil would never be sanctioned." During the rest of the meal, which is taken in silence, I've opportunity to study this new gentleman. By my wager, he's older than his sister by at least ten years, and with those same hooded, dark eyes. But where Miss Dorothy's are like pools and full of expression, her brother's left eye has a slight tic, serving to spoil the lustre of both. And where her countenance is serious, his is mournful.

After we've supped and settled at cards in the withdrawing room, Mr Henry, arranging his with an agony of slowness, suddenly voices displeasure at Robin's absence. "Who is this companion Robin has found to join him in his adventures?"

Sir Peter says he believes William Temple akin to the Irish branch of the family, which have long been known for unwise allegiances. "I believe his grandfather was involved with my Lord Essex against Queen Elizabeth. If memory serves, his neck just missed the axe. This young man, however, seems untainted by family treachery. Indeed, I believe him to stand staunchly for king and country." I smile to myself, supposing Sir Peter has forgotten the unpleasantness at a certain supper, when I for one thought the whole might end in crossed swords. It seems Mr Temple has cast his net and hauled in this entire household. Sir Peter adds Mr Temple has proved a jolly guest. "His enthusiasm and wit have lifted all our spirits."

Mr Henry looks thoughtful for a moment, before remarking that he cannot wait to meet this paragon of a youth who is staying under his father's roof and of whom we know nothing. Then, looking hard at my lady, he remarks: "I have never known you play so poorly, sister. Are you unwell?" Miss Dorothy declares the candles run too low for her concentration. I am sitting right close, since I'm supposed to be learning this dull game, and even with my sharp eye I can scarce make out the cards. 'Tis also true my lady shows little interest – throwing down her hand with no deliberation and barely a glance. I wish this dreary evening would end so's we might make to bed. In the old days, I was never one for my bed. At the taste of a drop of wine, I would up and dance all night. But I'm not at home, where singing and dancing are common after supper and which I did so enjoy. No, since living with gentry I've come to realise unplanned jollity is not a dignified way of carrying on.

Just when I'm feared my eyes may close, in strides Robin and Mr Temple, all rosy cheeks and hot breath from their ride, and trailing mud across a fine French carpet. And it's as if of a sudden we shake ourselves awake. Even Mr Henry looks a bit livelier as he is introduced to our guest. "Ah, Mr Temple, this is indeed a pleasure.

I've been most anxious to make your acquaintance." And as Mr Temple bows and returns the compliment, I'm set thinking how his presence can light a room better than a whole host of candles.

I take my needlepoint to the withdrawing room window, the better to get the full morning brightness. I'm more than a bit pleased to be calling this dainty thing 'my needlepoint'. At home, there was no leisure to learn such a craft. Miss Dorothy, herself a rare wonder with a needle, has lately taught me stitching and I am becoming quite adept, even if I do say so myself. I'm just set making a perfect letter D when in comes my lady with her brother Henry. Soon as they enter, it's clear all is not well between them. My lady's colour is high, and I'm quick to note the shake in her voice. "You have no right to talk to me of this. I assure you, Henry, he has not paid court – and I have indeed not encouraged him to do so."

My face is burning. I'm unsure whether to get up or stay put. I bend close over my work. Mr Henry chides my lady for speaking too warm. "From what I've observed these three days, Mr Temple is not unaware of you. As your brother, I've both your welfare and my duty at heart." This said with some emotion. And there's no lack of feeling in my lady's reply.

"I'm wondering, brother, if there be any person that would suit your sense of duty. It's not the first time you've voiced disapproval of a man – several men – who you think would court me." Mr Henry declares he stands by his sense of duty and finds a similar one sadly lacking in his sister.

"Surely, after all that's passed, our father deserves to see his daughter well provided for."

"Well then," says my lady, "if your sole purpose is to marry me off richly, I'll say no more!" And with that, Mr Henry starts singing a different song, telling her it's only her happiness that concerns him and calling on heaven to witness that nothing on earth is so dear to him as herself. I'm fair flummoxed by this theatre and my stitches fly this way and that, till of a sudden I stab myself with the needle and cannot suppress a yelp.

My lady, focusing on me now, and I think wanting to relieve my whole awkwardness, bids me retrieve a book she left in the library. I'm happy enough to quit this room, with the air so stiff it's a labour to breathe. I leave Miss Dorothy staring out the window, absorbed, it seems, in examining every detail of the gardens, and her brother set neatening Robin's pamphlets, left topsy near the hearth.

I'm so thinking on that strained interview, I don't at first see Mr Temple seated behind one of the library's great pillars. When my eye does catch him, I note he's engrossed in writing and so unaware of me. There's no sign of my lady's book. Then of a sudden, and without looking up, Mr Temple says: "Why do you creep so, Jane?" I reply I've no wish to disturb his labours, and explain my quest. So Mr Temple joins the search. But although we are both diligent, the book cannot be found. I'm just about to up and leave, when Mr Temple says: "Surely on such a morning you should be enjoying the air, Jane?"

I'm all for agreeing, but mindful of my place, I say, "I am happy to stay close by my lady till she ventures out."

And settling back in his chair, Mr Temple says, "It cannot be true that on such a sunny day, a person of your beauty and natural attributes does not have ten or more swains banging the door. Don't tell me it's not so, for I refuse to believe it."

His exact words! To hide my confusion, I say: "Will you be wanting anything of me, sir?" And I have to stop myself bobbing like a kitchen wench.

Mr Temple then gives me such an engaging smile and says, very polite: "Not at this moment, Jane." And I manage to walk out the room in dignified fashion.

This unsettling morning has still to run its course. I'm just deciding if I should tell my lady her book can't be found and risk walking in on more bargy, when a household wench, who speaks not one word of English, comes running, grabs my arm and pulls me towards the kitchens, where there's a right stew of commotion brewing. Here's Noah, pale as a bed sheet, hovering round Robin – who is dripping blood all over a stuffed and trussed bird. Seems he was helping himself to a fingerful of stuffing, when said finger came in contact with Noah's knife, being used to spread a good load of goose fat over the whole.

I'm thinking I got here none too soon, since Noah is set to binding a deep cut with a filthy piece of cloth and with his old hands shaking like leaves. Meantime, the wench who fetched me sticks close to the door, pale at the sight of blood and ready to make off in a second. I soon take good charge, scolding Robin for his greedy ways and for never paying proper attention. Then I rip off the cloth with one tug, causing him to yell as if shot by Cromwell's guns. "You need to wash this first, else it will fester," I tell him. I take the daisies from a pitcher of water on the table and plunge Robin's hand in. I tell Noah to fetch a good fist of love-lies-bleeding from the yard (first time I've dared give Noah an order!) and I make a fair poultice and bind up the wound with a clean piece of muslin. I tell Robin a scratch like that never killed anyone. Many men, I've noted, are not as brave as their bragging when it comes to a bit of pain.

All this time, I'm holding Robin's hand and thinking it soft as any woman's, with fine long fingers – when that hand suddenly tightens on mine, and I see Robin is smiling. "Was worth any torture, Jane, to have my hand held by such a tempting one as yours."

It's not yet noon and I've had two compliments, one after t'other! In truth, those saucy words have served to lift my spirit. I know of no girl not pleased to be thought comely. And at least things aren't dull when Robin and Mr Temple are abroad. I think again on Robin's hand, so soft to touch. So unlike my own rough hands which always seem plagued with calluses. No doubt *his* hands would be less fine if they were employed in honest work. But though he's contrary as they come, Robin's at least easy in his ways. Unlike his brother, he's not prone to moody swings and finding fault wherever he looks. I do so wish I'd not been party to that ill discourse in the withdrawing room, though some of Mr Henry's words echoed my own disquiet. Mr Temple's coming has unsettled us all. And my lady, for all her denials, is far from unmoved by this gentleman's charms, which I must admit are plentiful.

A letter has come. William is to leave – and almost immediately. We're just risen when he tells us. "My father fears I've outstayed my welcome. He bids me move on to Paris." He says it lightly and with only the briefest glance in my direction.

Robin voices dismay. He's at a loss to know how he'll now occupy his time. "St Malo will become the dullest of towns! You must promise faithfully to stop here on your return." My father echoes this. Henry can scarce conceal his delight.

"Paris, Mr Temple – what pleasure! And no doubt you'll continue to other foreign parts? Will you leave tomorrow?" William confirms he'll be travelling on to Brussels and The Hague. He seems animated. A conversation then ensues on the merits of the Low Countries. I say nothing, for fear my voice fail me.

Henry intends to ride out with William as far as Avranches. He insists on accompanying him into town to buy provisions for the journey. Robin goes too. Jane and I are left to our needlepoint. Seated on either side of the hearth, we work in silence, the only sound being the French clock, chiming at two, three and then four hours. I wonder how Jane would react if I were to rip this sampler to shreds and throw it on the fire. "What think you, Jane, of this hasty departure?"

And Jane mulls this over before replying. "I think Mr Temple shows proper respect for his father's wishes."

Do you indeed, Jane! I wish just for once this girl would answer a question with simple directness. "It has not escaped me, Jane, that you don't wholly approve of William." At least I've caused her to redden.

"In truth, my lady, I don't approve nor disapprove."

"Come now, you can be honest. What is it that gives you that look whenever William is mentioned?"

And as if she's to have teeth drawn, Jane admits it. "I see he's a winning gentleman, but I find him a mite too sure of himself."

Well, at least she's now straightforward. We lapse again into silence. But I cannot let such a remark go unchallenged. "I can't imagine why a confident manner should cause such sourness. Would you prefer a bumbler who must tug his hair before every sentence?"

And Jane says: "It seems to me Mr Temple is too aware of his charms and uses them to his advantage."

"Explain what you mean. In what way does William 'use his charms', as you put it?"

"Well, my lady, he's properly bewitched this family, hasn't he." I bid her go and fetch some refreshment. For all her efforts, Jane is still apt to overstep propriety.

There's so little time, and no chance to speak since my brother watches my every movement. When William helps me from my chair at supper, offering his arm and briefly touching my hand, Henry is there, urging him to a beverage in the library. "We must make the most of your last night, Mr Temple."

Robin too is determined William shall have a fitting send-off. He sets up the harpsichord. "Play for us, Dorothy." So, I play, whilst the men sit at the fire and test their wits on one another, barely aware of my presence.

I excuse myself and go to my chamber. I write the note hurriedly and go in search of Jane. She is sitting alone in the gardens, close to the dry and decrepit little nest. "I must apologise, Jane, for being so surly of late. I'm not quite myself."

Jane is quick to reassure. "I'd wager there's a fair storm brewing. That's why we're a-jitter. My father always says when the sea starts churning, folk soon follow suit."

"Yes, Jane. It's the weather." After much hesitation, she agrees to carry the note.

When I come down, the kitchens are empty. At least I know Henry is safe abed, in preparation for the early start he has so carefully orchestrated. These past weeks, whilst remaining cordial in William's presence, Henry has used every opportunity to disparage him in mine. According to my brother, William is not only false but entirely lacking in responsibility. "Are you aware he quit Cambridge early – and without his degree? No doubt he prefers tennis to labouring at philosophy." William has lately beaten my brother soundly at several sets of tennis. His family, too, have not escaped censure. They are scheming opportunists and wholly without honour. Although when pressed, Henry admits knowing of this family only through our father.

I hear a foot on the stairs and for an instant, the kitchen is full of light as William holds up his candle to get his bearings. "Ah," he says. "Finally!" And for the first time in this long day, I feel calmed. He takes my hand and presses it to his chest. I can feel his heart, strong against my palm. "I'm entrusting this to you," he says. And this is not his usual teasing, challenging tone. His voice is earnest, uncertain. This is no longer a game. Is it what I want? He talks of plans to return. I'm barely listening. This man, who has come from nowhere, may well change my life, and my need for him takes my breath. I am powerless.

He will leave at daybreak. He makes me promise not to come down. "Let me remember you as you are right now – by the light of this candle."

And how will I remember you? By the touch of your hand? The warmth of your face against mine?

He tells me his father has received reports of our friendship. But not from a third party. "What I imagined were bland notes, failed, it seems, to conceal my true sentiments. My father knows me too well." So much for those strong words on following one's own heart.

We remain in the kitchens until both our candles are in danger of extinction. "I will find you," he says. "And I will wager ten pounds you will already be taken."

I accept the wager. "In the circumstances in which my family is placed, ten pounds will be much appreciated." *A man has but to touch a neck.*

Henry is back from Avranches in record time, and not one word of William's departure. I decide to ask nothing. After dinner, he corners me in my chamber. "Now Mr Temple has quit us and whilst the weather holds, we might plan an outing to one of the islands." Since I can't imagine anything less appealing, I don't reply. Then, no doubt thinking of the worst he can dredge, Henry suddenly informs me William is an atheist. "As we rode out, we talked of religion. It was clear from his remarks that Mr Temple is ungodly." He pauses so this may sink in. "Pressed on when he last took the sacrament, he admitted not for months. He often finds the *rantings* of the pulpit tedious. His very words."

I say I believe William to be a man who prefers to think for himself rather than follow the herd. "To say he is ungodly does him great injustice. I've often heard him praise our Lord, and most sincerely."

"It seems, Dorothy, you know more of this gentleman's mind than even Robin, whose friend he is said to be." My brother walks about my chamber, making careful examination of the books on the table and the trinkets on the dresser. "We might ride over to St Servan. There are things in that town that may interest you."

I wonder, wearily, what they could be.

"Did you notice how this gentleman and Robin have been so drawn to that place? Do you know why, sister?"

"It's obvious, Henry, you are set to tell me."

Henry, his back to me now, is staring down at the hearth. "St Servan is where certain gentlemen go for certain pleasures." And here, my brother dispenses with all delicacy. "The place is full of French whores who sell their bodies to any hapless fool willing to pay."

"Robin and Mr Temple went there to game and sup. Robin has told me as much." I say this casually. I refuse to let Henry see how deeply he has shocked me.

My brother gives a dry laugh. "I fear, sister, the gaming Robin talks of has little to do with cards."

In bed, I think again of the serving girl in the coffee house and the frank appraisal in William's eyes. *Breton girls are strong of body.* Was it to such girls he and Robin rode over fifteen miles? Did he seek them out at random or was there one in particular? What special arts did she know that drew him time and again on that journey? Not for the first time, I wish I were better versed in the mysteries of pleasing a man. I reach for the little miniature on the table next to my bed. The dark, unwavering eyes of my grandmother look back at me. They hint at a wildness not found in any of the women in our family. Is this what men desire? My mother has always had an open and modest countenance. I've never talked to my mother – or any woman – about the desires of men.

At Chicksands, when I was a child, pitchers of hot water would be brought to fill a tub in my mother's chamber. Her love of bathing was considered eccentric by the rest of the household. Once, I saw my father enter the room as the maids left. I stood so close to the door, I could hear the water splashing. When my mother cried out, I felt sure she'd been hurt. But something prevented me from opening the door and going to her. A sense that all was not as it seemed. I heard my father give a deep animal groan, like the horses gave when we shod them. Then my mother laughed, and except for the sound of water being disturbed, there was silence.

I push back the bedcovers and take off my night robe. The stone floor beneath my feet is icy. The only mirror is small and grainy. When I finally find the courage to hold up the candle and look into it, I can see only my breasts: childlike, and not nearly as full and round as my mother's or Jane's. I run my hand across my stomach and the wiry mass at the base. I remember the words of an old nursery maid at Chicksands: *There's any amount of disease might be got from doing that, Miss Dorothy. Don't let me catch you touching yourself there again.*

Back in bed, I try to imagine William's face; his tall, lean body. But the only image that comes is that of my mother and father behind a closed door with water splashing onto a wooden floor.

I sit at the window of my chamber, the better to see the carrier. It's over a week since William left and it has rained every day. Perhaps that's why no word has come.

The goblet is still on the dresser where it has been all night; the piece of steel soaking in what was once the palest of wines, now turned rusty brown. I've often watched my mother prepare what she terms the 'steel and wine cure'. She turned to it when her spirits were low – the war too painful to bear. My aunt once assured me attacks of the Spleen have always run through the women in our family. *If a man do find himself afflicted, he don't acknowledge or tell it – lest it be taken for womanly weakness.*

I remove the piece of steel, close my eyes and gulp the mixture down.

"I fear you are ailing, sister. Shall we send for the medic?" Henry is so solicitous, it is hard to believe the animosity we have both lately harboured.

"I have a slight chill, that's all."

"You must wear your shawl. Your cheeks are pale. You need sea air, Dorothy. We will take the carriage later."

Back in my chamber, I am barely able to reach the bed. No matter how desolate, I shall never again resort to this 'remedy'. Low spirits are surely more endurable than this unremitting nausea. As usual, Jane is quick to attend me. If she does guess the cause of my malaise, she hides it well. "Most likely it's something you ate, Miss Dorothy. They do say herring taken at this time of year can be hazardous."

What would I do without you, Jane?

When I finally come down, Robin is alone in the withdrawing room, trying to coax the logs to give more heat. "Have you noticed how cold this house suddenly is?" he asks. "And the evenings are drawn short. I think November the dreariest of months."

"What I've noticed is you no longer ride out to St Servan now that William has gone." I search Robin's face. His countenance is as open as ever.

"You know how I love the cards. But my luck is patchy at best. Without William's tempering influence, I fear I would lose the very jacket from my back." And Robin gives me a smile of such warmth, for a moment, I'm tempted to believe him.

I watch from my window as the carrier takes his time, stopping to talk to one of the grooms before slowly ambling up to the house. A letter has finally come. When I reach the hall, I'm dismayed to see Henry has already opened it. But it is not from William.

"Are you then expecting a letter?" Henry asks me. "I will tell the carrier to inform me if one should come, so you've no need to rush down in that manner and risk a tumble on the stairs." Henry reads the letter in the hall, a rare smile lighting his face. "It is news from England."

This entire day, Henry has been guarding a secret. More than once, I've caught him smiling when he thought himself unobserved. His manner is relaxed, almost fanciful. "Look how the gulls dip and sway over the roof. Is it possible that one day we humans might do the same? What think you, Robin?"

Robin is curt: "If I did not know you better, Henry, I'd say you were in love." And Henry blushes, another rare occurrence. By supper, our curiosity is well roused. As we go in, Robin whispers: "Seeing Henry in such whimsical spirit is enough to spoil all our appetites."

"I suppose we may eventually know the cause," I reply.

Finally, with us, his audience, seated at table, Henry seems set to reveal all. But not before further testing our forbearance. "Is not this wine excellent? This is your choice, Father? Or was it already in the cellars? There's little to say good about the French, but they do know how to stock a fair wine cellar."

Robin says: "For God's sake, Henry – tell us what makes you so smug."

And lifting and twirling his goblet to better examine the wine, Henry tells us. "We are to go home to Chicksands." My father half rises then slumps back into his chair. Robin commences scratching his neck. I'm too stunned to move – trying to wrap my mind around Henry's words. For a moment, none of us speak. Then, Henry says: "You must have known we've been negotiating. Well? Is this not the news we've been wishing for?" I finally ask how it came about. "There are advantages, after all, in a divided family," Henry says. I know he speaks of John Danvers. My mother's brother has stood staunchly for Cromwell's cause since the first days of this bitter war – a source of great anguish to my mother and aunt. Henry confirms our uncle has spoken on our behalf. "As a consequence, Cromwell has agreed we may buy back Chicksands."

Robin is incredulous. "Buy back our home? It's better we raise our own army and take what is ours by right."

Henry sighs. "Sadly, that is not the way the world moves. Cromwell has agreed we may return in exchange for £10,000. A substantial sum – but we must rise to it."

"A substantial sum indeed." My father finally speaks. "And one which is totally beyond our means."

I agree: "Such a sum would ruin us, Henry."

"We are already ruined," Henry says. "Once home, we can start to make the estate pay again."

"But who is to work it?" my father asks. "My bailiff has been gone these two years, cosying with the Puritan army, and we will be lucky to find a handful of labourers left thereabouts."

I tell Henry there is no possible way to meet Cromwell's demands. "Even if we sold everything we own, the very clothes off our backs, we still could not raise such a sum."

"I thought you, sister, would be joyous at this news." Henry is clearly irritated. "Of course we shall raise the money. Maybe, Father, instead of writing your tome on the siege of Cornet, you can write to His Majesty demanding the three years of wages he owes you." Seeing my father's defeated look, I reach across and take his hand. And Henry, softening, says: "We will sit tonight and ponder a plan. Uncle Danvers has already pledged a fair amount of money."

We are to return home. Henry is right: this is what I've longed for. Yet I'm terrified of what we might now find there. I'd prefer to be alone, but seeing Jane's worried look and despite the coolness of the evening, I propose a turn in the gardens. As we walk, I try to reassure her. "You must of course come with us, Jane, if you are willing."

Jane replies she'd be happy to set up in the English countryside. "I've oft heard of its beauty and of the abundance of creatures thereabouts."

Her voice betrays her anxiety, so I summon what has long been buried, and describe to her my home. I tell of the little chapel where monks and nuns once prayed; the walled rose garden, full of nightingales and butterflies in spring; the view of the meadows and stream from my chamber; the barns behind the house where Robin and I played as children. "But after so much upheaval, things will surely not be as we left them."

"My father always says change is a good thing, if you are determined it shall be."

"Change has been thrust up on us, Jane. The world is turned upside down. We are all changed."

CHICKSANDS PRIORY AND HAM HOUSE

Chicksands, April 1649

Sir

Your letter has finally found me – and I'm extremely glad to have it so will not chide you for the lateness. In truth, there are few persons I would rather hear from. But I received none of the other letters you say you sent. And this one has scant enough news. Let me ask what you have done all this while, and why you are in Holland when all thought you still in France? And what could keep you there so long – and why was I not to know you went so far? You'd do well to satisfy me in all this, else when we meet, I will so persecute you with questions you will be glad to go abroad again to avoid me. That is if we shall meet. Despite your certainty, nothing for me is ever sure.

As for the ten pounds you claim – it is not yet due. And I think it best you put it amongst your unpaid debts, as it is a very uncertain one.

Your humble servant

D.O.

Sir

Your letter scolds me for my brevity, whilst yours in reply is barely a page! Though to know you are returned to London, that you are well, and in a place where I may see you gives me great satisfaction. Now, as requested, you shall have my story. We came here to Chicksands almost two months since and I have not words to tell the joy of being home – nor the sad state we found. My mother's beloved kitchen gardens and the lavender she planted are all that has survived. She arrives from Chelsea tomorrow. Her health is such she may be unaware of the loss we have suffered. Robin talks of returning to France.

Forgive this tumble of words. Like my thoughts, my news is scattered. We are slowly piecing together our home, though my father's income has gone from £4,000 a year to barely 400. Since the death of the King, he keeps mostly to his chamber. To the last, he could not believe the axe would fall. And since that unnatural and shocking day, he has not spoken one word of it. We've all, in fact, been silent as sleepwalkers. Save that is for my aunt and my brother Henry, who talk of nothing but best ways to dispose of me – or as my aunt puts it: 'to present a good prospect!' I resist, for I would not have you so easily claim your wager.

You ask when shall we meet. I shall be loath to leave my mother whilst she has such little portion of health. But I should be in London in the autumn, which I certainly desire, because you are there.

Till then – I am where I was, still the same, and as always

Your Humble Servant

Madam

The arrival of your letter and to know we are to be reunited gives me the greatest joy since my return. It has set me in such good spirits, my sister, Martha, wondered if perchance we'd happened on a fortune. You mention we might meet in autumn. Well, in the first days of September – and despite Cromwell's edicts – there is to be a discreet gathering at Ham House. I have an invitation to hand this very evening, and will ensure you receive one shortly.

I'm sorry indeed to hear of your mother's further decline and your father's loss of spirit. I fear the times have drained the strength and hopes of many who had the misfortune to live through them. I send my remembrance to your father in the hope he will rally when men return to work the land and he may see his estate recover somewhat.

Adieu until September. I will wait for you by the river in Richmond. Shall you be very pleased to see me?

Your humble servant

William Temple

In the coach to Richmond, my aunt repeats her set piece: how she loves me dearly for my mother's sake, and a little for my own; how I'm without doubt the most wilful woman she knows; how I've a stubborn nature that I must strive to overcome. "You seem set to reject even a duke, should one see fit to ask for you." I finger William's letter in my pocket. Aunt Gargrave says: "I believe you are barely listening."

At Ham House, the hall and receiving rooms are crowded. The air is close and reeks of powdered hair and warm flesh. I seize my excuse. "I am in need of a little air." As I walk towards the gardens, I try to keep my step unrushed, my demeanour calm.

He is waiting for me as promised. Gazing at the river, he doesn't see me approach. He is taller than I remember and grown thinner. I watch for a few seconds before calling his name. He turns, and I see he is, after all, unchanged. The gleam to his eyes; the creases beneath them when he smiles; that barely contained energy I sensed when we first met. He puts his hand to my face. "What have we here? That same sad look I've carried in my heart."

"Until this moment, I've found little cause to change it."

"Well then," he says, "we must guard this moment carefully." He takes my hand and we stand looking across the river, crowded with boatmen transporting late-night revellers. I'm aware of the texture of his jacket against my arm, of the muscles beneath, of his breathing. He draws me into the shadows. We are awkward together. There is much to say, and no time to say it. Our words bang into each other. In a week, he will leave again for foreign parts. His father thinks it best. "England is good for nothing right now," he says. This time, Spain, then Italy.

I tell of my deep concern for my mother; of Robin's return to France; of my brother Henry's continued persecution, his stifling protection. "He swears it's all for love and care of me. I receive notes from him that those who did not know might think from a suitor."

He is quiet for a moment. "And actual suitors? I'm sure there are plenty of those knocking your door." I mention a new swain with impeccable credentials who will likely be hard to refuse.

It's almost true. My hands are cold, shaking. "You best go inside," he says. But neither of us, it seems, can break the moment.

I can hear my aunt calling from the terrace. He presses in my hand a carefully folded paper. "This is where you may reach me. For God's sake, write often and tell me all that passes. They will forward your letters." He vows to come straight to Bedfordshire on his return. "Promise me on no account shall I win my wager."

Aunt Gargrave is not pleased. "You shouldn't have wandered so. It's difficult to find anyone in this throng." My aunt is full of names and titles and who is present and whom she has yet to see. "The French ambassador may still appear. They say he's a sight to behold in these austere times." Like all around her, she is feeling the heat. "You'd think they'd see fit to open windows." My aunt complains, too, of the sparse seating. Her feet, always a problem, will be swollen by now.

"I will fetch some ale, Aunt. I'll be but a moment." I navigate my way back across the room. There is no sign of him. Is he still in the gardens? He cannot, surely, have left already. As I pass through the hall, the door leading to the river is still open. I slip out, but the huge candles lining the lawns are extinguished. Except for an occasional light from a passing boat, all is darkness.

Back inside, I look around for a footman, and through the open door of an anteroom I see William. He is laughing with a group of young men. I position myself where he might see me. But he does not look across. He's engrossed with his companions. One of them moves, and I see in their midst a woman. Even at this distance I can tell she is beautiful. My aunt is at my side again. "Really, Dorothy, can you not stay put in one place? Lord Rich's nephew passed and now you've missed the moment." Aunt Gargrave's eye is already scanning the room and drawn, like many other eyes, to William's group beyond the door. "How fine the Countess of Sunderland looks now she has quit her widow's weeds," she says. As we watch, William bends towards that eminent lady and whispers. She throws back her head in laughter. "'Tis unlikely she'll remain widow for long, with so many bucks to choose from," my aunt whispers. "Her fortune, of course, is no hindrance. Let us find somewhere to sit before we expire."

I see him just once more, alone, and standing by a window. He sees me too and smiles, and I think he is about to approach, but our carriage is already waiting, and in a second, we are gone.

On the way back to Chelsea, as my aunt snores in the corner, I open William's note and read it by the light of the coach candle. *Address your letters to Mistress Painter, next to the Bull in Covent*

Garden'. And for the second time this evening, I'm reminded that this man, who for so many months has absorbed my thoughts, is, in truth, someone I scarcely know.

CHICKSANDS PRIORY

1653

Soon as she came down this morning, I noticed: Miss Dorothy has finally shed those gloomy baubles. And without them black eardrops, she's got good colour back. Though she's still clad in mourning gown. "I'm considering wearing it for the rest of my life, Jane. You'll see how once I quit it, they will torture me with suitors again." Since her mother died, my lady's been spared that particular bargy. And when you think of the rum assortment previously paraded, it's little wonder she's in dread of it. Course, that's not the real reason for her stubbornness. No. All those letters I've taken to and fro the carrier answer to that. Still, I've stopped my fretting. Mr Temple's are now twice the number of hers, and I'm tempted to think his affections may after all be genuine. Though there'll be a right stew if Mr Henry gets wind.

I've noticed through all the grieving that brother keeps his careful watching, even when my lady is quiet with her stitching or at prayers in chapel. Right now, though, there's more pressing doings than Mr Henry and his odd ways. At home, they used to say 'death comes in threes'. And what with Lady Osborne passing and Sir Peter failing – and now Noah still abed at noon, I'm thinking there might be some truth in those old biddy words. When I take him some broth, Noah can scarce raise himself. He does manage to champ at me, though, for slopping the broth. I tell him straight he looks like parchment. "Miss Dorothy says you're to stay put till the medic comes."

He raises himself then all right, and spits on the floor. "I'll not be needing no apothecary. I'll be up and doing afore he gets here." Despite his protests, I tuck the torn blanket about Noah and prop the pillows best I can. When I look in later, he's sound asleep and the broth scarce touched. And he looks so unlike himself, I'm tempted to give him a poke to make sure he's still living.

The medic finds Noah sitting on the edge of the bed in his nightshirt. "I'm strong as a witch's brew," Noah tells him. And the good doctor confirms as much, though in more delicate terms.

"The heart is strong, but the bones are worn," he tells my lady. "Best get a lad for the heavy work." When he's gone, my lady bids me ask in the village. No needs for that. Will Hammer will be round afore long. As he's the cook's grandson, no one questions Will being so often in the kitchens. He's a strapping lad and forever hungry. Will's pleasant enough, though, and always does my bidding without being twice asked. Soon as I tell him the news, he jumps at the chance.

"I'd give my right arm to work at Chicksands."

"You'd not be much use then, would you," I say. But I share Will's pleasure. I thank the blessed Lord every day for setting me down in such a goodly place, though my lady swears all is spoilt by war. But where else could you step through such cloisters on your way to a chore? Or pray on the very spot where monks and the holy sisters knelt? As I wrote to my father, every chamber is bright as a silver sovereign. 'Cept Noah's. That's surely a sight different from my own pleasing chamber, high in the house and right next to Miss Dorothy's. But then I've my bobs and trinkets scattered. Except for a broken chair, table and slop basin, Noah's don't seem to have a single thing of his own. I'm thinking there's cosier cells down the gaol.

My lady's well pleased with Will Hammer coming. She asks who shall tell Noah. I keep silent. After a bit, she says: "We'll let my brother do it." At that, we're both set laughing.

There's yet another letter come for Miss Dorothy, and it puts such a flurry on her, I'm thinking a certain gentleman is bound to dismount any moment. Turns out it's not from that quarter at all. "Robin is on his way from France. Is not that wonderful news, Jane?" Minutes later, she's saying he's expected this very day. I'm thinking that's just like Robin. Where most folk would send a timely letter, his way is to have us all running like hens. I doubt there will even be time to change into that good grey afternoon gown my lady lately gave me, which I do think becomes me a little, even if I say so myself.

As it turns out, we're all still kicking our heels at the end of the afternoon, with supper waiting and Sir Peter brought down 'specially. Course, there's no sign of Robin. But at least this spinning day has got Miss Dorothy out of her mourning gown. Mr Henry comments favourably. "That soft blue brings out your complexion, sister. And it would set off your shoulders too if you would just cast off that dull shawl."

My lady's look is cold as her voice. "This dull shawl was our mother's, Henry, and I intend to wear it often. I may have quit my public mourning but I'll not let go her memory."

We are all seated in the hall and about to start the soup – a rich pheasant one and Robin's favourite – when we hear the horses. My lady jumps up immediately and I follow. Here he finally is: Robin, tousle-haired, calling for the grooms, and looking for all the world like he's scarce been gone five minutes. Though by my count, it's three months and two days.

"The two prettiest girls in England," and Robin puts his arms round us in that familiar way of his. "I'm surprised, Dorothy, they've not managed to bargain you off yet!" Then he turns to me. "And you, Jane – what have you to tell?" I'm properly irked that I cannot, for the moment, find my tongue.

It takes Sir Peter a good while to recognise this son. It's not until supper is over and we're seated in the withdrawing room that his head finally clears. Then he wants to know what Robin is doing here, though all day we've been preparing him. Robin takes his father's hand and with careful patience, explains his journey. And I note that, after all, Robin is not the same. There are those fine new lines at the corners of his eyes and around his mouth, and a serious cast to him unlike the carefreeness we're used to. But then Robin catches me staring and grins, and I see he's not lost his annoying ability to cause a person discomfort. He's soon set talking in his old spirited way. "Do you know who I caught up with in Paris, Father? Mr Temple –William – you remember him from St Malo? What pleasure he brought to that dull place."

Sir Peter looks blank, but Mr Henry remembers only too well. "I'd not encourage that particular acquaintance, Robin. I've reason to believe Mr Temple severely tested our hospitality." And he ups and pours himself more brandy. As for Miss Dorothy, she's worrying the edge of her mother's shawl with such awful concentration, I'm feared she might unravel it.

"Mr Temple sends you all his good regards," Robin says. "And, Henry, he bade me tell you he will be pleased to visit Chicksands when he returns next month." Nobody speaks, but I swear you could cut the air with a sword.

I'd no notion Robin and Will Hammer were so well acquainted till I witness them in the kitchens. "Will, is this really you?" says Robin. "Do you remember me? It was I who used to thrash you so soundly at toss and catch when we were boys."

"You had the advantage, Mr Robin, being the older one," Will tells him. "Reckon it would be a different story now, if you'll pardon my saying so." Will's likely right, seeing the size of him and the way he towers over Robin. The two of them fall into such a hugging and clasping of shoulders, I'm feared Robin's bones might crush.

"We'll drink to this happy reunion." And in a blink, Robin has two tankards and a flask of ale and is seated with his feet propped on the table. Will is about to do the same, till he catches my look and thinks better of it. "So, Will, how come you at Chicksands?" And when he hears the story, Robin chuckles. "I dare say old Noah's not best pleased."

Will is surprised at this. He tells Robin straight there's no side between him and Noah. "I think he's glad I'm come. Though he'd likely not say so. He's known me since my birth, and my father afore."

At this, my curiosity gets the better. "What was this wife of Noah's then?"

"She were called Susan. She died in childbearing, along with the bairn." To my mind, that's misfortune enough to turn any man sour. At least I didn't die alongside my mother. My father had me to raise, and I do believe that melted his bitterness.

With Robin back, the easy pace of life is soon disrupted. There's no telling whether he's in or out or will eat with the house or no. Just like the old days, those pamphlets of his are strewn everywhere. Miss Dorothy, of course, is in a right flurry. Seems with all those letters flying, a particular gentleman has not seen fit to mention his imminent arrival. "Help me sort through these gowns, Jane. They've been so long neglected, I've forgot what I have." She's concerned too for her hair. "My aunt writes the London fashion is plainer now they no longer follow the Queen." Even though it's unlike my lady to concern herself with such trifles, I'm right glad to see her spirit revived. I'm worrying my head, though, lest that brother should note the change.

Right now, it's Robin irking Mr Henry's mind. He catches him as we are all gathered in the withdrawing room. "Since you spend so much time at the tavern," he says, "maybe you can keep your straggling papers there." Robin's failure to answer further spoils his brother's humour. Mr Henry picks up a mess of pamphlets from the floor. "And is this what you are reading? This sedition against Cromwell, who holds all our fate?"

Robin says: "Thankfully, Henry, there are those still sure that fate may change." His brother gives one of those unpleasant laughs of his.

"And many of those dreamers are plotting in France, is that not so, Robin? Could that be the reason you pass so much time there?" And though I thought he had long since quit that childish habit, Robin is scratching at his neck.

It's a good thing I'd opened my window wide, else I'd not have heard the commotion. I'm just set thinking how still and tidy all is, and the moon fat and round as a newborn, and how the silence – which in truth used to hurt my ears – now sits well with me, when there's such a to-do, I'm feared some prowling creature's afoot. But then the moon lights the garden and I'm quick to see it's no fox nor stag disturbing the peace. No. And though it's hard to be sure, it's either Will propping Robin or t'other way. They're laughing and carrying on and I think best I get down there quick before they rouse the whole house. I put a shawl over my night robe and creep down quiet.

First thing I note is the smell of strong ale. Robin is worst off. Will is practically carrying him, and once in the house, I see there's blood on Robin's eye. "A fellow made a low jibe at his late majesty and Mr Robin weren't having it. He's surely got a temper on him." And Will starts chuckling. He stops short when he notes my mood.

I'm thankful Robin's room is on the other side of the house, well away from his brother, since there's enough noise to wake the cows. When we finally get him inside, it takes another effort to haul Robin onto his bed. Will holds the candle so's I can better see the wound. Turns out it's just a small cut and not as deep as I'd feared. I scold Will and tell him to get off home. "And woe betide you tomorrow if you come one minute late."

I take a cloth and some water from the pitcher on the dresser and dab at Robin's forehead. Seems I'm forever tending his ills.

Then Robin tries to turn on his side, ready to drift off peaceful as a babe. I do feel so angry with him for always putting his foot wrong and not changing at all with his years. I let the cloth wipe roughly at the cut till Robin groans and opens his eyes. "It's you, Jane," he says.

"You've luck enough it's just me and not the entire household." And I'm thinking: *Who else would be fool enough to see you right at this hour?* Through his stupor, Robin smiles. I tell him to lie quiet and let me do my work. And Robin laughs and takes hold of both my hands. I'm trying to work them free and I bid Robin stop his foolishness. But despite myself, I'm laughing too. Robin keeps his hold on me, though, and strong as I am, I cannot break it. And before I can put a stop to this bargy, he's pulling me down onto him. I say, "Don't." And then I say it more strongly. But Robin doesn't heed. I'm fighting now, but he tightens his hold on my wrists until I cry out. And in a blink, he reverses our positions so's I'm lying beneath him. I do manage to free my fingers, but though I struggle to raise my hands, he has my arms pinned to the bed. And the face above me is strained and urgent and has none of Robin's humour. And though the mouth on my throat is warm, it's the mouth of a stranger. I try to plead, but the breath has all gone out of me, and in a trice he has freed one of my arms and placed his own across my throat, pressing down so's I'm sure I will die. I feel his other hand beneath my nightrobe. But though I scratch at him, I cannot move. Over his shoulder, through the window, the moon remains full, and with no clouds to spoil its shape. But it's rocking now, back and forth, as Robin thrusts and thrusts. I close my eyes against the pain.

I lay quiet and still. It's only when Robin's breathing is heavy with sleep that I'm able to move myself. My hand is sore and shaking as I hold up the candle. I can't see Robin's face. It's buried in his pillows.

I'm slow getting back to my chamber. I twice lose direction and take the wrong stairs. I'm supposing it must be the candle flame making everything so strange and unfamiliar. When I finally find my room, I'm glad to see my bits and bobs still set straight and ordered. I leave the candle burning on the table close to my bed. I'm still clutching the cloth soiled from Robin's cut. I use it to wipe the blood from my legs. I lay awake till the candle burns itself out.

And the dark is so dark.

Chicksands Priory, Bedfordshire, June 25th

Sir

I could wish you a thousand little mishaps for coming so near Bedford and not seeing me. Would your horse had lost all its legs instead of only a shoe so it was not able to carry you further. And now there's no chance since you are already in York! Though I'm grateful to know you are safe with your father and sister after that hazardous journey.

Your father is right to counsel you to think on a good fortune when choosing a wife. Though for me, that would be poor enough reason to tie myself to another. And if your father has one in mind who is also fair and of good character, so much the better. You would do well to follow his advice rather than your heart, which you seem so certain will not mislead you. The heart may not be the best guide, especially when, as I fear with you, it becomes too easily entwined.

You say you hope to be at Chicksands before the summer is out. Well, I think you needs be quick so you may claim your ten pounds. I must tell you that some friends who have observed in my face some gravity as you do, have proposed a widower to me, with four daughters old enough to be my sisters and a great estate. And as fine a gentleman as ever England bred. I am more than a little pleased that I may at last have met one with wit enough for himself and me too! But I've not forgot you in your absence, and if your father's efforts prove unsuccessful,

I'm set on you having one of my step-daughters. You shall have your choice. They say all are exceeding handsome and come with a goodly fortune. I'm sure I would make an excellent mother-in-law. What think you?

You have missed Robin, who left as speedily as he came – all packed and mounted before any had risen. My brother Henry worries Robin is courting trouble in his dealings in France. It is true he is strong-headed enough to let caution fly. Did you gain any such notion when you met with him in Paris?

I've not been in town much on account of my father's health. My brother Henry is oft gone and I would not leave my father alone. I think Henry pursues some good alternative for me should the widower prove unreliable. I hear from my aunt that Cromwell's son is ready to make my acquaintance, which just shows what strange times we live in. I would, of course, not consider such an offer, though they do say he is of better character than his father.

Now, I have sent you a long missive here and I would ask you to oblige me with the same and not your usual brief lines. I need to know all your news, and some idea when we may expect you, which I very much hope will be soon. Until then, I am always your humble servant

D.O.

Chicksands, July 20

Sir

I am reckoning how many faults you charge me with in your last letter – and amongst them, I see I am `heartless, unmerciful, unkind and severe'. What must I do to mend all this? I fear it is the work of an age. Alas, I shall likely be old before I am good!

Seriously, if there was anything in my letter to so distress you, I'm truly sorry, but how could you imagine I was set to accept the widower? If it's so, then York has robbed you of your

humour. Of course, I wrote in jest. And if you could see what
a learned, insufferable, arrogant coxcomb of a fellow he is, you
would be laughing as much as I! His head is so full of little
philosophical thoughts, I wonder I managed to find a place
there. He told my brother had he offered £500 more, he would
have taken me, to the greater glory of my family. And I told
Henry if this gentleman accepted £1,000 less and promised
me complete control of himself and his estate, I would still not
have him.

So, there's an end to it. And you must on no account pursue
this ill-thought plan of leaving York immediately to come here,
although I long to show you Chicksands with the pear trees in
bloom and the meadows ablaze. But think on your father. I
would not be the cause of a rift between you, else I should hate
myself forever.

You ask for proof of the strength of my regard for you.
What more can I give – save to say you have reason to believe
I will always be your faithful friend

D.O.

P.S. Henry Cromwell wishes to send me a pair of greyhounds.
Have you seen these new dogs? They are said to be truly
beautiful creatures and HC swears he knows the best breeder
in England.

York, July 29

Madam

For God's sake, write to me in earnest and tell me all
that's in your heart. Let us have no more subterfuge. I am
past all that with you. Whatever you have brought me to and
how you have done it, I know not. I have always thought I
was never intended for that fond thing termed a true lover.
I can only say that as the world goes, I see little of value in
it besides you.

My father would that I stayed with him longer. Yet he told me he would not see me so discontented, and that if you desired my coming, he would not hinder it. So, I will be with you soon, when we may talk face to face, and heart to heart.

I look forward to a clear sky awaiting me in Bedfordshire. Till then, I remain

Yours. W.T.

P.S. I know nothing about these new dogs, 'cept they are capricious of mood and easily provoked. I trust you will not accept Cromwell's offer — nor any other he may make you.

"It seems Robin spoke true." Seated at our father's desk, Henry holds up a letter. "William Temple has the impudence to invite himself." I say nothing. "Do you take me for a fool, sister?" Still, I am silent. "Do you imagine I've known nothing of your continued contact?" My brother's eye begins to twitch.

"I am sure, Henry, there is not the smallest corner of my life of which you are unaware." In truth, I know William's letter has caught my brother by surprise.

"If this hasty visit heralds a declaration towards you," he says, "you can be sure I will never sanction it."

I tell Henry it doesn't lay with him to *sanction* anything. "Only our father has that right."

And there ensues the usual argument on family duty and my woeful lack of it. He declares the Temples as good as penniless. "No doubt a consequence of switching allegiance so often."

"Well, at least we know they're not hunting a fortune here." This remark further rankles my brother and serves to fetch up all that lay on his stomach. All the men I have refused are brought upon the stage like ghosts to reproach me. My few good qualities, it seems, only serve to highlight my lack of wits in this matter.

"Despite my counsel, you still harbour feelings for this man." And since this is true, I don't deny it. Suddenly more reasonable,

Henry decides to offer a little homily. "Look around you, Dorothy. People who marry with great passion soon come to lose it. Those are happiest who have least of it."

And I find myself in the odd position of defending a sentiment I've long been wary of. "You would condemn me to a life devoid of emotional joy, Henry. I will never agree to such a union."

Henry swears he is merely concerned with my future – and his. "I should not like to lose you, sister. Were you set in a well-established household, it's likely I could follow you there." A happy thought indeed.

"You think it enough, Henry, for a man to be 'well established'. By which you mean rich. But if I cannot love the man I wed, I fear I'll grow to hate him and myself." I'm mortified to find I am close to tears. My brother moves towards me.

"You know, Dorothy, no man could ever love you as well as I do." I can more easily cope with Henry's rages than these sudden bursts of sentimentality.

I go in search of Jane. My brain is so addled with this late discourse I've almost forgotten the good news. "William is finally to come, and in less than two weeks!" Seated in the darkest corner of the hall, Jane looks up briefly from her needlepoint and nods. "You must light the candles, Jane. Your eyes will strain in this gloom." She says nothing but dutifully rises and goes to the kitchens. No doubt this sombre mood means Jane still harbours resentment towards William. I swear there is a stubbornness to this girl that once set, will not be moved. When she returns with the tapers, I speak plainly.

"Would you were happy for me, Jane. God knows I need you with me in this. After all this time, you seem still determined to distrust William."

Even before she speaks, Jane's look tells me I wrong her. "I'm all for wishing your happiness, my lady. I did used to fret about Mr Temple, but I see he proves a proper gentleman and of some loyalty, and I'm thinking that's rare in a man." Jane returns to her needlepoint and I hide my surprise by busying myself with some roses that have been badly arranged on the hall table. When I look across, Jane is weeping.

"Are you ill, dear Jane?" I'm at her side. But, drying her eyes, she insists she was never better. "It's just these long summer days don't sit well with me." I don't tell her what an odd remark this is – or what an emotional morning it's been.

Since his health will not permit otherwise, it has become my father's custom to remain seated in chapel when all stand for prayers. So, Jane and I, on either side of him, don't at first notice his distress. It's only when we too are seated that I realise all is not well. My father remains slumped forward, not by choice, it seems, but because his limbs refuse to move. I put my arms around him. He tries to speak, but words too fail him. Jane and I attempt to lift him to his feet, but this fragile man has become heavy as stone, and seemingly unaware of his surroundings. It takes Will Hammer to bear him to his chamber, with Noah following close.

As Henry is in London, it lays on me to arrange the night. I tell Jane we must take it in turns to sit up. "With the help of you and Will, we shall manage." As it is, the three of us sit together, fortified by a pitcher of ale. My father sleeps. Except for an occasional barely audible groan, he is finally peaceful. Weariness and anxiety make me talkative. "Do you remember when we were children, Will? You and Robin would torment me so about my height!" And poor Will reddens. "I towered above them both, Jane, and those two swore I was destined for a giantess and would be likely forced to live in a cave."

"If you'll pardon, Miss Dorothy, it were mostly Mr Robin who enjoyed such jesting. I was just an onlooker." And Will, his usually reticent tongue loosened by ale, goes on to regale us with more of Robin's boyhood pranks, from riding the back of a bull to spoiling a shoot. "He set them birds aflying just a day afore." Even from this distance in time, Will's voice is full of admiration. "He knew how to delegate his doings, though. He had me keep watch in a tree for nigh on two hour."

I remark that for all his jesting, Robin always harboured softness for God's creatures. "He's like you, Jane." Jane says nothing. I wish she would tell me what ails her. I miss her good humour and laughter, which, although at times irritating, have become as familiar to me as air.

Henry has returned and brought with him a visitor – in the shape of Aunt Gargrave. "When we had news of your father, how would I not come?" As I embrace her, I know, of course, she is here as Henry's ally. But I'm glad she's come. Always, since a child, I've been sure all will be well if my aunt is present.

Although my father seems out of immediate danger, he keeps wholly to his bed. And since he still cannot speak, it is often impossible to fathom his needs. "It's that look of resignation that hurts my heart," I tell my aunt. And as I walk with her to her chamber, Aunt Gargrave recites the many potions brought from London.

"I have sought good medical counsel from those who know." One mixture in particular supposedly fortified the King's nephew, Prince Rupert, before battle. "It's a pity they didn't give it to the whole army," my aunt remarks. Then, taking off her travelling cloak, she comes swiftly to the point. "Now, Dorothy. Tell me about this Mr Temple."

"What is it you would know?"

"Come, Dorothy. Your brother thinks this man a fortune hunter whose intentions cannot be honourable since you have so little to offer." Choosing my words carefully, I give a brief sketch of William's character as I see it, omitting any mention of our long correspondence and growing attachment. My aunt looks thoughtful. "And he is handsome, no doubt," is all she says.

He is handsome indeed – and he is come! Coat dishevelled. His face heated from the journey. Whispering encouragement to his mount; his long, sensitive fingers caressing the damp mane before turning to greet us. Aunt Gargrave is the first to step forward. "I think we may have met, Mr Temple." And as he gives her the knee, William assures her they have not.

"Else how would I forget such a pleasure?"

The greeting with my brother is stiff, both men wary. "Mr Temple. I trust you journeyed well? Chicksands is somewhat off-route for visitors."

William replies there are many routes to be taken from York to London. "This one is the most pleasant."

"With so much still laid waste, most find it a sad sight," Henry says.

When William turns to me, he is nervous. "Miss Osborne. I find you well, I hope?" And he goes on to enquire about my father. As for me, I can scarce look at him. All my careful planning, the endless conversations with myself – all for nought. I am lost. He will stay only two days, and in our current disorder, I thought it enough. But already I wonder how I am ever to part with him.

"What think you, Jane?"

Yes, my lady. You are right, he still has a way with him." Jane, helping me dress for supper, is something of her old self. "He certainly charmed Lady Gargrave." I'm pleased to hear Jane laugh again.

"Let's hope he can weave his magic with my brother. I would so have them friends." But watching from my window as these two men return from a tour of the estate, walking several feet apart and without speaking, it's clear such bonding is unlikely.

Over supper, my aunt is eager for York gossip. "Tell us the rumours, Mr Temple." William says as in London, all talk is of Oliver Cromwell set to declare himself 'Lord Protector'. "Having dissolved Parliament by brute force, this man who swore allegiance to the people now intends to rule over his own chosen council."

"Well," says Henry, "in this sorry thing called a Commonwealth, Cromwell is as good as another." Seeing us shocked, he adds: "At least he is not declaring himself king."

"But you must know, sir," William says, "such an idea has been muted." And he reveals further disturbing news. "Come what may, it's said Cromwell intends to install himself in the palace at Whitehall."

In Henry's opinion, this is mere tattle. "Though I imagine your family have some privy to Crowell's thinking, Mr Temple." And I see William's colour rise.

"My father once believed parliament bent on working the people's will. When he saw Cromwell's true ambitions, and how things might go for the King, he withdrew support."

"You mean he changed sides, Mr Temple."

Before William can answer, my aunt steps in. "What say they of the younger son, Henry Cromwell? He seems cut from altogether better cloth."

In a flat voice, William declares the Cromwell family all fashioned from the same unrefined material. "We were together at Cambridge, where Henry Cromwell had little aptitude for study and none at all for making himself agreeable."

My aunt mulls this over before enquiring if Henry Cromwell, too, is destined to live at the palace. "Will the sons also benefit, do you think, Mr Temple?" She naturally considers it an outrage the usurper and his kin should dare seat themselves at Whitehall. "But what a triumph for those they marry." I am aware of the heat in this room; of the spreading dampness at the back of my neck and beneath my arms.

The subject of HC is not easily exhausted. "He left Cambridge early to fight for a cause he believed in," my brother remarks. "You too left early, did you not, Mr Temple? To tour France and other pleasant spots." Well pleased with himself, Henry pauses to let this statement take effect.

William says: "I would not do battle against my fellow countrymen, sir. No matter how just the cause."

My aunt is the first to weary of this jousting. "If someone would help me to my chamber…" And Jane, no doubt glad to be free of this toxic air, is swiftly at her side. As William rises and bows, Aunt Gargrave drops a curtsy – something I know she finds increasingly painful. But when Jane tries to help her upright, my aunt pushes her hand away. "You must see the little chapel tomorrow, Mr Temple. It's refurbished with newly stained glass, despite Cromwell's edicts."

My aunt and Jane are barely out of the room before Henry resumes battle.

"I thought you'd little time for the pulpit, Mr Temple?" Knowing where this will go, I try to divert the talk.

"You would not credit our trouble finding craftsmen willing to fashion those chapel windows."

But William is intent on defending his beliefs. "I truly think God is not necessarily the answer to everything."

My brother leans forward. "No doubt for some, God occupies a poor place compared to their own desires."

And William replies that for others it's a question of striving to recognise the will of God and what is wrought by man. "The Almighty gave us power of thought, sir, and I believe it's his will we use it."

My brother observes it rare to meet a man on such intimate terms with the will of God. There is silence. I fear it will last only whilst these gentlemen prepare for renewed combat. I too rise, leaving them to thrust and parry into the night, with my brother, I fear, set to gain most points.

I am scarce back to my chamber when, close behind, Aunt Gargrave is with me. "Shall we not talk a little?" And without waiting for a response, my aunt settles herself in a chair by the hearth. I remain standing. "He is surely personable, Dorothy." And my aunt bids me help remove her shoes. This then, is likely to be a long interview. "It's not hard to see why a young woman might become besotted." When I don't answer, she continues: "I expect any number have already succumbed to Mr Temple's charms."

And my aunt goes on to liken William to another charmer – her late husband, Richard Gargrave, known in the family as one with a weakness for drink and gaming tables, and dying in profligate circumstances. "He had a way with women, you see," she says, "and like his other excesses, it led to his downfall."

I am shocked at this comparison. "Do you think it right, Aunt? William – Mr Temple – has shown nothing but honourable behaviour towards us."

"Come and sit here by the fire." My aunt bids me take the stool and draw it closer. "I am merely saying there are certain men who from early youth find any woman is available to them."

"What are you suggesting, Aunt? That it is *I* who have behaved improperly?"

"Now, Dorothy, don't get on your high horse. I am suggesting the opposite. I see he is unsure of you." I tell her such imaginings would inspire poets. But I know it to be true. From the few glances we've managed, I've noticed this gentleman, always so confident and at ease, has developed towards me an awkward diffidence. Perhaps the cards have strengthened in my favour.

"It's the conquest, you see," my aunt continues. "That's what interests him." She adds that her late husband was of similar mind. "And once the battle was won, he had need of other victories. Yes, well…" My aunt's voice is suddenly weary. I help her from her chair. "Tell Jane to bring my shoes in the morning. I'll not further offend my feet tonight." In the doorway, she makes one more effort. "You could never wed him, Dorothy. There is not the money there. And God knows, you owe it to your father to see you richly settled." Yet again, it comes to this.

I lay on my bed, too weary to remove my gown. So, this is how it will go. I'll likely have not one minute alone with him. My brother will never look kindly on William. No doubt my father, too, if he were able, would be loath to sanction this friendship. Henry is right: passion unchecked brings only pain, which before this madness, I surely knew to be true. But what am I now supposed to do with all these feelings that threaten to overwhelm me?

I'm woken by Jane, staring down at me. "You should have called, my lady." She tells me it is past nine o'clock. "Mr Temple has been up and visiting your father this hour or more." It seems my brother too is asking for me.

"Tell them I slept badly, Jane. I will join them at dinner." But when the chapel bell strikes noon, I've still not risen.

It's full afternoon when Jane comes to me again. She's pleased to find me at my desk. " I was thinking we might have need of the medic." She fetches a fresh gown from the closet. "You are to meet the gentleman down by the old barns. I told him that were the best place to go undiscovered."

"I would have you go in my stead, Jane – and hand him this note."

Jane declares herself at a loss for words. "Here he is, finally come, and this is your chance, Miss Dorothy, if you'll pardon my boldness. The Lord knows if there'll be another."

"Then we shall leave it in the Lord's hands, Jane."

I needn't tell you how dear you have become to me. But I believe we have allowed our feelings to go against the tide by desiring too much. Under the mask of friendship, we seem to have conjured hopes so airy they cannot support reality. I write frankly, for you have said you would know all that's in my heart.

Since you came, I've wearied myself with thinking. But you have seen how things are. And I can see no end to our misfortunes should we allow this folly to continue. Better to yield to what we cannot change than to long for something we've no likelihood of ever gaining. I tell you plainly – I would not lose you. My hope is that we may continue a true friendship, made the more perfect by having nothing of passion in it. I will always think of you as a person I extremely value and esteem, and you may know I will ever be your faithful

D.O.

Sir John Temple's House, York

Madam

I came to you in good faith, in the surety that you returned my feelings, as your letters have encouraged me to believe. Your indifferent treatment has shown how mistaken I was. Indeed, my father doubts you ever had true regard for me, since he has seen me so discouraged.

Your abrupt dismissal has left me in despair and at a loss to understand what has wrought this change. You offer 'friendship', but you must know of the passion, the love, I feel for you. If all I desire is to be so cruelly snatched away, I see very little reason to continue this existence. Better to end it. Death would be preferable to a life devoid of hope and purpose.

I remain, as always, your humble servant

William Temple

Chicksands

Sir

Your letter pains me. You wrong me if you think I played you false. I am your friend as ever I was in my life! God knows how hard it was to see you ride away and knowing that I had so hurt the one person I wish the most well.

You ask what has wrought this change. It is as I wrote: I believe it senseless to struggle against life. If God has seen fit to satisfy our desires, we should have had them. And if – as you say – you truly love me, then I beg you preserve yourself from the violent passion you showed in your letter. I tremble at the desperate things you wrote. A thousand women would not be worth this anguish.

I will write often. Only death or some palsy of the hands could prevent it. As for me, you may be sure I am as wretched as you. I shall not blush to write that you have made the rest of the world indifferent to me. If I cannot be yours, they may dispose of me as they please. Henry Cromwell will be as acceptable as any other.

Your ever faithful

D.O.

"This is lies," I say. "No," I say. "No, this is not the truth." If I say it enough, it will not be. I give the letter back to Henry, unwilling to have it longer in my hand.

"I fear it is so, Dorothy." Henry's face is ashen. We cling to each other. We've need to sit close together on the hall bench. Incredulous, Henry reads the letter again.

Sir,

It is with great sorrow I bring you this unhappy news. Your brother Robin, who I've been pleased to call my friend these several years, has met with an accident as tragic as it was sudden, and which has robbed us all of a spirit which in our whole lives we rarely happen upon. On route to an island off the coast of St Malo, Robin fell from the end of the boat, and despite the best efforts of his companions to recover him, he was lost to them.

Be assured I feel your bereavement as deeply as I feel my own. I hope one day for the opportunity to relate the many reasons you may be justly proud of a departed and much-mourned brother and friend.

Your humble servant
James Blentworth

"No, Henry. You'll see it is a mistake."

"I showed anger when he left," Henry says. "I failed to tell him safe journey."

"He can swim," I say. "You forget how he swims. Behind the old barns. The pond. So, it cannot be true."

"My brother drowned and I failed to wish him safe passage." Henry sobs. My own eyes are dry. I cannot weep.

My offences to God are surely great. From that has come all misfortune. And now this sore affliction. Through God's gentle mercy may I bear it.

I'm standing in the pond behind the old barns. The water is up to my waist and I am naked. People watch, silently, from the field beyond. I cover my body with my hands as best I can. The water is rising. I shout for help. The crowd has thickened now, but nobody moves. Then Robin is there. He reaches towards me: "Take my hand." But someone pulls him back and prevents his coming. The water is almost to my mouth. I am sobbing. I wake suddenly to the sound of it. But the weeping comes not from me. It is muffled, indistinct, but full of distress. I realise it is coming through the wall next to my bed. From Jane's chamber. As I open the door to her room, I try to suppress the shameful sense of relief that it is not William we must mourn.

Best as I can, I try to rouse myself, but my body won't do nought. There's no energy to it. "Oh, my lady," and Miss Dorothy sits herself on the bed and holds my hand.

"Dear Jane, gentle-hearted as always." She pulls back the covers and lays next to me. "Did he suffer, Jane? Was Robin too in fear of such an end?"

"It's as you said, my lady. He hits his head on the side of the boat and so feels nothing." These are the words I know she would believe and I am determined I shall too. I think on that note, thrown on the fire. Just three words: *Forgive me, Jane'*. Never! I tore it up.

Tender as if I were a newborn, my lady puts her arms around me and rocks me. 'Oh, Robin!' She strokes my wet hair and face. She too is weeping. First time today she's shed a tear. She kisses me on my eyes. We stay like that, comforted.

Only time I've known the house this quiet was when they killed the King. Usually, the kitchens are so a-clatter with gossip and, giggling, I'm forced to have a word. Not today. Even the dogs in the yard have quit their scrapping and barking. They do say animals know when things sit badly. Mr Henry is the only one giving voice to his thoughts. "There is more to this, Dorothy. I shall go to France. I'll talk to these people." Not much good in that. Not now. I've my own jumble of thoughts, and one in particular lies heavy: *Robin, gone.* I sit on the kitchen bench to catch my breath. I'm still there when Will comes with wood for the oven.

"You're pale as parchment, Jane." Will fetches some leftover broth from a pot in the hearth, but I can't take any. "We must all keep up our strength," Will says.

I can scarce stop myself asking, *Why?*

I remember my father saying there was nought so base as bringing forth a bastard child. Back in Guernsey, there was a young widow, pious as they come – or so it were thought. That's till she was brought to bed and the midwife called. The day it was birthed, she stifled it with a sheet and left it in the church porch. She pleaded she'd lost her senses. She escaped the hangman but the magistrate locked her up anyway. My father said was a pity she weren't driven into the sea.

"What will you do, Jane?" It's Will who guesses. I know by his look there's no point denying. "I'm the oldest of twelve, Jane, so I know a bit about what's what."

"If you speak of this, Will, I am undone." I can't look at him.

I feel the shame well up in me. What *will* I do? I'm determined my lady shan't know one word. I daresn't think on my father. And I know there'll be tattle soon enough. Will tells of a woman just outside the village.

"My mother used her services twice." I say I've heard talk she's a witch. I say it light so Will shan't note my dread. "That's just old crone gossip," Will says. "She births bairns too, so she knows what she's about." He's not asked one word as to the fathering.

I tell my lady I've business in Bedford. She's not best pleased. "I'll be back in a day or two."

"With all that's happened, I truly need you with me, Jane." I manage to stand firm.

Will comes with me. "The house is yonder, across them fields." Hovel, more like, and inside not much better. A family and as many cats living in one room. Will asks if he should stay. I say better not.

"Come for her in two hours." It's the first time the woman's spoke. She's over by the hearth with her back to us, stirring a pot. I never could stomach the stench of herbs stewing. When she turns, I note the weary eyes and filthy apron. Will looks as if he can't wait to be away. I do admit feeling low when he's gone. I put my hand in the pocket of my cloak so's none shall note its shaking. I finger the silver piece I'd been saving to send my father. I'm hoping it will suffice. A small girl, dirty and barefoot and carrying a babe, stares full at me with her big, dull eyes. I'm overcome with shame. I try to smile.

We go outside to what most would swear is a broken shed. Turns out it's a bedchamber – of sorts. Nowhere a body would want to lay their head. I'm glad to be out of the eyes of those children, though. The woman takes a blanket from a chest and spreads it on the bed. It's so stained, you can't fathom the true colour. She bids me take off my cloak and gown and lay down. Only way I can bear this is to think on other things. Think on the sea. My father lifting me above the waves and then dropping me down so the water runs over my toes.

Best be angry. Angry at Robin for dying like that. Angry that things can never now be set straight – not that they ever could've been. Not such a terrible way to die, lying peaceful on the seabed. I should tell Miss Dorothy that. The woman is pressing and kneading my belly. "Will you be hurting it?"

"Ain't much there. Not even quickening yet." She bids me drink the herbs. I try to hold the cracked bowl but my hands are shaking. She finally ups and holds it for me. The mixture is thick and bitter. "We'll just open you up a bit." Fingers probing, going deeper. I cling to the edge of the blanket, screw it into a ball. Then something sharp and strange, and so painful. Despite myself, I'm crying out to my maker. "Don't go being a babby." The woman laughs. "Just my little jest."

I know by Will's face I look like something the dogs found. "Lean on me, Jane. We'll soon have you home." I'm having difficulty with this walking. Suddenly Will is carrying me. We move fast enough then. In through a door and onto a bed. I close my eyes.

When I open them, it's night. I'm in such pain, I'm thinking best to die right now. The candle by the bed is lit but I don't know where I am. A bare room with little comfort. In the corner, Will, slumped in a chair. I'm loath to wake him but the pain is too great. "Help me, Will." And he holds my head whilst I'm sick into a slop basin. "Where are we, Will?" Then, without him saying, I know. It's Noah's room. I remember how I'd likened it to a cell. Now it's me in the prison, where most likely I belong.

Next time I wake, two persons are hovering. "So much blood," someone says. Someone else is gently dabbing my forehead with a wet rag. It takes a moment to realise it's Noah. "Just rest, girl," he says.

"How long have I been here, Will?"

"Only a day. No one knows. This place is right cut off." I'm thinking they're bound to know soon enough. Not much chance of keeping secrets round these parts.

"What about Noah?"

Will tells me he slept out in the old barns. "He's been that worried for you."

"Do you think it were a boy, Will?"

"Best not think on that now. Best just carry on."

Dear Niece,

When misfortune strikes, as it so often has in this family, we must be ever mindful of our duty to rise above it, in perfect assurance of God's great mercy and love. But really, Dorothy, what was Robin doing on a boat in the middle of the ocean? He has too long been strong-headed and now God has seen fit to punish him, and we must all suffer. But oh, how I shall sorely miss those high spirits and quick wits of my beloved nephew!

I am perplexed to know Jane has chosen this very moment to journey to Guernsey, and with no word of her return. You'd every right to voice dissatisfaction at such an ungrateful arrangement. I am of the opinion Jane should count it lucky indeed if you agree to have her with you again.

I myself will be at Chicksands as soon as the weather permits. As it is, this late heat has put such a swelling on my hands and feet. Yesterday, I had to abandon my wedding bands. I felt it particularly when I supped at Lady Praxton's airless house on Charles Street, and would have left early had it not been for the arrival of Lord Southley and his eldest son. As fine a young gentleman as you could hope to meet, and with an estate to inherit that would please even the most particular woman. Added to that, there is a fair face – though not so handsome as to cause concern. I could not help but mention to his father how struck I was.

I think on you, dear niece, and pray God give us all strength in this latest affliction.

Your affectionate aunt
Catherine Gargrave.

P.S. There is such dancing in town as you wouldn't credit, despite Mr Cromwell's edicts, including a new one called Gavotte, that's said to hail from France. Last week, at Lady Chitworth's, all the young were partaking of it, including your Mr Temple, who proved most excellent proficient when he took to the floor with one of Lord Rich's comely daughters. Their jolliness minded me of my own youthful love of the dance — now, like so much else, long past.

I put the letter into the pocket of my gown and walk out into the gardens and across to one of the old barns. Inside, all is chilly and decrepit. It reeks with the scent of dead animals cooked over the open brazier the soldiers left behind. Some ancient toys thrown in a corner are the only reminder of the childhood games once played here. Forgotten beneath the skittles and hoops is Robin's beloved horse. I drag it out and gently wipe away the dust and mildew with some straw. The sad wooden face slowly emerges. I can just manage to sit on its narrow back, comforted by the gentle rocking. When we were children, this was never permitted. As captain of the King's Infantry, the rocking horse was Robin's privilege. I was ever destined for the humble foot soldier awaiting orders. And Robin was always loath to end the game, even when we were both exhausted. Child and man, he was anxious to experience life to the full. That's what I shall miss most. Robin's ability to live in each moment.

I take out my aunt's letter and read it again. William, of course, is the same. He's committed to the pleasures of living. This is what first drew me to him. He has too much energy and liveliness to let the anguish of love lost wither his heart. Would that I had such a gift. I unpick the horse's tangled grey mane and comb it with my fingers. I've no talent for forgetting the past. These last months, when forced to sup or play, I fear I cast a shadow rather than enhance the evening. Henry has said as much: "I swear you have become the dullest of guests, sister. Your company at table is destined to sour the merriest gathering."

But what good can possibly come of prolonging this misery?

Their jolliness minded me of my own youthful love… Aunt Gargrave writes. I must pull myself out of this torpor. I shall sever all contact. I'll no longer reply to his letters. I shall immerse myself in other things. I brush the grime from my gown and go out into the sunshine.

There's a figure running towards me. One whose long legs carry him like a giant across the gardens. He's calling my name, as if in greeting. But as Will Hammer draws close, I hear the urgency in his voice. "Miss Dorothy, your father – come quick."

I recall being in my father's chamber with Will and Jane, and how their presence calmed my anxiety. Now I watch alone, holding my father's hand. He's not stirred this entire evening. Oh, Jane, how I would welcome your presence now! We've sent to London for my brother and he will doubtless bring my aunt, but I fear they may come too late. The stillness is broken only by my father's laboured breathing. I draw close to him. "You have been the very best of fathers." I stroke the fragile, almost transparent, hand. "Would that I had your counsel now when I so need it."

Will says: "You should rest, Miss Dorothy. Me and Noah can take our turns in watching."

I am reluctant to go. "I would not have my father left alone, even for a moment." I lay down on my bed, determined not to sleep. But my body is suddenly heavy as lead. When I wake, it is morning.

Noah was with him when he died. My father was not alone. I thank God for that one small blessing. All is peaceful – except for the eyes with their imploring stare. Neither Noah nor I have coins to press against them. I bend towards my father and kiss his cheek. I whisper to him: "You can rest now, Father. It was enough."

Tomorrow, Henry and I will leave Chicksands. My eldest brother, John, will arrive to take up residence. It seems I must now depend on relatives who are not my friends and who consider they do me a charity. My aunt is taking the waters. Until she returns, I shall be obliged to pass from one to another. There will be little time for quiet grief. I walk through the rooms one last time. When I enter this house again, it will be as a guest. A strange thought, but not as painful as once it would have been. Chicksands and I are long separated. Others have left their mark. Now, a new family will breathe life into these walls. I know little of my brother John. At sixteen years my senior, he was seldom here for my growing years. I wonder if he too is about to have his childhood memories tarnished.

Our trunks are ready and stacked. All that remains is to bid farewell to those who've cared for us. I fear our departure will fall hardest on Noah. Henry says: "Well, old friend. I trust you will serve the son as faithfully as you served the father." Looking at Noah's weathered face, remembering his steadfast care through all our changing fortunes, I am overcome. But, as always, it's impossible to gauge Noah's thoughts. Even when I lean forward and kiss him on the cheek, he retains his impassive stance. The day of my father's death is the only time I've known Noah falter. A hand laid on my father's own cold hand; the familiar clearing of the throat prolonged for an extra few seconds.

Will is more demonstrative, grasping my hand and wishing me safe passage. "I'm right glad to know Jane will be with you again, Miss Dorothy. I'd be much obliged if you'd tell her my regards."

Once in the coach, Henry and I are silent with our thoughts. We don't look back.

BOOK TWO
MARRIAGE

LONDON AND CHELSEA

I open the scrap of paper again. My palms are all a-sweat. *Sir Henry Molle. Next to the new hatmaker in Jermyn Street.* I'm hoping this surly coachman knows his business. Truth is, I've been fretting this whole journey. Her letter was cordial enough, but I'm still not sure of my welcome. My father was loath for me to leave: *England don't sit well with you, Jane.* He knows nothing of my need to set things straight. Not that I ever could.

Keep walking straight forward then turn at the Dog and Duck. And I'm in the street with my bundles before I can blink. It takes at least ten minutes to find this cousin's house, and another few to summon myself to knock. Once in the hallway, I'm still all a-jitter. Miss Dorothy seemed set on my coming, but I still remember her displeasure when I up and left Chicksands.

Turns out all my fussing's for nought. My lady comes straight down the stairs and embraces me. And as far as I can see, there's no strangeness between us. "Jane, you cannot know how I've missed you." She holds me away from her. "Let me look at you." Next, she's telling me I've grown thinner. "Are you sure you are quite well?"

"Grand as can be, Miss Dorothy." And surely should be – with six months' bellyful of sea air. "You'll find me same as ever was and grateful to be back in your company." She's changed too. There's not that lustre to the eye. And I note she's wearing the same mourning gown that served for her mother and Robin. The poor thing's scarce been out of it this two year. "My father sends his condolence, my lady. He was always admiring of Sir Peter."

She squeezes my hand. "Come, let me show you this disordered house." There's truth enough there. Seems there's no good management to this establishment. *Cleanliness is next to godliness*, my father always says – and I pride myself on following that dictum. Not so folk in this house, judging by the mess of debris littering the kitchens. This cousin of hers is not to be seen, and I'm noting his manservants are either paying court to the kitchen wenches or lolling in the stables with the grooms. Sensing my discomfort, my lady says: "Being a bachelor, my cousin Molle has no notion how to run a good house."

Same as always, I'm back brushing her hair afore bed. We're both well pleased, and my mind is further eased when Miss Dorothy tells me her aunt is to return to London. "We'll soon be settled back in Chelsea, Jane." Good thing too. By my book. A cluttered house in Jermyn Street is no fit setting for someone of my lady's standing. We're so easy together, I don't think twice before asking how fares Mr Temple. Soon as I says it, I could bite my tongue. My lady stiffens. "I don't wish to speak of him." She does, though, and at some length. Turns out she's still receiving those letters – even though she's ceased hers to him. "If, as I believe, we are destined never again to meet, where is the sense of it?" I'm thinking there's never use trying to make sense of a heart.

Miss Dorothy's not best pleased I'm having to bed down with the kitchen wenches. As for me, I'm that tired, I'd be happy to curl up with the hens. I think I would be sound asleep this full hour were it not for the narrowness of this cot and the prattling of the maids. As it is, though, I'm still awake and tossing when all is quiet and the hall clock chimes midnight. My mind's too jumbled with thoughts. I'm surely thankful to be in good step with my lady again, but when I close my eyes, the blackness of that terrible night is upon me. I see Robin's face and that same troubled mess of happenings. And I'm back again thinking what I might have done different.

It's after breakfast when I finally lay eyes on Sir Henry Molle. I almost collide with him in the upstairs hallway as I take my lady's tray down, since no one else seems inclined to do so. And this cousin is of such expanse that I've needs to squeeze by him as we pass. He follows me into the kitchens. "Welcome to London, girl." And giving my bob, I thank him kindly for the privilege. "You'll find this house quite full of noise," he tells me. "People come and go. Indeed, we are oft times three to a bed." This said with a hand on my arm. I brush it off, casual as you like.

"I fear my lady may find that insupportable, sir." I say this as coldly as I dare. "At Chicksands, we were well used to our privacy."

Sir Henry Molle's laugh is akin to a horse. "Ah, child, in this house, privacy is hard come by. You'll have needs to get used to our ways. It's share and share alike."

This is one gentleman I shall be avoiding.

Considering she's lost interest in the doings of a certain party, Miss Dorothy spends a deal of time waiting on the carrier. Most often, it results in some dull note from Mr Henry or a long missive from Lady Gargrave – either one likely to spoil her humour. "My brother will arrive from Bath in two weeks, and my aunt writes she will remain at Epsom for the rest of the month," she tells me. "Happy news indeed. Meantimes, we may die of discomfort." I'm thinking far likely it will be from an excess of dirt. But it's not my place to chastise these wenches for the slovenly things they are, and no good thinking cold looks will move them. No, they're too busy preening and gossiping to take note. Sir Henry Molle seems oblivious to the advantage being taken. Seems his sole concern is to be abroad as much as possible.

"Now that you are to stay longer, Dorothy, I will take you and your companion to Spring Gardens," he says. "Do you know these pleasure gardens, girl?"

I tell him I've not had the privilege. "But they do sound particular, sir."

"Indeed so. And you shall see just how particular they are." And the cousin gives one of his neighs.

My lady is finally rewarded for her patience: a letter's come with that seal I've so oft seen. "There's talk of his family moving to Ireland," she says. "I think that the best possible news." She says it, but her face betrays her. "He writes he would see me one more time."

"It might sit right to have a proper farewell, my lady." I'm minded of Mr Temple's own pale look when I gave him that note at Chicksands. "I will leave immediately," was all he said.

My lady is adamant. "No, Jane. William and I shan't meet again. What possible good could come of it? No, I am determined to keep my resolve."

Jermyn Street, March 1654

Sir

Your letter arrived this morning, and I am glad indeed if the move to Ireland shall mean new opportunities for your father. How sad to learn your life in London has been dull beyond endurance. You say you've lost all spirit for town distractions. But do you truly never venture out? That is hard to believe. Compared with my own previous country quiet, London seems full of a thousand pleasing diversions and I am constantly abroad.

My aunt is at Epsom, where she continues her campaign to dispose of me. A new suitor is set to make an appearance. Though when he calls and sees me in my mourning gown, he'll likely scuttle off again. If, as you say, you would see me one last time, you may if you please. You know where to find me. When you see my look you too may wish you hadn't come. Though I shall be very glad if you do.

Till then, I remain as always...

I will see him just once more.

I'd forgotten how his presence fills a room. Especially one as cramped as this. As he gives the knee, I am aware of the scent of his skin – the luxury of his hair so close to my hand. "I see your cousin is fond of books," he says.

"He deems it fashionable to keep a library." To my knowledge, cousin Molle has little interest in the content of these shelves.

William expresses his sadness at the death of my father. "I always remember his generous hospitality at St Malo – and the happy time I spent there." He speaks with sincerity, but he doesn't look at me. Nervousness makes us both formal. I enquire after his journey; he asks about my aunt's health. His father, he tells me, will leave for Ireland in a week. "He's set to become Cromwell's new Commissioner to Dublin."

"That sounds weighty indeed."

"And obviously not destined to meet with your approval." He walks about the room, examining various objects. Then, still without looking at me and seemingly absorbed in the charms of a small silver box, he enquires if I intend to accept what he terms 'this eager new gallant'. "No doubt he's a man of ample estate and fortune to finally satisfy your family." He looks at me now, his eyes as cold as his voice.

"This is just another of my aunt's 'good prospects'." I say it as lightly as I am able. "I hear this gentleman is of such pomposity and gravitas, it pleases none to be in his company."

"And should he declare himself? No doubt it might amuse you to keep him dangling."

"You do me injustice, sir. No matter how great my indifference, I'd never knowingly trample on a person's sensibilities." I know my voice is shaking.

"You'd little concern for mine, Miss Osborne. Even my father has commented as much."

"He is wrong to judge me harshly and with so little knowledge of me!" As usual, I speak in haste and too warmly. "You cannot know how it cost me to have so wounded you – or my misery after you left Chicksands." He is at my side, my hands in his. And all the grief and disorders of these past months well up in me. Despite myself, I am weeping.

His voice is solicitous now. "Dearest, I've been as wretched as you. But it matters not if we are to be reunited. Will you consider it? Shall we not be wed? If you refuse, how are we both to endure?" I cling to him.

And amid all the upsets and surprises of this day, I hear a voice that is mine telling him: "Yes."

"I'm thinking Mr Cromwell will soon see fit to close this place." Jane's voice is as disapproving as her face.

"Are you not glad, Jane, to walk somewhere where you need not clasp a sprig of lavender to your nose?"

"Begging your pardon, my lady, but I'd rather be where we can see what's afront us." Spring Gardens arbour walks, twisting this way and that, make it impossible to see what's ahead. Examining her mask, which she is stubbornly refusing to wear, Jane says: "I've still no notion why we need *these* things."

"It's as I told you. It is deemed appropriate masks should be worn so's all might be equal-footed."

"I'm thinking it's a rum sort of pleasure garden where a groom may pass the time of day with a person of quality." Jane glances back to where my cousin's men, frisky as colts, walk a few paces behind. Cousin Molle, anxious to reach our supper box, has strode ahead, leaving us to keep pace best we can. As we turn a corner, we almost collide with two gentlemen coming in the opposite direction. One is a thin youth in gaudy attire. Even with full mask, I recognise his flamboyant air. Thomas Chillingwood is a friend of Henry's. But it's his companion who gives me pause. A man as tall as William, and with that same unruly dark hair hanging loosely about his shoulders. For a second, I'm filled with confusion. But when he speaks, this gentleman's voice is dry and hard, with none of William's warmth.

"What have we here? Two beautiful women legging it alone. Do you not fear to be compromised?" The two men stand stock still in front of us. There's no hope of passing them. Thomas Chillingwood draws closer to me.

"I do believe we have Miss Osborne – Henry's sister. Miss Osborne, may I present Lord Montcroft." His companion gives an exaggerated bow. I respond with a brief bob. Jane remains upright. She has put on her mask. Cousin Molle's grooms stay close, kicking their heels, unsure of the situation. Behind them, a line of impatient strollers. Still, the two men do not move aside.

"Your brother has talked much about you, Miss Osborne." The tall man leans towards me. "And your passion for a certain gentleman. The matter has caused him some grievance, I believe." No doubt sensing my consternation, Lord Montcroft laughs.

"Your secret is safe with us, Miss Osborne. As, of course, is your brother's secret." With that, the men move aside and allow us to pass.

We continue, quickening our pace, towards the Grand Walk and our supper box.

Jane says: "I wonder what was meant, my lady, 'bout Mr Henry's secret?"

"Really, Jane, surely you know better than to heed the tattle of such men!" When she doesn't reply, I feel the anger well up in me. "And why did you not curtsy? The gentleman is, after all, a Lord of the Realm." Even as I say it, I'm aware how absurd this sounds. We continue in silence, my mind filled with my brother's treachery. How could Henry reveal our private discourse and my deepest sentiments to two such feckless men? Through all our differences, I've assumed Henry is as loyal to me publicly as I am to him. In truth, my name has no doubt been bandied at every London soirée. "I think I will never forgive this of my brother," I tell Jane.

Two weeks ago, in that same room where I gave my pledge to William, my brother and I had been close to reconciliation.

When, trembling, I stood before Henry and declared I would indeed marry William, his reaction had been, if not approving, at least one of calm acceptance. Whether through weariness of the subject or resignation at our change in circumstances, he showed little opposition and put no obstacles my way. "You know my sentiments, but I would only ask you delay this marriage until our lives are more settled." As he embraced me, Henry added, "Let us not lose one another, sister." Now, it seems, he's chosen to vent his true feelings in public. By the time we reach the supper box, I'm determined William and I shall be wed as soon as possible.

Awaiting us there is wine, plus ale and a cold collation of meats and salads. None of which I have appetite for. Cousin Molle is examining everything with care. "At four shillings apiece, I would hope they've prepared only the best of fare." I glance at Jane, knowing she will be shocked at such expense. But she looks away, no doubt still smarting from my foolish reprimand. As a footman prepares to serve the food, cousin Molle struggles to squeeze his ample body into one of the dainty chairs provided. He undoes the buttons of his doublet and beckons Jane to the chair next to him. "Come, girl, sit here and I will tell you who is who, for those masks don't fool me." I'm mortified when, peering into the crowd, he adds: "I swear the place is full of strumpets tonight." Across from me, I see Jane's mouth tighten.

"They look like just young girls to me, my lord, dressed in their best and enjoying the air. Same as us."

Even with his mouth full of food, cousin Molle manages a raucous laugh. "It's something headier than air they're gulping from those flasks, child. And something a deal more potent they'll be seeking later." I see Jane glance at my cousin with distaste. Sitting across from me, she's no longer the diffident, merry girl with the nervous laugh who came to me in St Malo. In truth, across from me is a woman – no longer a girl. And that, I think, has wrought the change.

We sip our wine and listen to a troupe of Italian players, their strange, wild songs so unlike our own careful music. I'm minded of my exotic grandmother and those challenging dark eyes. According to Henry, there are rumours of Italian blood. On that, my aunt has steadfastly refused to be drawn. Now, it seems, Henry too has a secret. It surely concerns a mistress. If unbeknownst to any of us my brother is betrothed, I will feel only relief. What completely undoes me is his cold indifference for my own good name.

Sir John Temple's house, Dublin

Dearest Heart

It was with no little surprise I received your letter. That you propose we should marry as soon as two months hence is such unexpected news it has me not quite knowing if I'm on foot or horseback. You say it's with difficulty you imagine yourself a bride – albeit you will be the most beautiful ever – but how, I wonder, will I fare as bridegroom? I confess until this moment I've given it little thought. Best, perhaps, to put thought aside and let the tide carry us. I will leave Dublin for London immediately. But there is still much to discuss, and I pray we've not set the date a little too hasty.

Dearest, let us resolve to live life to the full and not be concerned what others may say or think, so long as we understand our own hearts and conscience. I worry that for all your independence of thought, you oft have too much regard for the opinion of others. For myself, I intend to embrace all that life may offer, regardless of the conventions of this world. This is how I would live. And should you make me absolute master of your person, as you have promised, this is how I would hope to carry you with me.

I'm relieved you are finally at Chelsea. Now you are under your aunt's protection, I'm no longer tormented with thoughts of where you might be and with whom. I am happy to have her blessing, even though you say it is half-hearted. I am sure when she realises how strong my passion is, and how it has ruled me completely since first knowing you, your aunt will forgive my lack of resource. My sister, Martha, is also wary, since she thinks none can care for her brother as she does. Once she knows you, she will, like all who know you, fall in love.

My dearest dear, I am yours.

P.S. When will your brother come to London? My father would meet with him there regarding the settlement.

Alone with my aunt, I determine to speak plainly. "The truth is, I can barely endure the idea of being Mrs Bride in a public wedding."

"You have chosen your course, Dorothy. We must observe what is proper."

"I know there must be Cromwell's 'civil ceremony' and of course I want to receive the church blessing. All I ask is it should be quiet." When my aunt doesn't reply, I add: "I would if I could, but with Robin and my father both gone, I don't think it possible to display myself in a grand celebration."

"For goodness' sake, niece." Irritated, my aunt prods the wolfhound at her feet, causing him to heave his great body from the hearth. "There will be nothing *grand* in these austere times. Merely a small gathering of family, as your father would have wished, if after all this secrecy and deception anyone deigns to attend. How else would you have a wedding?"

What I would have is that William comes here one morning and the two of us go to church and get married. The rest of my dreaming sees us embarking on a long coach ride, dining at an inn by the way and retiring to lodgings where none know us. "I'd have it simple," I say.

My aunt leans towards me and takes my hand. "You are as close to me as any daughter," she says.

Unsure how to reply, I say: "This was your room, Aunt, was it not – when you were a girl?"

She squeezes my hand. "As you very well know, I shared it with your mother. Being of similar age, we enjoyed such giddiness as I blush to remember."

"Then you surely understand my own giddiness at this moment."

"Stubborn, yes. But none would describe you as giddy, Dorothy."

"Then why does this wedding, that I've so longed for, fill me with trepidation?"

"None can answer that, child." My aunt's voice is weary. "Save to say it probably has little to do with the rituals of a single day." Before I can reply, I'm seized with such a bout of coughing, my aunt is obliged to send for ale. She informs me I'm experiencing what she terms, 'prenuptial spasms'. "It is not uncommon on the way to the altar. And it is not too late to halt proceedings." Then in that way she has, my aunt abruptly changes the subject. "Now, Dorothy." And reaching into one of the many pockets of her skirts, she produces a little package. "My mother gave this to me when I married. Now you shall have it."

I recognise at once the necklace in the miniature. As I hold it up, the sumptuous jet beads glisten in the firelight. "I will treasure it always," I tell my aunt. Sensing she is about to leave, the old dog staggers to his feet – with almost as much difficulty as his mistress. "You are wrong if you think I doubt this marriage, Aunt. I know William to be a good man."

"None of us know who we are marrying, Dorothy, until it is too late."

For Mr William Temple
Next to The Bullock Inn, Dover Street.

Now you are here, we must both be patient, for it cannot be helped. My cold is such, I would not wish my worst enemy to come near. You say you're willing to risk the consequences, but I fear the sight of me, and my ungraceful bouts of coughing would send you catching the first boat back to Ireland! Poor man. And after such an uncomfortable journey. Do you think it best to leave me and start a new adventure?

For Mr William Temple
Next to The Bullock Inn, Dover Street.

Here comes a note again. You are like to have an excellent housewife of me. I am abed still at noon, having slept little for some aches and weakness that kept me tossing. Nothing but your note could have roused me from this torpor. You shall hear from me again after we have dined.

Farewell. Can you endure that word? No. Out upon it. I will see you soon.

A red coverlet wrapped tight and with no space for air to get by – Lady Gargrave swears by it. "The colour helps sweat out the poison." She'll have nought with these new continental practices favoured by Mr Henry, and I'll wager she's got good counsel. Light bedclothes and cool cloths seem no match for the pox. Never thought I'd be glad to hear that word uttered. But with Miss Dorothy taken with such fever, our minds were dwelling on graver news. Lord knows, though, those blisters are surely fierce. Lady Gargrave says they'll be bursting soon enough. "Then we shall have an end to the fever," she says. "I've seen enough of the pox to know so."

I'm surely thankful to be in Chelsea with lady Gargrave in good charge. I've need to attend Miss Dorothy, though, since the wenches here seem bent on keeping themselves at a distance. I stepped right up for that. I told Lady Gargrave: "I'll go full face to that good lady, day or night, and be grateful for the chance."

Mr Henry's no use, forever pacing the hall and anguishing. He won't go near his sister's chamber. Not like a certain other gentleman who can scarce be persuaded to leave it. Mr Temple's stood fast, even through the terrible nausea and vomiting that's rendered my lady near senseless. He's content to sit for hours putting the sponge to her poor mouth, which is so infected with blisters, she can scarce open it. The gentleman's jumpy as a jelly fish, though. "Fetch the aunt, Jane – I do believe she's stirring." Or: "Think you, Jane, we should change the bedcovers afresh?" And all times smoking on his pipe to afford a tad of protection. He's insisting everyone chew baccy, which in God's truth I can't stomach. No. I prefer to cover my face as lady Gargrave has told me. And I'm not much bothered by the smell – 'specially with the rose oil scattered.

As for the wedding, it's put off till the Lord knows when. What with my lady's condition and the number of persons knocking, none's got time to think on it. I've noted in all the comings and goings, few venture beyond the hall. That cousin of hers confined himself there, staying all of three minutes with a kerchief clamped to his face.

Her brother and Mr Temple seem bent on avoiding each other. Except for a few bows and mumbled pleasantries when they pass, I've scarce seen them exchange a word. Just a snatch of conversation regarding the settlement, and there seems disagreement enough on that. I'm thinking it's a rum time to be talking such things. And they're careful not to sup together, Mr Henry preferring to eat at the tavern.

So, with Lady Gargrave early to her bed, it's just me and Mr Temple in the kitchens tonight, neither of us with appetite. Still, I tell him straight he'd best take some nourishment if he's to keep his strength. "If you'll forgive the liberty, sir, I've not seen you eat all day." And since there's none else to do so, I dish us both some broth and bread.

"Tell me, Jane, is this the first time you've seen it – and is she very much worse than most?"

I tell him I'm happy I've never laid eyes on the pox before and, Lord willing, hope never to again. "But please, sir, sit and eat. No good can come of pacing."

"I'm looking for wine, Jane. Or does the aunt keep it hidden?" I go to the back pantry, as I oft saw Robin do, and take out the wine I know he favoured. I remember the careless way he would fill the tankards, slopping the ruby wine onto the wooden table. I can still hear him laugh, see his smile. "You must drink too, Jane," Mr Temple says.

"My eyes would soon close, sir." He pours me a tankard anyways, and as he gulps his own, I note he's still not touched the broth.

"Those pustules," he says, "is it not strange they are so numerous?"

I tell him they'll soon be scabbing. "They'll do their job, sir."

"But afterwards, Jane. Shall she be very marked?"

By his anxious look, I know this is no slight question. "Miss Dorothy will ever have her beautiful soul," is my careful answer. And seeing this is no great comfort, I add the blisters oft leave little mark. "At home, I heard of a woman you'd never known had suffered, 'cept for some pits on her cheeks and forehead."

Mr Temple pours himself another good tankard of wine, then, in a flat voice, he says: "You are right, Jane. The beauty is in the eyes and no pox shall destroy that. If God spares her, we shall marry by Yuletide. I would have an end to uncertainty."

His look is bleak enough, and I can't help but note how dishevelled Mr Temple is. "Was your man too affright to accompany you, sir?"

"He's scuttled back to Dublin, Jane. If you know of another, speak plain, as you tend to do."

I've no need to think but a second. "Begging your pardon, sir, but I know of no better person than Will Hammer. I'm minded he'd give anything to be back near Miss Dorothy."

And in that way of his, Mr Temple's spirits lighten in a flash, and he laughs. "By the way you speak of him, Jane, I believe this must be one of your beaux."

I soon put Mr Temple right on that count. "Will is younger than me by years, but as good a boy as I know for decency and hard work."

I'm right mortified when he laughs again. "My suspicions are always roused when a pretty woman protests – especially when her cheeks are burning."

It's true he's made my colour rise, but I won't let him set me back. "Well, you are wrong, sir. I were just trying to help, and only since you asked." And I ups from the bench and clears the entire table in a trice, even though Mr Temple has not yet finished his food.

"Come, Jane, you're too fiery by half, and you have a streak of broth in your hair. Come, let me wipe it off."

"Thank you, sir, but I'm capable of doing so myself." With that, I'm out the door. I'm glad I said my piece. I'm determined never again to let a gentleman wrong-foot me.

"Seventy-five, seventy-six – we'll soon reach one hundred, my lady." It's the first time this full month I'm able to brush her hair and I'm marvelled that with all this sickness, it's thick and glossy as ever. But when I tell her so, she closes her eyes and sinks back on the pillows. She's still weak as a kitten. Her voice is strong, though.

"Fetch a mirror, Jane."

"Best wait a day or so till you get your good colour back." She'll not be put off. I fetch the small, silver-backed mirror and hold it up to her. My hand is shaking. She stares for a moment, then runs her finger down the side of her face. She doesn't speak.

I'm glad they've chosen Christmas Day to go to church. 'Specially since Mr Cromwell's seen fit to ban the festivities. His god is surely different from mine, or any right-thinking person who believes in praising the Lord with music and revelry. Back home in the old days, there'd be bunting out and flagons of ale or wine for the neighbours, with my father playing the pipes into the night. And far as I know, the Lord found it all very pleasing.

My lady couldn't be persuaded on a new gown, even though her aunt urged it. "My blue will suffice." Looking at her, I do admit it's the just colour. It takes from her paleness. And lady Gargrave is a fair magician with that special powder I watched her mix.

"We'll just dab it, Dorothy, and you shall see – the scars will scarce notice." All the same, she goes to the hall chest and takes out a veil, gossamer thin. It covers my lady's face without completely hiding her features. "You look as fair as any bride in Christendom, niece."

I determine to add my own few words, which I've been practising this full week. "And my lady, if I may say so…" That's as far as I get before Lady Gargrave interrupts.

"We've scarce time for speeches, Jane. I fear this journey will be long enough as it is."

It's a good hour by my book. St Giles in the Field is not somewhere this family would normally frequent, surrounded as it is by low taverns and vagrants. For a moment, I fear Lady Gargrave may refuse to leave the carriage. "Really, Dorothy, is this the only church in London still willing to give the marriage blessing?" We've need to pick our way through the mess of people propping themselves round the church steps, most with hands out. Lady Gargrave holds her nosegay that close to her face, it's a wonder she don't suffocate. Once inside, though, all is good order. I'm pleased to note this is one church that's not lost its pomp and finery. And with so many candles lit, I'm thinking it's as fine a setting as should be.

Mr Temple's party are already in place and a deal more numerous than our own small gathering. By their similarity, there seems a good load of his relatives milling. The old man with the jolly face, I'm taking to be his father. He's tall as his son and has those same dark curls, though a tad faded. And I'm supposing the girl sticking close by Mr Temple is his young sister, though she looks a deal older than fourteen years. I note too she's blessed with that same family handsomeness. Mr Temple is at the centre of his group, looking spruce, and a sight better than I've seen him this month or more. I put that down to Will Hammer, towering over all, and attending his new master like a clucking hen. He comes straight to me. "Thank you, Jane. I'm sure it was you secured me this goodly post." And I note, despite his rosy blushing, Will is becoming more man than boy.

Our own party is less by far. By look of it, we're down to six. Sir Henry Molle is grandest in full periwig and fine frock coat. I'm surprised to note Chicksand's own parson ready to give the blessing. He do seem a-dither and a sight different than his usual nose-aloft self. I can't help but smile to see him here in London, out of sorts as a fish on a platter. I'm supposing he journeyed up with my lady's brother. It's fitting Sir John should be by Miss Dorothy, especially since there's no sign of Mr Henry. I know this won't sit well with her. Despite their estrangement, she'd have wanted him attending. She's never one to let a grudge spoil the day.

A short blessing, that's all was expected. Seems nobody told the parson. With Miss Dorothy still weak and me paining in these dainty shoes she's bade me wear, he takes his sweet time to deliver a lecture on wickedness. Still, by looks of it, my lady's bearing it well, straight and graceful and a sight more composed than the bridegroom, who's forever adjusting his apparel. He's still not collected when it comes to the signing, dropping the quill before it reaches the page. Will saves the day, stepping forward to retrieve it and holding the book still for the signature.

Mr Temple has arranged this dinner, and I fear it may not pass muster. Throughout our journey through Soho, Sir Henry Molle and Lady Gargrave have been fretting. The cousin especially is at a loss to know what good food could possibly be available in this part of town. "I cannot understand why they didn't consult. At a word from me, my own quarter would have provided the best cold lobster and wine in London."

Lady Gargrave is worried by the look of the place. "It appears to be no more than a common tavern." I do agree. By my book, this dreary setting doesn't fit right for a gentry wedding. But same as the church, inside is better than out. And with the upstairs room set aside for our purpose, and decked with so many flowers and the sumptuous food on display, even Lady Gargrave is soon in jolly mood.

I'm glad to be seated next to Will. It's first time I've set eyes on him since Chicksands, and I'm pleased to note there's no unease between us. I'm that eager to hear all of the house, and he to tell it, we barely manage to do justice to this feast. Will says Noah's found things hard. "There's no bonding between him and the new master like there should be."

I'm troubled to learn Noah's taken to the tavern for his comfort. "That's not proper, Will." I'm remembering Noah's poor quarters, where he tended me so gently. "'Tis a pity he never took himself another wife."

Will says: "Do you s'pose it will be you at the altar 'fore long, Jane?"

"I don't think I could stomach it, Will. Even if there were someone fool enough to take me."

There's a pretty speech, if a tad booming, from Mr Temple's father, whose gift to the pair is their own house on his Irish estate. He welcomes my lady to his family with such feeling that all applaud his words. None more heartily than Lady Gargrave, who, seated right next to the old gentleman, has received some good attention. Not to be bested, Sir Henry Molle makes his own flowery speech. And with the wine flowing, I'm thinking I'm not the only one whose mind drifts. He has a dull monotone and none of the warmth of the previous speaker. Mr Temple for one seems to have lost the flow. He's preoccupied gently lifting my lady's veil and arranging it off her face. He kisses her on the cheek, and I note at this distance her face is clear and smooth as you like. I can't help but think Mr Temple be the lucky one winning such as her.

I'm minded of that first time I saw her, in the gardens at Castle Cornet. "This be Miss Dorothy," my father said. "Sir Peter's daughter." It was the eyes that struck. Huge, almost black. Solemn, though. "You do speak French, my dear?"

My father answered for me. "Indeed she do, Sir Peter. And first one in our family to read and write it with ease, even though she be a slip of a girl." I remember blushing at the boast. Later, my father said I should have given the knee. "Them's not used to our rough ways." He was proud of me, though. Dare say he wouldn't be now, if he knew my shame.

"Is all well with you, Jane?" Will presses a kerchief on me, and I'm angered to find I'm close to tears.

"Seldom better," I tell him sharply. "And first time I've known the likes of you sporting a fancy kerchief."

My lady's cousin is still droning on, and it takes a moment to realise he's launched into a ribald story 'bout a bride and a wedding chamber. I'm wondering what Mr Temple's family make of such crudity, though all do seem to be laughing. I'm struck again as how gentry often ignore what's proper and allow themselves to lapse into undignified behaviour.

Will is first to the coach, and up on post next to the coachman. I do envy him being party to this wedding journey, which is secret, according to my lady's wish. In the doorway, she takes my hand. "Dearest Jane, I'll see you in Ireland. Though at this moment, I would you were travelling with me." I'm set back to feel how cold her own hand is. Taking my moment, I do manage to give my few words.

"If I may say so, my lady, I'm happy to be of service, and I wish you a joyful wedding day." She has not put back her veil, and I'm more than a bit pleased to note Lady Gargrave's powder has done its work. As she walks to the coach, I'm thinking all must be noting Miss Dorothy's radiance. So I'm properly taken aback when crowded in the doorway to wave them off, a voice next to me says: "'Tis a pity her beauty is so spoilt." And those blue eyes of Mr Temple's young sister, Miss Martha, stare straight at me. "My brother cannot be wholly indifferent to that loss."

"We'll have them build the fire," he says. "And I will fetch some wine." As the door closes behind him, I feel the chill. The candlelight plays on the walls and the bed. A green velvet tester; a dresser; two chairs; an oak chest. We are here at my insistence. *"Let us stop where none know us."* I take a candle and move it closer to the mirror on the dresser. The light casts itself on my face, pale and mottled. I am no longer myself. I am a wife. What was forbidden is about to become natural and proper. A duty. Not for the first time, I wish I were better versed.

He sends the maid away and moves me closer to the fire. "Mustn't let you catch a chill." His voice is nervous. But the fingers unlacing my bodice are swift and sure. "We shan't need the candle," he says. And we are plunged into darkness.

I've never before felt the strange warmth of someone's skin against my body. Unfamiliar hands, gentle, but insistent; fingers probing. My body reacts in a manner completely separate from my mind. My own hand, reaching out – caressing him.

He sleeps deeply, still and straight, his head turned slightly towards me. At dawn, careful not to wake him, I touch his face. It's as unfamiliar as my own body feels. Relaxed in sleep, the creases beneath his eyes have smoothed. I put my hand gently against his mouth. I can feel his warm breath on my fingers. His chest is lightly feathered. When I move my fingers there, he stirs. I slide my hand down next to his and lay with my head close to his chest. He changes positions, turning away from me and towards the window.

I've long known the hazards of this voyage. When William sailed to Ireland, I could not rest until he was safely landed. Now that we make the journey together, I'm calmer. But I shall not be persuaded to go atop. "The water is steady," he says. "You may trust me – you will not come to harm." I remain seated in a corner of this cramped cabin. "I wish you to see the coast of Ireland," he says. "I would not have you miss such beauty." Finally, he goes alone. Since Robin died, I have vowed never again to stand on the deck of a boat. The sea will always take what it wants. All man's powerful reasoning will not prevent it. *You may trust me,* he said. But what use is that against such an irrational and cruel force? Trust. Such a tiny, definitive word. I've always set such store by it. I've been slow to realise the heavy weight of such a little word on those it is bestowed. Only yesterday I told him: *I trust you with my life.* But will he not crumble under such a load?

IRELAND

1656

In my dream, the women gather. Jane is amongst them, and Martha. They move towards the bed. One of them takes hold of my arms. An older woman pulls back the bedcovers, searching. But I'm too strong for them. I break free and clasp the bundle close. The woman presses a great weight on my stomach, causing me to cry out and loosen my hold. The bundle unravels into pieces of rag, covered in blood. "The boat is waiting," the woman says. I awake – and remember. God has seen fit to deliver me of a son. He lived but an hour.

The air in Carlow is soft, though always tinged with a slight chill. Here in the gardens all is lush green from the summer rain. The roses, though, are wilted from the downpour. They lack the resilience needed to survive. Such a vital ingredient. As always, Jane is solicitous: "Are you sure you're well wrapped, my lady?" She tucks my wrap firmly about me.

"It's been two weeks, Jane. I cannot stay forever like this. Who is to manage the household?" She assures me all is ordered.

"Miss Martha may be scarce fifteen, but she can step right up when it comes to managing a good house. Shall I fetch you out some delicacy, my lady? A coddled pear might sit well."

"Stay and talk with me, Jane." We sit looking down across the valley towards the town. "Do you ever doubt your faith?"

"I'm ever sure of the good Lord watching over us," she says, "and I know his great plan is beyond our understanding." How often have I heard such words – and voiced them myself.

"But supposing there is no Great Plan. What if the Lord has turned his back?" We are silent together. No doubt Jane considers this blasphemy. Her voice, when she finally speaks, is firm.

"Begging your pardon, my lady, but I think such unsure thoughts are down to your bereavement."

A good word, though not quite fitting. There is, I think, no fit word. "Tell me again how he was, Jane. I'm sorely in need of knowing." If I could just once have held him.

"It was the cord, strung round his little neck. The midwife did try…"

"But how was his look?"

And Jane's face softens. "He were the most beautiful boy, with the darkest hair, and a good mass of it. And he opened his eyes only once and looked straight at me, steady as you like. I'd wager, my lady, he went peaceful back to his maker."

"Thank you, Jane."

William has been gone a week and there's still no letter. Jane is not surprised. "The carrier is that slack between here and Dublin. I'll warrant a letter lies forgot in some tavern."

He came to me just before leaving, fetching soup from the kitchens. "You must eat, dearest, if you are to regain your strength." We did not mention our son. We had not the words.

I'm woken by footsteps crossing the hallway. Taking my candle, I'm halfway down the stairs before realising I am without shoes. A dim light is coming from the kitchens.

Martha doesn't, at first, see me. In the candlelight, I watch her, seated at the table, hunched over a book, her bare arms smooth as satin, her dark hair tumbling about her shoulders. "It's late, Martha. What study could absorb you at this hour?"

As I move closer, I see it is my ledger. "My dear." I try to keep the anxiety from my voice. "I myself will deal with the household accounting." Having failed in my most cherished duty, I've a great need to fulfil all others.

Martha looks up and as ever, I'm struck by the beauty of this girl. "William has given instructions you are to rest," she says.

"I've rested enough. I'm not ill."

"You soon will be if you walk shoeless on these cold floors."

I lean over her and as firmly as I'm able, close the ledger. "I'd not have you strain your eyes on such tedious work."

"I have been taking care of my father's household since I was twelve."

"Then your father must have need of you back in Dublin. You have aided us enough these past weeks."

She reaches into her night robe and takes out a letter. I recognise the seal. '...*thus it would please me greatly to have you stay until my return*'.

"When did it come – this letter?"

"William gave it me this past week, when I was in Dublin for the funeral blessing."

My son is put beneath the earth in some corner of a Dublin churchyard and none saw fit to mention it. "Why was I not told, Jane?"

"You've been that weak, my lady. All thought it best you should rest quiet." At least Jane has the grace to redden.

"And the baptism?"

"Done by the parson before the mite were born. When all became aware of its peril. Do you not remember?" I remember nothing save the pain and that first faint cry. And then the silence.

William has returned, bringing with him his father. In the hallway, Sir John comes straight to me. "My dearest daughter, your loss pains me more than I can say."

'*Loss.*' Yes, that's it. That simple word. Too overcome to reply, I squeeze the hand that takes mine.

I follow William into his study. Being close to him calms me. When he's abroad, I often come to this room. Sitting amongst his books, I'm almost able to breathe his presence. Now, I've need to hear his voice. He is preoccupied, poring over his correspondence. "Shall we not talk a little?"

"Dearest. We can talk later. The ride back was an age. My father is no longer able to gallop the countryside." Rising, he leads me to a chair by the window. "Come, sit with me whilst I attend these duties." His hand caresses my hair, my face. "Your colour is back. I would have you near so I may look at you."

You would look at me, but you cannot talk to me.

At table, discussion is kept light. Sir John expresses surprise that Jane is not yet wed. "I'll wager it's not for want of suitors."

William chuckles. "If Will Hammer had his way, I'd warrant we'd have a wedding before summer is out."

I note Martha studying Jane closely. "They say if a woman waits past twenty, she'll oft remain an old maid," she says.

William says: "Never fear, Martha. We intend to marry you off long before that. Now tell us, Jane, why you won't take poor Will."

Throughout this discourse, Jane has kept her demeanour. "I'm thinking there's no man I'd like well enough to go to church with."

This remark solicits more mirth, especially from Sir John. "I see you are hard on us gentlemen, Jane. Maybe you need to be courted with songs and verse."

William says he intends to pen an ode on Will's behalf. "We shall find a way to melt you, Jane." Martha remarks William's poetry is the best she knows. Sir John fears it displays too much sentiment.

"What think you, my dear?" It takes a moment to realise I am being addressed. Sir John has need to prompt me. "Dorothy? On the subject of William's poetry?"

I say: "I wish to see the place my baby is laid to rest."

The table falls silent. Then William says: "Dearest." And Jane looks as though she would reach out to me. But it is Sir John who eases my mind.

"Of course, my dear. You must come to Dublin as soon as you are able."

A tiny mound against a churchyard wall. *'John William Temple'*. My baby son, who slipped in and out of my life before I could hold him close. The grave is so small, it's completely hidden by the blossoms I place on it. I take a handful of dirt from beneath the flowers and put it in the pocket of my cloak. I pray God the earth lies gentle on him.

Sir John's house is so full of people, Jane and I must share a chamber. "Bring me some wine, Jane," I say. "White wine – to help me sleep." I finger the piece of steel, hidden from sight and carefully transported from Carlow.

"I wouldn't know where to look, my lady, and it's too late to disturb the kitchens." Jane's voice is firm. She is not prepared to help me. I want to plead with her. To make her understand that any amount of nausea would be preferable to this unrelenting darkness.

"You are fortunate, Jane. You have never suffered loss."

Do you doubt your faith, Jane? My heart went out to her. She's doubting hers all right. And who would blame her? Times when 'God's Will' don't seem a just enough answer. Times too when a lie sits better than the truth, though I never used to think so. *He*

opened his eyes, I told her. Weren't true, of course. Poor mite could scarce breathe, let alone look about. It all sits so heavy. I say as much to Will on our evening walk. "If only she were able to shed a tear." He says the master's shed enough for both. "How do you know that, Will?"

"At night, in his study. The wall's that thin next to my room."

I say I've never seen a man cry. "Nor should I care to."

"Tears is a womanly thing, Jane. A man don't usually give way. But when the heart's that full..."

"But he's shown none of it, Will." To my mind, Mr Temple's demeanour has been a tad too merry of late.

"You can't always judge by what the eye sees, Jane." We're quiet on the way back to the house. I'm thinking there's a lot of sense to Will, seeing how young he is. And I'm back to that terrible night. Not many lads would have stepped up for that. No babe for me to mourn, though. Just a torn bed sheet soaked through with blood. Will by side of me. *I'll stay till you sleep easy, Jane.*

We're scarce back in the house when there's a calling for Will from the withdrawing room. "Better get there quick," I say. Miss Martha's not one to be kept waiting. Will rushes through the hall – he don't waste a minute. I'm thinking said young lady is summoning him a sight too often by my book. And I'm truly irritated that beneath Will's new manliness there's still the gullible country lad.

Will's not the only one to jump at Miss Martha's say-so. Whenever she's here, which is oft enough, she has half the household tripping over their shoes. I must admit that young lady do have her share of family charm. But as I'm finding to my cost, it can turn on a penny if she's crossed.

I'm coming downstairs when she catches me. "Good morning, Jane. Be so good as to exercise my dogs." I tell her straight I'm otherwise engaged.

"Begging your pardon, Miss Martha. I'm called on to accompany my lady into town. I'll gladly summon one of the grooms." This news, delivered with a bit of a bob, is not warmly greeted.

"I wish you to do it, Jane. The dogs are affright of those ruffians. I'm sure my sister will not mind waiting whilst you attend me."

As I struggle to keep three snappy hounds in check and stop them running at the sheep, it's that word *attend* sits most ill. My lady has told me many a time my job is not to fetch and carry. And though she herself oft forgets and sends me running, I pride myself on being no one's drudge. No, after so long with my lady, I'm sure of my place. And it's not as a person beholden to a slip of a girl, thank you very much! I've a mind that young lady's a sight too indulged. And it's not just Sir John who panders to Miss Martha. I've yet to hear Mr Temple refuse his sister any request, however inconvenient. "William, I'm partial to a special new rose water," she'll say. "Will you write to London and enquire where we might find it?" And in a trice, she's dabbing said potion about her person.

I'm thinking on all this as I chase these unruly creatures back to the house. And I'm further irked to see the carriage out front and my lady no doubt waiting in the hall. My gown is full of mud and there is no time to change into something more fitting. As feared, my lady's not best pleased. "I've been pacing these fifteen minutes, Jane." And out of breath as I am, I'm quick to relate my story. But if I'm thinking she might sympathise, I have, as my father would say, another thought to come. "Of course you must do Miss Martha's bidding," she says, "but you could have sent word?" She's truly out of sorts, so I say nothing. But I'm chiding myself for having forgot how gentry always stick together when it comes to fairness – and I determine to do better by myself next time.

We've not taken the carriage to town in an age, and if it weren't for the scolding, I'd be well pleased to be out and about with my lady so mended. "Since we're set down in this place, we must strive to know it better," she says. Truth is, these surroundings are dreary enough. The countryside is pleasing, but all is spoilt by the scramble of hovels about.

I tell my lady straight: "Outside London, I've scarce seen such a motley arrangement."

She's quick to agree. "And it's a miracle people remain in such good cheer."

I've reason to doubt that, given our hostile reception in town. Even before we climb from the carriage, a goodly load of unsavoury persons has gathered, including children, all with hands out and eyes cold. I'm surely glad Will's up on post so's they can note his size. As she steps down, my lady has her hand at her purse. "I can resist anything but beggars," she says. And I note she's close to a tear.

"If I might make bold, my lady – I'm of the opinion they shouldn't be encouraged." Back home in Guernsey, such creatures would be driven from town and with good riddance. When my lady tosses the first coin, there's such a pressing in on her, I fear for her safety.

"There's hunger here, Jane. How would we turn our backs?" I'm thinking we'd be foolish indeed to do so. And I'm right glad when Will finally takes things in hand and chases the vermin off, no doubt to ply their play acting on other upright folk. For all her good sense, Miss Dorothy can be gullible. She's no less so when we move to the market, paying a stony-faced woman twice their worth for a lace shawl and a basket of strawberries.

"Don't you wish we were back in England, Will?" I'm watching him buff Mr Temple's riding boots. I'm thinking it's scarce worth it, given the mud and rain in this place. Will says no offence, but he's content to stay put.

"I've found I'm partial to foreign parts, Jane. 'Specially with such a goodly master."

"But those townsfolk, Will. And the heathen language."

With some force, Will says: "It's their own God-given tongue, Jane. And any road, you scarce notice it with all the English hereabouts."

"A good thing too, else our ears might refuse to do their work." When Will don't answer, I say: "Them townsfolk were ready to cut our throats soon as look at us."

Will just laughs. "If you'll pardon me for saying so, Mistress Wright, you're apt to make a very harsh judgement."

"I've heard Sir John say oft enough that only a fool would trust an Irishman."

"Just because Sir John wrote it don't make it true," Will says. And I'm quick to ask what writing that is. "Thet book Sir John wrote that lies in the master's study. Did you not know of it, Jane? It claims boggy land is bound to breed rebellious souls."

"Then it must be right. Sir John is one gentleman who knows what he's about. Cromwell didn't honour him for nothing." Will raises one eyebrow at me, and I'm so minded of Robin's way of looking, it causes me to catch my breath. "Never knew you had a nose for books, Will Hammer. Never knew the likes of you could read."

"There be a lot you don't know about me, Jane Wright." And this mocking tone is something new in Will. "In truth, despite your scolding nature, I'd be content any place you were." Before I can say another word, he's packed away his rags and is up and off.

It's the second time this week my lady and I have fetched up in town. And since it's of an evening, I'm content one of the grooms is up on post next to Will. Mr Temple was not best pleased at this outing. "You are not fully recovered, my dear – and the rain hasn't ceased. The roads will be dark and full of mud." But weak as she still is, my lady's mind is set on hearing this preacher from London.

"Will you come with us, William? They say this Mr Marshall has swayed Parliament with his sermons." Mr Temple stands fast, declaring more fool Parliament for heeding Puritan rhetoric, and that no creature of Cromwell's shall sway *him*.

So here we are, crammed into a crowded hall, my lady pale, with me and Will on either side, and myself forced next to the groom, who smells so strongly of horse dung, I'm obliged to hold my shawl to my nose. Other side of Will is Rebecca, the new kitchen maid. I still don't know how a slip of a wench put herself forward for this outing. Time was when a maid knew her place.

And this William Marshall, with his white hair as unruly as his whiskers, is as angry a preacher as ever I saw. He is pleased with nothing. And it seems what makes the blood boil in him, is the likes of my lady. He's repeated as much several times. *If there were no kings, no queens, no lords or ladies, no gentlemen nor gentlewomen in the world, it would be no loss to God!* And some in the crowd say, *Amen.* I note my lady has lost what little colour she had and I do believe she's trembling.

Turns out I'd no needs to worry. Soon as she gets in the coach, my lady is full of more humour than I've seen this many a day. "God forgive me," she says, "I had such a do to look soberly in that place. I was as near laughing as ever in my life."

"I'm happy you weren't offended, my lady."

"Goodness, Jane, he is so famed I'd expected rare things. But did you ever see a man so wrong-headed? And everything repeated forty times. Surely he doesn't always preach so?" And she laughs. "I fear he will do little towards bringing a person to heaven and a great deal towards sending them to sleep!" She's still in merry mood when we reach the house, recounting all to Mr Temple. "You were right not to attend, William. His sermonising was absurd, and all listened as though he were St Paul!"

I'm properly glad to see my lady so recovered in spirit, and I can tell by his look Mr Temple too is content with this sudden change of weather. But when the laughter continues, accompanied by restless pacing and sudden quick movements, we are both disquieted. "Dearest, you will tire yourself. Let me help you to your chamber." Mr Temple bids me fetch some ale and honey. It's only when my lady is quiet on her pillows, warmed and peaceful from the brew, that we both feel eased. I make to leave but Mr Temple gestures me to stay put. He's sitting on the bed, her hand in his. "Pay no heed to that dolt of a preacher, my love. I will write you a special prayer. One that shall restore you." We stay until she finally sleeps. At the top of the stairs, Mr Temple turns to me. "I am feared lest this heralds another of her disorders, Jane."

I promise to keep close watch. "I'll not be leaving that good lady for a second." In truth, it's more than that by far, since when I return to kitchens, I'm caught up with Will and the groom. "I hope you're looking to your work, Will Hammer."

Will says he won't be needed yet. "Mr Temple is likely to spend an hour or two in his study."

"Well, mind you go quiet on the stairs. My lady's already abed, being spent with that preacher's ranting." And Will casts me an odd look.

"We was mulling on that sermon, Jane. We found it worthy of some talk." I look at the groom, slumped on a stool, seemingly incapable of moving, let alone talking.

I say: "Do you think it just then, Will, to go insulting the gentry?"

"He weren't insulting nobody, Jane. Only reminding we are all equal in God's eyes, despite fancy ways and titles."

I'm taken aback to hear Will speak like this. "Would you then put yourself up on the same footing as Mr Temple and Sir John?"

Will ponders this before saying, "No." But he's a mind God would. "It sets you thinking, Jane."

"That's your trouble, Will Hammer. You think too much."

With my lady in her bed for two days, Mr Temple is set on fetching the medic. "There's no fever, sir," I tell him. "Only a dampness of spirit that, begging your pardon, I think comes from her late sorrow." And I tell him I've a mind she took up her duties a tad too early.

"Should we send for Miss Martha, Jane, to help with the household?"

I'm quick to have my word on that. "If I might say, sir, I'm thinking it would be a pity to disturb Miss Martha when your good lady is sure to be up and doing in a trice. Me and Will can manage well till then." I'm determined to avoid another outing with them pesky hounds.

❀

I'm proved right about my lady. Mr Temple has written his promised prayer, and when he summons the whole household to partake, she's up and clothed and with colour fresh as a rose.

"In these fanatic times of so many sects, it is important you all may join in." Mr Temple has a fine voice for a prayer. Everyone is gathered in the hall. *"This prayer is designed to contain everything that is necessary for any of us to know or do."*

Despite the fidgeting and giggles of the serving wenches, all heads are finally bowed. All, that is, except Rebecca, who stares straight ahead. I'll needs keep my eye on that young maid. For myself, I'm right transported by Mr Temple's words, which are full of praise for the Lord and his goodness, and for the necessity of a life of humble service in his name. And not one word said against kings or gentlewomen. My lady too seems well pleased and much revived.

"What thought you then, Will?" We're down in the kitchens, hungry after our morning walk.

Will says he thought it a goodly enough prayer to satisfy all. "The master has a powerful way with words."

But for all Mr Temple's abilities, I'd have been glad to hear a proper church parson recite them. "It's a wonder we don't have one in the house, Will, same as at Chicksands."

Will says he's thinking there's only one way to get the parson here. "And that's if you and I stand up before him, Jane. What say you to that?" And this is not the Will of late, but a mumbling lad. I turn to the hearth and give a good stir to the ham stew. When I look back, I note we've both reddened.

"I'd say you'd gone soft in the head, Will Hammer – which in all honesty, I've always thought you were."

I dream I'm in church in a bridal gown that (to my shame!) I'm set to unbuttoning. My father is there with demeanour sour enough to turn the milk. I know it's a dream, and I struggle to pull myself awake. But the dreaming pulls me back and I'm at home in Guernsey, dancing with someone I don't know. He's tall, with a cap pulled low so's I can't see his face. I'm thinking it must be Will. He twirls me that fast, I start to fall. And when he bends over me, I see, despite the size of him, this is Robin. "I've been here all the time, Jane." Then, of a sudden, I'm full awake – and for a moment, I can still hear that voice. I'm pondering my dream all day. Strange – that tall man, and my ease when I thought it were Will.

When the letter arrives from her brother, my lady don't hesitate, even though Mr Temple considers a journey to London too taxing. "I cannot abandon my aunt in time of illness," she tells him. "Henry writes with some urgency and his letter has taken over one week to reach us." I blush when my lady adds: "All will be well since Jane shall be with me." I'm bound to admit those words are sweet to me.

I'm in the kitchen, folding my lady's gloves in the trunk, when Will comes in. I don't look up from my task, though I know he's watching me. "Don't ask again, Will, for I'm vowed never to wed."

"Why, Jane? Everyone needs to wed. If only for the comfort it brings in frosty times."

"I'm cosy enough, thank you. You're just a young lad, and I'm past the age to be thinking on a husband." I busy myself with gathering my lady's night robes, fresh from the tub. But Will continues to press me.

"I'm thinking we rub along quite well, Jane, despite your bickering nature." He ups and starts towards me. "And I'd pledge to always take care of you."

I move to the door. "And how would a bit of a lad like you do that?" Will laughs. And amid my confusion, looking at his great height, I'm forced to smile at my words.

But in a blink, Will turns serious: "I think there be other reasons you refuse me, Jane." And neither of us can look at the other.

It takes a moment to find my voice. "There are reasons enough, Will Hammer. Now get off and find yourself a wench young and silly enough to take you."

I never thought I'd be happy to see the arrival of Miss Martha, bursting into the kitchen with hair flying and rosy cheeks. "My brother sent word you will go with my sister to London. I rode straight over. I will take care of his needs whilst you're gone."

I know my mouth has dropped. "You rode here from Dublin on a horse, Miss Martha?"

Well, there were no cows fit to carry me." And Miss Martha laughs and Will laughs too. She bids him tend her steed, and Will's off and whistling as he goes. I'm supposing his words of late are quick enough forgot.

"Is there food, Jane? I've such a hunger after that journey."

I settle her with some cold ham and bird, even though it's not my place to prepare food. "I'll bid the maid ready your chamber," I tell her.

Turns out there's no need. My lady is in the kitchens before Miss Martha can take a bite. She's holding another letter.

"We are too late, Jane. My aunt died these three days past."

I go straight to her. "Oh, my lady."

"She was put in the earth yesterday." In a trice, we are both clinging to each other. And in her grief for that good woman, my lady is finally weeping.

"What sad tidings, Dorothy." We both glance across at Miss Martha. I'd almost forgot she was there. To my mind, her voice betrays only disappointment.

I hadn't known I would do this. Try as I might, I cannot stop the tears. What exactly am I weeping for? My aunt? My poor dead baby? All the dead, quaffed like candles? I'm like a country laid waste by war. Perhaps I weep for myself. Martha, too, is obviously distressed. "Will you not now be leaving for London, Dorothy?"

Jane says: "Miss Martha came to help whilst we were gone. I'm thinking she won't be needed now." As she so often does, Jane speaks too bluntly.

"Of course you must stay for a few days, Martha. It will be such a comfort." And although her smile is wan, I think I've eased her mind. I should like to put my arms about this motherless girl, feel the warmth of her young body. But Martha doesn't invite such intimacy.

For several days, I cannot look again at Henry's letter. When I do, I see he is proposing a visit. *My dear sister, I've great need to be near you. Can we not put aside what is past and be as once we were?*

Would I could remember such a time. In my mind's eye, Henry was always as he is now. As children, where Robin and I were boisterous and wilful, he was sensitive and remote, preferring the company of my mother and my aunt to ours. As a man, he tried, as far as he was able, to protect them both from the harsher realities of the war. I believe in these past few years, with our parents dead, Henry has become the son my aunt always wished for. His sense of loss must be as deep – deeper – than my own. And despite all that has passed between us, I too have a pressing need for my own kin.

"Will you not agree to it, William? Now that all is settled, what sense can there be in continuing this feud?" William is unmoved.

"I will not reopen this particular wound, Dorothy. I would not have the harmony of our little home disturbed."

"I would never ask anything of you that would do you disservice. But please, I beg you remember Henry is my brother, and almost all that is left of my family. I would have him near me at this time as I know my aunt would have wished."

"I am your family now, dearest. And as my wife, it's your duty to trust in my judgement."

My duty? It takes a moment to digest this. "I believed it my duty to be your helpmate, not to bend to your will when there is difference of opinion." Seated at his desk, William begins to leaf through his correspondence.

"We all have our duties, Dorothy. And mine is to protect you from decisions you may come to regret."

I'm reminded of a similar conversation with my brother, one in which William was cast as the interloper, set to destroy the peace of a family. I am, it seems, always in need of protection. As William applies himself to his papers, it's clear this audience is over. But I find I can't let go. "You remember what we wrote in our letters? We agreed that love and friendship must be based on equal share."

"I don't remember those precise words, Dorothy." William doesn't look up. "Of course I believe in freedom of thought for both men and women. Have I not always said so? But as in all enterprises, surely there must be one who leads and one who obeys?"

"If friendship is to survive, there can be no such distinction of power," I say. "No, if we are friends, we must both command and obey alike." He looks up now, and we stare at each other in silence. "This is a truth, William."

"It's not my truth, dearest."

As I walk from the room. I wonder how we've wandered into these waters. I fear as usual I have spoken too hastily, treading without thought, until the tide carried me beyond my depth. Is William right? Is perfect friendship between a man and a woman only possible if one commands and the other obeys?

Jane is brushing my hair for the night when William comes to my chamber. "Thank you, Jane, I will attend my wife now." He takes the brush from her. As Jane leaves, I wonder if she too is surprised by this nocturnal visit, the first since our loss. He brushes my hair slowly and with great precision, smoothing each stroke with his palm, letting his fingers linger against my neck. I'd almost forgotten the blessed warmth of his hand. I move it down to my breast. "Are you sure?" he asks. "I would not want to hurt you."

In truth, I've never been so unsure of my body. In these past weeks, there's been little respite from bleeding. But my desire to bring him close is greater than any discomfort I might fear. "Yes," I tell him.

If pain renders me unresponsive, he is, I think, unaware. And even in his passion, he is gentle, considerate. To feel his skin next to mine, his mouth on my body, to feel again we are one, brings such peace to my heart, dispels all doubts. "Dearest," I say. We lay entwined; his arm about me, his leg across mine. "I'm so happy to be reunited. I spoke too heatedly earlier."

He turns his damp face to me. "No, Dorothy. It is your independence of spirit that has always drawn me. It's what I most cherish in you."

"Then my brother might come?" I say it almost without thinking.

We are finally agreed that Henry may come for two days. This is not the straight, open talk I've always believed in. This is another kind of power. One that is new to me and that I am loath to admit to.

Waiting in the hall to greet my brother, I'm determined this visit shall be a time for mending what is broken. We'll walk together in the gardens and wonder at nature, as our father taught us. I'll show Henry the careful little molehill, a mark of our latest, half-blind resident. I'll take him to the honeycomb hanging silently against a courtyard wall, its stillness giving no hint of the busy work taking place inside. Together, we will remember all we've lost and the necessity of holding fast to what remains.

These musings are soon forgotten when Henry is finally here. "Ah, sister!" As he steps into the hallway, I see my brother is not wearing mourning. He is clad in a bright coloured jacket atop a gaudy waistcoat. And Henry is not alone. Without the mask he wore at Spring Gardens, I do not immediately recognise Lord Montcroft. He is younger than I imagined. Hardly more than a boy. But as he gives me the knee, I sense the same mocking arrogance that was so disquieting that evening.

"Miss Dorothy, or should I say Mrs Temple?" He takes my hand. "And where is this paragon of a husband of whom we hear much?"

"He is in Dublin. He'll return later today." As I try to remove my hand from Lord Montcroft's grasp, I'm thankful William is not here to witness this arrival. My brother insists on a tour of the house. His mood is jovial, a rare state for Henry. If I did not know him better, I would assume he'd broken his journey at several taverns.

"I congratulate you, sister. It seems you keep a pleasant household. One in which a man may be at ease."

"But it's remote, is it not, Mrs Temple?" And Lord Montcroft has the impudence to peer into my bedchamber. "Don't you feel a trifle separated from the world?" Without waiting for a reply, he adds: "This room is surely a mile from Mr Temple's own. Maybe he enjoys a nocturnal stroll." I feel myself redden and turn instinctively to my brother. But Henry is laughing – as if he's just been told an amusing story.

I'm relieved this supper is taken amiably. I'd reason enough to fear the air might be more volatile. When William returned from Dublin, bringing with him Martha, he did not hide his displeasure at news of our extra guest. "Of course I know of Lord Montcroft, Dorothy – the whole of London is acquainted with his reputation. But I fail to see what brings him to my door."

"It's but a short visit. I would so have it peaceful."

And he's done his best to ensure this. Even when Lord Montcroft remarks on his seeming lack of occupation, William refuses to be provoked. "I'd not join Cromwell's employ, my lord. I find gainful enough employment in my essays and translations. And I have my gardens and orchards to attend." Before another word can be uttered, Martha leaps to her brother's defence.

"My brother is thinking of standing for the Irish Parliament," she says. "And his writings are of the greatest distinction. At my request, William has recently translated Virgil."

Lord Montcroft looks at Martha as if seeing her for the first time. "What can one say in the face of such admiration? You are obviously destined to be a man of letters, Mr Temple." He glances across at Henry. "Hardly an occupation to advance your fortune, though."

"I'm of the opinion improvement of the mind is a far nobler end than the advancement of fortune." William's voice remains measured.

Lord Montcroft laughs. "Noble ends are usually reserved for those who can afford them, Mr Temple."

I'm expecting my brother to join this baiting, but Henry seems content to leave the stage to his young friend. Indeed, my brother's demeanour throughout this supper has been one of acquiescence and flattery towards the table in general, and Lord Montcroft in particular. "It's amazing how Monti can always guess the correct year of any splendid grape. It is one of his many talents." In truth, Henry is as unlike himself as ever I've known him. He even sings William's praises. "Mr Temple's attributes also know few bounds, my lord. His prowess at tennis is still celebrated up at Emanuel, I believe." But my brother then adds: "At the expense of your Greek, no doubt, Mr Temple?"

Lord Montcroft also considers himself something of a master at what he terms *jeu de paume.* "What a pity you've no court, Mr Temple. I should have been delighted to challenge you to a game."

"And you shan't be disappointed." William continues to play the agreeable host. "My Lord Ormond keeps a court a mile or so from here. He graciously allows me to make use of it."

Will Hammer is called upon to make a fourth, and Jane, Martha and I are summoned to witness this match. It takes two carriages and an hour's drive through ceaseless rain to reach Lord Ormond's estate. By the time we enter the damp, chilly courts, all are in sombre mood. Except Lord Montcroft, who readies himself by discarding his jacket and swishing his racquet at an imaginary ball, which he lobs towards Will Hammer. "I see you have bagged yourself a strapping lad, Mr Temple. I fear Henry and I will be sorely challenged to keep pace." This proves true. Although Lord Montcroft is the superior player, he's a reckless one, often sending the ball crashing into the wall of the court in his efforts to wrong-foot his opponents. In contrast, William is precise, with none of his usual impetuosity. His shots are less daring – but steady, determined. His strategy, it seems, is to wear the other down.

This match is between just two men. Henry and Will have little participation. On the few occasions the ball is lobbed Henry's way, he either sends it into the net or misses it completely, accompanied by groans from Lord Montcroft. Will fares better by his lordship, eliciting a "Bravo!" whenever his great height enables him to return a particularly high shot. But for most of the match, Will ambles aimlessly about the court, unfamiliar with the rules of this game.

Towards the end, William too has shed his jacket. Despite the chill, both men are sweating profusely, grimly determined not to cede the match. Next to me, Jane says, "This is more battle than sport."

"Let's hope it ends with few casualties, Jane."

William has saved his best shot for last. As Lord Montcroft chases the ball unsuccessfully across the court, he curses obscenely. I feel Jane stiffen. I glance across at Martha. She is all smiles, applauding her brother's victory. And his lordship soon regains composure. "Well done, Temple. It was a fair win. Though I fear the presence of your young Greek god severely hampered us."

Martha and I ride back with Henry and Lord Montcroft. Despite my brother's best efforts to engage his friend in conversation, that gentleman is sullen, replying only with a terse word or a shrug, before focusing his attention on Martha. "Tell me, Miss Temple, what does a beautiful young woman find to do in these parts?" And Martha, blushing, admits she has a great thirst for London.

"If my father didn't take me there every few months, I fear I would die of boredom."

"We cannot allow that. Next time you're in town, you must allow me to escort you to Spring Gardens. Your sister will vouch they are anything but dull, and I would be pleased to acquaint you with the delights to be found there." Martha demurely accepts.

"Sir John, of course, will expect to accompany you," I say. I notice my brother has turned away from this discourse and is staring dejectedly out at the countryside – where there is little to see save mist and rain.

The clock in the hall is chiming three when I wake, but it's not the chimes that rouse me. From somewhere in the house I hear raised voices. I feel my way across the room and light my candle by the embers of the fire. As I cross the hallway, the voices become clearer: my brother's, agitated; Lord Montcroft's, goading. I hear him laugh. There is a figure on the stairs ahead of me. As she turns, I see it's Jane. Her voice, when she reaches my side, is hushed and anxious. "I stood at the door of the withdrawing room, my lady, since I thought one of the gentlemen might be ill and need aid."

"Is Mr Temple there?"

To my relief, Jane thinks not. "I heard only Mr Henry and his lordship, my lady. And if you'll excuse the liberty, from what I could tell, they both be in their cups." For a moment, Jane and I stand on the stairs, unsure what to do.

"We'll return to our chambers, Jane. And please say nothing of this."

"I'm not given to gossip, my lady."

Neither Henry nor Lord Montcroft appear at breakfast. Martha, Jane and I eat in silence. This is broken when William joins us. "I hope you were not disturbed by the loudness of our guests last night." His eyes, when he looks at me, are accusing.

Martha says she was woken by the noise. "Your brother sounded distressed. What was amiss, I wonder?" I say I think it was no more than light-hearted banter that became a tad heated. William laughs, but there is no mirth in it.

As Henry and Lord Montcroft prepare to leave, I determine to speak to my brother alone. I find him in his chamber, which is in some disorder. Bed covers are scattered on the floor, and a half-empty brandy flask stands on the table. A tankard has rolled into the hearth. The carriage for Dublin is due to depart in less than an hour, but seated on the bed, my brother is still in his night robes. I'm alarmed to see how pale and drawn he is. "Are you unwell, Henry?"

"I fear so, sister. I fear I am somewhat undone."

I sit next to him on the bed and take his hand in mine. "Talk to me, Henry, please. Tell me what is wrong."

"Would that Aunt Gargrave had not died. Would that you and I had stayed together, Dorothy. Things then might have been more ordered. As it is, I must wander alone."

"Nonsense, Henry. You were always Aunt Gargrave's best-loved nephew. You are set to inherit the house in Chelsea you know so well. You will continue your work with war veterans. You have much to look forward to."

"Only grief, Dorothy. I look forward to only grief. I have lost my compass, you see." I put my arms around him. And this brother, usually so dour, so stoic and stern, whom I have always regarded with trepidation, puts his head on my shoulder and weeps like a child.

William is solicitous, arranging my shawl carefully about my shoulders and lifting my hair free of it. "We will walk in the gardens. I would see this honeycomb of yours." The sun is just beginning to fade, pale and watery on the horizon. The grass is damp and pungent. There is no wind and the earlier rain has left a freshness in the air. All is silent. William says, "I'm sorry, dearest, for the hurt I know this visit has caused."

"My brother is not himself."

"We are all mortified to find him in such questionable company, but it is not Henry who worries me, Dorothy. I'm concerned lest this visit should result in another attack of the Spleen. I'd have you rest for a few days, as a precaution."

The honeycomb no longer sits snugly in the corner of the wall. It lies on the ground, abandoned. "It is Henry who risks illness. I sense such despair in him. I so wish to help him."

"Dearest, you cannot help him. Your brother, I believe, may have chosen a way of life both unnatural – and unlawful. If I'm right, I think it will render him permanently wretched. I hope you will now agree I was right to advise against this visit." This said slowly, as though addressing a child. "I cannot forbid you to see him again, but I would urge you to think on the consequences to your own well-being." William moves the honeycomb with his foot. It's no more than a hollow, empty shell.

I am suddenly overcome with weariness. My brother, it seems, is lost to me.

Martha says: "I would ask you something, Dorothy." I bid her come sit next to me.

"My dear, you may ask me anything."

"In the kitchens, there's much talk of 'pederasty'. Can you explain what is a pederast? It's such a strange word."

"Indeed it is, Martha." I peer more closely at my needlecraft, holding the sampler up to the light, as if to check the stitching. "And one I am unfamiliar with."

Martha bends over her own sampler, a slight smile playing on her lips. I sense she knows very well the meaning of that particular word.

SHEEN, SURREY

1661

"You take him, Jane – lest I clasp him too hard."

"Reckon he can withstand a bit of roughness, my lady. Reckon he's a good strong lad." And I hold out my arms.

Jack Temple – a good strong lad. A tiny life force, grabbing my finger, tugging it to his mouth. Five dead babes, and now a miracle. I'm thinking it was boggy air caused all that grief and I'm silently thanking my maker for setting us back in the blessed English countryside. God's will, none of us needs ever put foot in Ireland again. "Reckon it's the freshness in these parts makes him so lusty, my lady."

"Yes, I do believe he may be thriving." She's not fully trusting. Not yet. And who would blame her? All those losses and she scarce shed a tear. But there was that dullness to her eyes, those deepening lines around her mouth. Truth is, this whole household were a-jitter afore Jack Temple took that first breath. Mr Temple couldn't stay put. Soon as she got her pains, he was pacing. "I'm at a loss." He pulled on his riding jacket.

"Please stay with me," I heard her say.

"I know not how to help you," he replied. He mounted up and made for the tavern. Said gentleman was humming a different tune next morning. "What think you? Is it not the best boy you ever did see?" So high were his spirits, for a blushing second I thought Mr Temple was going to press me to him! He could scarce be persuaded to quit the house, and I'd wager save for that summon to London, he'd still be here.

"Mr Temple's properly smitten," I say to my lady. "Think we'll see a deal of pampering from that quarter."

"Put my son in his cradle then, Jane, lest we are tempted to do the same." As I swaddle the mite and lay him down, I'm thinking on all the work went into fashioning this goodly bed. I wonder Will found time, given his load. He's diligent, though, Will Hammer. I'll say that for him. I'm barely done rocking the babe asleep when my lady bids me go and see if the carrier's come. "I think I heard the wagon, Jane."

"They'll scarce have got beyond Putney, my lady." It's the second time this morning she's sent me running. I'm thinking Mr Temple would be fast-pacing it straight to Whitehall without stopping for vittles, let alone letter writing. It's not every day a body's summoned by a king. "Truth be, my lady, I can scarce wrap my thoughts round this London outing."

"It's surely fitting a monarch should recognise the worth of a good subject," she says.

"Begging your pardon, but it's not Mr Temple meeting the new king that plays on me." No. I'm thinking that's only proper, given my lady's breeding and her family's closeness to the Royal Cause. "It's a king finally back in the palace at Whitehall that has me reeling."

"It's what God decreed, Jane. Our country in rightful order again."

Yes: *Rightful Order.* Miss Dorothy always has a way with her words. Everything as once it were. "I've heard the maypoles will be back in force this year," I say. "And there's talk a body can scarce move in London for all flocking to the new playhouses."

"Well, make haste, Jane, and see if there's a letter that tells us more."

I've not far to walk. This house is scarce big enough to toss a cat. Truth be, Chicksands was a deal more fitting for persons of quality. The gardens were twice the size. Still, this house do have its charms, being right near the river and all. I'm thinking Sheen is as fit a place as any for a child to grow. The closeness to London is no small thing neither, given the current goings-on.

My lady's not the only one dwelling on London doings. Soon as I go through the kitchens, Rebecca's quizzing me. "Do you think Will might meet the King, Jane?"

"I'll warrant His Majesty won't be passing the time of day with a manservant," I say. "I'd hope Will Hammer knows to mind his manners and keep his place." And Rebecca gives me one of her closed looks before turning back to cleaning the pots. There's never any guessing the girl's thoughts. She's like old Noah: secret as the grave.

"How fare the little ones, Rebecca?"

"Spirited as can be." This said without looking up or stopping her work.

"Good job you're young and hale then," I say. In all honesty, Rebecca looks far from hale. I stare at her stiff white cap and straight little back, and wonder again how this tiny wisp of a thing ever managed to bring forth two strapping twin boys.

"Still no letter, Jane?" Lady Dorothy's not best pleased. "Are we never to be told about this new monarch?"

"They do say this King Charles is handsome as they come, my lady, and with curls to match Mr Temple's own."

Leaning over the cradle, she strokes the babe's dark hair. "I do believe my son shall be blessed with that same handsomeness. What think you, Jane?"

We've been waiting on their return all day, but it's past midnight when I finally hear the horses. Then Mr Temple's voice: "Call the grooms, Will, before these horses expire." I'm thinking someone needs rouse the cook. Once her head's lowered, she can sleep like the dead. Turns out I've no cause to fret. By time I get myself down, the kitchens are a-clatter of pans and there's enough candles to light a feast.

I'm surprised to see Sir John walk in with Will and Mr Temple. "I caught the first boat from Dublin, Jane. I'd not have missed this chance to meet our beloved new monarch." I smile to myself, remembering Sir John's previous partiality for a certain Mr Cromwell.

Mr Temple is already ushering his father towards the stairs. "Come and meet our other new monarch, sir. Named for you, and with those same strong lungs."

I tell Will to help himself to leftovers from the pots in the hearth. I daresn't ask this surly cook to do it. By the way she's banging about, I can tell she's in no mood to be up and doing this time of night. Will is unaware. He dishes hisself a bit of cold fowl and cabbage and tucks his long legs 'neath the table. "You wouldn't credit, Jane, what times London's seeing, and the King said to have magic powers of curing and all. We could scarce move at Whitehall for all the sick crowding in."

"Well, I hope you've brought none of it back here, Will Hammer." My mind's on that babe.

"I was so close to the King I could have touched him." Will don't seem too cheerful about it.

"I trust he didn't note your gloomy look," I says. I'm thinking most persons would be a deal more jolly at such an honour. "In goodness' name, tell me, Will. Is this King Charles as dashing as they say? We've been waiting these two full days to know his words."

"His words were amiable enough. But he'd a cold eye."

"You should keep such thoughts to yourself," I say. "Talk like that could land you in the pillory."

"All I'm saying is, we've still to wait and see if this truly be a man of the people as some claim." And Will is shovelling food in his mouth with speed, talking as he does so.

"It's a good thing His Majesty didn't have to watch you eat. That's sight enough to freeze any eye." Will grins at me, and I'm remembering the boy he once was. And not so long ago neither.

We hear Sir John come bellowing down the stairs, full of the babe and the family likeness. "You can see William there, and I flatter myself that strong nose comes from me." I'm thinking there goes the way of men. Never a mention a boy might follow his mother. First thing I noted when Jack Temple looked up at me were those deep eyes of Miss Dorothy.

Sir John claps Will on the shoulder: "Mr Temple shan't need you more tonight. Go home to Rebecca and your boys." I turn away and busy myself pouring a jug of ale for Sir John. I've got nothing against Rebecca. No – she's a good little worker. But there's not much joy to her. I scarce recall a smile breaking that pale little face. And Rebecca's stubborn as a mule. Still, I dare say they're content enough. I hear she keeps a clean house. Not that I've set foot in it.

"The King smiled on Will, Jane. He's tall himself, but he thought he'd encountered a giant!" As I turn and watch Will hotfoot it out the door, I note he can still redden up when he's object of a joust.

All smiles now, the cook serves Sir John his coddled eggs and receives his usual fulsome compliments. "These look hatched warm but an hour ago. Methinks it's all in the preparation," and he beckons me to table. "Come sit with me, Jane. If you don't mind keeping an old man company."

"It's my privilege, sir." I'm that tired, and all this eating has pricked my appetite. I watch Sir John break into the egg and mop the yellow juice with a chunk of bread, and for a giddy moment I'm tempted to up and get my own portion. I soon pull myself straight, though. I'm not one for forgetting what's proper.

"The King looked kindly on us, Jane. My son was wise to return for this new reign. He's well set to enter the field of diplomacy. I dare say he'll see a foreign posting 'fore long."

"You mean they're bound for leaving England, sir?" I'm wide awake now and none too careful with my words. "Do you think they'll be returning to Ireland?"

"Further afield, I'll warrant. With His Majesty's good grace, that is." After a moment, Sir John adds: "And God's too, of course."

I'm too unquiet for sleep. I can't find a comfortable way to lay myself. My mind is abuzz with Sir John's news. I'm thinking Lady Dorothy's still too fragile for a foreign journey. I'm wondering if she knows of these plans. Chances be, she may not need me, what with the new nursery maid and her other wenches. And anyways, I've little taste for more foreign travel. But then what? I still have Guernsey. Though since my father died, I've no proper place, nor reason to be there. I do miss the sea. But far as I know, I've no relatives left to cast me a net. Then there's the babe. I'd be that happy to watch him grow. Truth is, I feel completely wove into this family.

There's been no mention of foreign parts this entire day, though I've kept my ears tuned. I'm expecting some talk when we gather for supper. But Sir John, for one, is occupied with lauding the new arrival. "I never saw an infant so alert in my life. I can see greatness there, mark me if I'm not right." He's generous, too, in praise of my lady. "You have a motherly glow, daughter. Is that not so, William? Methinks there'll be other hearty babes now to join young Jack."

There's much talk of the King, both gentlemen being favourably impressed. Sir John, in particular, can find no fault. "I sensed the substance of the man. This monarch is not of his father's ilk. He shan't alienate his people. I'd wager his game is to serve our country well."

Mr Temple's more cautious. "We spoke but a moment. 'Twas not possible to weigh his worth. The man keeps his cards close. But there was a sharpness to his eye which points to a keen mind."

I can't help note the lack of reverence. These two gentlemen, and even Will, speak of the King as a person of their own standing and not as our Most Gracious Majesty. Times have surely changed. I'm remembering how Sir Peter would scarce allow himself to remain seated when the old king's name was mentioned. I'm mulling on these thoughts and just biting into my pear when Sir

John says: "William and I have news to relate." I ready myself for what's to come. But turns out Sir John's tale has nought to do with travel. "Martha is to be betrothed to Sir Thomas Giffard." Across the table, I see my lady searching her mind to put face to name. Mr Temple obliges.

"Do you not recall, my dear? Tom Giffard is that callow lad from County Meath who has been pursuing Martha since we set up in Ireland." By the flatness in his voice, I'm thinking he's not overjoyed with this arrangement.

"Come now, William." Sir John is tetchy. "The Giffards are extremely well established. Martha will be set with a goodly estate."

"I've no quarrel with a good fortune and I daresay Martha shall relish terming herself Lady Giffard. It's the boy that troubles me." And Mr Temple beckons a wench to bring more wine. "I sense a weak character. One that will be no match for Martha's own strong will." Sir John don't seem troubled: "He's young yet, and with a good wife by him will likely come to prove himself. What think you, Dorothy? Is it not time Martha was wed and well set?"

My lady looks thoughtful. "What I think is of little import, Sir John. What are Martha's thoughts?"

Seems like a full minute afore Sir John can find a reply. "Why, I believe she has a good enough fondness for the lad."

And my lady says: "Then I think if there is some fondness on both parts, and a willingness to respect the other, this is fair basis for any union."

We are all surprised at these words, given the passion with which my lady approached her own nuptials. Mr Temple in particular looks properly put out. "Knowing Martha as I do, I think such a tepid arrangement may quickly pall," he says.

"You are ever the romantic, William. Martha's not a girl to be ruled by sentiment," and Sir John chuckles. "If things do sour, I dare say there are enough chambers in that castle to avoid clashes."

The rest of the meal is taken in silence. Soon as it's over, Mr Temple and Sir John retire to the library.

My lady is still quiet when we are back in her chamber. "Let's sit and read, Jane." This room is cramped and the candles don't cast much light. What with that and the heat of the fire, I can scarce concentrate on this romance she's given me. Seems I've read the same sentence ten times. Truth be, I'm not much of a one for books. I can't see the merit of them. Stitching is more to my liking. With stitching, you've always got something to show for the effort. When my lady finally puts aside her tome, I'm quick to follow.

My head is still full of foreign lands. I'm thinking if the posting were on French shores, we just might settle with ease. I'm wondering is this an apt moment to broach the subject. But Lady Dorothy has her mind on other matters.

"It's strange, Jane, that a gentleman of Sir John's nature, who wed, it's said, entirely for love of a woman and would take no other when she died, should not seek a love match for his daughter."

"I suppose, my lady, fathers are more clear-eyed when it comes to daughters." Then, I add: "Begging your pardon, but I think there was some surprise with your own words at table, since you had the happiness to follow your heart." Straight ways, I'm wondering if I've spoke too plain. But as she rises and crosses to her dressing table, I see my lady's not set back.

"Yes, Jane. It was my good fortune to wed for love. But I've always known the value of calmer sentiments." And seating herself, she begins to remove her baubles. "I'm convinced tolerance and quiet compromise may also serve a marriage well." She stares down at the pearl eardrops in her hand, as if trying to gauge their weight. After a moment, she says: "Of course, I'm lucky to be so blessed."

I help her prepare for bed. And since we're easy together, I don't hesitate to say what's occupying my own mind: "If you'll pardon my asking, be it true Mr Temple shall have a foreign posting, as Sir John told me?"

Soon as I says it, I wish I hadn't. "You must know, Jane, I cannot discuss such matters with you, and I'm surprised Sir John did. You shall know of any arrangements at the appropriate time." And although I apologise profusely, my lady remains out of sorts. "You may leave me, Jane. Please tell the nurse to bring my son."

As so oft happens, I've not handled things as I should. Seems however open our talk, I've still to learn when to speak and when to keep my counsel. I've just reached the door, when my lady softens: "Have no worry, Jane. In all probability, our next foreign journey will be for Miss Martha's wedding. Shall you be happy to see Ireland again?"

IRELAND

The rain lashing against the coach has finally begun to ease. We stare out at the sodden Irish countryside. Jane says: "Well, my lady. If you ask me, nothing's changed."

I would have been content to stay by Sir John in Dublin. But William was adamant. "We shall be more comfortable in our own house. I wish my son to see those magnificent orchards."

As we approach the gardens, I bid the nurse raise Jack to the window. *When you are grown, your father shall show you how to plant a tree.* I say these words to myself. I would not tempt fate. My walk through the rooms is slow-paced. Having just mastered the art, Jack is intent on walking with me. His little hand in mine connects me to the moment. I'm not, as I had feared, dragged immediately back into the past. I've always thought this house too large. Now, even with the rooms half empty, it seems smaller, strangely oppressive, as if in our absence it has turned inward on itself and taken on the weight of sadness we knew here.

William's study still contains several books. He's also left behind some of his own works. Piled on the shelf are his writings from the early days of our courtship. I take down a pamphlet and leaf through. It's the essay he handed me years ago in the gardens at St Malo: a young man dying of love for a heartless woman. His inability to find words to tell her. I remember how dismissive I'd been. Now, as I turn the pages, I see the writing is, in fact, filled with intensity: the work of a passionate young man. I place it carefully on the desk, next to an open letter from William to his father.

> ...*I implore you, Father, think further on these proposed nuptials. We know little of this family beyond their wealth and the solitariness of their estate. Martha is surely too full of life to be shut away in a remote castle in the depths of Ireland at a distance from her own kin. My sister has an appetite for living which it would be great sadness to see crushed. From the little I know of Giffard, he is as unremarkable as any man I ever met.*
>
> *To my mind, Martha would make an excellent wife to some aspiring diplomat ready to take on the world...*

The letter is dated more than a month ago, but obviously never sent.

Jack is fretful. The effort of walking has tired him. I take him in my arms and walk to the window. The mist has cleared, giving way to a view of the valley and the hills beyond. As always, all is verdant after the rain. "This is Ireland, Jack. Is it not beautiful?" And I hold my son close.

It's the first time I've seen Martha all year, and for a moment I'm truly startled. She is thinner than I recall, and there are dark circles beneath her eyes. Her face, though beautiful as always, has lost some of its youthful bloom. The creamy freshness of her skin has given way to a sallow dullness.

As he greets his sister, I see William too is dismayed. "My dear..." He puts his hand on Martha's arm and keeps it there as we move towards the dining hall. When he helps her be seated, it's with the care one might render an elderly relative.

William says: "Well, Father, is it true we are not to meet with this bridegroom until the church?"

"Come, William, you've met Thomas often enough." Sir John

is obviously irked by William's tone. "In a few days, you shall be brothers. There will be a lifetime to become better acquainted." Martha says nothing. She's to be married in less than a week, yet her demeanour is of one who has suffered misfortune. William may be right. This union, regarded with such satisfaction by Sir John, may be a deal less palatable to his daughter.

The men talk of affairs at Whitehall. Sir John is anxious for news of William's progress at Court. He declares himself astounded the King has not yet called for him. "There are enough fools wandering the continent on so-called diplomatic missions. His Majesty needs clever, honest men working his cause." Sir John wonders if William is passing enough time in London.

"You should ask my wife, sir. She complains I'm seldom at Sheen."

I wonder if this remark requires me to respond. Evidently not, since Sir John ignores it, saying: "We shall ride over to my Lord Ormond in a day or so and take his counsel."

William has sworn me to secrecy regarding his dealings at Whitehall. Sir John is less discreet. "You must keep your ear closer to the ground. Lord Ormond mentioned there's soon to be an opportunity in Spain." This delivered in a voice that might be heard from here to London. Jane pushes aside her plate, having eaten little.

William says, "We shall all be relieved to know the future." This is true, and I would not have Jane disquieted before I am able to speak with her. Wherever we go, I shall need Jane with me. I can scarce imagine life without her.

Jane says: "Begging your pardon, my lady, but if you're not wanting me more tonight, I'll make for bed." Her head, she tells me, is still set on that rocking coach.

And mine on those swirling waves. "Why is it, Jane, these short sea voyages always seem so hazardous?"

"It's likely the sea letting us know its strength, my lady. My father always said, "The ocean's there to remind us we're of little import." Comforting words indeed.

I sit for some time with my candle burning. The fire casts a warm glow, but I feel the chill. Even in summer this chamber has a dampness to it. I've a longing for William. What would happen, I wonder, if I were to go to him? If I were to open the door to his chamber, approach the bed and lay beside him? If I were to take his hand and guide it to my body, so he might know, without words, how to comfort me? How would William react? In eight years of marriage, I have never once made the walk from my chamber to his. I have always waited.

Lying alone in this bed, memories come flooding back. I am in Ireland, this place where I bore and buried so many babies. Those tiny, mewing creatures, whose faces, try as I may, I cannot recall.

We're at the church early, Jack in his little breaches and new frock coat, Jane in my blue gown – which becomes her more than it ever did me. Sir John sits beside me. His gout prevents him escorting his daughter from the house. William will bring Martha into church. The bridegroom is already in place, sandy hair brushed neatly about his shoulders, eyes fixed firmly on the ground. Sir John leans towards me. "God willing, Thomas will soon conquer this shyness. It does not become a man."

"Dat." Jack points his tiny finger.

"Yes, Jack. Flowers." Daisies and anemones, garlands of them on either side of the altar; beside every pew. Churches are once again celebrating in style. I bid Jack look at the array of flowers decorating the heads of women gathering in the church.

When Martha enters with William, she too is wearing her floral crown. "Rosemary, Jack, and lily of the valley." Despite her pallor, Martha is a beautiful bride. Soft rose is always flattering, and the delicate tone of the dress sets off the darkness of her hair and the vivid blue of her eyes. But as she passes, clinging tightly to William's arm, I see the tension in her face, and my heart goes out to her. I well remember my own wedding day and how sorely I missed my mother. Martha has no memories of maternal love to sustain her, but she may well long for the warm presence of the woman she's no doubt pictured all her life. I am Martha's close female relative, but I've not been a good sister. Character, and now distance, has separated us. As Martha takes her vows, I make my own promise. In future, I shall do all I can to strengthen the bond.

Jane says: "Looks like the Lord's smiling on this union, my lady." Sunlight streams through the windows of Sir John's dining hall, casting its rays on the fine damask table coverings and those of us gathered there. The viol and lute player are forced to move their instruments to a cooler corner. "Nice to see Miss Martha looking so lovely."

"It's Lady Giffard now, Jane, but yes, you are right." Seated between her father and William, Martha is easily the most beautiful woman in the room. And although still pale, as the music begins, she's more relaxed, no doubt relieved to be free of the formal ceremonies. When the musicians strike up a lively jig, Sir John bids Thomas bring his bride to the centre of the room. Martha is as skilled at the dance as any Frenchwoman, but poor Thomas is no expert. However he concentrates, the intricate steps defeat him. His performance, accompanied by much blushing, is soon cut short by Sir John, who bids other guests join the couple. The dancers crowd onto the floor, amongst them Sir John's grooms, who also misstep themselves but are too jolly to care. By my side, a small voice says: "Me!"

"Yes, my lovely. You shall dance too." And Jane sweeps Jack up. For a second, I'm filled with anxiety. But as my son laughs and skips with pleasure, I determine to conquer my fears. I will leave Jack in God's good hands. I look about me at those still seated. All eyes are turned to the bride. With her face animated and cheeks now flushed, she is suddenly the young girl I first met on that day of my own wedding. Even Will Hammer, seated next to Sir John's steward, cannot take his eyes from the dance. But when I follow his gaze, I see it's not Martha drawing Will's eye, but Jane, the blue dress twirling as she lifts Jack in the air; the sunlight playing on her hair.

As the couple leave, I push my way through the throng to take Martha's hand. "There'll be a letter awaiting you at Castle Jordan. Let us stay close."

"The wind is up, Dorothy. Your hands are cold. You should go inside." And they are gone.

In the coach carrying us back to Carlow, William is silent. I say: "Are you now more at ease with this union, dearest?" When he doesn't reply, I add: "For all Thomas's youthful demeanour, I think him a good and kindly man."

"You are ever the optimist, Dorothy." William's voice is close to anger. "How can you imagine this marriage will be anything but a disaster?"

My mother used to tell me I slept like a feather: the slightest noise would wake me. It's the same to this day. And although it's not yet dawn, when the door of my chamber creeks, I'm instantly conscious of it, and of the warmth of William's body as he comes next to me. I turn to him. "Dearest." But he does not speak. And his lovemaking has an urgency I'm unaccustomed to. I try to catch my breath, to adjust my body to his. I am left behind. But sensing his need, I reach up and take the dear face above me in both my hands, trying to draw him closer. By the chink of dawn light, I see William's eyes are tightly closed. For a moment, I wonder if he is truly awake.

He stays till morning. Both of us unable to sleep.

Leaning on one of his servants, Sir John is already waiting at his door when we arrive in Dublin. "You will take some nourishment before you leave? It's as well to board a boat with a satisfied stomach."

I think it will take a deal more than food to calm *my* anxieties. William says: "Sir, you will find any excuse to keep your grandson near you!"

"I have but one, so I shall needs make the most of him. God willing, I shall soon have more." And Sir John gives a raucous laugh. But, seated at table, he shows little interest in Jack, engrossed instead with strategy for William's next trip to Whitehall. "Lord Arlington is your man. You must put more effort to courting him. They say he's ever about the King, and a shrewd player of palace games."

I've met Lord Arlington only once, on one of my rare trips to London with William. At Whitehall, he insisted on showing me the King's new private sitting room, where, with a hand on my arm, he'd confided: "It is here the King enjoys his mistresses." The room was claustrophobic, decorated in heavy crimson damask with several dark couches. Lord Arlington put his face so close to mine, I could smell his stale breath. "You are a beautiful woman, Mrs Temple. William is a lucky dog."

Sir John says: "I believe Lord Arlington is the most agreeable man."

Jack begins to whine. He is restless and bored with our company. I bid Jane take him into the gardens. Sir John watches as they leave. "I'm surprised Jane never wed," he says. "She surely had her chances." And William laughs.

"I'd wager many, sir. But I fear Jane's expectations were raised too high."

For some reason, these words anger me. "Please do not be concerned for Jane. I've known her long and well and she has never shown the slightest interest in any man's attentions." The men are taken aback. "Jane is happy with her state. Not every woman feels the need of a man's company and protection." I'm aware my voice is heated and both men are laughing now. They cannot know how surprised I am at my own words.

I'm still pondering this when one of the grooms comes with a letter. As he reads it, Sir John's face loses colour. He stares at it for some time as if trying to understand the words, before passing the letter to William. It's from Edward Giffard – Thomas's brother. William reads it aloud:

> *My dear Sir John,*
> *The news I bring is painful for me to write. A week ago, my brother Thomas fell ill with a malaise, which, although we employed the best medical advice, none could identify. After four days and nights of fever, and always being attended with much compassion by his family, the Lord saw fit to relieve him of his earthly pains. Thomas left this world on the 15th of May. We pray God have mercy on his dear soul.*
> *Yours in Sorrow, Edward Giffard.*

The 15th of May! Barely two weeks since Martha became a bride. For a moment, no one speaks. How can we possibly find words? Sir John slumps in his chair, suddenly shrunken. "Why is it," he finally says, "in this advanced age and with all our great knowledge, we cannot put a stop to these infernal illnesses?" His voice is cracked and dry. "Our young are snuffed out with scarce a moment's warning." Wearily, he adds, "Though ours is not to question God's will."

I look across at William. There's a small red patch just below his cheek. "Martha must return immediately," he says. "She cannot stay alone in that place."

We are silent again, before I say: "We will keep her close. She shall come and live with us at Sheen."

SHEEN

Them Irish boats do dip and rock. By time we were home, my lady looked sick as a dog. I deemed she'd have need of a few days in her chamber. No persuading her to that – not with all there is to do before Miss Martha arrives. "My sister will be in deep mourning," she says. "I wish to make her surroundings as pleasing as possible." Will and those yard boys have been heaving furniture about all week. If you ask me, this house wasn't built to shelter so many. I'm wondering Miss Martha don't go back and live with Sir John. That Dublin house is a lot more suited. Still, I must admit fate has dealt badly with that young woman – having a new husband up and die so sudden. I've not always seen eye to eye with Miss Martha, but I'm surely saddened by her plight.

Mr Temple's fetching his sister from the boat. He's taking Will with him. "Good job you're strong," I says to Will. "I'd wager Miss Martha won't be travelling lightly." I'm proved right on that. It's a wonder one coach could hold so many trunks and mantles. By time they're unloaded, they're spread about the entire hall. My lady goes straight to Miss Martha and puts her arms about her.

"I am so happy you've come," she says, adding she's sure her sister is in need of rest.

Miss Martha declares she's not one bit tired. "I'm eager to see the house. Perhaps Jane can tell someone to unpack my trunks." And tossing aside her cloak, off she rushes, peering into rooms and demanding to know where will be her bedchamber.

"She's been thus animated since we came from the boat," Mr Temple tells us. "I fear it's the shock of all that's passed. We must treat her with care."

Miss Martha's just as lively at supper, declaring her pleasure at being on English soil again. "Of course, Castle Jordan was very grand," she says, "and I dare say with work it might have been rendered comfortable. But there was a gloom which was hard to abide." I'm thinking that's not surprising, seeing as how a young husband fell sick and died soon as he got there. Miss Martha prattles on about the awful Irish weather and the dampness of the castle bedchambers. She don't say one word on that young man's sad demise. Maybe it's too painful to speak of.

Perhaps sensing this, Mr Temple says, "My dear, you must now endeavour to forget the whole sad time." He raises his wine: "Welcome to your new home."

My lady don't say nothing. Seems she's at a bit of a loss. I'm thinking she's as startled as me by Miss Martha's demeanour. 'Cept for her mourning gown, she don't look a tad like the grieving widow we've been expecting. She's all bright-eyed and a good deal hardier than she were at her wedding. "You have rescued me, William," she says, "and I intend to devote myself to being of help to you." After a bit, she adds: "And of course to Dorothy."

We're about to retire to bed when Miss Martha beckons me. "Would you come with me to my chamber, Jane, and make sure all is arranged for the night?" I don't object, seeing as how she just got here.

When all is set and I'm about to leave, I feel duty bound to give my condolences. "I was right sorry, Miss Martha, at news of your sad bereavement." And I note her face cloud over.

"Thank you, Jane," she says. "I appreciate your words." Then turning away, she adds: "But I should remind you to address me now as Lady Giffard."

From: Temple Court
To: William Temple
Next to the new Coffee House, St James Street, London

Dear Heart, thank you for the two baskets of excellent grapes that came with your letter, though in honesty, I would rather have you here beside me dearest, than any amount of the sweetest fruit. I'm glad things finally progress easily with my Lord Arlington, and I'm relieved you have Martha with you to attend your needs. But some here say London should be avoided. The carrier told of forty-five dying of plague in Cheapside in the space of a day! A good reason indeed to make haste home.

I fear you will find me grown dull here alone, and doting much on little Jack. Try as I may, he makes me grow too fond. For indeed, he is the quietest, sweetest, and best little boy that ever was born. Except for Jane, he is all my entertainment, until I have my dearest home again.

As your instructions, I shall be very careful of myself. But all say I shan't come soon. My cousin Molle was here lately with his wife. After four children, he deems himself a regular tome of knowledge, and declared that I am, as yet, some time from the event! I'm also reassured by Jane, who has found an excellent midwife in the village for when I have need.

My cousin and his wife had hoped to find you here and both declared you a very errant gad-about! I'd advise you to come quickly to save your reputation. But mostly because you know how extreme welcome you will be. Jack bids me send you a little kiss, and there shall be twenty more from me when you come.

Your own,

D. Temple

We were all woken by the knocking: it's not oft a letter comes in the night. Mr Temple's scarce back from London and now he's off again. And to Lord knows where. Not even time to plant them cherries he's set his heart on. The pages are spruced and wandering about the kitchens half asleep. My lady looks that fatigued. "All I know is it's at His Majesty's behest," she tells us.

I hold Jack high so's he can watch the coach pull out. Jack's crying and carrying on. He don't want his father to leave. I tell him no needs to take on. "He'll be back in two shakes of a lamb's tail." Jack's not having it, tries to wriggle free. Not like Will's boys. Minding their manners; stiff little soldiers as their papa waves goodbye. Rebecca's that particular, I'm surprised they don't salute.

Miss Martha says, "God speed their journey," and my lady adds, "And keep them safe." It's the secrecy that plays on her, not knowing where they're bound. Though chance be Mr Temple finds hisself on some leisure outing. They do say the King's that capricious.

As we go back to the house, I note there's some difficulty in my lady's walking. She's not truly big yet, but I'll wager we'll be running for the midwife afore the week's out. I urge her take some nourishment. Please God grant her one more healthy babe! Soon as she's seated, she's eating with relish. "If all goes well, I think we may finally know a foreign posting." This, without me asking nought. Though after three years of Mr Temple to-ing and fro-ing, I'm no longer fussed about foreign parts. What comes will come.

"Well, it cannot be soon enough." Miss Martha's not in good humour. She's mortified Mr Temple wouldn't take her with him on this outing. "I'm pressed to know who will care for his needs."

"With two pages and Will, he's well served." My lady is firm. "You are invaluable to him – to us all – Martha, but this journey is for men. It may be hazardous. William would never agree to put you in danger."

These words serve to further prick Miss Martha's fancy. "That's exactly why I should like to be there. There's little enough adventure in Sheen."

I'm thinking good thing too, given my lady's present state. And the thought jogs me. "I'd best make sure the lying-in needs are met, my lady. If you and Miss Martha will excuse me."

Miss Martha's quick to turn her tongue on me. "I must remind you again, Jane. I am to be addressed as Lady Giffard."

I hand the sheets to a maid and chide her sharply when she don't turn tail quick enough. "Don't stand gawping. Get them up to the birthing chamber." Truth be, it's myself I'm chiding for getting on the wrong side of Miss Martha again. I still can't think of her as widow. Two years out of mourning and she's back as sprightly as ever, and every bit as wilful.

This groom surely took his time. Not much good scolding him for his lateness. Best get him off quick. "Ride fast," I tell him. I'm affright lest the babe come before the midwife's brought.

Miss Martha's thinking the same. "What will we do, Jane, if she doesn't arrive?"

Since I've no fit answer, I busy myself reassuring my lady. "Rest easy, she'll be here or I'll know the reason why!" I pass the damp cloth over her forehead.

"I fear for my baby, Jane. It does not move." And my lady grasps my wrist. At that same moment, such a spasm of pain overtakes her, she almost tears the sleeve clean from my gown.

Miss Martha takes her other hand. "Hold tight to me, Dorothy."

I've a mind to murder that groom, and the midwife too. Two hours gone and still not hide nor hair of them. And my lady's screams are like limbs being torn from her. I'm feared lest God has destined this babe to join those other poor mites. Supposing it's turned wrong? "Is there nothing we can do to help her?" Miss Martha is as white as the birthing sheet.

I tell her it's just the way of it. "Nought to be done till the Lord wills it." And my mind is reciting all I know: Hands 'neath the babe's shoulders, lift him out gentle, best not pull. But if he's turned wrong, it would take a midwife to turn him right, and even then...

"My hope is fixed on God." My lady's voice is faint, but she's calm now, despite the pain, which is worse than any I'd hoped to witness.

Miss Martha says: "You shan't die, Dorothy." Her voice shaky; grasping my lady's hand so hard, as if willing her own strength into her sister. I hold the cup for my poor lady to take a sip of ale. What else to remember? Cut the cord clean with a knife and tie it close. Catch the leavings in a bucket. Don't forget to swaddle the babe well. All this assuming the Lord spares it – but if feet comes first. And without the midwife ...

Finally, we hear her, panting up the stairs, calling for slop bowls and rags, rushing through the door: a big woman, her face almost purple. I note beneath her cloak she's still wearing her night robe. I hands her my shawl. First thing she does is ask for ale, downing the tankard with scarce a breath. I keep my counsel for the sake of my lady. The ale is surely fortifying, though, since the woman soon takes good charge, totting up how things be, and telling my lady: "It shan't be long now, mistress." She gets busy with her tools. Not much there, except a crochet stick with a brutal-looking hook. She sees me staring. "I shan't be using it lest the mite dies and I've needs to fish it out." I glance at my lady, feverish and with eyes closed, hopefully unaware of this comment. Seeing my look, the midwife softens: "Methinks the fruit will fall of its own accord."

It's another fourteen hours before she's proved right. And with constant prayer and praising the Lord, my lady has endured, though by my life I don't know how – her poor body broke as if from the rack and no strength left in her. Once, she raised herself on the pillows and says: "I commit my soul to God, and that of my baby." And she implores us all to look to little Jack.

By late afternoon, she's rallied just enough, and, soon after, we're finally able to thank the Lord for his merciful dealings. There's blood everywhere and a bucket full of leavings on the floor.

The midwife, weary as a dog, examines it. "I oft rest it on the mite's head to insure good eyesight." My lady groans. Of all those births, this was the worst. And I'm feared lest providence snatches the tiny thing before we can swaddle it.

"You have a daughter, Dorothy," Miss Martha tells her sister.

This midwife's not shy of giving orders to the cook: "Milk, with camomile and sugar, the yolk of an egg, all mixed well. Give it to her soon as she wakes." And seeing the look of Miss Martha and me, she orders up some for us. It must be the tone of voice, for the cook sets to without a single complaint. The midwife breaks her own egg into a tankard of ale.

The sun is going down, and Miss Martha and I are still at the kitchen table, neither of us able to move ourselves. I can't help but marvel at her. Cheeks glowing again, she don't look much the worse for wear. "Well, Miss – your ladyship. Begging your pardon for saying so, but I was rightly admiring of the way you stepped up." She looks at me in surprise.

"This is my brother's child, Jane. My niece. There's nothing I would not do to help it survive."

I lay in my bed and give thanks for this tiny new life. But I can't stop my mind dwelling on that crotchet hook. I'm taken right back to that dreadful night. Pushing something inside me, so much pain. My own little mite, fished out. And thrown – where? In with the slops, no doubt. *Not much of it. Not even quickening yet.* A tiny creature thrown away like a bit of old rubbish.

Miss Martha says: "We must get word to my brother. I'll write to Lord Arlington."

"My dear, what possible good could come of that?" My lady is still weak, but her voice is firm. "William is on the King's errand. We must not trouble him with domestic worries."

"I hardly think the plague a 'domestic worry', Dorothy!"

For once, I'm agreeing with Miss Martha. Just the word chills my bones. My lady remains calm. "One man sick in the village does not warrant us to panic. We've yet to know the physician's word."

"If you'll pardon, my lady, there's talk of shutting off the house of that saddler," I say. I've heard mutterings, too, of swelling of the neck and blackness of the skin, but that might just be old biddy prattle. My lady's thoughtful. I'd wager she's thinking on Jack and that tiny babe.

"We'll stay put until we know more. Make sure we've enough provisions, Jane." She's adamant everyone takes baccy. "And be sure the servants living in the village move into the house. Tell Rebecca to bring her boys tonight."

Not much use trying to reason with Rebecca. Down in the kitchens, she bids me thank Lady Dorothy, "but the boys and I shall be best in our own home."

"Do you think that's what Will would want?"

"Will's not here, Jane," she says. "And in his absence, I must make decisions as I see fit." I never come across a kitchen maid who gave herself such airs.

It takes two medics and a surgeon to confirm what we've all been expecting. Not much help to the saddler. He upped and died yesterday. None knows where they've buried him; there's rumour the sexton came in the night. My lady refuses to stay abed. "I cannot lay in my chamber when such trouble is afoot." She's still not sure what to do.

Next thing we know, the magistrate's knocking, anxious to tell us what's what. "The saddler's business has been closed, his house shut up for twenty days," he says. He's a little bird of a man and even more nervous than we are. My lady asks if there are children in the house. He thinks there be seven. He's glancing at his timepiece. Seems this gentleman's not eager to dwell on the plight of the saddler's family. My lady is, though. She asks what they'll be doing for nourishment.

"Food will be taken by the watchmen." The magistrate's restless to be off.

My lady says, "I will tell the kitchens to prepare some baskets and take them down to the village." This gets his attention quick enough.

"I implore you, Mrs Temple. All must stay in the house until the pestilence passes." He takes a step closer to her. "We cannot risk the spread of this amongst our gentry." Soon as he's gone, my lady bids me tell the cook to prepare bread and ale and cheese to take down to the village. "Surely it is unchristian to lock people in their own homes," she says.

The cook's not sympathetic. "Serves them right for trying to hide the truth when all knew it were the plague."

Jack's that stroppy with life indoors. "I want to see the horses." He won't be distracted with toy ones neither.

"Come and look at your sister. I do believe she's smiling."

"I don't like her. Give her back, Jane, and play with me."

Miss Martha's first to suggest we venture out. "It's been over two weeks." She's saying what all are thinking: with no more sign of the pestilence, chances are it were but a single case.

My lady's still cautious. "We'll wait a few days, just to be sure."

Miss Martha's fit to burst. "Methinks we'll soon go mad with all this being cooped up and praying."

We send a maid down to the village to test the air. I almost have to push her out the door, and seems she's back soon as she went. "There be folks walking about, but always in the middle of the lane," she tells us. When I ask if she called at Will's house, the girl admits she didn't go that far. "But I passed the saddler's, on the other side, and 'tis still tight closed." She tells of little ones crying pitifully at the window and their mother shouting at any who passed of their need for more vittles. My lady is moved almost to tears.

Miss Martha points out that like all who came with us from Ireland, this particular maid is in the habit of exaggeration. "Tomorrow, I shall walk in the village and see for myself."

Good job she don't, 'cos we soon gets news bad enough to set us more of a-jitter. It's a groom who brings it, having heard over the wall of the stables. The house next door has been taken with the sickness. Miss Martha's soon singing a different song: "We must go to London, Dorothy. Lord Arlington will know what to do."

My lady doubts London is the safest place. "Would it be best to remain close together in the house?"

"If you shan't come, Dorothy, at least allow me to take the children. I know my brother would want them away from here."

The matter's soon decided for us when the cook comes running to tell of the sickness crept into our very house. Seems the maid we sent to the village was taken badly in the night and is collapsed in the kitchens. I've my doubts the plague would come on so quick, but no one wants to take the chance. One kitchen wench already has her belongings packed, and the cook is preparing to journey to her cousin in Dorking.

My lady tells me to gather up the other servants and inform the stables we shall leave for London. She's determined Rebecca and the boys shall come too. "Send one of the grooms to fetch them, Jane."

The grooms are readying the horses for our departure, and none is anxious to set foot in the village. "I'll not risk my health for a stubborn wench and her brats," says one.

"Well," I say. "Just proves what I've always known, that men are never as brave as their bragging!" And to shame them, I declare I'll go myself.

I'm glad Will's house is at the end of the lane, set back a bit from the others. I'm thinking it might give them a tad of protection. It's a poor enough dwelling, though, and once inside, I'm set wondering it took Rebecca so long to open the door, seeing it's just one big room with a smaller one at the back. I must admit feeling a strangeness being in this house, and since Rebecca don't offer it, I look round for a chair. Except for a pair of low stools, there's only two to be seen, and the boys are occupying both, seated at the table, poring over an open bible. Looks like the only book in the room, even though

I know Will is fond of his reading. It's obvious Rebecca don't give a penny for bits and bobs, since except for Will's carpentry tools, all surfaces are scrubbed clean and bare. I'm wondering if Will misses the bright, pleasing rooms he had before.

Rebecca finally offers me a cup of ale and some meal cake. "I shan't take my boys into that sinful city. We'll stay here and pray the good Lord spares us." I know it's no use arguing with her, but for Will's sake, I try.

"We're all in God's hands, Rebecca. But you must do what's best for these little lads."

Rebecca's not convinced. "This pestilence is punishment for the King's wicked doings, and we must all suffer the consequences."

I've little time to dwell on those incautious words. Once back, I'm busy sorting baccy whilst my lady and Miss Martha set mixing cordial for the maid, and for her friend, up from the village to tend her. A yard boy, too, has opted to stay. It's not hard to fathom his motive. "He's sweet on that kitchen maid," I tell my lady.

All are anxious to leave, and in the blink of an eye we are piling onto the coaches. Inside and out, there's a tangle of arms and legs and bits and bobs. I'm surely glad to be with Miss Martha and my lady. Except for the children and the nurse, we've the luxury of a bit of space. We're just about to set off when my lady remembers that little miniature of her grandmother. "Fetch it for me, please, Jane. I would keep it with me."

Lord knows why she's so attached to this odd image, but I puts it careful inside my cloak and makes to leave. As I pass the kitchens, I hear a laugh. And there's the kitchen maid, brazen as you like, sitting on a bench, swilling ale with the yard boy. I'm tempted to deliver a few choice words, but there's a calling from the coach. I make do by giving the two of them one of my looks.

Seems like we'll have a straight run through to Putney Fields. Not so coming in the other direction. A cluttered mess of coaches and carts and walkers are stretched from here to Christendom, all bent, it seems, on high-tailing it in the other direction. When we stop at a cross lane, my lady leans out the coach as if she would converse with a traveller heading towards Epsom. Then, thinking better of it, she pulls her head back in again. Strikes me none of us is sure where we're heading. Miss Martha would make straight to Whitehall. "We must find Lord Arlington."

But my lady declares we'll stop at Chelsea. "I'm sure my brother will assist us." Considering they haven't set eyes on each other these years, I'd not wager it.

There'll be no reunion this particular day neither. The Chelsea house is closed up, with not a soul to be seen, and likewise all the houses thereabouts. We sit silent, waiting for the other coaches to draw level. I can't take my eyes from the overgrown gardens and shuttered windows. I'm wondering if my lady too is recalling the bustle and brightness that was once her aunt's home.

We make for a tavern where Robin passed many a merry day. "All must be sorely in need of sustenance," my lady says. But the tavern too is shut and bolted. She bids the coachmen rest for a moment, and everyone spills out onto the field. A groom and two maids declare they'll go no further, and set about walking back across the lane to Putney. The coachmen lay on the grass, spent from the journey and the prospect of no ale houses at the end of it.

A woman pokes her head out of an upstairs window of the inn. "You'll find nought but sickness in these parts. Best get back where you come from."

Bold, as always, Miss Martha shouts back that we are making for Whitehall, "where we are known at Court."

The woman cackles. "You'll find few friends in that quarter. The King and his arse-wipers passed by on their way to Oxford a two-week ago."

Once back in the coaches, my lady gives instructions to make for Jermyn Street. "We'll go to my cousin Molle."

Soon as we reach the city, she's doubting her plan. Streets usually a-throng with folk are all but deserted. To hide my disquiet, I catch up little Jack and take him on my knee. He's happy enough to nod off, the sun already being low in the sky. My lady remarks that London is strangely altered. "As if the whole city is weeping." A few preachers on corners shout about sin and the need for repentance, and an old crone hobbles alongside our coach offering to do her magic. Miss Martha bids me shut down the blinds.

There's noise enough once we reach poorer parts. And it's dismal indeed. Terrible shrieks and crying from the houses, and when we roll back the blinds, we see every other one with a red cross on the door and *Lord Have Mercy on Us* writ bold. Folk hanging out of upstairs windows, calling for help. People running through the streets, and near the Haymarket, I see one poor soul, half naked, shouting of a vengeful and angry god. And everywhere a strong smell of burning. My lady bids us keep our shawls over our mouths. On all street corners, you can see rough-looking watchmen, none that I'd be happy to encounter in a dark alley. Jack's crying. The babe's crying. The nurse is pale as parchment. She keeps trying to cover the babe's face, as if to shield it from the horror. None of us can find words for what we witness.

When we reach Jermyn Street, it's clear things are no better. One of the grooms knocks long and hard before rousing a servant from next door, only to be told Sir Henry Molle and family left for Hertfordshire three days ago, along, it seems, with most of the street. The man is not best pleased to be left behind. "Far as I know, they've locked most of the inns and taken the ale with them."

None can think of a plan. All are putting trust in my lady. It's the first time I've seen Miss Martha close to tears. "You must decide, Dorothy. Otherwise, we shall surely perish. Would that my brother were here!" That's when I remember the Dog and Duck, that tavern where the coach dropped me off all them years ago.

In my worst dreams, I never thought my lady would be forced to share a tippling house garret with her servants and three belching coachmen. I'm surprised she don't utter one word of complaint. Miss Martha do, though. "The local magistrates shall hear of our conditions." She's angered we didn't stay the course for Whitehall.

"Surely there's someone left at Court who could have provided better accommodation."

The landlord brings up some bread and cheese and a good quantity of ale. He's surprised we deemed it suitable to come to London. "They're saying over a thousand died last week. The pit at Aldgate alone took more than 400 bodies in one day."

I ask the landlord if he can't provide two beds. But my lady insists she and Miss Martha shall share the floor with the rest of us. Miss Martha don't say nothing. She's likely lost for words at such a rum suggestion. I make sure the ladies are set apart, though, and I bid the coachmen give over their jackets to the mistresses. My lady looks right beaten, and her voice is flat. "Tomorrow, we shall return to Sheen."

I finally manage to curl up next to one of the maids. On my other side, seated on a stool, the nurse gets out a huge titty to suckle the babe; there's no modesty left in her. But all are too tired to care.

I'm lying here mulling on what we've seen this terrible day and thinking how it's worse than anything we knew in the war. I don't usually hold with the poor. If you ask me, their plight is due to lack of gumption, downright idleness. But recalling those dismal shrieks and cries of mourning, I find myself sorely grieving with them, and praying the Lord to remove this torture.

I was never so glad to be home in Sheen. And as I could have predicted, the plague patient is rosy as can be and with no sign of the deadly sickness. "No purple lumps come up, then?" I say. "No coughing or green vomit?" At least the wench has the grace to blush.

When word of our lack of servants gets about, Rebecca finally returns, bringing her boys with her. She's that smug when she hears of our woeful outing. But her smirking is quick wiped when I tell her without the cook, she's the one who'll have to get food to table.

Tired as they be, my lady and Miss Martha set to making big pitchers of cordial from an old Sir Walter Raleigh recipe. "Make sure all take it every day, Jane," my lady says. "With this and the baccy, we should be safe." She's also burning bergamot about the house.

Of a sudden, Miss Martha stops what she's doing and says: "Let's vow to stay together and never leave one another until this scourge is over." And before we know it, we're all three clinging one to another and with enough tears flowing to flood the kitchens.

To: Lord Arlington, Secretary of State
From: William Temple
Brussels, 14th November, 1665

My Lord,

You do me much favour in expressing satisfaction with the outcome of this secret assignment in Brussels, which has taken more months than we both imagined. I fear I was, in the end, unworthy of the trust you put in me, being unsuccessful in persuading others to join His Majesty in his campaign against the Dutch. But if, as you write, His Majesty's plans are altered and he is well pleased with this outcome, I shall count myself fortunate indeed to have served him in this.

The offer of the residency at Brussels is one I have long hoped for, and I thank your lordship with a full heart for the opportunity to prove myself equal to such a high diplomatic posting. I will return to England immediately and prepare my family. As for His Majesty bestowing on me the further honour of a baronetcy, words cannot convey my appreciation and most humble gratitude.

On a personal note, thank you for reassuring me as to the health of my dear wife and sister and their blessedly serene sojourn at home in Sheen whilst the plague raged. The world of women is a tranquil one indeed.

I thank you also, my lord, for news of the birth of my daughter. My wife, I know, was anxious to present me with another son, but for myself, I am relieved and overjoyed to know this child is safe born and healthy.

With grateful thanks for all your lordship's efforts on my behalf, I remain

Your humble servant,

William Temple

BRUSSELS

1666

William is nervous. "May I suggest the claret now, my lord? Or there is some passable brandy if you prefer." Watching as Lord Arlington downs yet another goblet of wine, I sense it is quantity rather than quality that interests his lordship.

William continues to hover. I, too, am not at ease. "You must be in need of nourishment, my lord, after such a long journey. I can't imagine what delays the Countess."

Lord Arlington chuckles. "The Countess of Sunderland has never arrived at the proper hour in her entire life, Lady Temple."

I say, "I've yet to meet this eminent lady." I don't mention that painful long-ago moment at Ham House, watching through an open door as a beautiful widow captured William's attention.

Martha says, "When my brother was a boy, he wrote poetry to the Countess." William points out that every young gallant in England was likewise engaged, but Martha continues to tease him: "How many, I wonder, kept her portrait by their bed? And you should have seen, my lord, how he blushed in her presence!"

Bidding the footman bring him more wine, Lord Arlington says, "You'd best take heed, Lady Temple. It seems you're about to welcome a rival." And he gives a raucous laugh.

"I cannot wait to meet this person all speak of with such

admiration." I know my voice is cold. Even Jane looks at me in surprise. Hastily, I add: "God grant she's found happiness after her long widowhood."

Martha says, "Widowhood is not necessarily such a dismal state, Dorothy."

There are voices in the hall below. As we rise to greet the Countess, I feel instinctively at a disadvantage, my palms damp, my hair sticky against my neck.

She comes straight to me. A tall, smiling woman, handsome rather than beautiful and a deal older than I'd imagined. "Ah, the beauty who stole young William's heart!" I had not expected such directness. I stumble out some words of greeting.

William is more fulsome. "My dear friend, what a pleasure!"

Lord Arlington, too, seems well acquainted with our guest. Bowing over her hand, he asks, "So, how are we to address you this evening? Is it to be 'Lady Sunderland'? Or do you prefer plain 'Mrs Smythe'?"

"Come now, you shall call me 'Doll', as you always have. And I shall address you as 'my lord', for I know it pleases you." She apologises for her lateness. "We could not help but stop and marvel at the pristine streets. No need to clutch at nosegays in this city!" She's travelling with her daughter-in-law, a pale, sad-looking young woman. Mr Smythe, we are told, is at his house in Suffolk. "My husband doesn't take kindly to foreign travel." Lord Arlington remarks it is rare to see two women touring the continent alone. "For heaven's sake, my lord!" The Countess is scornful. "Women are changing. Haven't you noticed? Besides, we have a whole army of servants watching our every move. Sadly, Anne and I are seldom alone."

William leads the two ladies in to supper. "Now you are *Sir* William," the Countess says, "Anne and I will need mind our manners. We've grown rough eating from street sellers this entire journey."

I'm relieved when William places Martha next to Lord Arlington. She will no doubt charm him, and in a manner I would find impossible. His lordship, too, seems well satisfied. Leaning towards her, he says: "So, tell me, my dear, how you are enjoying Brussels."

Martha replies she finds it pleasant enough. "If only all were not constantly worried by the French. Do you suppose, my lord, they are truly set to capture this city?"

"Word has reached us that *you*, Lady Giffard, have already done that. Temple, this sister of yours is said to melt the hearts of all who meet her." Martha blushes. I see Jane too looks flustered; no doubt disquieted by such empty, honeyed words.

The Countess turns the conversation to tapestry. "All say Brussels has a rich repository."

I mention the Spanish ambassador's fine collection. "We viewed it this very week."

And in that intimate way she sometimes adopts, Martha adds: "But there was one work I found distasteful." She describes the offending scene: King David casting a lustful eye on beautiful Bathsheba, reaching out to her, anxious to lead her to his private chambers. "I was surprised the ambassador felt it fit to display, and that you, Dorothy, lingered so before it."

"It wasn't the subject that held me, Martha." I search for the right words. "It was the execution. I thought such rich colour and texture might only be found in a painting. You agreed with me, didn't you, Jane?"

Loyal as ever, Jane says: "I never did see colours mingled so pleasingly. It's a miracle what folks can do when they set their minds to it."

But Martha won't let go. "Surely you cannot approve of such a work, Dorothy? When we were children, I was forbidden to read those particular bible passages."

I say the story has a just moral. "David and Bathsheba incurred God's anger and spent the rest of their lives repenting and atoning."

Lord Arlington finds this amusing. "Then you think adultery forgivable, so long as one repents?" I wonder if this warrants a reply. "Ah, but God did not forgive them, Lady Temple." And Lord

Arlington leans across the table towards me. "Would you expect your husband to pardon *you* if he found you in adultery? Wouldn't you say he would be justified in banishing you forever from his sight?"

With some heat, I say: "Of course I cannot imagine any such situation, my lord. But I do know many husbands would feel it their duty to banish wives for such sinful behaviour, even though they themselves might well be guilty of the same impropriety, and without censor."

In the silence that follows, I fear I have spoken too hastily. But it seems Lord Arlington enjoys my unmeasured words. "You are that rare creature, Lady Temple, a woman who knows her own mind. What say you, Temple?" Looking across, I see William has reddened.

It's the Countess who rescues the moment. "We should dearly love to see this wonderful work. Do you think the Spanish ambassador might be prevailed upon?"

I say, and firmly, "The tapestry is exquisite. Your ladyship will find it a feast for the eyes."

Martha remarks it was the grandeur of the ambassador's residence that drew her own eyes. "It's thrice the size of ours, William. How can that be?"

"Well, for one thing, I am not Spanish, and therefore not in such an exalted position in this city. Neither am I an ambassador." And William glances at Lord Arlington. "I'm of a humbler hue, Martha."

Martha is not convinced: "Surely England's Representative is worthy of a grander setting?"

A voice I know to be mine says, "The difference, I think, Martha, is not one of title, but of monies earned. It's likely the Spanish coffers enable their envoys to be well-set, whereas the English are ever in arrears." I know this turn of conversation will discomfort William, but I cannot stop. "A diplomat must often reach into his own purse to maintain his household and entertain in the manner expected of him." Is it the wine that makes me speak so freely?

Again, the Countess comes to my aid. "It's well known we pay our diplomats poorly and rarely. My lord, can't you prevail on His Majesty, who all say is guided by your excellent counsel?"

It's Lord Arlington's turn to look discomforted. But he's obviously adept at turning difficult conversation into banter. "Alas, when it comes to monies, the King keeps his own tight hand on the purse strings. Try as I might, I've not been able to loosen it. Were it not so, I should be a rich man instead of poor as a churchmouse!"

"Not quite, my lord," the Countess remarks. "They say your London house is only slightly less grand than the palace at Whitehall."

"You must know, my dear, Doll, my house and the palace barely escaped destruction from the Fire." There is more than a hint of testiness in his lordship's voice. "The cost of rebuilding London makes it a poor time indeed for diplomats to be complaining of lack of funds."

Talk of the Fire enables the conversation to move on. Lord Arlington describes the terrifying destruction of St Paul's: "Boiling lead, pouring from the roof and running through the streets. I hope never to see the like again." He recounts witnessing scores of citizens jumping in the river to avoid the flames. "The King stood steadfast, though. We asked him many times to leave for Oxford, but he insisted on staying amongst his people, even during the Fire's worst excesses."

The Countess remarks there are those who believe the Fire to be God's punishment for the King's own excesses. And before this can be taken further, William applauds Lord Arlington's courage during those terrible days. "News reached us even here, my lord, that you yourself also stood steadfast."

I glance across at Jane. I'm wondering if she too is thinking on London's suffering in the midst of the plague, when both his lordship and the King fled to safer climes.

The Countess declares the whole of England aware of Lord Arlington's bravery in times of crisis. "One only has to look at your face."

His lordship fingers the small black patch on the bridge of

his nose. "Oh, this. This is nothing." And with obvious relish, he launches forth on his encounter with the severe edge of a sword whilst fighting the late king's cause at Andover.

"I do wonder," says the Countess, "if it might be prudent to expose that wound to the air so's it might finally heal. Unless, of course, you wish us all to be ever minded of your suffering." For the first time this evening, Lord Arlington appears at a loss for words.

As William and his lordship retire to the library, I lead the Countess and her daughter-in-law to the nursery. The children are still awake, Jack astride his little wooden horse, Diana quiet in her cradle. The nurse says, "It's that hot this evening, your ladyship, I've let little Nan lie cool without her blanket."

Suddenly animated, the Countess's daughter-in-law bends over the cot making cooing sounds to the baby. Turning to Jack, she ruffles his hair. "A brave knight riding to battle." It's the first time she's spoken this entire evening.

The Countess and I remove to the anteroom. "Anne misses her children," she tells me. "She was loath to come on this journey, but there's some trouble with my son and I felt she should get away. Men can be the very devil, can't they?"

We sit together, quiet and easy in each other's company. This is not the woman I long ago conjured in my mind. Based on little more than a glance, I'd determined the Countess of Sunderland to be haughty and cold. Nothing could be further from the truth.

"William is a good man," she says, "but he's impetuous, always has been, and apt to believe everyone as honest as himself. I see he's extremely admiring of Arlington."

"Lord Arlington has been a great support. We owe him our good fortune to be here."

The Countess laughs. "Lord Arlington has one aim in life, my dear, and that is to improve his own good fortune. You would both be wise to remember that."

When the women have gone, I return to the nursery. Diana is asleep and Jack put to bed. He reaches up and touches my hair. "You are beautiful, Mama." I take his little hand and hold it against my cheek. Once again, I thank God for the bountiful gift of these children; the joy of watching them grow stronger each day. Despite myself, I am beginning to trust in their future. My head tells me I should remain cautious, but the blood sings a different song.

Downstairs in the hallway, Will Hammer, vigilant as always, waits quietly on his master's needs. "Are Sir William and his lordship still in the library?" I ask.

"They've just called for more brandy, my lady."

This then, is likely to be a long evening. "Is all well at home, Will?"

"I believe so, your ladyship. Though news takes its time to reach across the water, and Rebecca's not much of a one for letter writing."

"Would she had agreed to come with us. It must be hard for you to be separated from your boys."

"I'm truly grateful for your concern, Lady Dorothy, but if you'll pardon my saying so, with such a goodly master, I count myself lucky indeed to be here."

When William and Lord Arlington finally emerge from the library, Martha and I are waiting in the hall. As a footman helps him into his cloak, Lord Arlington expresses regret at missing the departure of the Countess. "Her marriage continues to cause a stir, as you no doubt know." And fuelled by wine and brandy, he leans unsteadily towards us. "All say she married this person of no account out of pity, which is a pitiable thing indeed!" Amused by his own words, Lord Arlington roars with laughter.

As Martha and I retire to our chambers, she says, "Lord Arlington is truly the most engaging man. I'm mortified the Countess behaved so prickly towards him."

I say the Countess is a woman who speaks her mind. "Isn't that a good thing?"

"In my opinion, it's never a good thing for a woman to speak her mind." Martha is adamant. "There are other ways to turn a conversation to our advantage."

It's almost midnight when William comes to my chamber. He slumps into a chair. "I put it to his lordship that the Dutch, not the French, are our natural allies and we would do well to forge an alliance. He agrees but fears the King's allegiance will always lay with France."

"Couldn't you write directly to His Majesty," I say, "and set out your reasoning?"

William is scornful. "Such a move would reek of disloyalty towards Lord Arlington."

"Do you trust him to pass on your advice to the King?"

"I would trust him with my very life, Dorothy. I know him to be a man of the highest integrity." There is irritation in his voice. "It was obvious you do not share my good opinion."

"Dearest, I must apologise if I misspoke. I've yet to learn the subtle language of diplomacy, which his lordship employs so well."

"There is merit in speaking straight, Dorothy. There are enough false words bandied in the name of diplomacy." William yawns and closes his eyes. "I would only urge you to think more on when it is best to keep silent."

As I sit opposite and watch him drift into sleep, I study William's face. Little has changed over the years. A few more lines around the eyes, but the strong, determined chin remains intact, the well-defined cheekbones, the eyebrows that I traced with my fingers on our wedding night. I should like to reach out and touch them. But with pain in my heart, I realise the shared intimacy that allowed me so easily to caress my husband's face seems to have slipped away, without, perhaps, either of us noticing. "Dear heart," I say, "come to bed. You are exhausted."

"I'm not asleep. Merely thinking." Wearily, William gets up and walks to the window. "There's one more thing: Lord Arlington believes the French will probably attack sometime during the next few months. He suggests you return to England with the children." I'm too stunned to reply. "I think he is right, Dorothy. I'd be loath to put my family in danger."

The children. I try to arrange my thoughts: They must go, and quickly. "Martha and Jane shall take them. I'll stay here and look to your needs."

"No, Dorothy. Lord Arlington thinks you should return with our children."

"But who will manage your household?"

"Martha shall stay with me."

"Is that also Lord Arlington's suggestion?"

"You need to sleep, Dorothy. We are both tired. We'll talk more of this tomorrow."

I go to him and take his hand. "Come to bed with me, William, please."

"I'll leave you in peace, my love. So you may get some rest." And he is gone.

So, I'm to be banished. Why is it I can't stay silent when a conversation fails to go my way? Martha is right. By now, I should have learnt that women rarely win an argument with confrontation. All those youthful clashes with my brother Henry surely taught me that. However unpleasant I find Lord Arlington, I should have smiled and kept my counsel.

Lying in this huge bed, I long to feel the warmth of William's body next to me. His arms about me, shielding me from these choppy waters that I'm so inept at navigating. I think again on the tapestry: David and Bathsheba, willing to risk everything, even the wrath of God, to lay in each other's arms for even one night. I lean across the bed and pull the pillows close to me.

Sitting with our needlepoint, Martha says: "I shall miss you, Dorothy, and more than I can say." I am surprised and touched by the feeling in her voice. Moments of intimacy are rare between us.

"And I you, dear sister. But I'm relieved to know William will be well cared for."

"My brother and I are always content in each other's company." She puts away her work. "Although William does sometimes say the oddest things. The other day, I heard him tell Will Hammer he believes no woman should make love past forty! It's as well the Countess did not hear!"

When she's gone, I continue to work on my sampler. In less than a year, *I* shall be forty.

The door to Martha's chamber is ajar. I call her name before entering. I'm inside before I remember she is gone to town on an errand. The room is pristine, the china plates and small figurines Martha so favours all pleasingly arranged. The drawing, said to be by Mr Holbein, and acquired by William this very week, already hung by the bed. On the table, Martha's books, piled neatly. Next to the books, two letters spread open and placed carefully side by side. One written in Spanish; the other, I think, a translation of that same letter into English. It's addressed to Martha.

I've always tried to avoid deceit. But I must admit to a low interest in other people's correspondence. The letter is from Gabriel Portella, a Spanish archer late in William's employ, now retired to his family home in Antwerp. It is signed: *'Your most humble servant and lover'*. Words I find hard to connect with the dour old man who tutored Martha and I in his native language. He's thanking Martha for the gift of a sword hilt:

> *So, Madame, I thank you deeply for this gift, which has melted me near to tears, though thankfully not in your lady's presence. Am I to believe you a saint or an enchantress? You have made a deeper wound in my heart than any cavalier could have done. Since I touched this enchanted hilt, I feel the blood in my veins grow warm and love, so long banished, returning in triumph to kindle a violent flame. Oh Lady of My Soul, how you have undone me. But a little hope will relieve these sufferings. Just a word, dear lady, a gesture…*

The translation, in Martha's own script, is precise and neat. The original is scrawled across the page in a hand I know so well. It's written by William.

I read the letter again, trying to understand. A jest, no doubt – part of the easy playfulness that exists between William and his sister. The sort of jesting he so enjoys. But is it a jest? Perhaps it's indeed from Portella. Soldiers are seldom scholars, and the old man is surely not capable of penning such a warm epistle. No doubt he begged William, always amenable, to write it for him. A kind act on William's part, towards a faithful old archer who has become besotted with his sister. Yes.

Though it is addressed from Antwerp. So perhaps it is, after all, a jest.

I put the letter back on the desk, exactly as I found it, neatly aside the original. What made me look? Base curiosity. I hurry from the room, overcome with shame.

"Talk to me, William. Sit with me."

"Dearest, I've yet to send these dispatches. Time is pressing."

"Why is it we never talk?"

"Dearest, we talk all the time."

I watch as he signs the documents with his usual flourish of the quill. Bold, heavy letters across the page. I say: "What has become of Senor Portella?"

William remains engrossed in his work. He does not look up. "I imagine he is enjoying his well-earned retirement," he says.

"Are you still in contact with him?"

He looks up then. "No," he says. He finishes packing the dispatches. He's impatient, anxious to end the conversation. But I cannot let the moment go.

"Why must I return alone to England with the children, William? Why don't we send Martha?" Even to my own ears, my voice sounds petulant, childish.

"We've discussed the reasons. It's Lord Arlington's decision – and mine." He's already at the door. "I have sent for the passports. Let's have an end to this constant questioning."

The passports have still to arrive, despite William's best efforts. Every day we are delayed increases my anxiety for our children – until Lord Arlington writes that the King's own yacht shall be sent to bear us home. Once again, we shall be in his lordship's debt.

Jane and Will Hammer stand either side of me on the deck of this grand boat as the coast begins slowly to fade. I'm thankful to have Will with us. His size alone gives a deal of reassurance. No doubt noticing how my hands grip the rail, he seeks to distract me from the swirling ocean. "Look, my lady, you can still see them." Two tiny figures: William and Martha, standing close together on the shore, until the morning mist swallows them and they disappear.

SHEEN

First thing I see when we turns into the carriageway is Rebecca standing with the cook. Never thought I'd be pleased to see those gloomy faces. Will's boys grown tall, running towards us. They've spotted their father up on post. Rebecca pulls them back. Nothing much changed there. Soon as the horses halt, Will's jumping down and scooping up his boys. Then he hugs Rebecca. No thought for my lady, waiting to be helped from the carriage. Not like Will to forget his manners.

I put my nose to the air and smell the honeysuckle. "I'm surprised you've got time for a walk, Will." We stop and look at the new orchard. Except for a couple of thin shrubs, there's nothing much to admire. "If Sir William wants this worked on afore you return to Brussels, I'm thinking you'd better get on with it."

Will's not fussed. "There's time enough. I wouldn't miss a chance for our walking. Reckon you and me's covered a good few leagues what with here and foreign parts."

"I'm partial to a walk," I say. "Even if it do mean having to listen to your fool prattle."

"Shall you be missing Brussels, Jane?"

I tell him I shan't miss that fast foreign tongue. "It fairly undid me. I'm thinking Brussels would be much improved if they all spoke in English."

Will gives that irritating laugh he's lately developed. "What *I* think, Jane Wright, is that you never change. Though if you must know, I'm right glad of it."

And I'm right glad to be home. I can't vouch the same for my lady. Twice I've woke in the night to hear her pacing. I've noted the darkness 'neath her eyes, too. A letter came from Sir William this morning. She's been waiting on it all week. "They are planning a journey to Holland," she tells me. "Sir William and Lady Martha."

Sounds rum to me. "Wonder if that's wise, my lady? Seeing as the Dutch don't like us."

"Sir William would never put his sister in danger." Her tone is sharp. "He will, of course, have made sure all is secure for the visit."

I'm quick to apologise for my doubting.

Seems we've been settled longer than three weeks. Seems almost like we never left. Still, we could do with a few more willing hands. My lady says, "Rebecca is doing the work of two." I'm bound to agree, and with no complaining neither. "Please enquire if all is well with her, Jane."

Rebecca's that closed she'd probably think I was prying. I decide to ask the cook, who's not sympathetic. "Rebecca's young enough to cope with a few extra tasks. Only one needs a hand in these kitchens is me." And she heaves her great bulk into the chair by the hearth. "I've my rheumatics, which flare something cruel from all this bending and reaching."

I say, "It's just that Lady Dorothy mentioned how Rebecca's always that thin and pale."

"She's strong as a horse, that one. If she be pale, it's for lack of sleep, down to all them late-night meetings. Tell her ladyship that."

"What of these meetings, then?" My curiosity is well wetted.

"Dissenters, they calls themselves. Troublemakers if you ask me." And I remember Sir William talking of persons worshipping without a parson.

"Have they knocked here?"

"Lord knows how many times they've been in and out this house since you were gone." She spits into the hearth. "Nasty creatures. Thin as beanstalks, every last one of them."

I'm mulling this over when I'm back with my lady. "Seems Rebecca's fine with the workload," I tell her. "Seems she's a regular glutton when it comes to hard work." And since the day is drawn in, I busy myself lighting the candles.

"What's these Dissenters then, Will?" He's quiet for a moment as he coaxes a vine away from the wall.

"There's a lot of them in these parts, Jane." He bids me hold the string so's he can tie the plants. "Them garden lads don't know a thing about fruits. These vines needs more sun if they're to do their duty."

"Who are they, these people? What's their business?"

"To praise the Lord, Jane, but with more humility than most. Round here they call them Quakers, 'cos it's said they truly tremble before the Lord. Reckon they be good people."

"I've heard Rebecca goes to their meetings."

"Aren't nothing wrong in that. She's just listening to their words."

"Well, I hope them words don't go insulting the gentry, like that old gnarly preacher back in Ireland." Will don't answer. Seems he's properly distracted with his vines.

Time was, Lady Dorothy would have been passing hours in the gardens with Will, giving orders to those idle lads. Now, she can scarce be coaxed from her chamber. I've twice seen the empty wine goblet next to her bed, with the piece of steel, plain as you like and all browned. I've had to bite my tongue. I've noted, too, she's taken to wearing gloves since that unsightly rash appeared on her hands.

"Begging your pardon, my lady, but I'm thinking you're not

yourself. I've not seen you eating right since our return." In truth, I'm thinking it's more than vittles has taken her spirit. "Are you quite sure you're well, my lady? I'd be happy to get the medic up from the village."

"Perhaps we'll journey to Epsom," she says. "The waters may yield some benefits."

I'm pleased to know of this diversion; they do say Epsom is best place for a scurvy spleen. Young Jack's not happy, though. *"Moi aussi,* Mama. *Ne me laisse pas seul ici!"* He's grown ever more clinging since our return. And it's hard to get him to say a word in English, though in Brussels he'd speak nothing else. Jack do have his stubborn streak.

I'm already abed when there's a knocking, so quiet it's a wonder I've heard.

"What are you doing here, Will?" And I'm thinking good thing I've flung a shawl over my night robe.

Will says: "Can I come inside, Jane?"

"It's not proper. Not at this hour."

"It's important, else I'd not have come."

I tell him best we get down to the kitchens, and quietly too. "I hope this is something I should be knowing, and not a matter don't concern me." I take my candle and Will follows with his.

He walks about the kitchen, moving in and out of my candlelight, jumpy as a bullfrog. "Thing is, Jane, looks like we're set on leaving England, me and Rebecca and our boys." I'm wondering if this means she's finally agreeing to Brussels. Will soon puts me straight. "The New World, Jane. Rebecca's put her mind to it. Her brother's already well settled there."

It takes a moment to understand what he's saying. "Is this them Dissenters or whatever they call themselves?"

"I wanted to tell you first, even before the master."

"But why, Will? They do say the sea churns something terrible on that voyage. And what of Sir William? What will he do if you goes off like that?" My thoughts are all over the place.

"A gentleman can always find a willing servant," Will says. "I've a mind my prospects might be better over there."

My candle's none too steady. I put it down on the table. "It's a dangerous place. All say that. Some are even returning, kissing the ground when they're safe back."

"The thing is, well, I'll surely be sorry to bid everyone goodbye." And Will looks down at the floor, as if he might find some words there. "'Specially you, Jane."

"You and me are like brother and sister, Will, and always shall be."

"No, Jane, I am not your brother. Neither do I have a brother's feelings towards you, as you very well know."

There's still a few embers in the hearth. I give them a good poke. We'll likely be catching a chill, standing about like this. "Rebecca's a good girl." Will's voice is shaky. "She's straight as they come, and a wonderful mother. It's just..." He fiddles with the button of his waistkit, undoes it, fastens it again. "Well, if you was to come too, I'm thinking..."

"Reckon thinking's not what you're doing, Will Hammer. Wonder what your wife would say to such a thing."

"I've enough saved for us all to set sail, Jane. And you'd be all right. I mean, I'd always keep an eye open for you."

"My place is here, Will – with Lady Dorothy. I've been by her since I was a girl, and I hope to stay until they finally close my eyes." I pull my shawl close round me. These candles aren't good for much longer. "I hope you'll think more on this fool idea."

We stand quiet, with both candles running low, till I finds my tongue. "If you're determined to see this New World, as you call it, well, you'd best get off back to Brussels and tell Sir William." And we're just stood there, staring at each other, neither of us saying a word. "But I wish you happiness anyways, Will," I finally say. "I'll always wish the best for you."

I'm never one for coach outings, and this one's been that bumpy. It's my knees suffer most. When we get to the inn at Epsom, my lady says: "Lay abed awhile, Jane. Later, we'll walk in the town." Truth is, I've been feeling out of sorts since this morning, when we saw Will back off to Brussels. And I don't feel much improved when we're out and about. My lady's none too chirpy neither. "Tomorrow, I'll take the waters early, Jane, and perhaps you should too."

We stop at a baker and buy two sweet buns to cheer ourselves. The baker woman is full of gossip. "The King just left Epsom. You missed him by a whisker." She leans over and keeps her voice low. "There was more than one woman in his party, and none you'd want to keep company with." The woman sniffs. "He set two of them up over the coffee house and not a mile from his own dwelling." My lady, never one for low prattle, makes to leave. But this baker woman must have one more word. "Them weren't even pretty. I pity the poor queen. Still, shows he's a real man, don't it?" And she throws back her head and laughs, showing off a mouthful of rotting teeth.

We sup at the inn. And to revive ourselves, both me and Lady Dorothy partake more than our usual portion of wine, though I'm careful to sip mine slowly, as my father taught me. All the same, the ruby liquid does loosen my tongue. "Do you think it true, my lady – all they say about the King and his ways?" She toys with her duck leg, pushing it to the edge of her plate.

"I think, Jane, that I've little understanding of the things men do. They seem prone to make odd choices that they think will make them happy."

Glancing across the room, I see the grooms, not looking out for us as they should, but indulged in their own revelry with a girl from the inn. "Well, my lady," I say, "in truth, I'm never surprised what silly creatures men oft are." We both laugh, but when she reaches across and takes my hand, I'm set back by the warmth of hers. I note, too, her brow is heated. I'm praying it's the wine and not the onset of one of her attacks. This talk of His Majesty likely upset her. I'm thinking best change the subject. "Sir William will be right sorry to lose the likes of Will Hammer."

My lady is thoughtful for a moment. "But is it not admirable, setting out on a new adventure, willing to risk everything?"

"Some might fancy it foolhardy, my lady, 'specially leaving such a goodly posting."

"When we finally bid Will farewell," she says, "I thought how wonderful it must be to start one's life anew."

"Well, not a final farewell. He'll be back from Brussels afore they sets sail."

"No, Jane. Rebecca and the boys are to meet him in Yarmouth. They'll sail from there. Will won't come back."

For a strange moment, I feel as if I'm somewhere else. Looking down, at myself from a great height. My lady is speaking, something about the morrow, but my mind's not following. Then I see she's looking at me, expecting an answer. "I'm right sorry, Lady Dorothy. I didn't hear what you said." Despite a roaring fire in the grate, I'm cold of a sudden. I take up the goblet and gulp down the rest of my wine. Will, gone. Gone for good and all. Not coming back. Never. And I scarce bade him farewell. I search in the pocket of my gown, chiding myself for forgetting my kerchief.

"Are you all right, Jane?"

"Right as rain, thank you, my lady."

From: Lady Dorothy Temple,
Temple Court, Sheen

Dearest. I write in haste that this may reach you before you leave for Holland. I beg you take good care, especially since you say you will be travelling in disguise! The Dutch are not our friends and I fear what may befall you and Martha if you are discovered. I write in some trepidation, as we parted so coolly. Since returning home, I have searched my mind for all that might have been said different. I fear, as you have mentioned, I often speak without thought. I shall try to remedy that. I only ask we go forward as one, and in complete openness. I've come to the mind that marriage is a journey, and if it is to continue to flourish, it needs constant care.

I've received a letter from Lord Arlington, inviting me to attend Court in honour of His Majesty's birthday celebrations. I know you would urge me to overcome my reticence to that place, and shall therefore accept and be merry so's my presence shall in no way mar your reputation!

Dearest, I pray matters in Brussels shall soon be settled and I might be back at your side. Until then, I hold our children close.

Yours in love and affection,

D. T.

Something has changed since I was last at Court. The Great Hall, with its magnificent ceiling and paintings, though still majestic, seems somewhat shabbier. The carpets and curtains, once so exotic, are faded and stained. Perhaps rumours of the King's lack of finance are true. But there is something else, something indefinable. Next to me, Lord Arlington says: "You look anxious, Lady Temple. Does the sight of so many of the King's concubines discomfort you?"

"After our sojourn in Brussels, my lord, I'd forgot the splendours of the English Court. I feel as one fresh from the country." I'm pleased to be able to match him at this game of words.

"Yes, Brussels does tend to be a city of plodders. It lacks sophistication."

"Simplicity has its charms, my lord."

Lord Arlington laughs. "Tell that to the King's mistresses. You see Lady Castlemaine? She is wearing more jewels than may be found in the royal vaults, and still she's not satisfied!" He gestures towards a tall, beautiful woman standing by the King's chair at the gaming table. Her pale green gown is of the finest silks, jewels glisten at her ears and throat, and her expression is one of extreme petulance. Lord Arlington leans towards me. "After years allowing her to dip into the royal coffers at whim, His Majesty tires of her. The King's eye wanders to a little Parisian whore newly arrived from the French Court."

"I think you speak too frankly, my lord."

"Only to you, Lady Temple. As I recall, you prefer honest talk." This room is stifling. I try to move away, to put some space between myself and this man, but Lord Arlington remains uncomfortably close. "We should take our seats for the Masque, and then I shall present you to His Majesty." Guiding me across the room, he whispers, "One cannot blame the poor King. He has many a bastard child, but no legitimate heir from his barren little Portuguese wife."

The lute and guitar players have taken their places on the balcony. We are seated a few feet from the King, and at an angle that allows me to study his profile. It's of a once handsome man, now much worn, with jowly jaw and fleshy mouth. When he turns to talk to the young woman next to him, I see the lines criss-crossing his cheeks and forehead.

With much flourish, an Indian fire-eater is trumpeted in. Two young men follow, bearing an intricately designed chair. Once the man is seated, the assistants set about arranging coals on a hot brazier, a procedure too slow for some in the audience. Despite the presence of the King, there are jeers and shouts of impatience. But when the man proceeds to dine on various red-hot materials, including, it seems, brimstone, all are quiet. I hold my breath. I can barely watch. After a while, an assistant brings a tankard of what looks like boiling oil, which the man drinks with apparent relish. When he begins to munch on a glowing ember, the King calls for an oyster to be brought and placed on the burning coal in the man's mouth – where it sizzles. "Best you digest quickly," the King shouts. "I would roast an ox on you next!" There is laughter, cheers.

But nothing is as it seems. As the maestro rises and steps

forward to bow to the King, I note the sweat running down his face and arms, washing away particles of body paint. It is plain our exotic fire-eater is, in fact, a pale and puny Englishman.

The Masque itself is a long, complicated dance performed by various courtiers and three small girls, richly robed and covered in jewels. One of them, Lord Arlington tells me, is Princess Mary, the King's niece, daughter of his brother James. She is obviously the youngest of the three – yet appears to have a woman's wiles about her. She moves her body with grace and assurance, performing entirely for the King's pleasure, reaching out towards him as she dances and curtsying prettily whenever there is a break in the music. Is this truly a suitable pastime for a child?

Beside me, Lord Arlington says: "Many a young buck will be weighing his chances there."

"Lord Arlington tells me you have been in England for some time, Lady Temple. Why have we not seen you at Court?"

I note with surprise the King's brown eyes are clear and alert, and slightly mocking. They fit oddly into his sagging face, as if they had been placed there by mistake. "I've been dealing with matters at Sheen, Your Majesty."

"Ah yes. Sir William's beloved little house. If you are to stay longer, why not join us for the hunt?"

I thank him profusely. "But alas, I must look to the needs of my family."

The King has heard that William is visiting Holland. "It will please me greatly if he meets with my nephew there," he says. "I shall bid him inform that young man it would be our pleasure to welcome him in London."

I've met the Prince of Orange twice on his visits to Brussels. A shy, awkward young Dutchman, with unfashionable clothes and thick accent. I wonder how he would fare at this worldly English court. The king is already looking beyond me, preparing to move away, his attention caught elsewhere. "You must take great care of your husband, Lady Temple. His work is of vital importance to us."

Lord Arlington says: "We needs have no worry on that account, Your Majesty. Sir William has a devoted sister who panders to his every need. That is, of course, when Lady Temple is elsewhere."

The King laughs. "Dammit, Arlington, how is it that some men have the fortune of two good women, whilst others can't find one of any worth?"

As Lord Arlington hands me into the coach, I thank him for arranging the visit. "It was a truly memorable evening."

He leans towards me, his hand lingering on mine. "Your husband is a fool, Lady Temple, to allow such a handsome woman to travel alone."

From: Sir William Temple, Brussels
To: Sir John Temple, Master of the Rolls, Dublin

A thousand apologies for my delay in responding to your letter, which arrived after Martha and I set forth for Holland. I'm sorry indeed to learn of your disquiet regarding this journey, and can happily assure you all passed without incident since we travelled incognito throughout. With her usual spirit, Martha was enchanted with everything, especially our visits to the Dutch East India Company houses, where my sister marvelled at the exotic fabrics and artefacts. Suffice to say my purse was sorely tried in satisfying her desire for all she saw!

My own pleasure was to pass unrecognised amongst the ale houses and hear the freedom and liberty with which men speak so openly upon public affairs. And the frugality of the Dutch is something to be pondered. No man, it seems, would dream of spending more than he has coming in, and usury is, albeit, unheard of! A way of life our own country might do well to follow.

In both The Hague and Amsterdam, we were fortunate to meet with city leaders, men of principle and sincerity with whom we could speak frankly, and with whom I deemed it prudent to reveal our true identities. Most were of my opinion that a treaty between the English and the Dutch would serve both countries well. My passage to these gentlemen's confidence was aided greatly by Martha, who, as always, charmed everyone.

I've kept my most momentous news till last. My good Lord Arlington, to whom I owe much, writes that my residency here in Brussels is at an end, and that His Majesty, due in some part to my dispatches, is finally in favour of pursuing a peace treaty between England and Holland. Lord Arlington further informs me that in light of this, the King wishes me to carry things forward, and I am to be offered the ambassadorship at The Hague!

So you see, Father, our little adventure yielded more than exotic silks. And without my sister's support, I doubt I should have met with such success.

I shall write to my wife tonight and return home to Sheen in a month to prepare those dear pledges waiting there, who will surely be as joyous as I that we are finally to be reunited.

Your obedient and most affectionate son,

W.T.

It surely is good to have Sir William home again. Reckon he can still lighten a day when his spirit's up. And he's more than a tad pleased with himself right now. Which is only fitting since everyone's abuzz with this treaty of his. "My signature will be there soon after we arrive in The Hague," he tells us. "We may never again see Dutch boats invade our great river."

"God willing," my lady adds. She's justly proud. "All done in secret, Jane, and completed within five days!" I'm not for understanding the whys and wherefores, but if it means we're friends with the Dutch, I'm thinking that's good, seeing we'll soon be fetching up there. And I'm pleased to note my lady's spirits so revived and that glow to her we've not seen this many a moon.

I smile to myself when I pass the kitchens and hear the cook humming away. "Those in Brussels could learn from you," Sir William told her this morning. "None there knows how to prepare a breakfast fit for a man." She's happy enough with that, and there's not one word of complaint at having to step up for such a mass of Easter dishes. Whilst she's setting the picnic on the riverbank, me and my lady hide the eggs around the gardens.

We've not seen Sir Henry Molle and his wife this year or two, and as they come from the riverboat, I'm quick to note they're both of greater expanse than ever. So much so that Lady Molle can scarce get herself into a chair. It takes two wenches several minutes to set her comfortable. Sir Henry's four sons are corpulent too, but a deal more agile. They take to the egg hunt with such gusto, I'm feared our own mites shan't get a find – though Nan do go toddling after them, ready for the challenge. Not so Jack. He sits that close to his father, you couldn't drop a farthing between them. Unsure of himself as always, there's no persuading him to take part. "I shan't find anything," he says.

"Come on," I say. And I take Jack's hand. "We'll look together."

Seeing how I helped paint and hide these eggs, it's not long afore he's found his prize. He takes it straight to Lady Dorothy. "For you, Mama." Then he's back and sitting close as he can to Sir William.

No chance of Sir Henry Molle's lusty lads minding their manners and sitting quiet. No. They grab some duck from a platter and run with it. Like father, like sons, I'm thinking as I watch Sir Henry cram pork pie in his mouth. My lady's cousin is not my favourite person by a long shot, and it's my luck to be seated right by him. Supposing he might still have his frisky ways, I'm on my guard lest a hand or foot wanders in my direction. Though if truth be told, I can scarce recall the last time I had need to defend myself from mischievous hands.

The magistrate arrives late and, seated next to Lady Dorothy, picks carefully through the leftovers. "I must congratulate you, Sir William, on your splendid success. With both Holland and Sweden now our allies, we may finally be free of French influence." He's still looking at his timepiece every few minutes, like he's got some peculiar tic.

Sir Henry Molle's not for dwelling on treaties. He's wondering about Miss Martha. "Where the devil have you hidden that pretty little sister of yours, Temple?" And as Sir William explains it, she went straight from Brussels to Dublin.

"After such a long absence, my father was anxious for her company," he says. And Sir Henry declares any father would worry for the well-being of such a comely daughter.

He seems about to say more when, glaring at him, Lady Molle cuts right through: "This 'Triple Alliance', as all are terming your treaty, Sir William, will it mean more honours for the entire family?"

Sir William declares he has little interest in honours. "We live in an age when nothing is given without pandering, and I shall never bring myself to that."

Lady Dorothy says, "An earldom might mean more money for your purse." From where he's seated on the grass, Sir William reaches across and taking her hand, plants a kiss on it, right before everyone.

"What more shall I want if I have my dear wife and my little corner of Sheen?" Since he's been home, they are as two lovebirds.

The magistrate says, "Well, at least there's an embassy awaiting you."

And as a wench serves the hot cross buns, Sir William launches into talk of Holland and its citizens, saying 'tis well his wife be prepared for some peculiarities. "I never saw a country with such a curious obsession with cleanliness." He tells of supping at the home of some Dutch gentleman. "I had the very deuce of a cold, and you can imagine my surprise when every time I spat on the floor, a wench with a cloth was down to wipe it up!" He swears it were her sole task. "My host informed me had his wife been home, she would have turned me out for fouling her house!" This tale, told with Sir William's usual humour, produces great mirth, especially in Lady Molle, who laughs so hard it brings on a wheezing fit and a footman has to be sent running for more ale.

Only the magistrate fails to be amused. "Surely we should be commending the Dutch for their keen observance to cleanliness?"

Next to me, Sir Henry Molle asks, and none too quietly, "Who the devil is that fellow?"

We sit long in the evening and watch the candles being lit on the river boats. The children still running and playing Catch Me as the moon comes out, even little Jack finally enjoying himself.

The magistrate is first to depart, still looking anxiously at his timepiece. After he's gone, Sir William says the gentleman puts him in mind of a bird pecking at dull seed, "With one eye always elsewhere, in case there's a juicy worm to be had." I'm set laughing with the rest, though I do think this magistrate had good counsel on the Dutch. I've always found it irksome when folks up and spits wherever they please.

I'm early down to breakfast and who should be sitting there, bold as you like, but Miss Martha. "I arrived but an hour ago," she says. And in a trice, she's on her feet with arms outstretched. Miss Martha's never one for clasping folk to her, and since I've no notion what to do, I keep my own arms stiff to my side. "I've missed you, Jane. I've missed everyone. Are there coddled eggs? Could you arrange it, dear Jane?"

This whole day, Miss Martha's been full of talk concerning that Holland outing. At supper, she's still singing praises. "You will find much to your liking, Dorothy. William and I have already made many friends." Lady Dorothy just nods. She's hardly touched her apple pudding. Miss Martha declares she's never known such a good adventure as travelling unknown in a foreign land. "Luckily, we had two pages and my maid all familiar with the Dutch tongue." I'm thinking it must have been novel indeed for Miss Martha to keep her own tongue quiet for once. "Do you remember, William, that time you had me dress as your page with my hair tucked in a cap?" And right here at table, she pulls her hair up and back from her face to show the effect. "We slept on straw in a barn where none might find us. I've never felt such freedom."

Sir William looks none too pleased with the telling of this tale. No doubt he knows Lady Dorothy, always cautious, will deem it foolhardy indeed. But all she says is, "Freedom is such a powerful word." And she sits silent for the rest of supper. It's as if the light of these past days has gone right out of her and settled on her sister.

THE HAGUE

I'm thinking Sir William gave good counsel – seems these Dutch folks are martyrs to cleanliness. Never did see houses so neat as pins. And pleasing wide streets and waterways, not to mention all the English you hear spoke. My only grumble is the weather. The damp comes right out of the ground and seeps into you. And this cold can cut clean through. I'm supposing that's why the Dutch are prone to look a tad glum. The house, too, is not entirely to our liking, as Miss Martha was quick to point out soon as she set foot in it. "Did you ever see anything so tall and thin?" she says, "and with so little light coming in?"

She's not fussed, though. No. She's too busy swanning about them foreign embassies. Not so my lady, who's been ailing since we arrived. It's not just her ague. No – as so oft with Lady Dorothy, her spirit's brought low. She's always likely to be affected by the elements. Sir William has urged her to rest. "You must let Martha take charge until you've regained your strength."

My lady's not having it. "I myself will arrange the running of our household." She vows she'll be fine in a day or two. If you ask me, she don't want Miss Martha taking over, like said lady did at Sheen. As my father used to say, "Give some people a thread and they'll likely take the whole spool."

Still, there's no denying Miss Martha knows how to step up for an occasion. Which is just as well, 'cos it's not every day a house is told to expect a royal visit! Sir William's surprised. He's already well acquainted with the Prince of Orange. But seems that gentleman makes it a point to call on all new ambassadors.

Seeing as my lady's still indisposed, Miss Martha's not slow to put herself forward, ordering everyone around and telling the maids to spruce theirselves up. She insists Lady Dorothy remain abed, even though my lady's been set on making the effort. "It would not do for the prince to see the ambassador's wife so pale," Miss Martha tells her. And she's right stroppy with me: "Go and practise your curtsy, Jane. Your usual bob will not suffice." As always, her tone can truly irk. Still, when I'm alone in my chamber I do try to correct myself. Curtsying proper doesn't come easy to me, and I've no mind to be taken for a person who don't know what's what. I'm more than a bit nervous, though. Who'd have thought Jane Wright would be meeting a prince!

Turns out this prince is nervous himself. When Miss Martha drops her Perfect Curtsy, he stares straight down at his boots. He does manage a smile when little Nan steps forward, pretty as a picture, and in a gown to match her aunt's. And he greets Jack with a solemn handshake. I can't help but note how he's not at all dashing, like you'd expect from a soldier prince. No. Truth be, he's short and stooped and with skin the colour of an uncooked pie. A sad enough look for someone not yet nineteen. He don't stand on much ceremony neither. He's arrived with only two minions and greets us all with no fancy fuss. When I finally make my own curtsy, he's already turned and talking to Sir William. I'm thinking our English royalty would be a deal more proper. No doubt sensing his awkwardness, Sir William soon ushers him off to the library for some private talk.

Miss Martha's put out. She's used to receiving more attention. "Don't just stand there, Jane," she says to me. "Anyone would think we are unused to welcoming eminent guests." As we move to the withdrawing room, she adds: "It's odd how little elegance the Dutch often display." For once, I'm agreeing with her.

Sir William, though, seems well pleased with this visit. "I think I've won his confidence," he tells us at supper.

Miss Martha's not impressed. "'Tis a pity you couldn't improve his manners. He's certainly lacking in charming ways."

Sir William laughs. "He's a young man with no notion of social mores, Martha. No doubt the sight of you in that blue gown threw him into confusion."

"Walk with me through the house, Jane." Lady Dorothy's determined to be up and doing, though, if you ask me, she's still not herself. I take her arm on the stairs. There's enough of them to tire the strongest body.

"Lean on me, my lady." Even though it's early afternoon, we've need to carry a candle. "I'm thinking this place is a tad gloomy, your ladyship."

"We shall make it less so, Jane. Together, we shall make it a house a man is happy to live in."

I'm thinking it will take a deal more than talk to make this place comfortable. "Yes, my lady," I says. "We'll do it together." And she squeezes my hand beneath her arm.

I remember when he came to me in Sheen at Easter. The weather had been warm all day. We picnicked by the side of the river and watched as the light faded and candles from the boats reflected in the water. When the guests were gone, we walked along the riverbank. He took my hand and held it against his cheek. We lay together all night in my bed. He held me close, as in the old days. I thought my heart would burst. His lovemaking was gentle, considerate. I was unpractised. "We mustn't leave it so long," he whispered.

I must think on other things.

Panels of painted cloth, cushions, my virginals brought from Sheen, bright, new earthenware, green fabric for curtains, indigo for the walls.

"What think you of these designs, Martha?"

"What I think, Dorothy, is that these cushions are an extravagance."

"But surely worth the cost for such intricate weave."

Jane says, "Them woven images are very pleasing, my lady." And I explain the story of Esther pleading with the King to save her people.

Martha is unimpressed. She peers at the work more closely. "Why is it, Dorothy, you have such a taste for kings lusting after young women?"

I purchase six cushions.

"Do you remember our letters, William? How we promised there should be no secrets between us? We vowed to go forward together. Do you still believe those words?"

William looks up from his book and laughs. "The blood was certainly overheated," he says.

"We would write all we felt, all we hoped of life. We were able to hold each other close through those letters," I say. "I knew your heart, and you read mine."

"And we still hold each other's hearts, dearest. But we now have responsibilities beyond the ties that bind us."

The ties that bind us. That's not it, William.

I say: "In truth, I oft feel we know very little of each other."

"Would that I understood you, Dorothy!" Impatient, William closes his book. "You know all there is of me and have done for more than twenty years. I consult you on everything, I'm always pleased to concede to your wishes. Have I not encouraged you to change this house to your liking, no matter the cost? I think I may say I encourage you in all you do." He rises, anxious to be gone. "What more do you want of me?"

All of you, William. The whole of you. "I should like more moments alone with you," I say.

When he's gone, I sit in his study window and watch the boatmen plying their wares on the canal below. What William says is true. He is always solicitous, quick to grant me anything that he feels might make me happy – render me reasonable. What more do I want? Many things. To find a way back. To resurrect and cherish all that was once so precious.

I want your body on mine, gentle, as it was that Easter night. Is that so very wrong, William? Are these feeling perhaps a little unseemly for a woman my age? Should I pack them away in the bottom of a trunk with the lid shut tight?

I want a letter, William. A teasing, loving letter. The type of letter you once wrote with ease. A letter such as you wrote to your sister, Martha.

In almost three years, I can count on one hand the number of mornings I've woken to find this dark chamber infused with sunlight. I tell Jane it cannot be wasted. "I shall walk by the canal before breakfast. Given the climes here, there may well be fog before dinner." William always rises early, breakfasting alone and then straight to his study. This morning, I shall prise him from work and into the sunshine. We will walk together.

My first impression on pushing open the study door is one of confusion. It takes a moment to register the scene. William and his secretary, Mr Bloom, are bending over a young girl seated in a chair. I recognise one of the new kitchen maids whose name I do not know. The three of them are laughing. William is pushing the girl's hair back from her neck. There is a brief moment of fluster. "My dear. I was not expecting you to be down so early." But William is quick to regain his composure. "Geile here is being driven half mad with toothache and want of sleep. We are about to apply moxa – you will recall that remedy from the Indies that so soothed my gout?"

I note there is no sign of this miracle mixture about the room.

As if reading my thoughts, William says: "Given how noxious the aroma is, we shan't send for the cure until the last possible moment." When I don't reply, he adds: "I'm just locating the great vein under the ear where the book tells me it must be applied." There is no sign of the book. The kitchen wench, no longer laughing, stares down at the floor.

I say: "Would it not be best to consult the doctor? There are surely many approved cures for this condition."

After mulling this over, William agrees. "Perhaps we should try the medic first – though I am sure moxa will be the solution."

As I make my way to breakfast, I'm wondering how a girl with agonising toothache has the spirit to laugh so heartily.

At dinner, I ask William the doctor's verdict. He obviously finds the question irksome. "We decided to proceed with the moxa," he says. "The girl is now perfectly well, so there's an end to it."

"Have you noticed, Jane, how things are so rarely what they seem?"

"I'm not sure I follow you, my lady."

"Just when you think all is certain, all is ordered, you suddenly find you may have understood nothing. Have you ever felt that?"

"Can't say I have, my lady."

"But it's hard, is it not, Jane, trusting what we think we know?"

"Not sure I understand your meaning, my lady. By my book, all we can do is our best and try not to let ourselves down." We continue with our needlepoint. She's right about this pastime – it soothes the spirit. No need to talk. No need to think.

Jane says: "It's surprising that Miss – Lady Martha – has not wed again. Seeing as how she's so full of life and all."

How often have I had that very thought. "It is surely a private matter for Lady Giffard," I say. And aware I've spoken harshly, I add, "It's interesting, Jane, that all believe a woman can scarce exist without a man at her side."

Jane says: "It's just the way of things. By my book, a husband gives a person a proper place in life." Putting her needlework aside, she rises and begins preparing my chamber for the night. Seated at the dressing table, I study her reflection in the mirror. It's of a still handsome woman – Jane's face shows little of the damage wrought by time – but why haven't I noted those small, fine lines of strain around her eyes?

"You yourself have not married, Jane, and I've always believed you to be perfectly content."

"I've never found anyone fool enough to take me, my lady." The words are said lightly, but I'm aware of the flatness in her voice. I've been remiss. Concerned as I am with suspicions, absorbed with my own needs, I've assumed Jane has none. In truth, I doubt I've thought of her at all. If she'd stayed in Guernsey, Jane would surely have wed and known the joys of motherhood. By keeping her with me, I've deprived her of much. Martha, too, has been cruelly deprived of those same joys. A young widow, forced to depend on the good will of relatives. Yet I've failed to draw this sister close. I've allowed doubt and uncertainty to sour my heart.

The letter arrives with dispatches from London. As William reads it, I sense immediately all is not well. "It's from Lord Arlington," he tells me. "I'm to make all haste to London." He passes me the letter. It is short and curt, and with none of his lordship's usual flowery greetings.

I help him to pack his papers. "Why can it be," he says, "that I'm recalled so abruptly, and without explanation."

I reply all are aware of His Majesty's capricious nature. "Doubtless he calls for you on some whim." Neither of us believe this to be true. For weeks, rumours have been rife that England is once again dealing with France against the Dutch.

William and Martha's trunks are put aboard the boat. He'd determined to make this journey alone, but Martha was persuasive. How could I object? She will, I know, as always, look to his needs.

Jane and I watch until the boat joins the mass of others on the canal and we lose sight of them. "I fancy, my lady, Sir William should have liked you with him," Jane says.

Would I might believe this. "He thought it best we stay in place, Jane, lest his hasty departure should cause disquiet." Quite what is expected of me alone here in The Hague, with Jane, is beyond comprehension.

From: Lady Temple, The Hague
To: Sir William Temple, Temple Grove, Sheen

Dearest,

With what relief I received yours from Yarmouth telling of your safe passage despite contrary winds. It is strange, is it not, that I should now be abroad whilst you are at home?

By now, I trust you'll have met with Lord Arlington, and perhaps His Majesty too, and will no doubt know the reason for your hasty recall.

Here at The Hague, all are asking why you went so quickly, and some are of the opinion you'll not return. Yesterday, the Prince supped with us. He talked openly concerning rumours that His Majesty deals with the French again and that something is striking up between those two nations. The Prince thinks you are recalled because you are too great a friend to the Dutch.

Dearest, I hope you may soon be restored to us. Meantime, I do my best to present a good front and continue social events as though all were well. But I'm oft daunted. How I wish I had your ease of manner.

I'm reassured that Martha is attending your domestic

arrangements, and I hope, too, she has arranged a medic to counsel on your gout. To experience such discomfort at sea was truly unfortunate. Please promise to take better care of yourself.

Nan sends her best kiss, and Jack shall write to you after dinner. All here hope for a speedy reunion.

Your most loving D. T.

To: Sir John Temple, Master of the Rolls, Dublin
October 14

Father,

My wings are clipped! After three short years, I see my treaty dying before my eyes. I would not have believed it possible for the King and his ministers to change on a matter so obviously in the interests of our country!

After a series of meetings with My Lord Arlington, at which he treated me more as an inconvenience than a friend, it seems England will once again support the French king in future hostilities against the Dutch. At our last audience, having kept me waiting more than one hour, his lordship could find no merit in any of my diplomatic efforts. In the heat of the moment, I asked in the name of God what more could a man do? At which point, Lord Arlington flew into a rage, declaring: "I'll tell you what a man can do more; he can let the world know how basely the Dutch have used the King and declare publicly how Dutch ministers are rogues and rascals and not fit for His Majesty to deal with!" My answer was very calm: that I should always speak of all men as I find them, and so I should of the Dutch.

A stroll in Pall Mall with the King, though more congenial, touched mostly on the weather and my gout. Our only serious discourse concerned the Prince of Orange, and whether I thought him a suitable future match for Princess Mary, the King's niece. He begged me sound out the young man. Since

I'm a million miles away, I've needs leave that delicate task to my wife. Regarding my recall and the situation with France, the King said not one word!

So there, Father, be an end to it, and an end too, I dare say, to my foray into diplomacy. I apprehend weather coming that I'll not wish to be abroad in. I should rather retire to Sheen and tend my gardens!

Meantimes, the King refuses permission for me to return to The Hague and close my embassy. My wife must stay on and carry this burden of deceit as best she can. As you know, Lady Temple is fragile and given to debilitating fits of the Spleen. She's totally unsuited to stepping front stage and dealing with worldly matters.

We live in unsettling times indeed.
Your obedient son, W. T.

"It seems you are a perfect fit for Sir William's shoes, Lady Temple!"

The Prince of Orange is not known for his humour, but this is surely said in jest. "Forgive me, Your Highness. I am a poor substitute indeed for the keen mind and counsel of an ambassador."

"On the contrary. Our ministers are full of talk of your deft dealings. One went so far as to remark that on complex issues, 'a woman's sensibilities are oft more subtle than a man's'." To hide my confusion, I busy myself rearranging some books on the table next to me. The Prince adds, "There are even rumours that you sometimes help with those eloquent letters Sir William is famed for." Pray God these rumours never reach William!

"I assure your highness, the substance and flow of my husband's letters are down to his own elegant hand." The Prince looks as if he would say more but is overtaken by the spasmodic cough that so often plagues him. I lead him closer to the fire. "Come, let us sit in the warmth."

Looking about him, the Prince says: "You have given this entire house warmth. It was always the most unattractive residence. You've brought it to life. It's a pity Sir William had not more time to enjoy it." I don't mention my husband barely noticed the changes.

"Your Highness was asking about the Princess Mary. Well, I've seen her rarely, but all say she is finely bred and of good humour." I can still picture the unsettling Whitehall Masque.

"Character and a good disposition are qualities I prize highly, Lady Temple. I fear I'm not an easy person to live with." When the Prince blushes, it begins at his throat and creeps over his entire face. "I'd do my best, of course, but I will need a wife who is likely to live well with me." He speaks candidly, and with no affectation. "Trouble at home is something I could not bear. I fear I'll have enough of that abroad."

"The Princess is still a child," I say. "It might be prudent to watch and wait."

The Prince declares he is certainly not ready to take a wife. "And I doubt the English would ever accept such a union, especially since our two countries are so oft at war. I hear there's still no news of Sir William's return." The two of us sit quietly for a moment. Finally, the Prince says, "When I do marry, I would have a union of trust and honour, such as you and Sir William enjoy." How innocent this young man is.

Rising, the Prince says: "There is one more thing. I realise it's not usual in such matters to talk of personal particulars, but I would also have a wife who is, well, in some ways, comely." And there's that blush again.

Jane says, "Seems the Prince appreciates our English ways. That's the second time he's supped this week."

"It's our good Dutch kitchens," I tell her. "They know how to prepare his favourites."

"And I keep a sharp eye on those cooks!" Jane has no need to explain. Nowadays, everywhere is rife with tales of poisoning. If the Prince were to fall ill at our table, Jane and I would probably not leave The Hague alive.

"Come, Jane. Sit with me in my chamber and talk awhile." I suddenly feel full of vigour. My 'deft dealings' indeed! If only they knew of my trepidation whenever a minister or ambassador approaches me.

"It's odd, Jane, is it not, how we find ourselves alone in a foreign place entertaining a prince."

"With Sir William back in Sheen and all," Jane says, "and us left here without him."

"So you think, Jane, a woman is incapable of holding a fortress now and again?"

"Well, to be honest, my lady, I don't think no one can do the sort of work Sir William does. I think that's work fit for a man."

"Have you forgotten the war? Women were left to defend their homes oft enough and did not shrink from the task."

"Yes, my lady, but if I may say so, they weren't exactly alone, were they? What with bailiffs and stewards and all, I'm thinking there was always men to protect them."

"I can name at least ten women solely responsible for holding their homes safe against Cromwell's army." Jane does not answer. "I think you do women a disservice, Jane. It was said of my own grandmother that she could run an estate better than any man." Still, Jane is silent. I begin to find her company irksome. "Perhaps you do not know that my husband oft shows me his letters before sending them, and I might suggest a sentence, a phrase, here and there."

"Oh no, I've always known you to be a wonderful letter-writer, Lady Dorothy. And I think you've stepped up to things very well, given the difficulties."

"Yet you refuse to credit that in some circumstances a woman might, for a while, manage the busy work of a man!"

"Well, yes, my lady. I'd be quick to say you're capable of most things when you put your mind to it. I'm sorry. I didn't mean…" And I see she is close to tears.

"Forgive me, Jane. I've upset you."

"Oh no, my lady. It were my fault for misunderstanding. But since the hour is late, I think I'll make for my bed."

The room is cold with Jane gone. How could I have spoken so sharply to her? She, who all these years has been my friend and support? And, of course, she's right. My role here isn't of the least importance. Merely to smile and be pleasant, to keep up pretence without raising alarm.

This morning, Jack asked, and not for the first time, was his papa never coming back? What was I to tell him? The truth? That I fear it is more than the sea that separates us.

SHEEN

1671

Lord knows how we've got everything packed and stowed so quick, and by the King's own orders, no less. All these months of waiting and now we've to make for home within a week. Least I'd no needs take space in a trunk. This mantle's ample for holding my gowns and bits and bobs. Only thing I worry for is my miniature. I've been keeping it careful these past months, and I'm loath to damage it on the journey. I'm thinking I'd better put it about my person. I never thought on owning such a pretty thing. "It was crafted when I was a girl," my lady told me. "Sadly, I fear it's no longer a good likeness."

I'd begged to differ. "Oh no, my lady. I'd know you anywhere by those eyes!" I was properly overcome by such a wonderful gift. 'Specially coming so soon after a scolding. "You must forgive me, Jane," she'd said, "if I spoke too sharply." And I'd assured her all was due to my own awkwardness.

"Begging your pardon, Lady Dorothy," I'd told her. "I'm thinking you can do anything when your mind's put to it." As always with her, my misspoke moment was quick forgot.

"Forgive our sins, most merciful Lord. Into thy hands…" It's not the first time today Lady Dorothy's called on the Almighty. "If we get safe home, Jane, I'll never again put to sea." No good me telling her I've known waters more choppy than this. I plump up the pillow and wipe the sweat from her face. Poor thing can scarce raise her head for fear of vomiting. And considering this is the King's own craft, there's little enough comfort, stretched out on a narrow cot with only two thin covers. Jack sits close. He's taken such fright, he won't leave his mama's side. The nurse has retired to bed. Seems only me and young Nan's still got our sea legs. She's trotting about like a true sailor, even as we are tossed.

"I fear we shall all perish before we reach England!" My lady's voice is that weak. "Tell them to bring more ale, Jane. And please be quick."

Not much chance of finding a body to fetch and carry. Up on deck, all are frantic trying to take down the top mast 'fore it's torn to shreds, and bailing out water, which in places comes over my shoes. Folks are sliding about from the keeling, and all not tied down is hurled by the wind. I've difficulty keeping my own balance. I put my kerchief to my nose. Despite the winds, the stench from below is powerful enough to kill a goat. Seems Lady Dorothy's not the only one with a churning stomach. Someone takes my arm: "There's rocks ahead, best get below." I stay anyway and watch these strapping lads put their energy into guiding the boat just clear.

Balancing the ale best I can, I push the cabin door with my foot. "The sea shan't have us this time, my lady!"

She's enjoyed only a fitful sleep. I've kept vigilant in the chair beside her. Though to my shame, I do admit dropping off once or twice when things got smoother. "It's a fair morning, Lady Dorothy. See how calm it is now."

"I'll not look out, Jane." She vows she'll stay quiet till we fetch up in Plymouth. "Who knows how these waters may turn?"

Standing by the portal, Nan says: "Look how pretty!" Not much fazes young Nan. The nurse takes the children topside for a better view of the sunrise.

They're still there when the Captain knocks. Thinking he's enquiring for our health, I tell him my lady needs better vittles than were last offered. "A good broth and some cold beef would best restore her." I'm about to say more, when I note this captain's face.

"I would speak with you privately, Lady Temple." And I blush when she tells him all needs saying may be said in my presence. He's a solemn sort of person. A bit weather-beaten, and with one of them jaws that tells of firm resolve – though he's proper nervous now. "We're about to meet with a Dutch frigate, your ladyship. My orders are to fire a warning shot bidding any Dutch vessel crossing our path to lower its flag. And if they refuse, to open fire in earnest."

He's not kept waiting for a response: "My children – they must be fetched immediately."

"The men are clearing the decks now, your ladyship. All guests shall be safe below." The Captain seems to struggle with his words. "Should we open fire, it will be an act of war, and the Dutch will surely retaliate." My heart's going that fast. My lady don't say nothing. "It could become very dangerous," the Captain tells her, "and, well, I'm thinking of you and your children." Still, my lady is silent. "What I mean is, I would need your agreement before carrying out such an order."

My lady don't hesitate now: "If your orders are to fire on the Dutch – then fire you must. Without thought for us." My own thoughts are in a right state. Main one being: best ready ourselves to meet our maker.

Seems like Lady Dorothy's got that same idea. Once the children are back, and without telling the reason, she bids us all kneel and join hands. "We will pray together." The nurse, sensing trouble, starts to weep. She's too young to welcome heaven.

Nan says: "Don't cry, Beattie. God sees everything and you'll make him sad." This produces more tears, then Jack starts wailing too. I try to hide my fear for sake of the little ones, but my hands are shaking like leaves, and I can feel the sweat trickle down my neck.

My lady stays calm, though. "Into thy care we commit our souls, dear Lord." Them words surely toll heavy now. She bids us join in the *Lord's Prayer*. We recite it three times, and I try to empty my head of all save the words, but my mind won't let me. We're surely going to die – and in that same way as Robin. I've oft wondered how such dying feels.

We hear the warning shot. It seems to shake the entire boat. We stay fearfully praising the Lord for what seems an hour, but not a sound from above. My knees are paining me something terrible. I say: "Maybe them Dutch saw sense and lowered their flag, like the Captain wanted."

My lady won't take chances. "Help me move the cot so we may all sit close behind it." It's heavy enough, and with no man to help, takes an age to shift.

Jack keeps asking what's happening. "Why are we hiding, Mama?"

I says: "It's a new game, Jack," though I'd wager he knows different. It's stifling cooped up like this and still holding hands. On one side of me, Nan has dozed off. On t'other, I've got hold of the nurse. Our palms are that clammy, we're fairly stuck together. None feels like talking, and what with Jack whimpering and the nurse sniffling, I'm thinking we're a sorry sight. There's still only silence above. I'm starting to fear all but us have left the boat. Then we hear someone outside, and the nurse tightens her hand on mine till I fear she may break it.

The Captain helps my lady up off the floor. "All is safe now, Lady Temple." Quick to regain her dignity, she gives a small curtsy, though I note she's still trembling.

"The Dutch obeyed your orders, then, sir?"

"No, Lady Temple. They did not lower their flag. But I decided it would be right to hold our fire. I deemed my priority must be the safety of your party."

At these words, the nurse, echoing my own thoughts, pipes up: "Oh, praises be the Lord in his mercy. Thank you, sir!" And for a moment, I'm feared she's about to throw her arms around this man. Only Lady Dorothy seems less than jubilant.

When the Captain's gone, she says: "I pray that good man's concern does not cost him too dearly."

"You've grown thin these past months, Dorothy. I hardly recognise you." I'm supposing this be Miss Martha's idea of a cheery welcome.

Sir William's more fulsome, clasping my lady and the children to him in one big swoop. Soon as we're home, he's in great excitement to show us alterations to the house, made, he tells us, through Sir John's good generosity. "Come, Di, hold my hand and see what magic Papa has wrought."

None shows more surprise than Lady Dorothy. "It is twice the size since your expansions," she tells Sir William. His particular pride is his grand new bedchamber and study, all set apart from the main house.

Back in the kitchens, the cook's not keen. "I've told him, if he wants vittles late in the evening, he'll have to fetch his own. I'll not be walking that distance."

Lady Dorothy, too, is unsure. "The new rooms are lovely, William, but a trifle isolated."

Miss Martha don't think so. "Now that William intends to devote more time to his writing, he needs somewhere he will not be disturbed." I'm supposing she's got good counsel. Though it does strike me a bit peculiar for him to be so cut off from the rest of us. Still, I'm bound to admit, what with the new rooms and the extra acreage Sir William's purchased, the house does look grand indeed.

Sir William can't stop himself dwelling on our late adventures. "My wife has endured much, and all to end in a hazardous sea journey!" He's right proud of her, though, telling any within earshot how his lady bid the Captain fire when necessary. "It must be confessed there's some merit to this family. I made the peace with Holland, and my wife was like to have the honour of making the war!"

I'm bound to have my own word. "Lady Dorothy were braver than any I know of. I do believe no man could be as brave!" And my lady and I exchange glances.

As always, though, she's modest as they come: "There was more than one brave man on that boat. The Captain risked everything that we might be safe."

Sir William says: "Yes, and he's languishing in the Tower for his pains."

All are shocked at this news, especially Lady Dorothy. "Surely he must be forgiven for protecting innocent children?"

Miss Martha is quick to respond. "He betrayed our country's honour. What would happen to the order of things if all disobeyed commands?"

Lady Dorothy's not convinced. "Rules must surely be stretched to fit circumstance. Is it Christian to punish a man for following his conscience?"

"My love, our history is full of such examples." And Sir William puts his arm about her. "For my part, I rejoice at this captain's decision. But Martha is right. If we all failed to follow rules, there would be chaos."

"I remember a time, William, when your thinking was very different." And my lady beckons me help unload her trunks.

Temple Court, Sheen.

Your Most Gracious Majesty

Forgive me if I am unaware of the correct procedure in these matters. I write on behalf of Sir Richard Bellamy, lately captain of your majesty's yacht, Merlin, and now detained in the Tower awaiting your most gracious Majesty's pleasure. As Your Majesty is no doubt aware, during our voyage from Holland, that good man was faced with what was for him, an impossible dilemma: whether to fire on a Dutch frigate, as ordered, or to protect myself and my children against the violence that would surely erupt. Being a man of conscience and compassion, he chose the latter.

If I'd not been aboard that boat, due to Your Majesty's most gracious hospitality, Captain Bellamy would not have grappled with such a choice. I beg you to pardon a man whose only crime was to take pity on a nervous woman and her children – and whom I believe to be as loyal and steadfast to you, as my father was to your father, when my father stood on the side of the crown till the very last, at great personal cost.

I beg Your Majesty's gracious consideration and tolerance, and remain, as always, your very humble servant.

Lady Dorothy Temple

The afternoons are drawing in. It is not yet four o'clock, but Jane must light the candles. Martha is restless. "Isn't it odd? Wherever we are in the world, we are always hovered over our needlepoint!"

Jane says, "For myself, Miss – your Ladyship – I'm that pleased knowing how to work these dainty things."

"Well, I'm happy for you, Jane, that you find such a boring pastime pleasurable." And Martha stabs at the sampler with her needle. "Why must we always be so dull?"

It seems we are not to be dull for long. There are quick footsteps through the hall. Even as William enters the withdrawing room, it is plain all is not well. He comes straight to me. "This, from Arlington." He waves the letter close to my face. "It appears your friend Captain Bellamy is to be released from the Tower at your behest." Jane, making her excuses, gathers her sewing and leaves. Martha remains.

As for me, my dismay at William's agitation is tempered by relief at the news. "I'm so happy to know this!"

"You astound me, Dorothy! To write to the King; to have it

delivered to the palace and tell me nothing!" I have rarely heard such anger in William's voice. Even Martha looks uneasy.

"Forgive me, dearest." I try to control the tremor in my own voice. "I did not want to involve you in a matter I felt purely a concern for my own conscience."

"Well, you have indeed involved me. It seems the King saw fit to pass your letter straight to Arlington. You may imagine my humiliation." He reads from the letter: *Your wife is a woman of singular character, Sir William. It's rare for a wife to take matters into her own hands so completely as to write to a monarch!*

Martha is pale. "I'm sure Dorothy acted in good faith. Lord Arlington's words may well be admiring."

"Lord Arlington's words, Martha, tell me 'tis a pity I cannot control my wife!"

There's little chance of sleep. Rising, I pull my shawl over my night robe and sit close to the embers of the fire. At supper, he spoke not one word to me, and retired directly after. In seeking to right a wrong for which I was partly to blame, I've been thoughtless and misguided. Why did I not tell William of my plan? Ask his counsel? Had I hoped, in my pride, to deal with this entirely alone and therefore reap all gratitude? Matters must not be allowed to fester.

There is a light coming from his study. I knock before entering. William is seated, poring over a map spread across his entire desk. And he's not alone. A new young maid from the village stands by his shoulder, also engrossed.

"I've been showing Bridget where our household journeyed. The exotic places she missed by insisting on being born too late." His tone is playful. All anger, it seems, forgotten.

I say, "You should to bed now, Bridget. Lady Giffard will require your services early tomorrow."

This is the first time I've been in William's study at night. The fire is lit, and many candles give a glow to the dark, panelled walls. All is warm and welcoming. But I suddenly find the room oppressive.

I feel a spark of anger that William is so recovered from our earlier encounter, whilst I have suffered such soul-searching. "I'm sorry you took offence at my actions, William. I was thinking only of that poor, good man imprisoned in the Tower." These are not the soft words of remorse I'd meant to deliver, and I know my voice is cold.

"What's done is done, Dorothy. Of course, I understand your reasons. But if I may say, your actions are oft too hasty, only to be regretted later."

"I regret I caused you anger, but I cannot regret my letter, since it has resulted in Captain Bellamy's release."

"And at what cost to my standing with Arlington – and perhaps His Majesty? I would ask you think carefully on that!"

"You once pressed me, William, to follow my own conscience and not be concerned with the opinion of others. You wished me to be of 'independent spirit', a characteristic you professed to admire in a woman. But if I cannot sometimes follow that independence of thought, it's in danger of withering. In fact, I am oft in fear of disappearing altogether!" We stare at each other. Both, it seems, amazed at this outburst.

"I only ask your complete loyalty as my wife."

"And you have it! If you feel I've let my conscience override that loyalty, then I'm sorry. I have always striven to be the person you may trust above all others. I've loved you deeply and faithfully, William. And I am still as moved by the touch of your hand as I was when we first met. But in truth, I rarely now feel that touch. I sometimes wonder if indeed you have need of me at all. Perhaps you would prefer to start a new adventure!" William concentrates on the careful folding of his map.

"Some things are best unsaid, Dorothy. You are tired, that is what makes you speak so. We shall not talk further tonight."

I wake as the clock in the hall chimes nine. I don't rise. I shall not go down to breakfast.

I'm woken again by a small knock. This is the first time Bridget has come to my chamber and she hovers uncertainly at the door. I bid her come inside. "I see you have a note. You may bring it to me." And, seeking to put her at ease, I add, "Are you happy to be here as Lady Giffard's maid?" The girl reddens and stumbles out some words of gratitude. She bobs two or three times before leaving the room. She cannot be more than fourteen years.

The note is from William:

Dearest, you are, and ever shall be, my anchor. Without you, I should be constantly adrift.

I hold it close. Recalling my own blunt words, I'm truly saddened. But I cannot bring myself to regret them.

BOOK THREE
TILL DEATH
US DO PART

WHITEHALL AND SHEEN

1677

If the bride looks less than radiant, it's hardly surprising; so many days of weeping have taken their toll. I wonder if there was ever a more sombre wedding; a more ill-matched couple. Just a few weeks past, the bridegroom visited Sheen and confided to me his eagerness for this moment. "You told me true, Lady Temple. She is all I hoped. I'm confident we shall live well together." Now, the Prince of Orange stands sullen and ill at ease, as if suddenly aware of the foreign waters he swims in. The bride keeps her kerchief clasped to her bosom, eyes fixed to the ground. Was it right, I wonder, to have a hand in this?

The King is doing his best to lighten the mood. As Prince William places a handful of gold and silver coins on the Bible, with the words: "With all my worldly goods I thee endow," His Majesty bids his niece scoop them up.

"Put them in your pocket, my dear! 'Tis all clear gain!" Just one of the many coarse remarks he's uttered this evening. It does nothing to raise the spirit of Princess Mary. Unable to contain herself, she begins to weep quietly into her kerchief. None move to comfort her. We are all too mindful of protocol.

She is just fifteen. Barely older than my own Nan. She could be my daughter. A month ago, summoned to the palace, I found her in high spirits, both nervous and flattered that a foreign prince had asked for her hand. I'd been happy to assure her that Prince William was both honest of nature and true of heart. Now, as I watch her stumble through nuptials binding her to a man she barely knows, and whose native language she speaks not one word, I wonder if these solid attributes are enough.

As the Queen leads her off to the bridal chamber, the Princess casts a desperate glance at those of us gathered. No doubt this is hardly the romantic moment she has dreamed of.

We crowd into an anteroom. "Will you join me in a hot posset and some cake, Lady Temple?" I've not seen Lord Arlington these several years, and since his favour has slipped, I did not expect to see him this evening. There are rumours he is in poor health. Yet except for a slight limp, and some obvious trouble with one arm, he's much the same. He still sports the black patch on the bridge of his nose. And he still delights in low conversation. "It's hard to imagine the night to come," he remarks, "given all the talk of Princess Mary's devotion to Sappho." Sensing my distaste, he quickly adds: "Gossip, that we should certainly dismiss, of course." This followed by a squeeze to my arm with his good hand. To hide my embarrassment, I comment on the décor of the room, the intricately designed ceiling, with its depiction of two rosy cherubs entwined above the heads of the King and Queen. His interest waning, Lord Arlington looks about the chamber. "I'd hoped to find your husband here. Perhaps you left him in the tender care of Lady Giffard?" When I don't reply, he adds, "Ah yes, we heard of Sir William's return to The Hague and his negotiations of this marriage." Lord Arlington chuckles. "Let's hope it doesn't prove fruitless for all concerned. Such a pity your husband cannot be here to witness the happy moment."

I say: "My husband and his sister are in Dublin where their father is ailing." At least Lord Arlington has the grace to offer condolences. But these are cut short by the entrance of the King, recently come from the bridal chamber and surrounded by his Corps Diplomatique.

"I told the prince, 'Go to it, nephew,'" he bellows. "'Go to it for England and St George!'"

My brother Henry is dead. William and Martha have scarce returned from Ireland and the sad task of burying their father when there is news of this further loss. William hands me the letter. My first reaction is one of disbelief. "How can it be that Henry died in Whitechapel?"

William says, "From what I've been told these past years, your brother's life was, at best, disordered."

"From what you've been *told?*" I'm full of confusion. "You were privy to news of my brother and I was not?"

"My dear," William says, "I would not for the world burden you with rumours and half-truths. Suffice to say your brother Henry seems to have set himself apart from London society."

How many times, over the years, have I been tempted to visit the house in Chelsea to seek a reunion? And yet I failed to do so. Unable to face the truth of what I might find, I preferred to keep away and let my brother swim alone. Is that what the Lord intends for those who by nature march to a different drum? "I have lost my compass," Henry told me. How many of us could echo those words? A 'disordered life', William says. Do any of us, I wonder, live a truly ordered life? I glance back at the letter, the impersonal words. Bread Lane, Whitechapel, above the Ship and Anchor. My brother died alone, above a tavern in a part of London where few would venture.

PALL MALL AND SHEEN

1679

William has held the lease on this London house since the death of his father. A haven, he reasoned, during the constant summoning to Court. Yet situated as it is, so close to St James's Palace, I doubt it has afforded much peace. I myself have rarely visited, and for that very reason. To know the King keeps mistresses is one thing, but to overlook the very grounds in which he parades them lays too heavy on the stomach. Yet here I am, at William's insistence, about to spend a glorious summer day closeted at 81 Pall Mall. He refuses to tell me why my presence is so needed, and judging from the knowing glances that pass between them, Nan too is party to this mystery.

She bids me close my eyes, and I'm slowly guided up the winding staircase and along the hallway. We move to what I sense is the withdrawing room. William says, "You may open them now." It takes a moment to find my bearings. As ever, this room is filled with light from the floor-to-ceiling windows. All else, it seems, is changed. Some of the furnishings I recognise: chairs brought over from The Hague, cushions and throws. But here in London, they look unfamiliar – as does the room itself. The walls, once drab grey, are now a delicate green. They are hung with paintings I remember from Ireland, long since stowed away. There are two enormous tapestries and new virginals, more ornate than any I'm accustomed to. They stand alone and are decorated in the French way, with intricate carvings. The occasional tables I recall from Sir John's house in Dublin.

"Do you like the changes, Mama?" Nan cannot contain herself. "It's your birthday gift. Papa has given you this house for your own!"

"Dearest," William says, "let me show you the other rooms, all newly decorated, I trust, to your taste, though there is still work to be done." As we walk, it is obvious much time and money has been devoted to this transformation.

"Look, Mama, this is your new bedchamber. Isn't it beautiful!" Nan takes my hand and leads me to the dresser with its set of silver brushes; the same ones, I believe, that sat upon Aunt Gargrave's dresser all those years ago. She pulls me to the windows. "And, look, you can see right down into His Majesty's gardens. You will think yourself a perfect duchess!"

"You arranged all this in secret, William?" And he admits he was not entirely alone in the enterprise.

"There was more than a little help from Martha. She, of course, has a better idea of popular tastes than her brother."

"And me, Papa, did I help too?"

"It could not have been done without you!" And William takes our daughter's hands and twirls her about the room. Given their obvious enjoyment of the moment, I've not the heart to be less than enthusiastic, declaring I'm almost too overwhelmed to speak. "But shall we not all be together here?"

"Of course, whenever we can. But I so rarely use it and my father's will has enabled this new decoration. Your own London house, my love, to stay and go as you please." And William collapses into a chair. "You wear me out, Di. That damned dancing master has taught you too well!"

Laughing, Nan favours us with some intricate new steps. "May I sometimes be here with you, Mama? I long to know more of London."

William says: "And perhaps you will occasionally entertain your country dolt of a husband!"

In the coach on the way back, William slowly eases his leg onto the seat opposite. The gout, never absent for long, is once again beginning to plague him. "I fear my dancing days are over."

Nan will not counsel it. "You dance like a young man, Papa. You are surely better than Jack. He is a very oaf at his steps and turns."

William closes his eyes. "After six months in Paris, I think we may see some changes there." In a moment, he is asleep.

Nan continues to chatter, heady with the air and promise of London. I make appropriate sounds whilst my mind runs circles around the events of the day.

What has happened? For several weeks, I've sensed something afoot. More comings and goings than usual; conversations that ceased when I entered a room. But a house just for me, and so lovingly arranged. Why? Questions flood my brain. How often am I to be here? I've friends in London, but they are few. Diana will obviously enjoy it. Jack too will no doubt welcome time in the city. And what of William? Now that we are once and for all to be settled back in England, his intentions are to distance himself entirely from Court, so shall Jane and I be often alone at Pall Mall?

The house has been made beautiful – even if its position is not to my liking. How many men of my acquaintance would present their wives with such a fashionable London address? Yes. I should consider myself lucky indeed.

So why am I not grateful?

"What think you, Jane?" she says. "Is it not the handsomest house in all London?"

I say, "It is indeed, my lady." In truth, what strikes me is this family's fondness for rushing places. One minute, Sir William tending his vines, the next, back at The Hague. Seems the King can't sleep comfortable unless he's got Sir William running. The whole family in and out of Holland too. And now, just as we're finally settling… "Will we be doing much to-ing and fro-ing, my lady?" My joints pain me at the very thought.

"I'll need you near me when we are here, Jane. You shall have the chamber next to mine." There's no doubting my good fortune there. This room is as pleasing as any I've known, and overlooking the King's own gardens and all.

"It's surely grand, my lady, and with everything just so." Still, I'm wondering what she would want with such a house, seeing she's never shown much liking for London life. I'm bound to admit the air is a tad sweeter here than elsewhere in this city. I never saw so many sweepers-up. I'm supposing that's due to the King so oft nearby, none wanting to offend his royal nose. Truth is, only scent reaches you when you come out the door is the strong aroma of the coffee house. I've peered in once or twice and my jaw surely dropped at the number of grandly clad gentlemen with nought to do but sit and smoke all day. Still, I'm supposing it's better than the tavern.

Seems, too, we've some important neighbours. "The crowd's that thick outside number 78," I tell my lady. "Wonder who they're waiting on." And I'm shocked when she tells me it's Mistress Eleanor Gwynn, dwelling, if you please, but two doors down. Even I know who Nell Gwynn is, thanks to the cook's prattling back in Sheen. Nowadays, all are aware of the King's goings-on. I admit, though, I'd not mind catching a glimpse of that particular lady.

But it's not a day for pondering. No, not with young Jack arriving fresh from Paris, and Sir William and Miss Martha expected back from their Holland journey. My lady's in a proper state. "Do we have enough provisions? Would you look to the kitchens, Jane? I so wish this to be a celebration."

I'm curious to know what Sir William will make of this son, come back almost a man, and with the nicest of French manners, stepping from the coach and bowing to his fellow passengers like a proper young gentleman. Something our English gentry are not always noted for. Jack's grown tall these months and lost that displeasing slouch of his. There's no doubting he's not the nervous lad was sent away. I'm a tad daunted by this change, and eased when, seeing me and Lady Dorothy, he fair throws himself at us. Seems he's holding back a tear, whereas the old Jack would give way at the drop of a hat.

My lady's free enough with her tears. She'd never have parted with Jack if Sir William hadn't insisted. And she's not about to leave his side now. Seems all she can find to say is: "You've grown so handsome." Not like my lady to be at a loss for words. Even Nan's not her usual self – shy when Jack enquires how goes her lessons and music.

By dinner, though, the two of them are back to their old easy jousting. "So tell me, Nan," says Jack, "about this tutor of yours. Mama wrote all the young ladies have set their caps for him. I'll warrant that includes you!"

And Nan reddens up like a strawberry. "You will see when he comes, Monsieur Gore is not handsome or tall, and he has a nose too small for his face."

"Well," says Jack, "since your nose is also small, and since you are scarce higher than a dwarf, you should make an excellent couple!"

We're all set laughing. Even Nan can't keep a straight face. Turning to me, my lady whispers: "There's something of Robin in Jack, is there not?"

It's so long since that name was mentioned, for a moment, I've needs to catch my breath. "Yes, well, it's all family, isn't it," I say. Truth be, I don't see one scrap of likeness. I can still picture Robin and that saucy look and that smile of his that could light the gloomiest room.

It's taken two days for Sir William and Miss Martha to get from Holland on account of inclement weather, and I've scarce seen Miss Martha so the worse for wear, her thick hair dull and limp and her gown more than a bit soiled. She's soon set on retiring for what she terms '*un repos*', bidding Bridget go with her. That young maid don't look too chipper neither, but Miss Martha can't do nought without Bridget in attendance.

I'd wager Sir William's leg is paining him, but seems he's determined it shan't spoil the sight of master Jack. Sir William makes great doing of holding Jack by the shoulders and declaring he won't own this stranger. "Tell me, sir, what have you done with my son?"

He's still marvelling after supper, when the tables are set for cards. "Your sojourn in Paris sits well on you, Jack, as I knew it would." It adds to Sir William's good humour when he beats his son at nearly every round of Basset. I must admit, now and then, with the wine flowing, cards can bring about a jolly evening. Least, that's until Miss Martha, all neatened now, and with hair curled perfect, makes her crude remarks.

Sir William says, "They talk in The Hague of a mutual content between the Prince and Princess of Orange. I would never have merited it, but I'll wager, after all, this is to be a love match!" Seeing my lady cheered, he adds the Princess's greetings. "She would meet with you, Dorothy, when she is next come to London."

And that's when Miss Martha pipes up: "The Prince and Princess of Orange are the oddest couple. 'Tis common gossip at The Hague – Prince William retires to bed in woollen drawers which he seldom removes."

Across from me, I note Lady Dorothy stiffen. As for me, I fix my eyes on my cards, not knowing where else to put them. Even Sir William seems discomforted. "Common gossip, Martha, is best left unrepeated." Nan and Jack don't think so. They're delighted at Miss Martha's tale. And Jack, no doubt thinking to best his aunt, treats us to a few low words of his own.

"News of our own majesty's doings reached us even in Paris," he says. "They do say Mistress Gwynn is the ribald one." My lady tries to put a stop to this displeasing talk, telling Nan to concentrate on learning the game and Jack to look to his cards.

Miss Martha, though, declares herself eager to hear more. "Do tell, Jack."

And he surely does. "'Tis said a crowd recently surrounded her coach, calling Mistress Gwynn the Catholic whore. Whereupon she leaned out and said: 'You are mistook, good people. I'm the Protestant whore!'"

These words are not warmly greeted by Sir William. "I believe in France, as in England, it's considered impolite for a gentleman to make coarse conversation in the presence of women." Jack, discomforted, stares down at his plate and for a moment, no one utters another word. But as so often with Sir William, his mood turns on a penny. "Dammit, though, if these aren't good tales! I heard tell Nell Gwynn is quick with her wit." And in a trice, all are laughing fit to bust.

All except me and Lady Dorothy. It don't take much to see she's mortified. "Is it wit, I wonder, to use such unseemly language?" she says.

Miss Martha says: "Come, Dorothy. Why must you always be so prim?"

And Sir William answers for her: "My wife is of modest nature, Martha." I'm thinking it's the first time I've ever heard a hint of tetchiness in his tone with his sister.

It's gone three o clock, and we're still waiting on this tutor. The others left for Sheen two hour ago. Sir William's a stickler for time. He declared he'd no intention of waiting on the whim of a Frenchman: "Let him come on alone, tomorrow."

This didn't suit young Nan. She begged her papa let her wait, and my lady, always soft where Nan's concerned, said she too would stay. Though when the three of us are seated alone in the withdrawing room, with nought to do but bide our time, it's obvious my lady's not best pleased. As for Nan, she can barely be still, running to the window every few seconds. "I fear he may have met with an accident."

Lady Dorothy don't think so. "More likely, Monsieur Gore is a poor timekeeper." She'd been looking forward to that journey to Sheen with young Jack.

We are about to go in for supper when we hear the knocking. Nan is up in a trice and, making to the door, almost collides with the maid. She hands my lady a note. As she reads it, Lady Dorothy sighs. This proves too much for Nan. "Please, Mama – is it or is it not from Monsieur Gore?"

"It seems your tutor is indisposed and down with a cold. He will not, after all, be travelling with us to Sheen."

Nan's not done gazing out the coach since we set forth. Not like her to be so silent. My lady notes it too. "What must we do to cheer you, Nan?"

Nan's quick to respond, and with some spirit. "You may invite Monsieur Gore to stay at the house when we are next in London, Mama."

My lady's not much taken with this idea. "I believe he has his own comfortable quarters."

"No, Mama. His lodgings are damp. He has told me so. And that is why he has a cold."

Me and Lady Dorothy exchange glances, and to lighten the moment, I say, "I'm thinking them French are a sight less hardy than English people." And Nan gives me a glare would freeze the duck pond.

Soon as we arrive at Sheen, she makes straight for her chamber. And despite my lady's bidding, Nan don't come down for supper. Sir William's quick to voice concern. "I noted her pallor as she stepped from the coach. What think you, Dorothy?"

My lady assures him all is down to fatigue. "The journey tired her. We'll let her rest."

This serves to exasperate Miss Martha. "For goodness' sake! All can see what's wrong with the girl. It's a problem of the heart."

That sets young Jack off. "I knew it – Nan is pining for her Frenchman!"

It takes Sir William a full moment to digest these words. He has a good swig of his wine before reminding us that Nan is not yet fourteen years. "She's but a child and too young to be troubled with affairs of the heart. I will not counsel it!"

Miss Martha says, "It seems, William, you have forgotten what it is to know passion!"

Sir William looks properly put out, and as if he would turn this whole conversation, comments on the succulence of the cherries. "What think you of these? Picked fresh from our own gardens."

Miss Martha won't be stopped. "I well recall you pining after the Countess of Sunderland, William. You were barely able to eat!"

If I didn't know my place, I'd like to remind this table of a certain other gentlewoman who caused Sir William to lose his appetite!

Sir William says: "I shall think again on this tutor." And he heaves hisself up from table, leaning on his chair for support.

Jack's looking spruce in his new frock coat, which he's forever tweaking at. Don't know who's more a-jitter, him or Lady Dorothy. "Don't forget, Jack," she says, "never turn your back in His Majesty's presence, and only speak when you are spoken to."

Sir William says, "It seems I am to be upstaged by my two fashionable companions!" Looking at Miss Martha, I must admit she's dressed and quaffed a treat, though it's hardly surprising, considering all the preening went on this morning.

We're all in the yard to wave them off, young Nan jousting Jack till the last. "'Tis as well you keep your gloves on, else His Majesty may note your bitten-down nails!" She's back to her old self, and none is more pleased than Sir William, who clasps her to him afore boarding the coach.

"Soon, Di, I'll have the pleasure of presenting *you* at Court!"

There's no sign of Nan at breakfast. I'll warrant it's down to my lady's words last night: "There are any number of suitable tutors here in England," she told her. Seems that Frenchman is to be sent packing.

I take a tray up to Nan's chamber. "Come now," I says. "Still abed on a good autumn morning?" And Nan do rouse herself to eat a little and ask the hour. "Time enough you were downstairs." She complains of a cold. "I expect that Frenchman passed it to you," I says. And at the mention of him, young Nan turns into her pillow and quietly weeps.

My lady says: "If she's not better tomorrow, we shall send for the doctor." Seems that cold tincture hasn't done its duty. But then I never did put much faith in medicines.

"I'm thinking it could be fresh air Miss Nan's in need of. She's scarce been out the house these past days."

"Jane, you are right. Tell the cook to prepare Diana's favourites. Tomorrow, we'll picnic by the river."

Seems the Almighty has other plans. I'm just up from my bed when the heavens open. Down in the kitchens, the cook's her usual cheerful self. "That's today washed out then." She adds it's not the day for picnics anyways. "What with Miss Diana taken bad in the night." I'm on my feet in a trice and asking after my lady. "She'll be still with her," the cook tells me. "A groom's rode off to fetch the doctor."

"It's merely a cold, is it not, Jane?"

"Yes, my lady, and a body's oft a tad feverish with a cold. That medic will put it right."

First thing he asks is if young Nan has suffered recent upset. And when my lady tells about that tutor, the old man's soon chuckling into his beard. "Young ladies can be very vulnerable to a grieving heart. There's nothing more likely to unbalance the humours." He's a tall, straight-backed person, and after a good exam of the patient, he's quick to reassure us. "No more than a little distemper of the blood. Keep her well wrapped. A broth laced with brandy and a posset of barley and lemon balm should see a speedy recovery."

He's proved wrong on that. By supper, Nan's still tossing. Me and my lady sit close by her, but try as we might, we're not able to tempt her with vittles. Lady Dorothy's not taken much nourishment herself. I fear she's given over to dark thoughts. She won't leave Nan's side. So when she bids me send for the medic again, I do so without a word, even though I'm thinking said person won't be best pleased at this hour.

The gentleman's a tad weary but not put out so's you'd notice. He's surprised, though, to note Nan still feverish. "We will try a purge and some dandelion cordial," he says. Poor Nan weeps as he applies the enema. And no coaxing can get her to take the cordial. The medic turns to Lady Dorothy. "I fear we must compel her." And weeping herself, my lady bids me help hold down her daughter's arms whilst the gentleman, pushing a spoon in Nan's mouth, forces it open and pours the cordial down her throat. Nan don't offer much resistance. But it's not a moment afore she vomits the mixture up.

My lady says: "I'll send for my husband. Jane, tell the grooms."

"The fever has to take its course, Lady Temple." The medic gathers up his tools and potions. "I'm convinced this is only a disorder of the humours. We'll wait until morning. If deemed necessary, I shall apply the leeches. Keep the room as dark as you are able." This purge is as brutal as any I've known. Even though we've changed the bed sheets several times, Nan's still not done. Finally, spent with voiding, and curled like a babe, she drifts off.

I've not seen leeches applied before, and it's a most dreadful thing. He takes them from a little jar in his bag, six of them, and gently lifting Nan's night robe, attaches the writhing creatures to her chest and thighs and belly. My lady turns to the window. She can't watch. I do, though, not able to take my eyes from this horror. "You may hold her hand," the medic says. My lady turns back then, and I note her nails dug right into the palm of her own hand, almost drawing blood. She gently strokes her daughter's hair, murmuring to her throughout.

I'd my doubts such torture would work, but within two hours it do seem the fever has dropped, and Nan finally lays more peaceful. After a short sleep, she's sitting up and taking the broth prepared by my lady. "I do believe we've seen the worst," I say. I bid Lady Dorothy take some broth too. "Else that medic will be back to tend you!"

Though still weak and of no good pallor, Nan remains peaceful all morning, and when Sir William rushes through the door, all dishevelled from his ride, I'm the one able to give reassurance. Clinging to him, my lady is too overcome to speak. Sir William is not alone. He's come with one of the King's own physicians. "When he knew the reason for my hasty departure, His Majesty insisted," he tells us. And this gentleman is eminent indeed, robed almost as grandly as the King himself. I'm thinking young Nan is in good enough hands now.

The cook always steps up for an important guest, and after a good meal of fowl and fresh-caught salmon, and a long rest, this gentleman goes straight to work, demanding to know what cures have been applied. He's scathing enough when we recite them. "Many of my colleagues are still caught in the old ways," he tells us.

Rousing Nan from her rest, he proceeds to listen and tap and look into her eyes and down her throat, telling us our own medic was right about one thing: "The blood is heated and unbalanced. I shall apply another purge and let more blood, but in the new approved way I oft use at Court."

My lady is ready to object, but Sir William silences her. "Hush, my love. Let the gentleman do what he must." He bids my lady wait outside. "You stay, Jane, in case Sir Thomas has need of assistance."

I'm reassured this physician has a Sir to his name. I'm not eased, though, when he opens his bag and takes out a small knife with a fierce-looking blade. Nan is quiet, holding her father's hand and gazing up at him. I'm thinking she's too wearied to object. Though when this medic makes three quick cuts in the middle of her arm to open the vein, Nan do cry out. As for Sir William, he looks as though that knife went clean through his heart.

It's all over in a trice, though the blood did spurt, and I'm glad my lady were spared that. When Sir William bids her back in the room, she goes straight to Nan. Having caught a good cup of blood, the physician applies a poultice of vinegar and mint to the wound, and Nan sets up a low moaning. "Can't you see how it pains her!" my lady says. "Is it not possible to give some relief?"

"The arm will sting for a while, but it will cleanse the wound well," Sir Thomas tells her. "Now I shall apply another purge."

Sir William insists my lady retire. "I will sit with her through the night," he tells her, though he hisself looks that wearied.

"Reckon that physician knew a trick or two," I say. And I'm off to the kitchens in search of replenishment for my lady. When I come back in her chamber, she's on her knees. "I fear the Lord is preparing to take my child,' she says, "and it's more than I can bear. Pray with me, Jane, please." I'm happy to oblige.

We're both up at the crack of dawn. Making our way to Nan's chamber, I say, "Chances are, she'll be wanting a good breakfast this morning."

Sir William has pulled back the curtains to let in a chink of watery light. He's seated in the corner, his face grey. As she approaches the bed, my lady cries out. Nan has kicked back the covers. Red pustules cover her neck and the lower part of her face. "It's the pox." Sir William's voice is flat. "How is it none could tell?"

Seems like we've been living in our sleep these past days. Three medics called, but none able to ease things. Nan's too weak to fight. Seems there's nought to do but watch and pray she rallies. By time Jack and Miss Martha return from London, Nan can't even cry out, so swollen is her throat with pustules. I take it on myself to keep young Jack from the patient, knowing my lady would surely die if he succumbed too. But there's no keeping Miss Martha out of the sick chamber. "My brother will have need of me," she says. None, for the moment, has need of me. It's an agony not to be in that chamber but only right the family should be private there. My lady has scarce left it. And when she do go to and fro the kitchens, she's blank-faced and dry-eyed. Not so Sir William. You can hear his weeping clear through Nan's door. It's truly a terrible sound.

I can't help but berate the Lord for this weight of misfortune, even though I know full well it's wicked to do so. It's not the first time I've been given to question God when all seems so unjust.

Jack and I sit in the kitchens, both of us not talking. Looking at him, I see a small boy again, biting his nails down to the quick. I fetch some leftovers from the hearth and bid him eat, but Jack hardly touches them. "She will recover, won't she, Jane?"

And I hear myself say: "Yes, if it be God's will."

I'm surely glad of the distraction when young Bridget comes in. She takes one look at us and fetches three tankards of the master's best wine. "None will object at such a time," she says. If this were a day like any other, I'd be questioning how a servant gained access to a master's private wine cabinet. Truth be, though, this good ruby wine is indeed restoring. Bridget takes my hand on one side and Jack's on the other. There's nought to do save pray.

We're still sat there when Sir William comes to the kitchens, ghost-like in his crumpled white shirt. "She's bleeding from the throat," he says. "There's no longer hope."

Me and Bridget hang the black cloth through the house. Despite the gloom of it, I'm glad of the task, pushing my mind to getting each piece just right. Not dwelling on anything else.

The coffin is of no great size; young Nan were small for her age. Come summer, she would have been fourteen years.

William has gone. He travelled with Martha and Jack to London. He could find no peace here. His study is strewn with books and papers. There is an air of neglect. I sit at the desk and stare at the painting placed above the mantel. A gift for William's birthday. The paint is scarce dry. I should like to reach out and touch her; the soft blue folds of her gown; her reddish-brown curls, so like my mother's; the small hands, reaching towards me. But Nan's face is unsmiling, sullen at being compelled to be still. I try, but fail, to picture her as she truly was, dancing through life. Would that a painting might blot out the present and restore my memories.

On the desk, set apart from the debris, is the letter I helped her write.

To: Sir William Temple, English Embassy, The Hague
From: 81 Pall Mall, August 1679

Papa, I have delayed writing to you till I could tell you I'd received all my fine things, which I have just now done. And I think I will never stop giving you thanks for them; they have made me so very happy. Everybody that comes to my new chamber admires them above all things (though not as much as I think they deserve). And now if Papa was here too, I should think myself a perfect pope!

Monsieur Gore and I rub along mightily well, and he makes me believe I shall come to something at last — that is if he stays, which I don't doubt he will, because all the fair ladies will petition for him!

We are rid of the workmen now, and this house is ready to entertain you when you come, and when nobody shall be gladder to see you than
Your own most obedient and affectionate daughter,

Diana Temple

Across the top, William has written: '*My Di*'.

I hold the letter close to my face. I can almost smell the warmth of her young body. *Oh, my daughter, My precious, beautiful girl.*

SHEEN AND PALL MALL

1680

At the top of Richmond Hill, I bid the coachman halt so Jane and I might look down at the river below. From here, you can clearly see the damage wrought by the flood. Mud and debris cover the fields and gardens close to the water. A group of herdsmen, boot-deep in filth, are attempting to free a cow, sucked into the mud. The animal suddenly deems it best to lie down. When the earth gives way beneath you, the line of least resistance often seems the only choice. "The poor thing's probably bagged up with milk," Jane says. "It's a wonder it don't drop dead from the stink must be in them parts." To add to the dilemma, the swirling grey river continues to threaten the banks, as if any moment it might choose to resume its onslaught. Jane says, "I fear you are cold, my lady. Shall we not make for Sheen?"

"I would take a moment." I recall the last time we witnessed such a flood, years ago at my aunt's house in Chelsea. "Do you remember, Jane? We were about to sail for the Isle of Wight."

"I surely do," Jane says. "And if you'll pardon my saying so, it were a journey of some adventure."

With my brother abroad, there were always adventures. I say, "I so oft think on Robin."

And Jane, no doubt mindful of my recent bouts of melancholy, brusquely changes the subject. "That was the moment we fell in with Sir William," she says. "And if I may say so, 'twas the beginning of all happiness."

The beginning of all happiness. Dear Jane. Of course I remember that moment. What was it he said? *Your lips are like cherries!* Yes, that was it – or some such foolishness. We were both set laughing. It was his laugh that first caught me. That, and the way a strand of hair had fallen loose about his forehead. Later, the brush of his fingers on my neck. Those small unguarded moments which draw us close to another, and are sadly lost and forgotten along the way. How can we know how providence will change us? Though I see little change in Jane. Her open face may be less smooth, but sitting opposite me, I still see the pretty, guileless girl she once was. Life has set Jane apart and spared her the turmoil it so often inflicts. But then, I note her wince with pain as she moves slightly in her seat, and I am forced to acknowledge the truth: Jane and I are two elderly women suffering all the discomforts of age. I bid the coachman make haste for Sheen.

Now and then, when things are quiet, I do still think on Robin. It's his jesting I'm apt to recall, and that quick way of turning any gloomy subject to fun and setting all laughing despite themselves. I truly thought the Lord had freed me of that other painful memory. But when that name is mentioned unexpected, I can still find myself back in the dark place. There's things you can never make tidy and right, however hard a body tries. Best not think on what can't be changed.

If it were down to me, I'd rather gone straight to Sheen and no stopping, but Lady Dorothy were set on this detour. She's properly fascinated by a flood, long as she can view it from a distance. Even so, I noted her fright when the waters below got choppy. Not so me. I'm always pleased to see nature at its wildest. I'd enjoy it more, though, if my knees weren't suffering. It's a fair journey from Pall Mall to Sheen, and it surely can be brutal. There don't seem no good way of seating myself. My lady's concerned. "When we are there, Jane, you must rest." She's always quick to sense another's discomfort.

Once in the house, my aches are quick forgot. The hall is brimfull with garlands of holly and rosemary and other pleasing greenery, with Sir William and Miss Martha waiting on us by a roaring fire. There's even a Yule log at the ready, and big bowls of apples set out on the tables and stuck with cloves like we had at home when I was a girl. Seems we're set to celebrate Christmas in style again. It do raise my spirits. I'm about to comment on the festive feel when I note my lady's paleness. Miss Martha notes it too. "The Lord wouldn't want us to grieve through another Yuletide, Dorothy," she says. And Sir William steps up smartly and takes my lady's hands.

"My dear, come to the fire." He agrees with his sister. "Martha is right. It's time to celebrate a little. Jack will be here tomorrow."

Leaning across to warm her hands, my lady says: "Yes. We must be cheerful this year." She says it, but her eyes don't show it. As for me, I can't help thinking the Lord will find it pleasing indeed to note the house so bright and welcoming again. I'd wager Lady Dorothy could well get her spirits back once Jack's come from France.

Down in the kitchens, even the cook seems to have caught the mood. Rosy as an apple, and with sleeves rolled to the elbow, she's showing a wench how to stuff and truss the birds ready for tomorrow's roasting. As ever, though, she's soon given over to grumbling: "I can't be expected to keep my eye everywhere. If them birds spoil, there'll be no Christmas cheer for you." I'm thinking even without the capons, there be a goodly enough spread. Big jars of boiled calves' tongues – which I do admit I'm partial to – collars of brawn, pork pies, a hock of ham and a huge plum and beef pottage, all set ready on the tables amongst a goodly display of sweet pies and cakes.

It's a sight different than last year. With such a weight of sadness still on us, Christmas was gloomy indeed. My lady took to her chamber throughout, whilst the rest of us ate and drank with scarce much relish. In the evening, we gathered in the hall and listened in silence as the wassailing lads struck up their singing outside. But there was no inviting them in to warm themselves and sample the mince pies. No. However sweet their song, we kept that door tight shut.

Seems this cook's got more on her mind than tomorrow's dinner. Soon as the maids are out of earshot, she can't wait to tell: "That Bridget's gone and got herself wed."

"Well!" I says, and I wait for more. But seems the cook don't know much.

"Some's saying he's a gentleman," she tells me. "I've my doubts as to that."

I'm left curious all afternoon. It's not easy, hunting down Bridget. She's ever at Miss Martha's beck and call. I'm going down to supper when I finally catch her, and then only passing on the stairs. "You're a dark one, getting wed like that and not telling no one."

Bridget's quick to fault me. "You and Lady Dorothy are seldom here to tell. It weren't no secret. Sir William gave his blessing, and Lady Giffard attended me at Richmond."

"But who is he then, this Mr Johnson?" I says. "I never did hear you speak of him."

"He's a merchant, Jane. So he's oft voyaging." And Bridget don't offer one more word.

My lady too is curious. At table, she asks Miss Martha straight: "What is known of this groom?"

It's Sir William who answers: "Methinks he's a good enough cove." Turns out said gentleman deals in fabrics.

Lady Dorothy would have more. "But shall you then lose Bridget, Martha?"

Her sister looks properly put out. "Mr Johnson will spend much time voyaging. Bridget shall continue as my companion. Is that not so, William?"

And Sir William confirms it. "Bridget shall stay. It is settled." He's quick to change the subject, bidding us all raise our goblets to the season and give thanks to the Lord for his continued mercy and grace. Seems there's to be no more talk of Bridget and her nuptials.

I'm still dwelling on these doings when I'm abed. A gentleman merchant wedded to one of our maids! Don't think I've ever known the like. It does irk me, Miss Martha referring to Bridget as her 'companion'. By my book, that's surely stretching the truth. Bridget certainly don't enjoy the sort of position I'm favoured with. She don't have a pleasing chamber to herself. And she's never invited to eat with the family like I am. And far as I know, she's still called upon to help round the house and do the sort of menial tasks none would ask of me. No. What Bridget is, is a maid! She's right about one thing, though: me and Lady Dorothy are more oft in Pall Mall than home here at Sheen. Not surprising we don't know what's what. When young Nan was taken, my lady could scarce be coaxed from this house. Was as if staying put might bring that angel back. Now when we come, seems it just serves to remind her of that terrible time. She never do go near Nan's chamber.

I'm down in the kitchens helping turn the jellies from their moulds when Jack arrives. Being still clad in my morning gown and cap, I think best not up and greet him. So it's not till we're all gathered in the hall before church I finally sees him. And I'm so taken with surprise, all I can manage is "Oh!" Jack's sporting a careful moustache and a full set of whiskers.

"What think you, Jane?" says Sir William. "Has my son come home in manly fashion?"

And finding my voice, I say: "Indeed he has, sir. I scarce recognise him." Course, it's not true. Above the beard, Jack's face is little altered. That same pale, soft, young lad's look and hooded eyes, so like his mother's. But where hers are steady and sure, his are as anxious and uncertain as ever they were. As for manly, I'm thinking Jack looks like a boy who's found some play-box whiskers and stuck them on his face. My heart goes out to him.

There's enough of us for Christmas dinner to warrant setting up two extra tables. Everyone squeezes in, from Sir William's steward and grooms, spruce in their church-going jackets, to the chambermaids and the young 'in-between' wench. Squashed next to one of the garden lads, she looks too overcome to say boo to a goose. There's more moving-up once the dishes are served and cook and the kitchen wenches join the feasting.

I'm surely thankful there's plenty of space at our table, where I'm seated next to the parson, whom I've no wish to press against. And I'm more than a bit surprised to find myself opposite Bridget. I've never known that young maid seated at top table, not once! She surely do seem at ease, chatting to the magistrate in very forward fashion. Not that he's paying attention. No. The magistrate's eyes are all for his new wife, who a person might be pardoned for thinking were his daughter. She's pretty enough, but with one of those mouths that tells of petulance. Still, at least the magistrate's not checking his timepiece every few minutes.

What with the cook's good fare and the wine flowing and everyone in party mood, I'm silently thanking the Lord for this merry day. I'm relieved to see my lady in better colour, and absorbed in quiet conversation with Jack, their heads close together. All's well till the parson takes the opportunity to remind us all of our wickedness. "To God be the praise," he says. "And may he grant this day be one of humility and atonement for our sins."

Sir William says: "Come, sir, surely the Lord would want us to be joyful in celebrating Yuletide?"

Helping himself to more pork pie, the parson don't think so. "Indeed, it's the very moment to don hair shirts and reflect on our misdemeanours. I pray the Lord deliver us all from our gross evil."

This certainly puts a damper on jolly conversation. My lady says, "We are surely flawed, sir, but evil? What of children?"

The parson don't hesitate. "We are all born corrupt, Lady Temple. But in his great mercy and love, the Lord strives to sanctify the young and make them his own."

This don't satisfy my lady. "Are we really to believe," she says, "that the suffering of children is part of God's 'great mercy and love'?" None speak. Some at the other tables also cease their talk and look towards us.

The parson, unused, I'm supposing, to finding himself crossed, looks properly mortified. "My good Lady Temple, though we lament the death of a child, it's often indeed a great mercy sent to us by God." I note Jack put his hand on his mother's arm, and I'm surely wishing someone would put a hand over this parson's mouth. My lady just stares at him coldly. She don't say one more word.

It's Miss Martha who breaks the silence, telling the table at large how she and Bridget are about to set off for Ireland to finally inspect them properties her father left. "My brother insists on accompanying us," she says. "William thinks two women travelling alone cannot be trusted to avoid adventures!" There's general laughing all round. 'Cept for Lady Dorothy. I'm thinking she's as surprised as me at news of this outing.

The rest of the meal is taken with money talk. The parson's eager to recount his success at ale-brewing. "As you know, my living is small indeed. If it weren't for the generous patronage of parishioners such as Sir William... I have prayed the Lord make me more profitable, and the Lord has heard me. My ale, if I may say so, is finding great favour with the villagers!" The magistrate says he knows well how poor a man's purse can be, since his own stipend is lowly indeed. By the richly-robed look of his wife, I'd wager most of it goes on her person.

There's cards in the evening, and dancing for those who can still move, with fiddle tunes provided by one of the grooms. By the time we're making for our beds, Sir William's French clock has already chimed midnight. On the stairs, I hear my lady say, "I too should like to see Ireland again." And in the light of the candles, I note Bridget glance across at Miss Martha.

Sir William don't encourage the idea. "This is not the opportune moment, my love. My father's estate is sorry indeed and in need of much attention."

Seems this journey to Ireland is to be sooner than anticipated. "We must sail whilst the winds favour us," Sir William says at breakfast. "We shall leave tomorrow."

As I watch Bridget try to stuff everything in one trunk, I'm set wondering on the amount of things Miss Martha always seems to require. "Anyone would think you were going for a year," I say.

"It will likely be a long visit, Jane."

I can't help but voice my thoughts: "What if your Mr Johnson should come and find you gone like that?"

And Bridget says, "He understands my duties to Lady Giffard."

"Oh," I say, "that's good then." I'm thinking said gentleman must be tolerant indeed, him being newlywed and all. I'm dwelling on that look passed between Bridget and Miss Martha on the stairs. Could be, seeing as how she now has her own properties there, Miss Martha intends to settle back in Ireland and take Bridget with her. To my mind, that would be no bad thing.

But where would that leave Mr Johnson?

We've no sooner seen the party off, when Jack, too, announces his departure. Lady Dorothy's stricken. "Must you go so soon? Surely the embassy can spare you a few more days!" As Jack explains it, it's not his lowly clerk's work taking him back to Paris but the plight of friends.

"They are Huguenots," he tells us. "No doubt you've heard of their difficulties, amongst much, the threats to close their schools. Some dread they shall have to convert to the Papist faith for the sake of their children. One friend has seen her family home looted."

My lady declares herself ignorant of such happenings. "But what can you do, Jack?" And I note the question worries her, as do Jack's reply:

"I am pledged to help them leave, Mama."

Lady Dorothy don't mince words: "If you care for your friends, I beg you not get involved! Enlist the help of someone higher in the embassy."

Jack is properly set back. "I thought you, of all people, would understand my need to stand against such injustice!"

"And I do, Jack! You see suffering and your heart wants to put an end to it," my lady says. "I had a brother, before you were born, who I believe to have paid for such sentiments with his life." I'm fair flummoxed by this turn of conversation. My lady's always claimed Robin's drowning were an accident! Of a sudden, I feel the need to sit, and make to leave. But Lady Dorothy insists I stay put. "There's nothing you should not hear, Jane," she says. And softening her tone, she tells Jack, "I'll speak to your father. He may see fit to mention the matter to the King."

Later, she tells me, though fearful, she's proud of Jack's Christian thinking. For myself, I find it wrong-headed. 'Specially if Jack's set on these persons coming to England. You can hardly move in London now for all the foreigners, often strange-looking indeed, and many not speaking one word of English. But Jack's his mother's son – too soft-hearted by far.

Lady Dorothy remains standing in the driveway, long after she's waved the coach off. She bids me ready us for our own journey. "We will leave within the hour and return to London. I shall not stay here alone."

Good thing we high-tailed it back to Pall Mall. Soon as we're in the house, one of the maids hands my lady an elegant-looking note, the reading of which puts her in a proper dither. Seems the Princess of Orange is staying next door at the palace. "She wishes to visit tomorrow, Jane."

We're still in a state come morning, what with the baker not bringing them special cream buns my lady ordered and her fretting over the coldness of the house. I'm quick to reassure her. "The fires shall all be lit, my lady." I'm thinking since she's coming from The Hague, chances are this princess will be well used to a bit of chilliness.

We're spruced and gathered in the hall in good time, servants too. My lady's insisted all shall be present. First thing I note is how tall this princess is, a good head or more than Lady Dorothy. And graceful too, with a stance straight as an arrow. But even as I concentrate on making my curtsy, I can't stop my mind jumping to that short prince, and what an unusual-looking couple they must surely make. Though she don't stand on ceremony, clasping my lady's hands and calling her 'dear Lady Temple', the princess is a lot more regal-seeming than that spouse of hers, coming with a good entourage of maids and two splendidly clad footmen.

They've been closeted in the withdrawing room an hour or more, and my lady has twice called for fresh beverage. Not so the Princess's footmen, who've refused all offers of something for themselves in the kitchens. They prefer to stay, soldier-like, in the hall. They're so nose-in-the-air, they've got the rest of us creeping like mice. I'm thinking life in the palace must be dreary indeed. The ladies finally emerge, the princess much animated and Lady Dorothy looking well at ease.

I've been wondering all day if she'll confide something of this visit. I know better than to ask. I pride myself I've been long enough with Lady Dorothy to know when to await her counsel. It's not until we're alone in her chamber after supper, she finally tells me straight what a delightful person this princess has become. "I found her much changed, Jane." And after a moment's pondering, she says, "It's interesting, is it not, that a marriage begun so indifferently should in time blossom?" I'm searching my mind for a just reply, when she adds, "I believe the Princess Mary had low expectations, so any happiness must be threefold. Maybe that's the secret."

Finding what I trust are apt words, I say, "All seems to the good, my lady. The Princess certainly do seem lively."

"Yes, Jane, she's lively indeed." I am taken aback when my lady adds, "Her liveliness puts me in mind of my own Diana." It's the first time since those dreadful days I've heard my lady mention her daughter's name.

It was with difficulty I finally persuaded her to be seated. She preferred to dart about the room, inspecting every object in a manner some might deem unseemly. It was impossible, though, not to be touched by her girlish enthusiasm. "You've such a delightful house, Lady Temple. All is warm and hospitable."

Once seated, she talked easily and freely, and I was startled at the intimacy of her conversation. She mentioned her husband frequently. It's obvious she holds him in high regard. "I hope I'm proving a good wife. I've always had little understanding of the world of men." This said with great frankness. "My sister and I grew up without their company. Our household was ever full of governesses and ladies of the Court. We seldom saw our father." She recounted her trepidation when sailing to Holland with a man she scarcely knew. I told her word had reached us of her popularity amongst the Dutch. For a moment, I thought she might rise and throw her arms about me, so great was her pleasure at this.

"The Prince has been wonderful patient with me," she said. "And I think the people now accept me. I believe there is trust between us." I told her how precious I think that is.

She offered condolences for the loss of my daughter, as many others have done. But her words were so sincere, for a moment I had to turn away. She asked if I were aware of her own loss. "I'd come little more than four months, Lady Temple, but I felt the baby quicken, I'm sure of it." As she talked, I sensed the depth of her attachment to this unborn child, and I told her how well I understood.

When she made to leave, she took my hand. "I will always remember your words regarding the Prince before our marriage," she said. "I now know how honest and wise they were." At the door, she turned to me. "It's impossible to love him more than I do. I pray he doesn't love me less."

Jane says, "They're a long time in Ireland, my lady." I tell her the work is proving more complex than expected. William and

Martha have been gone more than three months. The letter I just received is like the others he has written: full of idle workmen and irksome delays. They tell me nothing. How does he fare? Is he anxious to be home? Does he, I wonder, sometimes miss my company? I doubt it. This past year, I've stayed mostly here in London. I've lived in a wilderness, unable to share my grief or lighten the sorrow of those I care for. William and I have yet to speak of the loss of our daughter. It lies between us like a stone. It's fallen to Martha to provide the succour and strength I lack. As always, she has risen to the occasion.

I take out the other letter I received this morning.

The Hague, April 6, 1681

My dear Lady Temple,

I have writ you two letters today, but will send only one, lest you deem me too tiresome a friend. I hope I might call you friend after our meeting, which I think on with such pleasure.

I am alone here, the Prince being abroad again, and most probably at battle. Every day, I wish for a letter to tell me he is safe. Most of my ladies-in-waiting are now returned to England and are replaced by Dutch women I scarce know. Though I would never question the Prince's wishes in this matter, I am very in need of friendship. How I wish you were still here in The Hague where I might see you. But I've resolved to put melancholy aside and tell you of the possibility I am again with child. I'll not talk of it, lest it should bring ill luck. But please pray for me, Lady Temple. The prayers of such a good woman will surely bode well with our Lord. And send me a note soon as you are able, telling me how things fare with you. With my deepest and most true regard,

Mary Princess of Orange

A letter from William and a letter from the Princess. One revealing nothing, the other almost too much.

If this absence from William has taught me one thing, it is the necessity for change. Beginning with myself. The anxiety. The endless doubt. The lack of trust in anything I once held true. It must cease. It's as if my mind were constantly readying itself for some fresh horror, so that forewarned, the blow might be less brutal. What I know for sure is that William is a good man. Despite the human flaws that afflict us all, he is an honourable man. I must, *will*, prise open my heart. We can no longer be as we once were – the pain of life has seared us too deeply. But we can go forward together, holding each other close with care and understanding.

They are to come at last. Jane and I arrived at Sheen two days past to prepare. I am determined all shall be as welcoming as it was at Christmas. Jane confirms all his favourite dishes are prepared. "I'd warrant the cook is well pleased, my lady, even if she shows the opposite. She likes a bit of busyness."

"Yes," I say, "things are quiet with Sir William gone." Without him, this house seems empty and too large. When William is here, his very presence fills every room.

It's almost midnight when we hear the horses. Despite the hour, I bid Jane rouse the servants. I wait at the door. Only the relentless rain prevents me from greeting them in the driveway. I barely recognise the figures alighting from the first coach, so tightly are their cloaks drawn about them. Once inside, William and Martha push back their hoods. It's plain to see their fatigue. William comes to me immediately, my hands in his, his face against mine. "Dearest, I am so glad to be home." At any other moment, my heart would be singing at William's obvious joy at this reunion. But my attention is fixed on Martha and her pale, drawn face.

"Martha, dear, come to the fire. You must take some nourishment." From behind her, I hear a sound. Bridget stands a little apart, swamped in a cloak too large for her. But the faint familiar sound comes not from Bridget, but from somewhere inside the cloak.

William says, "Ah, yes. There was no end to our adventures. Bridget even took the opportunity to give birth. Pull back your cloak, Bridget, and introduce Lady Dorothy to little Esther Johnson."

Such a tiny creature, no bigger than a man's hand. I longed to hold her, to feel that little body warm against my heart. That was my first thought, blotting out all misgivings. Those came later, lying alone in this bed.

I remember Aunt Gargrave saying it was always best to kneel when praying. That the beseeching position intensified the prayer. I've not prayed for so long, heavy with certainty that God has turned his back. The wooden floor is rough and cold against my night robe.

Dear Lord. I know myself to be unworthy of your blessed grace, but I beg you to cleanse my spirit and remove from me this burden of disquiet and uncertainty that threatens to engulf me. Help me recognise the good that is surely everywhere, and to cast out unkindly thoughts that sees untruth and falseness where there is none.

The cook says: "Well, that explains it, don't it!" And though I keep my counsel, I'm bound to agree. It surely answers for them quick nuptials. The cook pours two tankards of ale. She's ready for a good tattle. "Do you suppose Lady Giffard knew then?" she asks. "Afore they set off for Ireland?"

I remember that look on the stairs. But it's not my place to discuss our gentry with this cook. I comment instead on the babe. "It's a pretty thing. I never did see such a mass of dark hair on such a little mite."

"Thank the Lord it don't look like its mother," the cook says. And I picture Bridget with her large, flat face and flaxen hair. I'm thinking this Mr Johnson must be handsome indeed. The cook is prattling on: "I always knew that wench were no better than she ought," she says, "and there's still not hide nor hair of Mr Johnson, whoever he be." I make to leave. But she must have one more word: "If it were down to me, I'd turn her out in the lane, brat and all."

I'm thinking Sir William's too much of a gentleman for that. Still, I'm taken aback to find Bridget given the chamber next to Miss Martha's own. By my book, that's taking charity a tad too far.

Turns out it's as well Bridget is on hand, Miss Martha being so poorly and all. Seems that journey fair done for her. It's not like Miss Martha to stay abed once the sun's up, but for the past two days, that's where she's been. My lady's concerned. I hear her ask Sir William should she send for the medic. He don't encourage it. "The crossing was rough. Methinks she will recover soon enough." Meanwhile, Bridget administers to the patient, even though it's plain she's spent from lack of sleep herself.

I never do hear that baby cry, though. I mention as much to my lady. "Seems good as gold." My lady just nods. She's said little enough about these doings. Chances are she's properly shocked at such goings-on. My lady's a stickler for propriety.

Soon as she's up and about, Miss Martha's back to her old self and quick to issue orders. "Jane," she says, "fetch my wrap and day book from my chamber." In the absence of Bridget, I've little choice. That tone still irks. Never so much as an if-you-please! I'm more than a bit heated when I pass Bridget's room. The door is wide open and she's seated on a stool in a state of some dishevel, with the babe in her arms. I make to pull the door closed.

"Come, Jane," she says, "come and see the babe. Is it not the most beautiful child in the world?" Despite her tiredness, there's a rosy glow to Bridget that I've oft noted in young mothers. All I can see is a little dark head, and tiny fingers moving on Bridget's bosom. Then, of a sudden, it moves its head, opens its eyes and stares up at its mother.

Going downstairs, I'm musing on that scene. It must be wonderful indeed to hold your own babe close like that. To feel its little fingers warm on your skin and that special gaze, just for you.

I've almost reached the hall before I realise I've forgot Miss Martha's things.

SHEEN

1685

It's a kitchen wench back from the village who brings the news. "They're saying the King's dead." Just after, a boatman crosses the river with a note for Sir William confirming it. There's been prayers published all week, so we knew to expect the worst. Still, Sir William's properly shaken: "I walked with His Majesty in the palace gardens not ten days ago," he tells us. He's hard-pressed to know why all them doctors failed to restore the King. "Surely with their great knowledge, something could have been done?" He orders the black bunting put about the house. Then he gathers all the servants in the hall. He tells us it were something called *apoplexy*, whatever that is. Some starts weeping, including the cook, who, far as I know, never had one good word to say about the King. Sir William says, "King Charles is dead. Long live King James." From what I've overheard this day, seems he's got his doubts. "Most know this new sovereign to embrace the papist faith," I hear him tell my lady. "I fear he may alienate the people. It's a pity, with all his children, King Charles had no legitimate heir save his brother."

Down in the kitchens, things are gloomy indeed, with the wenches snivelling and the cook so overcome she's in need of wine. Luckily, she's had her fill by time Sir William walks in. He tells us even on this sad day, the Lord will be expecting all to fulfil their duties. "We can best please God by going about our daily tasks." He recites the *Family Prayer*. No matter how many times I hear it, it always wells me up: all as it should be and everyone in their place. That's surely an apt message on such a day.

It's calmer in the kitchens after them words. 'Cept for little Hetty, who is running about in her usual high-spirit way. Bridget never does nought to upbraid her. Still, I'm bound to admit a softness for Hetty. She's a child with the sweetest of tempers. Sir William scoops her up and sits hisself down on a bench with Hetty on his knee. "Well now, Esther," he says, "I'll tell you a story." And he proceeds to relate a child's tale about a king ruling over a great island, till: "*one day the Lord feels lonely and takes that king to heaven to sit by his side.*" I'm doubting this last bit, considering all that's been said about King Charles. But little Hetty's well pleased. She reaches up and touches Sir William's face. I oft think Hetty has eased his pain for losing Nan.

We're scarce recovering from this gloomy day when there's a letter further churns the spirits. I'm sitting in the window seat sewing with my lady when Sir William brings it in. "I'll not permit this!" he says, and whilst my lady reads it, he's set pacing the room. "Jack shall not marry without my permission!" I'm quick enough to make myself scarce. Young Jack to wed? Far as I know, there's been no talk of a Paris wooing.

Down in the kitchens, word's already spreading and there's plenty of loose tongues. "Let's pray the Lord it's not some Frenchie," the cook says. "That would really bring on the master's gout."

It's not till Bridget comes down that we're treated to some proper news. I'm supposing she got it from Miss Martha. "It's one of them Huguenot persons Mr Jack's so fond of," she tells us. "'Tis said she's an heiress, so I don't know why the master's complaining."

At supper, Sir William's still fretting. But since nobody asks me to leave, I sit quiet, not knowing what else to do. "Our late majesty made contact several months ago, so this family will surely be granted permission to leave," Sir William says. "Jack has no need to wed the daughter to get them here."

Miss Martha agrees with her brother. "To marry someone of whom we know nothing is foolhardy indeed," she says, adding it would be most disquieting to have a Frenchwoman in the family.

Acting the peacemaker, my lady points out that Jack seems to harbour a real attachment for said person. "He would not give his feelings lightly. She must be a girl of good qualities."

Sir William swears it shan't happen. "I myself shall have a hand in choosing Jack's wife." I glance at Lady Dorothy, wondering if she too is dwelling on all them letters Sir William once wrote to her. Don't think old Sir John had much say in that story.

Sir William hardly eats, but I'd wager he's drunk more than his usual portion of wine. When he tries to get up from his chair, he plonks back down double-quick. A servant is summoned to offer an arm, but Sir William shakes it off. As he heaves hisself up again, he says: "I shall write to the embassy tonight and leave for Paris by the week's end."

That cook foretold right: Sir William's not suffered an attack of gout for more than a year, and now of a sudden, it's come on thick. One minute to bed with mantle packed tidy, this morning unable to move his foot. Two medics have failed to ease the pain, no matter how many poultices are applied. My lady says not much chance of journeying to Paris now. "He'll need patience and abstinence," she tells me. I'm thinking Sir William might manage the last, but as for patience, he's never had much of that.

I'm soon proved right. After one day abed, Sir William's talking about curing himself. A page rushes down to the kitchens. "He's set on doing it the Indian way." We all know what that means: searching out that strange moss he brought from Holland with an aroma worse than horse dung. My lady and Miss Martha are against it. Lady Dorothy don't trust the source and Miss Martha can't stomach the smell. But there's no deterring Sir William. I'm surely glad not to be in that chamber when it's applied. I've seen it done before, spreading that foreign stuff onto his major toe and then setting it alight till it burns clear through to the skin. Our noses are soon affronted with the vile stink and Sir William hollers from here to Christendom when the scorching reaches the flesh. Next moment, he's shouting for as much garlic as can be found to put on the wound.

It's been four days of torture for Sir William, with umpteen applications of the 'moxa' as he calls it. And it's been dreary indeed for the rest of us, all tiptoeing about the place, propping doors open to let the smell out and air in. So, this morning, there's rejoicing indeed when Sir William manages to put foot to ground without much pain. By dinner, he's hobbling about, and more than a mite smug. "I'll nail my flag to the Eastern ways any time," he tells us. And he praises the Lord he's able to make for Paris on the morrow.

Turns out the Lord has other plans. My lady's down in the hall when the carrier comes. Soon as she sees that letter from Paris, she's jittery. "We'll wait till after breakfast to give it him," she says. I make for the kitchens and take my vittles there. But even though we're a good distance from the hall, we can still hear Sir William roar. Seems young Jack's already wed. And to a woman called Marie, with one of them foreign family names no one can pronounce!

SHEEN AND LONDON

Marie du Plessis Rambouillet. Marie Temple. Dark hair and the fairest complexion. A beautiful young woman indeed. Stepping from the coach, Jack can barely contain himself. "Mama, allow me to introduce my wife! When you know her, you will love her as much as I do." I'm hopeful this shall be true. Marie has arrived with her mother, a woman of noble bearing, and more than a little austere. Before we are inside, she is enquiring of the house.

"Does it have a chapel, Lady Temple, where we might give thanks to the Lord for delivering us from the jaws of evil?"

"Why is it necessary," Martha asks, "for that girl to carry her prayer book wherever she treads?"

"She's endured much for her faith, Martha," I say. "We must make allowance."

William is less tolerant. "They find fault with everything. Even the privy closet doesn't suit." All, it seems, is rough and crude after Paris. "I pray the Lord," William says, "that Jack has not let his conscience mar his future happiness."

At supper, as Jack helps his wife be seated, I note his hand gently brush against her hair, whilst her own hand reaches up to touch his arm.

It's love, William. Can you not recognise it? Do you not remember?

We walk in the gardens. "At least here we can avoid the mother's incessant chatter," William says. "What think you, Dorothy? Would they be more content at Pall Mall?"

Pall Mall. The house I never wanted has become a haven. A place to find tranquillity without the disturbance of memory. Should I forfeit my own peace so that William might have his? I say, "it's early days. Perhaps it's best for now they settle here at Sheen."

Whilst Marie and her mother are at prayer, I'm finally able to steal a moment with Jack. "Is she not lovely, Mama?" he says. "And of the sweetest nature." The words are warmly spoken, but with some uncertainty.

"She's lovely indeed, and obviously devout and good. And you, Jack? Are you happy?"

Save for two things, he tells me. "I feel a great lack of gainful employment. I'm now of an age to think seriously on a life of diplomacy. Papa could so easily smooth the way if he chose."

I remind him of his father's distrust of that profession. "He would say it's a world peopled with those muttering falsehoods to those who know them to be so."

Jack is unimpressed: "He is still oft at Court, so let him find me a position where I may be of assistance to the new monarch." He rises and goes to the hearth, leaning his hand against the mantle, his restless stance so like Robin's. "Marie is accustomed to the very best finery," he tells me. "Her family has lost much. I want to relieve their plight; to cover her with all that is as beautiful as she."

I am careful not to smile. "Jack, dear, I think it is best you talk to your father."

That, says Jack, is the other difficulty. "He's barely spoken a dozen words to me since we arrived. I know he disapproves of this marriage. I fear he has lost all regard for me." I'm hard-pressed not to reveal what William is engaged in this very moment: struggling to finish the memoirs that shall be dedicated to this son he loves so dearly.

In truth, William has taken to spending much time in his study, often not joining us for dinner or supper. "His work is in great demand," I tell Madam du Plessis, by way of an excuse. "He is frequently approached for his essays."

"A true believer, as Sir William must surely be, should always dine with his family," she replies. "Christ showed us the way when he broke bread with his own family of followers."

Marie says: "Your father does indeed spend much time alone with his work, Jacques. He is missing the novelty of this fairly good English meal."

"Not always alone," Madame du Plessis says. "That child is often with him. Is she a relation, Lady Temple? She surely bears resemblance to the family."

Fortunately, I don't have need to reply. Martha is quick to jump in. "She is the daughter of my companion, Madame. My brother is fond of the company of children."

Madame du Plessis thinks Esther precocious. "It's always good that a child should know its place. Especially the child of a servant." I note she and her daughter exchange glances.

I've a sudden overwhelming desire to get away from this house.

When my mother was declining, Aunt Gargrave said: *She has chosen to die*. With the end of the war, many were unable to face the new disturbing truth of things. They lived in a constant state of denial. *They chose to languish rather than live*. However disturbing, the truth must be faced and uncertainty banished. Whilst Jane packs the mantles, I go in search of Esther. I find her alone in the kitchens, sitting on the floor, playing with a wooden spinning top attached to a string. I'm struck by her determined little face, her complete concentration. Each time the top slows, she pulls on the string at just the right second to set it spinning again. She's found a way to prolong the game. Standing in the shadows, I study her lustrous dark curls, the expressive blue eyes beneath thick brows, that familiar curve to her cheek. Stepping towards her, I say: "Will you walk with me, Esther?" And with that trust children ever have, she rises and places her tiny hand in mine. "Where shall we go?" I ask her.

She doesn't hesitate. "Horsies," she whispers. We walk towards the stables. It's the grayling pony that draws her. I lift her in my arms so she might caress its neck and face. Stretching out her long fingers, she does so, in that intuitive, careful manner I've so often seen William employ.

Amidst a tumult of feelings, there's a sense of relief – as if a weight is suddenly lifted. There is no doubt. This is William's child.

He does not wish me to return to London. "I'll come back soon," I say. "There are matters need attending."

William presses me. "What things? Stay until we may travel up together." Of course, I know why he is so solicitous. When I don't answer, he finally says: "Dearest, please don't leave me here with that wretched Frenchwoman. The girl I can tolerate – just. But her mother!"

Sitting by my window overlooking the King's gardens, I watch the breeze play amidst the rose bushes. Unlike his brother, King James is scarcely here, preferring the palace at Whitehall. This view I once despised, I've now come to love for its silence and beauty. The abundance of flowers and greenery it brings forth each season reminds me of the gardens at Chicksands when I was a child. A place of escape when all was turmoil.

When you finally cease denying a truth that changes the world, how should you deal with it? A man seduces a serving woman; a child is born. Hardly a novel story. Does love enter into it? I picture Bridget's plain, strangely incurious face, her voluptuous young body. I've always believed passion to be a madness, with scant connection to love.

I recall that moment in Brussels when I pushed open a door closed to me; another door, pushed open in The Hague. I remember my confusion. I'm surprised how calmly I face this present situation. There's no anger. Only sadness for what once was and is now forever lost.

A note has come from the Princess of Orange. As always, it lacks discretion:

> *My dear Friend,*
> *I've not had word from you for near one month. I've great need of your good counsel. The Hague is full of rumours regarding the situation at Whitehall. The Prince tells me Parliament is unpleased at what they see as my father, the King's tolerance for the Catholic believers he gathers about him. The Prince thinks England will not stand for it. And my sister, Anne, writes that our stepmother the Queen becomes arrogant and treats all 'cept her Catholic priests and handmaids with haughty disdain. Remembering what passed with my grandfather, I fear for the future of the crown.*
>
> *Your ever-faithful friend, Mary, Princess of Orange*

I have, of course, heard these rumours. But it's hard to fathom the country would once again set its sights against a king. Surely not even Parliament would have the stomach for that. But I understand the Princess's anxiety. As the King's presumptive heir, she has much to disquiet her. She is young, and despite her happiness in marriage, somewhat alone. If she were closer, I might be of help.

Jane is as surprised as I am. "I'll go to the kitchens and make sure we have a good load of supplies," she says. Neither of us knew William and Martha were planning to join us here at Pall Mall. Bridget, of course, is with them. In the hall, she steps forward and bobs. "I hope you are well, your ladyship." I nod. I cannot bear to look at her. Thank God the child is left at Sheen.

William whispers to me: "You have been gone too long." And whilst Martha and Bridget retire to unpack the mantles, he takes my hand and leads me to the withdrawing room. "Sheen has become more than a little crowded." He talks of taking a lease on Moor Park, a country house near Guildford. "Martha and I will inspect it before returning home," he tells me. "It might be prudent to retire there in the summer months. The air is said to be beneficial for the gout." Things at Sheen must be sorry indeed.

At supper, I ask for news of Jack. According to Martha, he is akin to a lovesick errand boy: "He runs to and fro for those Frenchwomen without letting Marie move a finger."

William says: "Tell Dorothy of your suspicions, Martha."

"It is obvious the girl is *enceinte*. What else would explain Jack's hen-clucking and her constant taking to her bed?"

Marie with child? It is possible. And my child perhaps set to become a father, with all the joy and heartache that will bring.

He comes to me in the night, placing the candle on the bedside table. I believe this is the first time William and I have lain together in this bed. My immediate reaction is to recoil. But in the candlelight I see his face. And what I see is defeat. I move across the bed to make room for him. There's a strangeness, an inability to find the right positions for our bodies. But once we are entwined, his arm about me, my head resting in the curve of his neck, the awkwardness passes. "Dearest," he says. "I fear I've not always been the very best of husbands." I move my hand to rest in his. "You surely are aware," he says, "of my very deep regard for you." And just for this moment, I know it to be true. He draws me closer. We do not caress. We are at peace.

SHEEN AND PALL MALL

1688–1699

Two little girls at play in the gardens, sweet as pie. Still can't put my mind to it: young Jack a father. Not that he's not properly devoted. No. What gives me pause is Jack's still more lad than man. Result being, he gives too much rein by far to them Frenchwomen. My lady is worried. "He'll not find his feet without satisfying employment." She's said it more than once. We all know Jack's been badgering Sir William to grant him some good introduction.

That wife would be pleased enough to see him somewhere foreign. "Jacques should follow you, Sir William, and become an ambassador," she says at supper. "Then we might travel and not always needs be in this Sheen weather."

Sir William don't agree. "That's not a life to suit an honest Englishman," he says. "And I will tell you, Marie, if Jack were to follow me, you would end at The Hague, where the weather is a deal worse than Sheen."

The mother asks: "Why should we not hope for Spain?" And Sir William takes a good swig of his wine. Young Jack says nothing. It's my lady who comes forth. Glancing at him, she says: "I'm sure my son will find the right path for himself."

But this Madame must have the last word: "Jacques should always put Marie and the children first," she says. "That is the Huguenot way."

Once the Frenchwomen are off to pray and Jack out of earshot, Miss Martha makes no bones about her opinions. "Living with those two, I can well see why England has been so oft at war with France," she says.

Sir William do love those granddaughters, though. Always in the gardens inventing games for them. That's when he's here. Which is not regular. He's taken to passing weeks at that gloomy Moor Park. My lady finds the journeying too taxing, and even Miss Martha don't like going. But thanks to young Hetty, Sir William's seldom there alone. Now that his eyes are grown rheumy, he's glad enough to have Hetty along reading to him. "Esther's a clever child with her books," he tells us.

My lady and I are preparing to return to Pall Mall when she glances out her chamber window. "It's a boatman, Jane, coming across the river." We both stand and watch, caught by the speed at which the man wields his oars.

It's not a ten-minute later when Sir William calls us to the withdrawing room. "The King has been forced to leave London," he tells us. "The crown has been offered to his daughter, the Princess of Orange." We've known for some time there was a load of trouble brewing. But nobody thought the King would be cast out, let alone that young daughter brought to the throne. "He's wrought this on himself," Sir William says. "The King has never ceased to flaunt his papist leanings."

Miss Martha thinks the birth of the King's new son may have stirred the pot. "There's talk the Queen was never with child. That the babe was brought to the palace by stealth and baptised Catholic," she says.

Sir William don't give much heed to this. "What is truth or not is no matter now," he says, looking over the letter. "Prince William has already arrived in London. The dye is cast." Seems this princess were set on refusing the throne lest it were given joint with her husband, which strikes me as being very proper.

Sir William bids us pack the mantles. "We shall all return to London," he says.

This don't suit the Madame. "Marie and I will have no part in these English upheavals," she says. "We shall remain here with the children." Strikes me there's relief all round. Even Jack don't disagree, telling his wife 'tis best she stays put during this turmoil. Her mother says: "Jacques, make sure you push yourself forward with these new monarchs."

We surely find Pall Mall in a mess of disarray. Household chores neglected whilst everyone prattles in the kitchens on the state of things. I soon have a word. "If this house isn't shipshape within the hour, I'll know the reason why – and don't let me catch you skiving." Given this family's standing with the Prince of Orange, I'm thinking we might well expect a visit.

Seems the whole town's a-jitter with rumours. First, we hear the King is dead, then that he's up and taken refuge in Ireland. There's tales too, of goings-on at Whitehall, 'specially since the Princess arrived. Some are saying she's a deal too delighted with her new position than is seemly. Miss Martha heard tell the Princess insists on sleeping in her stepmother's bed. My lady don't believe a word. "I know from her letters the anguish the Princess of Orange must feel at her father's plight," she says.

Since the crowning's set to take place in the early morn, we were up past midnight preparing. But tired as I am, watching my lady board the coach for the Abbey, I'm thinking all that sewing were worthwhile. She looks a proper picture in that same blue dress she wore to Court a few years back. Though since she's grown thinner, it's took a good load of last-minute stitching. Standing in the door, Jack says, "Mama will cast this new queen in the shade."

Miss Martha's quick to get her twopenny in: "It's strange how my sister is drawn to old clothes." Since she's not invited to the ceremony, Miss Martha's mood is sour indeed. We all gasp, though, when Sir William makes his way down the stairs. It's the first time he's worn his trimmed cape, and I'm bound to say it becomes him a treat. Sir William's still a handsome man, despite his ailments.

The bells have been ringing all day, and the air is so full of the stink of bonfires, we're quick to place lavender about the house. But there's a good festive feel abroad. Even Miss Martha has caught the mood, challenging Jack to a race in the lane, accompanied by shrieks and shouts. I'm surely glad those Frenchwomen aren't here to witness such undignified behaviour.

When my lady and Sir William return, we're waiting in the hall – servants and all. None wants to miss the day's news. First thing Sir William does is take off his cape. "This thing weighs a ton."

My lady says it were nowhere near as heavy as the Queen's crown. "It was enormous, and bejewelled with every precious stone. The poor woman was so exhausted, she could scarce rise from the throne." The new king was said to have coughed his way through the entire proceedings.

Sir William tells the oddity of Dutch soldiers guarding the couple throughout, and how it was novel indeed to see two monarchs crowned at one time. "So begins the reign of William and Mary," he says. "Though obviously the governing will be entirely in William's hands." I'm thinking strange how kings come and go and are quick forgot. This is the fourth in my own life, and one who through God's good grace I've been honoured to be in the company of. I wish my father had known that. But I can't help thinking of this queen's own poor father, dead – or somewhere in the wilds of Ireland. Don't know which is worse.

Jack would make haste for Sheen, but he's loath to leave before his father is summoned to the palace, which is expected. "Please, Papa, speak to the King on my behalf." Seems Jack's asked that at every meal.

All feel sure Sir William will be offered a high post just like he were with the last kings. "I shall, of course, refuse," he says at table. "Nothing would induce me to play those palace games again."

When the letter finally comes, Jack is down in the hall before the carrier is out the door. But Sir William is promising nothing. "We must wait on the King's plans for our country," he tells Jack. If you ask me, he's thinking Jack's not ready for big responsibilities. Soon as he opens the letter, Sir William stops short. Turns out it's not for him. The letter is from the Queen. It's Lady Dorothy invited to the palace.

I'm shown to her private sitting rooms. It's the first time I've been in this part of the palace. As with the other rooms, these are dark and claustrophobic. When she enters, I've barely dropped my curtsy before she's apologising. "I trust you will forgive me for greeting you thus," she says. "This whole place is gloomy indeed. We shall not remain here. The Prince's – the King's – health will not endure it. We'll go where there is good air. Words cannot convey how glad I am you've come, Lady Dorothy." This all delivered so fast, her words trip over one another. "Are you well? Let us sit. There must be no ceremony."

Once seated, there's a moment of awkward silence. To relieve it, I say, "Your Majesty is looking well indeed." These are words I immediately regret. The Queen is pale, and since I last saw her she has gained considerable weight. Her face has become jowly, giving her an appearance beyond her years.

She senses my falseness: "Lady Dorothy, I've many around me who would flatter and speak untruth, let us promise never to do so. I'm so in need of a true friend who might be trusted to speak plainly."

For the next hour, she talks. She tells me of the sadness of her lost babies. "I fear I shall never now bear him the son he longs for." She confides her deep guilt regarding the fate of her father. "I've been so torn, Lady Dorothy. My first duties must be to God and my husband. Tell me you agree with that." I assure her I do. "I'm aware my father can never forgive this treachery," she says. And her face is overcome with misery.

Carefully, I say, "This is nothing you could change." I tell her England would never endure what was perceived as a return to Papism. "This is not of your doing. Your task now is to be the very best queen you are able, and for you and the King to support each other through the journey."

"I'm not sure I'm ready for this journey, and if indeed I can be a good queen. I am unsure I know how to be a queen at all." She rises and comes next to me, taking my hand.

"You are honest and true and you can and will be strong," I say. "Look how you captivated Holland. What more could England wish for?" And feeling it necessary, I add: "Please tell me how I would help you."

"You will help me by being my friend," she says. "But unlike a true friend, I've talked only of myself. You've told me nothing of how things fare with you."

"I have a son. His desire is to be of service to Your Majesties." Have I spoken too rashly? It seems not.

"I will mention it to my husband immediately," she says. "The Prince – the King, that is – is always amenable to my suggestions. And we shall meet again soon, Lady Dorothy." As I am about to leave, she says, "My mother died when I was but nine years. I still think of her every day. I've never found anyone I could confide in so completely."

Back at Pall Mall, I am relieved to see a letter finally come for William. He asks little about my audience with the Queen, his mind fixed on his own with the King tomorrow. "What think you, Dorothy?" he says. "I fear it will be Secretary of State again. How many times may I refuse?"

I tell him what he would hear: "As many times as it takes to remain away from Whitehall. You've your writing and gardens, which you have oft said are your true passions." It seems this entire day I'm called on to reassure.

Preparing for the night, I confide to Jane some of what has passed. "I'm fearful for the Queen, but with the Lord's good grace, she shall rise to this. I believe her to possess inner strength as yet untapped."

"Yes, my lady. But it's of no great matter, is it? That Dutch husband of hers will see England good."

"She's the King's daughter, Jane. The rightful heir to his throne."

And Jane says: "But it's lucky we've still got a king, isn't it? I'm thinking England always fares best under a good, strong man."

Of a sudden, I am bone-weary.

"He's not easily taken on this mantle," William tells us. "The King confided his first thought was to stay in Holland in the countryside he loves." A reaction, William says, he can well understand. "But he is still the serious, thoughtful man I remember, and I believe him to be of great resolve. He shall, I think, do well leading our country."

Martha says: "Let us pray he becomes more king-like in the process."

At table, William tells, at some length, of the King's urging him to accept the secretaryship. "I needed all my power not to be persuaded," he says. "I've agreed instead to always offer advice on any matter he wishes." Though disappointed, His Majesty was, apparently, grateful. Not one word is said regarding the Queen.

After we've eaten, William ushers me to the withdrawing room. "I would talk with you alone." Once I'm seated, he paces the room. "A strange thing," he says. "Quite without my asking, the King brought up the subject of Jack. He asked if my son might be interested in a position of some merit. I began to wonder if His Majesty has psychic powers!" My surprise is genuine, that this new queen, with all the duties thrust on her, should be so quick to keep her promise. But I'm startled when William tells me the position available. Minister for War, although an honour, is not what I had in mind. William, too, is unsure. "I fear this would be beyond Jack's capabilities." After a moment's thought, he adds, "I shall refuse on his behalf."

I say, "Such opportunities are rare. There may not be another. Perhaps we should not stand in the way of his ambition." William says he will sleep on't.

Jack's enthusiastic reaction dispels all misgivings, although he's immediately worried he shall disappoint the King. "If you remain true to yourself, then nought can go ill," I tell him.

William adds the necessity of not appearing doubtful before His Majesty. "He lacks confidence himself. He will not appreciate the lack of it in others."

In the night, I awake to footsteps passing my chamber. I put on my robe and go quietly down the stairs. I find Jack alone in the kitchens, staring down at the tankard of wine before him. "You'll need a clear head when you meet with His Majesty," I say.

He doesn't look up. "What I need is Marie with me," he says. "She must come immediately."

"Would it not be best to begin this new position free of distraction?"

"We are as one, Mama. Marie is as necessary to me as breathing."

When William hears the Frenchwomen are to come, he makes plans to return to Sheen. "This house is too cramped," he says. "Jack has need of space to prepare himself." When I agree, he adds: "Best you stay here, Dorothy. Marie and her mother know little of London. They will need guidance. Jane shall stay with you."

The Queen wishes me to accompany her on an outing. Cooped up here with Marie and her mother, I am more than anxious to oblige.

I spread my gowns across the bed and onto the chairs. None is suitable. I call for Jane. She comes slowly. I know her joints pain her, but there is no time to offer sympathy.

"The Queen wishes to visit a coffee house. We must go incognito. It's important we are not recognised." Avoiding the disapproval I know Jane's face will convey, I busy myself examining the frayed hem of a cloak. "I would borrow your plain muslin morning gown, Jane."

"I fear it will be too large, my lady."

This is so like Jane, ever ready to put forth obstacles. I'll not be crossed in this. "The Queen wishes this outing, and I would have your grey gown, and there's an end to it."

Jane says: "Yes, Lady Dorothy." She doesn't move. She can be so infuriating.

"I know you think this foolhardy, so why not say, rather than adopting this unpleasant stiffness?"

"Well, my lady, then, yes, I do think such an outing might be a tad unwise. If you were recognised, or if the Queen should be found out – well, respectable ladies don't visit such places. I think Sir William would be the first to say such an idea was foolhardy indeed."

I turn to face her, angry she should speak to me thus, and I am taken aback to see how pale she is and how she clasps at her hip, which is obviously paining her. "Jane, please sit whilst we talk. Tomorrow, we shall send for the medic to attend you. There must be some ease he can offer."

"I think it's you who are unwell, my lady. I fear you may have fever."

"Bring me your grey morning gown, Jane. And please do it now."

The Queen has chosen this venue because she can come unrecognised. It's unlikely we shall encounter someone from the Court amongst the fruit sellers and street performers of Covent Garden. As arranged, a small dark coach, curtains drawn, waits in the shadow of the church. As I walk across the square towards it, I have a moment of uncertainty. Surely this disreputable spot is no place for a queen. Then I recall my words to Jane this morning: *I'm beginning to believe that every moment of our lives needs to be fully lived.* How few times have I practised that!

The coachman jumps down and opens the door. Inside the cramped coach, I can only manage a cursory bob. The Queen bids me sit next to her. She's wearing a black gown with high white collar. She might be a dissenter or a nun. My gown, as Jane predicted, hangs on me like a sack. We both sport tight-fitting white caps covering our hair. We look at each other and are reduced to laughter. What a relief to laugh.

"You do know, Your Majesty, how risky is this outing? If you were to be recognised…"

The Queen replies she has always wished to see the inside of these establishments men flock to. "The King believes they are hot beds of sedition," she says. "We shall see."

Amongst the long tables already filled, there are two or three smaller ones. I proffer our coin for entrance and we settle in a corner with a good view of the entire room. We are the only women present. But though conversation halts for a moment, except for an occasional hostile glance, we soon become almost invisible. The stench of smoke and coffee beans pervades, taking me back to my previous visit to such a place. I recall the downy fair hair on the arms of a Breton girl, William's appraising glance.

The atmosphere is, if anything, more vibrant than that long-ago morning. Here, all appear to know one another. They shout across the tables. "What news from France?" "Tripoli?" Pamphlets are passed and commented on.

Someone remarks on a critique of Mr Congreve's new play: "The man who wrote this is a dolt, with little or no humour."

We watch, fascinated, as a churchman enters. The Queen whispers: "I do believe he's a gaitered bishop!"

Seating himself at the middle table, the cleric asks the room at large if they have heard the latest concerning Hoare's Bank. "The deuce is," he says, "they are moving from Shoreditch to Fleet Street. I have my every penny there. What can it mean?" From the irreverent replies he receives, it dawns on us this is not a churchman at all, but an actor from one of the nearby playhouses.

Someone says: "This is what you do. You go down to Drury

Lane. Beg them to take you for a proper wage and stack your money beneath your bed." There's a great whoop, followed by applause.

The Queen is enchanted. "What freedom they have to say anything and everything! If I were at Kensington now, I'd be sitting working my needlepoint, surrounded by women I have no wish to talk with."

A sullen young girl finally comes to our table. Two minutes ago, she was laughing and jesting with the men. I say to the Queen, "In my experience, coffee is akin to drinking syrupy soot!" We order two cups of chocolate. I tell the Queen of the Women's Petition Against Coffee. "It states the drink makes men as fruitless as the sandy deserts."

The Queen is amused, but it gives her pause. "When marriage is barren, women usually blame themselves – is that not so, Lady Dorothy? How interesting they are now pointing the finger at their husbands."

I draw the Queen's attention to an old man sitting across the room, staring at us. "He's done nothing else these past several moments." The man finally drops his gaze and engages in conversation with a group of younger men, who hang on his every word.

"Maybe he thinks we are actresses," the Queen whispers, and we laugh. Then, peering again at the man, she says: "I do believe it's Mr Dryden, who once read his poetry at the palace."

My first thought is, I shall write to William. He will be interested to know I was in the company of such a great literary figure. My next is one of panic. "We must leave immediately, Your Majesty. It seems he may have recognised you."

I wait to see her safely into the carriage. As it is about to pull away, she glances at me with a look of utter fear. "I pray I'm not undone, Lady Dorothy." Then, staring resolutely ahead, she adds: "But I will not let it spoil my one afternoon of freedom."

I bid my coachman drive through the park and then around by Somerset House. I would not go home yet – I feel such sharp dismay. The Queen is right to be anxious. She is young and inexperienced. This outing was rash. I should never have encouraged it.

Jane comes directly to my chamber to help free me of this ugly gown. "You gave good counsel," I tell her. "This outing was a grave error." Jane says nothing, engages in unpinning my hair from the cap and brushing it out. "I'll go to Sheen tomorrow," I say. "No good can come of staying here. You must stay in my place, Jane, and make sure all goes well with the women." As always, Jane is eager to oblige.

When I tell him I am to leave, Jack is barely listening. With Marie at his side, he is poring over his first assignment for the King. My son no longer needs me. This is how it has to be.

The weather at Sheen is temperate. I take long walks beside the river. I've little heart to be in the house. Martha passes the time sketching or playing the virginals. Bridget is ever with her, as is the child.

As for William, when he's not confined to his study, he's greeting the friends and officials who daily appear. They come to plead that he change his mind regarding the secretaryship. "They accuse me of depriving the country of my talents and experience," he tells me. "It's a quandary, Dorothy!" I can see this to be true. William is a man who in worldly dealings is ever principled and trustworthy. But I cannot help but think he enjoys this predicament. A momentary return to front of stage.

We have been several weeks without news, but this morning there is a note from Jack. It's not a happy one.

> *Sir,*
> *My first assignment for His Majesty has not proceeded well. I fear he'll not honour me with another. With too little knowledge, I pressed the King to trust a man who,*

though I could not see it, was completely unworthy. On my recommendations, His Majesty sent one General Hamilton to Ireland to persuade doubters there to support the new crown. To my shame, Hamilton has now joined forces with those who strive to restore King James. I fear, Father, I must offer His Majesty my resignation. I've failed all – not only my king and country, but those I hold dear, you and Mama and my beloved Marie, whose devastation at my weakness and ineptitude is more than I can bear.

We sit in silence. It is William who breaks it. "I should never have agreed to this posting. I let myself be persuaded against all good judgement."

If he is blaming me, he is right, and he does not know how deeply I blame myself. "Surely," I say, "the King will forgive one error that could not have been easily foreseen?"

Martha agrees. "Jack is too sensitive," she says. "He must learn to be more robust."

"I advised him it would take months of watching and learning before wading into the fray," William says. "Jack was too anxious to make his mark." He declares he will return to Pall Mall. "I shall persuade him to stay the course."

Martha prefers to remain at Sheen. "Jack would not want us all fussing. He will soon see it is a matter of little consequence." Knowing my son, I doubt this.

We are about to board the coach when I see a boat newly moored on the river beyond the gardens. "This will delay our departure," William says. And I realise his failing eyes cannot identify the man hurrying across the lawns. When I tell him it's the magistrate, his irritation grows. "What the devil can the man want?"

As he approaches, it's clear the magistrate is perturbed, his usual careful appearance dishevelled. Of a sudden, I remember another man hurrying across another lawn: Will Hammer coming with news of my dying father. I've a moment of deep foreboding. I should like to board the coach now and set off at once, before this man reaches us.

The magistrate is short of breath and pale. He is clasping some letters. One bears the royal seal. "Good day, Sir William. Before you read these, I fear I must relate the terrible news I bring."

Sensing his unease, William says, "'Tis best we go inside." And the magistrate follows us back into the house.

I've passed this courthouse many a time; it's less than a five-minute from Pall Mall. But I never thought to see the inside of it. I'm surely glad Sir William's here, though I can't fathom how he endures it. At least my lady's spared. Too poorly to leave Sheen, that's what Sir William told us. The Lord only knows what I'll say when I do see her. I'm thinking there's no words will comfort my lady.

When the coroner questions me, I say it were a day like any other. "Just your usual Thursday, sir, Your Honour. Least till after dinner." I can tell by his face this is not the answer the man would have. "All engaged in preparing food and eating it," I add. I'm that nervous.

The coroner is impatient. "But it's true, Mistress Wright, is it not, you were the last person of the household to see the deceased alive?" *The deceased.* Oh, dear Lord! Jack, what have you done? How could you do such a wicked thing? Try as I may, I can't stop the tears. I glance across at Sir William. He too looks overcome.

The coroner says, "Try to collect yourself, Mistress Wright. Tell me how you found this gentleman's mood."

"He were very quiet, sir. He didn't say much."

"Walk with me to the river, Jane," he'd said. "I have some errand." As we walked, only once did he speak: "I've failed in everything, Jane."

Thinking this just Jack's usual uncertainty, I'd said: "Well, by my book, there's never much sense crying over spilt milk 'cos there's always more in the milk churn." My very words. And they were brusque indeed, seeing as my mind was occupied with them Frenchwomen, and my misery at being left closeted with them at Pall Mall. If only I'd known how troubled he were.

There'd been a load of harsh words, most coming from that Madame. Jack were not himself for several days, but I'd no knowledge why, seeing I wasn't invited to sit at table. The Madame made that very clear. "We have things to discuss, Jane, that are private to the family." I remember wishing I'd not given her the satisfaction of seeing me redden.

Next up from me is a waterman, jumpy as an eel. Seems it's not the first time he's been before this coroner, who says, "So, Mr Cody, here we are again."

The waterman clears his throat. "Well, Your Honour, I still don't rightly know how it happened. One minute, he were seated behind me, quiet, like the woman said, but very gentlemanly." He waits for the coroner to say something, and when he don't, this waterman stumbles on. "Well, as Your Honour knows, them waters up near the Tower can get that choppy, and the winds were making an awful din. I thought I heard him say something, but no chance to turn around."

Here he stops again, and the coroner says, "Continue, Mr Cody."

I note the waterman run his tongue over his dry mouth. "Well then, it weren't till Bert Crowe pulled his boat alongside that I knew of the awful thing. 'Young gentleman jumped in,' Bert told me. I turned then all right, and saw the note left on the bench with one shilling atop. We turned our boats and started pushing our oars down far as we could to try to reach him but weren't no good. Bert said he'd seen him come up once with hands in the air as if he would save himself. Then he were lost. I'm thinking he must have put stones in his pockets, Your Honour." The coroner takes a moment to consult his papers. Then, he bids one of his clerks read the message Jack left in the boat:

My folly in undertaking what I was not able to perform has done the King and kingdom a great deal of prejudice. I wish him all happiness, and abler servants than John Temple.

Whilst I'm mulling this over, the coroner declares, "It's clear John Temple committed self-murder."

Terrible words indeed.

And worse to come. Some common person shouts: "Crime! A sinful crime!"

And Sir William, seated a few chairs from me, turns and says, "A man may surely dispose of himself as he pleases!" Them words ring out. And even though I know he don't mean them, as his friends usher Sir William from the courthouse, I can't help but feel shame on his behalf.

Walking back to Pall Mall, the cold bites through me. There's ice on the trees and on the windows of the coaches. As I pass a hat shop, a man's intent on clearing the frost from his doorway. He bids me good evening. "I 'spect the river will soon ice over," he says. "With luck, we'll have one of them Frost Fairs."

A Frost Fair, with its booths and food stalls set upon the river and fiddle-playing jollity and laughter, and people dancing on the ice. And all the while, somewhere beneath it, young Jack lying dead.

MOOR PARK, SURREY

Her Most Gracious Majesty, Queen Mary
March 1689

Your Majesty,

I give you most heartfelt thanks for your kind letter and the sense you have of my affliction, which truly is very great.

I strive to reflect that since this unbearable burden is laid upon me by the hand of Almighty, and surely merciful, God, who always proportions his punishments to the support he offers, I may hope to bear it as I ought. Especially as one who has in many ways deserved it.

The strange times I have lived through might well have taught me what this world is. But it seems I've needed closer examples of the uncertainty of all human blessings. That having no tie left in this world, I may better prepare myself to leave it.

Your Majesty's most humble and obedient servant,

Dorothy, Lady Temple

The hand of a merciful God? Where is my son's body that I might mourn him? Oh, dear Lord, I pray the end came quickly. Did he strive to save himself? Like Robin, Jack is an able swimmer. Is there not the smallest hope he had strength enough to swim further upstream, and even now may be safe, too defeated and shamed to yet return home? *Dear God, I pray you forgive my unworthiness and lift this pain from me. I beg you, Lord, allow me some small hope.*

From the bureau, I take out the letter brought by the magistrate:

> *'Tis not out of any dissatisfaction from my family, from whom I have received infinitely more friendship and kindness than I deserve, that I do myself this violence. I've long tired of the burden of this life, and it has now become insupportable. From my father and mother, I've had all the marks of tenderness in the world. And I wish them, and all my friends, health and happiness and forgetfulness of me. The only regret I leave the world with, is that I shall leave my family for some time (I hope but a little time) in affliction.*

I read the words over and over, the better to acknowledge the truth. No. There is not the slightest hope. Like Robin, my beloved son lies dead beneath the waters. I turn the letter over. On the back, I write: '*Child's letter he wrote before he killed himself*'.

I've seldom known such a silent journey. Even Miss Martha don't say two words. Just sits staring out at the countryside, which is bleak indeed. My lady's asleep in the corner. Her first proper rest these several weeks. It was Sir William's decision we should retire to Moor Park. "I shall no longer remain at Sheen," he told us. And in a trice, he'd upped and signed that house over to his daughter-in-law. I'm thinking it held a tad too many memories.

As we fetch up in the carriageway, I'm struck this is a rum sort of place to recover our spirits. The outside is dreary enough, facing a thick wood and with a strange creeper invading the walls. But inside is even gloomier, with not one room, far as I can see, offering a tad of cheery light. If you ask me, we make a grim party, following Sir William through these chambers. He bids us look out the window at the wild and unkempt gardens. "I shall model it on the Dutch way," he says. "I will create something of beauty." I'm hard-pressed to credit how.

Since we've left the cook behind at Sheen, there's one been hired from a near village. She's so old, she can scarce lift a platter. I admit, though, once tasted, her beef pottage goes down a treat. Seems at least we're set to eat well. Which is all to the good, since there's not much else to cheer us at table. Sir William's always been the master of lively conversation, but only memorable thing I've heard him say of late is how much happier his life would have been had it ended at fifty.

"Shall we be returning to Pall Mall?" I ask my lady when we're stitching. And I've no words to describe the stricken look she gives.

"I've not one living child," she says. "I've a great need those left should stay close."

As I light the candle in this chilly chamber of mine, I'm wondering who lived in this place afore us. None that were happy, I'd wager. It's like this house got broken. I'm thinking maybe it's fitting, seeing this family too is properly broken.

As if things weren't bad enough, now there's this Mr Swift come. I still can't fathom it, seeing how Sir William already has an able secretary. And this new person isn't one to keep his opinions to himself or confine them to Sir William's study. No, Mr Swift booms them across the house, and not in a refined manner. Only person he's soft with is young Hetty, whose tutoring he's been put in charge of. "Esther don't become you," he tells her when we're all gathered in the hall for prayers. "It's too plain by far. I shall call you Stella, meaning star. That's much more fitting." Forward words indeed to deliver to a child of eight.

My lady says we must be tolerant. "You've a tendency, Jane, to judge too harshly. Mr Swift is young and has come straight from Ireland. Like many there, he is gifted with words. He'll be of immense help transcribing Sir William's essays."

I'm thinking it's one thing to be gifted with words and another to use them sourly. I'm supposing his being reared-up in Ireland makes Mr Swift so uncouth. Even Sir William's been quick to note his ill qualities. "Jonathan shall not sit at table with us," he says. Miss Martha declares she should indeed hope not.

"His manners are cruder than the horses'." Upshot is, Mr Swift's put to eat at the servants' table. And he's not one bit happy with it. Glancing at his stormy face after dinner, I'm thinking he looks ready to breathe fire. Still, I must admit he do seem to be tutoring Hetty well. When Sir William quizzes her, my head's reeling at young Hetty's knowledge of her verbs. Since that child were rendered fatherless, Sir William's taken a keen interest in Hetty's well-being. That's all to the good, seeing her own mother don't pay much heed. Bridget's happy enough to let others take the reins. In truth, that girl don't show a tad of feeling for anything. It's surely hard to think of her as widow woman. Since she got news of Mr Johnson perishing at sea, I've not seen one sign of grief. And since none of us were familiar with said gentleman, it seems poor Mr Johnson's not been mourned much at all.

I still remember the cook's raised eyebrows at Sheen when she told of his sad demise. "Another one lying with them fishes," she said. "If you want to believe that."

For all his shouting about the place, this Mr Swift don't seem hardy, always suffering attacks of unbalance and difficulties with his hearing. By my mark, he's poorly more than he's well. So when my lady bids me take some broth to his room, I can't rightly refuse. I knock twice, but he don't open the door. I'm finally forced to kick it with my foot. Mr Swift's up and doing and sitting at his desk, dressed, as usual, in cleric robes, though far as I know he's not been ordained. He do look pale, though. "Come now, sir," I say. "You need some vittles inside you."

He's his usual surly self. "It's more than vittles are needed in this house." He goes on to lash out at Sir William. "He sometimes remains silent and looks coldly for days, and I am driven mad, Jane, thinking of all the ways I might have slighted him." All this delivered in such uncertain schoolboy fashion, I can't help but feel for him. Seems he's not so cock-certain as he'd have us all believe.

I say, "Sir William's oft in pain. He suffers from many ailments." And I find myself patting Mr Swift on his shoulder. I harden up quick enough at his next words.

"Sir William is strong enough in some quarters, Jane." And I note the meanness in his voice. "I trust you've heard the rumours regarding Stella?"

"I don't hold with gossip, Mr Swift." And at this, I'm quick out the door.

Seeing as how I'm neither deaf nor blind, I was well aware of the sinful talk in those kitchens at Sheen. As my father used to say, "There's some folks gets through life casting aspersions on others." It surely made my blood boil to hear Sir William's good character and Christian motives so maligned. Now this Mr Swift brings these spiteful lies to Sir William's door, with no thought for that poor man's honour, let alone his present grief. I pray the Lord such untrue, wicked tattle never reaches my lady's ears.

Moor Park's a lot less roomy than Sheen. There's little chance of finding yourself alone, lest it's in your bed. That's why I've taken to a stroll in these gardens now and then. They're still a tad bleak, but I'm bound to admit Sir William's making good on his plans, drawing up an enormous map for the workmen, who've already made way for paths and bushes and even created a small pond. The grounds still have a chill, though, 'specially when a body's walking alone. I pass a young vine, newly planted close to the wall, and for no good reason I'm set thinking on Will. I've not let myself dwell on Will Hammer this many a moon. But looking on these tiny vines, I'm minded of his big hands when he tended those at Sheen – and the easy way we had of walking together of an evening. A person could always feel safe with Will and trust him for his straightness. You only had to look at his good, honest face to know Will Hammer weren't one to deal in lies. It still pains me I shall never more see him. Course, I never did pay heed to that tom-fool stuff about us being wed.

It is rare for William to come to my chamber in the afternoon, and I'm flustered he should find me so dishevelled. As I rise from the bed, he says, "You're pale, Dorothy. You're in need of fresh air." I note the concern in his voice. "Come," he says, "walk with me in the gardens and see the progress we've made."

The men are working on a series of gravel paths, twisting this way and that and destined to separate the pristine flowerbeds. Tulips and foxgloves are already beginning to bud, and each rectangular bed is surrounded by an arrangement of miniature box hedges. All is perfectly ordered. As a girl, I admired gardens left in wild profusion like the one my father enjoyed at St Malo. Now, I prefer the comfort of a careful garden – a sign that even amid the chaos of human existence, we can occasionally control nature. The herbs, too, are flourishing, laid in neat rows of mint and sage, borage and basil. As I examine a pot of newly flowering garlic, William says, "I fear this desperate melancholy may throw away your health, Dorothy. You must learn to moderate your grief." I pluck some basil and rub it between my fingers to release the perfume. We walk on, and William points out where he shall place his intended water features. After a moment, he says, "I too mourn our children, and as deeply as you. But through it all, I believe we must submit and trust in God's will." *Submit and trust.* How he's changed from the questioning young man I once knew.

At one end of the garden there's a canal surrounding a tiny wooded island, reached by a series of little bridges. "I shall reinforce the bridges," William says, "but the isle is too thick to clear." On the way back to the house, he says: "There is much poverty and disease in this world, Dorothy. When you think how God has dealt with us, what he has given, we should surely fall on our knees. If Christianity teaches us one thing, it's the need to moderate our passions." This little lecture could have been delivered by Aunt Gargrave.

As is his habit, William has arranged his study at the far end of the house. But even though the walls are solid, the raised voices of William and Mr Swift, locked in dispute, carry. The entire household is alert to their arguments, which in this past year have been many.

Martha says, "Why does Mr Swift not quit the house and return to Dublin instead of constantly threatening to do so?" Indeed, the relationship between these two men defies explanation. It's obvious that in calmer moments, Mr Swift is in awe of William. The few times we've talked, he has expressed this with all the enthusiasm of a young man towards a distinguished mentor. And William, I know, enjoys wearing that particular cap. He's pleased with Mr Swift's writing skills, and intrigued by his fierce – and oft unruly – intellect. William is also, I suspect, disquieted by it. That, I believe, is the reason he refuses to eat with the younger man. Ever used to holding forth to a captive audience through an entire meal, William would surely find it hard to welcome a rival orator at table, especially one with such a sharp and cutting wit.

"The problem with Jonathan," he said recently, "is his inability to temper his thoughts." When I pointed out those thoughts were oft of a unique nature, William's reply was heated. "His ideas come tumbling out completely unchecked and oft in the most offensive manner. He's yet to learn the art of listening." My own experience of Mr Swift has been more favourable. I've taken to spending time in the new library, a sad room, still awaiting the arrival of William's books from Sheen. Sitting there amongst the rows of empty shelves brings an odd relief. Since no one usually comes, I've had little need to hide my grief – which still at moments overwhelms me. So it was a surprise to twice find Mr Swift there. Despite my craving for solitude, on both occasions I've been drawn into a discussion on literature. Mr Swift's knowledge is extensive, but he has paid careful attention to my own meagre preferences. A young man, I would say, who listens well.

This morning, carefully crossing the rickety bridge and onto the tiny island, I hope to be alone. One of the garden boys has cleared a small patch of earth for me, hidden by trees and bushes from the main gardens. We were surprised to find an ancient bench, a sign, perhaps, that someone else, a generation or so ago, chose this very spot to sit and contemplate.

I've gathered a good number of small stones for my purpose. Kneeling, I fashion them into two hearts on the smooth earth. When Jack was a small boy, he was ever trying, and failing, to draw a perfect heart. He'll not mind if mine too are a little lopsided. I've brought flowers. Just as I finish arranging them, a voice behind me says, "Lady Dorothy, may I assist you?" Mr Swift proffers his hand and helps me to my feet. I wonder how long he's been standing there. We sit together on the bench in silence.

Finally, feeling the need to offer some explanation, I say: "They are in memory of my dead children, the flowers." When Mr Swift doesn't respond, I add, "My son is somewhere at the bottom of the river, and my daughter lies alone in a cold tomb in the Abbey at Westminster."

Mr Swift says: "And you felt the need to create this small memorial." He sounds genuinely moved. "My father died before I was born," he tells me, "and my mother gave me over to my uncle's care. I was put to sleep in a tiny room at the top of the house. I remember feeling very alone. There were no paintings of my father. I had to imagine how he might have looked. So I built a little shrine to him and put it aside my bed. It was made of odds and ends, but I believed it brought us closer."

All this said in tones more tempered than usual. "Life has dealt you many blows, Lady Dorothy. Your countenance is ever sad."

I remember my mother running her finger along my cheek and saying the same. "I've lived through sad times," I tell him, "but I've also lived a life of much advantage. I've failed to fully appreciate this and the Lord has seen fit to punish me by removing my most precious treasures." *Why am I telling him this?*

Mr Swift says: "We mortals are tossed on a wild sea. I think the Lord knows you to be the good woman you are. And, if I may say so, a strong one. How lucky your children were to have such a mother." For all his bluster, Mr Swift is capable of showing deep and unexpected understanding.

In my chamber, I confide the morning's adventures to Jane. Ever practical, she says: "You were out there without your shawl, my lady? You should have taken me with you to help." She doesn't comment on what must surely seem to her an odd way to honour my children. She is, however, less accommodating on the subject of Mr Swift.

"Begging your pardon, my lady, but I fear he's not polite company for a lady of your standing."

"What an absurd notion, Jane! What exactly is 'a lady of my standing'? Someone so removed from the world, she cannot appreciate interesting conversation?"

Jane reddens. "I just meant Mr Swift is a lowly and uncouth sort of person compared to you and Sir William." I turn away so Jane shall not be aware of my extreme irritation.

Despite the distance from London, here at Moor Park, we are seldom lacking guests. The King has visited several times – usually unexpected – seeking William's counsel. Although still taciturn and slightly remote, he's no longer the shy, awkward young Dutchman I remember. There's a newfound authority to his bearing; a steeliness to his voice. But his old dislike of ceremony still stands and he is easy with whatever state he may find us. He's told me more than once: "I am here for your company, not your table."

Today, he's accompanied by his boyhood friend, Hans Bentinck, the newly created Earl of Portland, known in Court circles as 'The Wooden Dutchman', reflecting an austere and unbending nature.

But at table, both men are relaxed, the Earl enough to joust playfully with Martha over what he sees as her decision not to remarry. "You left many a broken heart amongst my countrymen," he tells her. "Even now there are those at The Hague would walk the waters if you should crook your finger."

Martha blushes and declares no man ever wrote her words of sufficient ardour. "Else," she says, "I might have been tempted."

The men are on their way to Newmarket, where, says the King, they shall, "race horses, gamble our money away, and get reeling drunk every night, to prove to my English subjects I am, after all, truly one of them!" I ask after the Queen, expecting the usual half-puzzled look and to be told she can be found 'engaged in household matters'. I'm surprised when the King says, "During our campaign in Ireland, the Government was entirely in her hands. She wanted of experience, but she attended all council meetings and conducted herself well." He sounds truly proud. But the Irish campaign was hard for her. "She'd a natural great sadness to see her husband and her father engaged in battle." He gave orders, he says, that King James was not to be hurt. "It's better the Queen knows her father to be chased into exile in France than dead by the hand of my army."

As we repair to the withdrawing room, the King takes me aside. "The Queen misses you, Lady Temple. She doesn't easily find friends. She would be overjoyed to welcome you when you are next in London." Dropping a curtsy, I assure him I should be honoured.

Before leaving, the King is anxious to see the gardens. "You have brought a small piece of my country alive in England," he tells William. "If only I could fly home like a bird, I would give a hundred thousand guilders for that." As we stand outside the house and survey the whole panorama of William's plantings, the King says, "In fact, I would give two hundred thousand guilders to be back there."

Martha, expressing tiredness, doesn't walk with us. She drops a deep curtsy to the King and a less formal one to the Earl, treating him to an amused smile as she walks away. Even at her mature age, Martha is still shrewdly adept in the art of flirting.

As William and the King stride through the gardens, the Earl and I follow at a distance. He compliments me on our hospitality. "His Majesty enjoys the tranquillity here," he says. "In London, his demeanour is usually dour."

This blessed tranquillity is rudely broken by children's laughter and a small shriek as Esther runs from one of the greenhouses carrying a basket of tomatoes and pursued by a young garden boy. She stops, flustered, when she sees us. "This, my lord, is Esther Johnson," I say. Quickly recovering her composure, the child gives a solemn little curtsy before walking back to the house in dignified fashion.

"Amazing," says the Earl, staring after her. "The likeness."

I'm stunned by this comment. Is the entire Court aware of the situation? With heavy heart, I repeat my chosen mantra: "Yes, she does bear an odd resemblance to my husband's family, even though she is no relation." As I say it, I feel shame at knowing the Earl must be aware of the truth.

The Earl himself blushes, searches for words. "Well," he says, "I was indeed struck... that is, there is... I think... indeed a likeness. To Lady Giffard, I mean. A great likeness."

I remember, when I first glimpsed the baby wrapped in Bridget's cloak, thinking how little she resembled her fair-haired mother. Martha was unwell. William would not permit me to send for a doctor. The cause of Martha's malaise was unknown, to me, at least. Sitting here alone in my chamber, I should like God to wipe my mind blank, to rid me of the power of thought. But I'm compelled to piece together this horror that has lodged in my head.

The letter, read secretly, all those years ago in Brussels. A letter written by William and addressed to his sister. *I feel the blood in my veins grow warm – love returning to kindle a violent flame*. Were those not 'words of sufficient ardour'? I recall being overcome with guilt at reading them. But was the guilt truly mine? *Oh, dear Lord, I beg you cleanse my spirit of these unworthy and wicked thoughts.*

Hans Bentinck was right – why has Martha never remarried, despite numerous suitable opportunities?

Is it not entirely normal for a young widow to wish to remain forever in the bosom of her family after such tragic loss? There are a thousand such examples. Could this outrage that twists through my mind be no more than base jealousy for a relationship forged by birth in which I could never be a part?

Almighty God, please help me.

As soon as the coach is out of sight, I go straight to Martha's chamber. They've gone into the town, William, Martha and Bridget. Something regarding a new printing shop for William's essays; I was barely listening.

As always, Martha's room is pristine. Books neatly piled, a gown placed carefully over the back of a chair, correspondence sorted into separate piles on her bureau. I look through the papers: notes to be answered, bills to be paid, letters for the carrier. I open the drawers of her dresser, the chest where she keeps her finest gowns, the cupboard next to her bedside. I have no shame.

A week ago, William talked of our duty to put in order our wills. Martha said she would make a draft that very evening. I open the bureau drawer. A sheath of poems Martha has tried her hand at; her small prayer book; old letters from her father; William's translation of Virgil, prepared especially for her. Some papers carefully folded. I open them up.

MY WILL: MARTHA LADY GIFFARD

There are many large bequests, some crossed through and changed. I flick through to the final pages:

> *...My two agate cups and saucers to Betty, oldest daughter of... To Betty also, my large Indian teapot... My pendulum clock and some pins to Mrs Burrrows... To my serving woman, Pritchard, my chocolate cup I usually drink in. The picture*

of our Saviour and the Virgin over the chimney piece in my chamber to my niece Becky Giffard...

To Esther Johnson, I give ten pounds with the hundred pounds I put into the exchequer for her life and all the interest that shalt have accrued thereof. I also bequeath her my portrait by Sir Peter Lely that hangs in my bed chamber that she may sometimes think on me.

I push the papers back in the drawer, unwilling to have them in my hands. Like a blind person, I feel my way towards the door.

My heart is beating as though it would escape my body. On the stairs, I meet Mr Swift – with Esther. The child gives a pretty bob and wishes me good day. Mr Swift says: "We are off to tackle Chaucer, Lady Dorothy. We've some raucous reading ahead."

William's study will be clear for an hour.

Unlike his sister, William is not well organised. Papers and books lay wherever – on chairs, tables and even the floor. Where to start? As I search the drawers and bookshelves, I tell myself over and over that a child is not to blame for its beginnings. Despite the beliefs of the pastor at Sheen, a child is innocent.

I've need to stop. To sit for a moment and calm myself. The chair by the window looks out onto the gardens and William's French sundial, newly arrived. He is enchanted with it. I force myself to dwell on that boyish enthusiasm, still intact after all life has dealt him. That barely contained buoyancy that won my heart so completely all those years ago. But try as I may, these things no longer have power to move me. I look across at the pile of letters on his desk. For a second, I'm tempted to walk away. To shut the door. But I cannot shut my mind. The need to know is stronger than the fear of knowing.

Carefully placed beside his other letters is an envelope. Inside is William's will.

God's holy name be praised, he's written. *His will be done...* I skim through the list of bequests, substantial ones for Marie and the children. Martha too taken good care of. Smaller thoughtful gifts for servants and relatives. But almost everything, it seems, should William die first, is bequeathed to me.

Except at the end. One sentence: '*To Esther Johnson, the lease on my lands in County Wicklow, Ireland*'.

I hurry along the hallway, wishing to encounter no one. But I'm not quick enough for the cook. She would discuss the day's menu, a daily ritual she enjoys. I listen numbly, nodding assent at every sentence. What would she think if I were to scream at her to stop talking? Despite a good fire, my chamber is cold. I lay on the bed, pulling the covers closely about me. Although it's not yet noon, I feel a great need to sleep.

But sleep does not come.

Jane says, "If you're really set on leaving so quick, my lady, should we try to get word to Pall Mall? The Lord knows what state we'll find there after all this time."

I tell her I should like to leave tomorrow. "We'll arrange everything once we are there."

"You're very pale, my lady. Are you well? This late-summer heat can play havoc with our dispositions." Despite myself, at these simple words of concern, I begin to weep. Jane is at my side in an instant. "What ails you, Lady Dorothy? Please tell me."

I've a sudden urge to unburden everything. The tears come freely now. "Dear Jane, always my friend." I take her hands. But how can I tell her of this anguish and uncertainty? Things too painful to confide.

At supper, Martha and William express surprise at this sudden departure. Martha thinks the diversions of London may be beneficial. William disagrees: "I would strongly advise against making the journey in this present heat," he says. I can scarce look at them.

After the meal, Mr Swift joins us at cards and I partner him. I've no concentration. The cards blur before my eyes. I should like to excuse myself and go to my chamber. As it is, I play badly. My hands are shaking; my head aches. Mr Swift and I lose time and again. I long for the evening to be over.

As we leave the withdrawing room, I apologise to Mr Swift. "I think your mind was elsewhere," he says. Then, making sure he is not overheard, he adds: "I promise to take good care of your little altar, Lady Dorothy. I understand your need to leave this house, but I hope we shall meet again." And he is gone.

I'm scarce in my chamber before William is there too. "Let us talk, dearest." How often have I longed to hear those words? Now, they are of little import.

"I'm tired," I say. "We've a long journey tomorrow."

William moves towards me. Takes my hands in his. "Sit, please, Dorothy. Tell me what ails you."

Everything, William. Everything ails and disquiets me.

We sit together on the bed. I say: "There's nothing in the least wrong. I've need of London air, that is all."

"I cannot forbid you to leave," William says. "I've been wed to you long enough to know the folly of that." He squeezes my hand. "But I think this sudden desire to run away is wrong, dearest. It will not heal the hurt in your soul. As I said lately, however hard we find the bitter losses we've suffered, if we're to survive, it's vital we moderate our grieving."

I move slightly away from him. "Yes, William. I remember. What you said was 'we must moderate our *passions*'. My voice is shaking. "Have you ever done that, William, moderated your passions?" The words hang in the air. We sit and stare at each other.

"How can you ask such a thing?" he finally says. "Tell me what you mean."

How can I tell him what I mean when I'm unsure myself?

"Throughout our marriage, I've tried to curb those passions that are unworthy of my regard for you," William says. "Isn't that obvious to you?" He sounds utterly sincere. "I've struggled, I admit, with my love of gaming. But in all else you may trust me. I've striven to live up to the love and esteem I have for you."

Oh, dear God, is it possible he speaks the truth? Could I, after all, be completely deluded? '*To Esther Johnson, the lease on my lands in County Wicklow, Ireland*'.

I say, "Nothing is obvious to me, William. I want to believe you, but I fear you have betrayed and defiled our marriage. I really must go to London. There's no help for it." For a long moment, he stares at me, stunned. As he walks towards the door, I long to call him back. To hear him tell me again these thoughts are untrue. To have him comfort me. But I've finally given voice to the demons that have for so long tormented me, and they are out there between us.

PALL MALL

1692–1695

This house has been so shut up, I'm thinking we'll never rid it of the musty stink. I says to my lady: "We could open windows if there were any good air about." She bids me do so anyway. But then there's the noise – street sellers shouting loud enough to deafen a donkey. "Pall Mall's surely changed since we've been gone," I say. Seems several low persons are plying their wares right next to the house. *"Pins, pretty pins, pretty maids"* – the woman's voice like a ship's siren. Someone else is playing jarring notes on a penny whistle, urging folk to buy his brooms and brushes.

I put it down to royal doings. With the Court moved to Kensington, I'm supposing there's little need to keep our street pristine. My lady don't seem concerned. "It's lively indeed, Jane," she says. And she leans out the window. Next moment, she has me running to fetch a rabbit from an old man dragging a brace on a stick. "And onions too, Jane. Tell the kitchen we shall have rabbit pie." It's been like this since we arrived. My lady has us all rushing this way and that. Servants rounded up and brought back in a blink. She can't stay quiet. "There's much to be done, Jane, and so little time." I've seen these restless moods afore, and they oft herald a bout of my lady's disorders.

I know Sir William was worried. As we left |Moor Park, he voiced as much. "I fear she's unwell, Jane. Send a messenger if I'm needed. And make sure she sups well. She's grown so thin." Wish I knew what put my lady so out of sorts. I'm wondering if it were that Mr Swift, with his vicious tongue. He's someone who dearly loves upending the apple cart.

I stuff the filthy creatures in my basket, full of vermin, I'll be bound. And I'd warrant the same applies to the peddler. As I drop the coins into his dirty palms, I try not to touch him. But the man grabs my sleeve. "I'll have a good young goat tomorrow, mistress – randy as they come." And opening his toothless mouth, he's coughing and laughing and wheezing all over me.

Soon as I get in the door, a maid's telling me a note's come for my lady. "Well, give it to her then," I snap. I'm in no mood for niceties. We're still not fixed on a suitable cook, and down in the kitchens, no one wants to prepare this rabbit. One kitchen wench says rabbit fur gives her the itch, and another is too timid to contemplate the blood. I say, and firmly, "Lady Dorothy shall have her rabbit pie." And rolling up my sleeves, I call for boning knife and cleaver. I've watched my father skin and clean a rabbit many a time. As I cut off the feet and the head and tail, the rank smell of the poor creature makes me retch. I cover this by saying, "It's like taking off a jacket." It's not, though. This animal's tough as old boots. I grab the shoulders and struggle to pull the skin down over what's left of the poor back legs. When I slice the belly open and reach in to pull out the innards, I have to look away. God forgive me for defiling such an innocent little creature. The young wenches are pale as parchment. Now for the heart and lungs; I plunge my hand in and cough to cover the waves of nausea. I'm supposing I must scrape the fat and sinews away. The knife is barely sharp enough. "There," I say as brusquely as I'm able, "you've got a good load of lean meat. Simmer for an hour with bayleaf and then make your pastry, and mind you bake the best pie ever."

I scrub and scrub at my hands, but the smell of that poor little thing stays with me.

My lady comes looking for me. "Jane, I've had a note from the Queen asking me to attend her at Kensington House. Come, help me choose a gown."

"She wants you today, my lady?" And when Lady Dorothy confirms this, I say, "The kitchens are preparing a good rabbit pie, like you fancied. Can you not take time to eat?"

And my lady says, "No, Jane – I must go. You have it." After my lady's gone, I go down to the kitchens. The pie is ready, and lovely and rich in colour. I congratulate the two wenches, who are justly proud. But there's no way any of us can contemplate a bite. "Take it out to the grooms," I say. "They've always got hearty appetites. They'll think Yuletide's come early."

The note is clear. I must take the back entrance at Kensington House – where there shall be someone waiting to show me the way. Why should the Queen desire such subterfuge? As often of late, I am aware of my heart pounding through the bodice of my gown. There's a moment of confusion when we find no one at the gate. My coachman will not leave until I'm safely inside. There's a bell. Someone comes immediately: "Lady Temple?"

Up some steep steps and along a corridor, then another. More steps. I almost stumble. I am breathing hard. Now, I'm in a dimly lit hall. A door is opened. The Queen comes straight to me. Like her husband, there is no ceremony. Nonetheless, I'm surprised when she embraces me. "Lady Dorothy, I have been so wishing for your company." I'm unsure what to do. Taking a moment to catch my breath, I look around. After the dimness of the hallways, all is light, airy, with rose-coloured curtains and pleasing French furniture. Chinese bowls, filled with flowers, are scattered about the room. It's in total contrast to the heavy claustrophobia of Whitehall Palace.

The Queen asks how I fare. How can I possibly answer? I remark on the beauty of these chambers. "The King mentioned they were arranged entirely to your instructions, Your Majesty."

"I'm sorry to bring you here in secret. The King is away and with him gone, I trust no one." I note the anxiety in her voice. "Everywhere is so full of intrigue." What is most troubling, it seems, is her relationship with her sister, Princess Anne. "She's completely under the spell of her courtiers, some of whom I believe would not hesitate to do us harm in hope of returning my father to the throne."

At Moor Park, with the comings and goings of William's friends, I've heard much talk of Princess Anne's increasing reliance on such companions. "Do you know the names of those you think would plot against you?" I ask the Queen.

She has suspicions, she says. "But I would not further alienate my sister by demanding she rid herself of these persons."

I say, "Sometimes the Lord calls on us to face a hard truth, and to act on it." I remember the four names constantly mentioned by William and his friends as enemies of the King and Queen. Should I tell her that her suspicions are right? William, ever cautious of Court intrigues, would advise against such rashness. But William is not here.

"I hesitate to intrude in such a delicate matter," I say, "but I'll write something for Your Majesty that may help you find the truth and share it with the King."

At the mention of her husband, the Queen comes and sits by me. As always, her words are intimate and direct. "I'm trying to understand this man who is the King, and also my husband," she says. "He is not true to me, Lady Dorothy. Did you know that?"

What should I answer? I've heard rumours that the King's mistress, Betty Villiers, followed him from The Hague to London and is now set in a house close to where we sit.

The Queen says: "I believe I was the last person to know. I fear it's because I've failed to give him a son." I see she is close to tears.

Would it help her to hear my own fears, so much worse than anything she could imagine? I think not. "The King obviously has high regard for you," I say. "He made this plain at his recent visit to Moor Park."

She stares down at her hands, folded in her lap. "He no longer comes to me at night," she says.

I sense her need to find some explanation for this pain. "I believe there is oft a difference, Your Majesty, in how a man and a woman perceive love," I say. "For us, it tends to encompass everything, our minds and our bodies. Men are perhaps more able to separate the two." I think a moment before continuing. "I had an aunt once, who said that for certain men, the chase is all, and when conquest is accomplished, they feel compelled to move on." Even as I speak, I know these to be empty, meaningless words. To put the King in this category is false indeed. It in no way fits the nature of that straightforward, reserved Dutchman. Am I then speaking of William? His story, I think, is infinitely more complicated. I've offered the Queen a pencil sketch, something easily erased. In truth, I have no idea why human beings do what they do.

The Queen seems satisfied with my little homily. She thanks me profusely. "I'm so happy you are returned to London," she says. "We shall see each other often. Now, come and let me show you the other rooms. Come and see the portrait Mr Murray has made of the King." And she leads me to her bedchamber.

Before leaving, I write down the four names and hand them to the Queen. "The first is most important, Your Majesty. The Princess should dismiss her, and without delay." Then I remember something: "When my daughter was a small child, she used to call Betty Villiers '*The Squinting Dragon*'." For the first time this evening, the Queen laughs.

In the coach back to Pall Mall, I marvel that hours have passed and I have not thought once of those at Moor Park. Then thinking of them, I spend the rest of the journey remembering.

There is another note from William. As in previous ones, he is anxious for me to return.

Dearest,

You are too long away. I trust all is well. Your brief letters tell me nothing. Do you remember those you wrote when we were young and unwed? You bade me burn them. Did you know I kept every one of them? They are locked in my escritoire. The reading of them still brings pleasure – and pain, too, when I think of all that has passed. Dearest, after all we've endured, it is important we face the future together, as one. We must end this rift that has come from I know not where. Those terrible words you uttered at Moor Park stung my heart. If I have caused you pain, I've done so unwittingly. I would come to you. But I'll not do so unless you desire it. You have my heart. God willing, I still have yours.

William has written me a love letter and it has come too late.

Jane pulls back the curtains in my chamber. "I do believe it's starting to snow," she says. "You should dress warm today, my lady." The first snow of winter. Yuletide will soon be upon us and William will expect me to return to Moor Park. Should I write and tell him of my poor health? I think not. A heart that beats too wildly, an occasional dizzy spell – these are as nothing compared to the debilitating and ever-increasing fits of gout he suffers. But I'm determined never to return to that house.

These back stairs have become so familiar, I could probably climb them blindfold. It's always the same young girl waiting at the gate. Small and unsmiling, she's never once looked me in the eye. I'm wondering what exactly I should tell the Queen. William's last letter was frank: *"Tis said the Princess Anne has written to her father begging his forgiveness and pledging allegiance to his return to the throne'.*

William has no idea I reveal the contents of his letters to the Queen. It is I who have steered our correspondence in this direction. With vague promises of returning to Moor Park, I've sought his opinion on a host of political matters. How manipulative I've become. It saddens my heart that marriage has taught me the necessity for such deviousness.

These musings are quickly forgotten once I'm in the Queen's presence. "You are pale, Your Majesty. I fear you are unwell."

The Queen denies it. "The only thing I suffer is fatigue."

She's arranged a supper here in her chambers; a cold collation of salads, meats and fruit. There's also a good quantity of wine. A small table is drawn close to the fire. As the heat of the flames and the ruby wine warms us, the Queen's colour returns. She tells me the King is once more preparing to leave, this time for Flanders. "It seems he's only happy when on campaign," she says. "I thought at least we should have the winter together. I fear I've not the strength nor will to pass more months alone with his scrapping ministers." I mention one or two I feel she may trust, but the Queen looks at me wearily: "I cannot think on it," she says. "I'm in need of rest." We have both barely touched our food. "Would you forgive me, Lady Dorothy, if I should rest for a moment?"

"Of course, Your Majesty." And, rising, I prepare to leave.

The Queen says: "No. Please do not go. Stay with me for a while." I'm reminded of the child I saw at her wedding. So in need of affection, reassurance. She must now be more than thirty. And with a start, I realise my own Nan would not be far behind. My daughter – the woman I will never know. How, I wonder, would she look now? She would be a woman with her own tastes and interests. Would she have found her heart's mate? My beloved Nan, snatched away without warning or reason. "Shall I call for your ladies, Your Majesty?" I ask. "To help you disrobe?"

She declines the offer, lying stretched on her bed. A long, pale statue. "Come, sit next to me," she says. This bed is enormous and hung with the most extravagant oriental fabrics. I sink down amidst silk pillows, and the Queen reaches for my hand. "Do you ever think of death?" she asks.

I tell her it's frequently in my mind. "Having lost those dearest to me, I pray to be reunited."

"I still pray for my mother," she says. "Every day. And every day I pray God make me ready for my own death as I ought to be." She tells me she's already written full instructions for her funeral. There is calm resignation in her voice.

"You are young," I tell her. "You have much life to live before you embrace such thoughts. Think how devastated the King would be to lose you."

I lean across and, forgetting for a moment this is the Queen, I push the hair back from her face and stroke her brow, as I would a child. As I used to do for my daughter when sleep eluded her. She says, "You were right, Lady Dorothy, when you said love is… indefinable. In his way, I do believe the King loves me. But as a companion, united in our thoughts. Not as a woman." We are both silent. Then she says: "In truth, even before the Villiers woman, he came to me very little, and only, I think, to produce an heir. I thought I might be repulsive to him."

I stroke the inside of her arm, her wrists. She takes my hand and moves it to the delicate white skin at the top of her breasts. The Queen's body is no longer firm, but her breasts pushed up by the bodice of her gown are as round and smooth as those of a young girl. As I gently caress this fragile spot, I'm aware of her vulnerability, of all our vulnerability. She reaches up and, pulling my face towards her, kisses me on the mouth. It is a chaste kiss, that a daughter might give a mother, but it stirs me to my depths. How long since I felt the sweet, soft warmth of another's lips against mine?

We lay close together, side by side. I think of the dour, unappealing Betty Villiers. At least she has produced no children with which to taunt the Queen. I close my eyes, and, immediately, the face of Esther Johnson swims before me.

After a moment, I say, "I will leave you to rest, Your Majesty." She does not reply. I lean across to look at her. She is asleep.

PALL MALL AND MOOR PARK

The Queen is ailing. At first, it were thought to be the pox, but then she rallied. This morning, though, down in the kitchens, there's fresh rumours of fever. The King's said to have cancelled his journeying and refuses to leave her side.

Lady Dorothy's anxious, unable to settle. Starting a new needlepoint, then discarding it, setting out alone on walks across the park. I finally say: "I'm thinking no news might well be good news, my lady." I don't mention the rumours in the kitchens.

"Could it really be so, Jane?"

Truth is, I'm doubting it. Once you call for nine medics, seems to me there's not much hope. Lord knows what hideous cures they've all set up. Remembering young Nan, I shudder at the thought. But knowing my lady's disquiet, I say, "Chances are she'll be right as rain afore they put forth a bulletin."

"Yes, Jane." She's reassured. "That's why we've not heard. She is recovering."

My lady has refused to leave London. "I'll wait till Her Majesty is well." It's not a decision I'm quiet with. No. I think a wife's place is at her husband's hearth. 'Specially at Yuletide and with Sir William ailing and all. Seems to me things have got quick out of hand, like that unwise outing to the coffee house. No good regretting things later.

We knew the news were bad when we saw them black-edged bulletins. My lady sent me running for one. Reading it, she says: "It's definitely the pox, Jane. Prayers are being said. If only I could go to her."

I note her red eyes and pale skin. "You're unwell yourself, Lady Dorothy. Let me get a fire built in your chamber so's you can rest a while."

She's not having it. Declares she'll take the carriage and ride to Kensington. "I will wait there till we know more," she says.

My candle's been run down for more than an hour, but I can't sleep. I'm tossing like a turtle in the pot. My head's taken with more than that poor queen. It's Lady Dorothy worrying my mind. Three hours she waited in that coach, and not one scrap of news. I was down in the hall when she returned. She'd been without her gloves and her poor fingers were froze. I warmed them between my hands, chiding myself for my rough palms.

I must have dozed off. I'm wondering what time it can be. It's still dark, but the hall clock is striking what sounds like mid-morning. It takes a moment to realise it's not the chiming clock that's waked me. No. It's the low, monotonous clanging of St James's chapel bell. I should rouse myself and put on my garments, but my bones ache in every place. I'm supposing that's how you know you're old, when you wake feeling worse than when you went to your bed. There's a tap at the door and in comes my lady clad only in her night robe. I'm up then all right and flinging my shawl about her. "Come now, Lady Dorothy," I says, "it's cold indeed to be about at this time of night and without your shoes." I try to lead her back to her chamber, but she stays rooted. I beg her at least to sit. "You'll be catching your death."

"Death is already about us, Jane. Can you not feel it?"

It's snowed solid for three days, but there's no children to be seen laughing and pelting each other. No. There's a silence 'bout this whole city, and all the coaches shrouded in black.

There's been word we might lose the King too. 'Tis said when the Queen died, he fell down in a faint, his grieving being so deep. I've always deemed that Dutchman a bit of a cold fish. But as Will used to say, you can't always trust what the eye sees.

My lady's stayed mostly in her chamber, sitting in the window, staring out at the royal gardens. I tell her there's folks crying in the street. "London loved her more than she imagined," she says. And that's the most she's uttered these several days. She declined to attend the funeral, even though there was a royal invitation. "I prefer to remember her as she was, Jane." Sir William too was not in attendance, owing to his ailments. I'm more than a bit shamed this family weren't represented. I'm thinking it's not proper.

Drawing back my lady's shutters, I say, "I surely wish you'd permit me send for the medic."

Lady Dorothy's reply is same as it's been all week: "I'm perfectly fine. Just sad at the state of things." If you ask me, this is more than her usual attack of melancholy. There's dark circles round her eyes and an unhealthy pallor to her cheeks. My lady has had the pox and, far as I know, a body can't suffer it twice. But I've wrote to Sir William anyways, even though it's not my place: *Please forgive these forward words… without worrying you unduly…* It took more than an hour to write. My fingers are that gnarled with pain, I could scarce hold the quill.

She's not left her bed for two days. Her sleep's fitful at best. I sat with her all last night. Once, she woke and said: "The King saw Nan was drowning. How brave of him to try to rescue her." She was sweating something terrible. I passed a damp cloth over her face and arms. She grabbed me by the wrist. "But the sea claimed her in the end," she said.

"Them dreams can oft seem real," I told her. I talked softly to calm her. "Reckon that queen was lucky having a friend like you. Reckon she knew it, too." I stayed pressing the cool cloth to her brow till she drifted to sleep. I put my candle close on the table by her bed so's I'd note any change.

This morning, the fever's dropped. No matter, I've made up my mind: I'll send a groom for the medic, with or without my lady's permission. I'm in search of a lad when I see the carrier coming. There's a note from Sir William, just a few words: *'Bring her to Moor Park, Jane – and at once.*

At dinner, she's taking soup. I've been worrying myself all morning how I'll persuade her to leave. Turns out, I'd no needs. When I tell her Sir William might desire her company seeing as how he's properly ailing, she straight ways says: "Yes, Jane. You are right. I have no more strength to stay alone."

It takes an age to get her to the coach. "Hold on to me, my lady. I shan't let you fall." The maids are all in attendance, along with a couple of curious neighbours. Knowing how she guards her privacy, I shield her best I can. "One step up and you'll be seated and at rest." I drape the blanket about her person and sit myself opposite. She goes straight to sleep.

When we get to Chelsea, my lady wakes and looks out. "We must visit my brother Henry," she says.

Gentle as I can, I remind her Mr Henry's been dead these years. "He's gone to a better place."

She looks at me sharply. "Do you still believe in such a place, Jane?" Knowing this blasphemous talk is down to her ailing, I don't say nothing. I just lean over and tuck the blanket closer round her. "Come and sit by me, Jane. I'm so very cold." I move across and my lady puts her head on my shoulder like a child, and in a blink, she's back asleep. Despite her thinness, her body leaning against me is heavy. I feel the pain go up from my shoulder to my neck, and my arm is numb. But I daresn't move. I'd not disturb this peaceful rest for the world.

Sir William and Miss Martha are quick in the carriageway

when we fetch up at Moor Park. One each side of her, and with the aid of a young maid, they help my lady into the house, Sir William murmuring to her throughout, "There, my dearest. You're at home. You shall soon be comfortably settled."

As he takes my lady to her chamber, Miss Martha turns on me. "You should have brought her sooner, Jane. And why were no doctors consulted?"

I'm too weary to defend myself. "I'm very sorry, Miss Martha," I say. And as she glares at me, I realise yet again I've addressed her wrongly.

Sir William and Miss Martha take turns sitting with Lady Dorothy during the day, and Sir William and me do it at night. Two medics can't be sure of the cause. They both want to bleed her. Even though my lady be weak, she's strong enough to refuse. Sir William can't persuade her neither. "Promise me, William," I hear her say, "you will not let them touch me."

Miss Martha can't credit it. "Why will Dorothy not fight?" she asks.

Everyone's creeping about the house. Even Mr Swift's not his usual bumptious self. "I'm truly saddened to see that good lady thus," he says to me. "I'm composing a poem for her."

I'm thinking fat lot of good that is. Down in the kitchens, young Hetty's near to tears. "Do you think they'll let me go to her, Jane? Perhaps I might be of assistance."

I promise she shall go in soon as my lady's a tad better. "She'll surely welcome a visit from you, Hetty."

Sitting with my lady at night, her eyes are open but she says little. I talk to her, quiet like, bringing forth all I can from happy memories of Nan and Jack. She asks for her grandmother's little miniature, and clasps it to her. Just as I'm tiptoeing out in the dawn light, I look back, and she says: "The end comes so soon, Jane."

The Frenchwomen have been sent for, and the granddaughters. Though Sir William swears we shan't lose her. "I shall not let it happen." His moustache is unkempt and his waistkit crumpled. He hasn't slept all week.

My lady's stopped talking altogether. It's hard to tell if she's asleep or awake. This morning, I'm kept from the room. Only the family are permitted, which I know is proper, but if I could just once see her. I pray someone's holding her hand, assuring her the Lord be with her. Soon as I'm alone in my chamber, I drop to my knees, pleading with God not to take her.

I've been hovering by her chamber all day. Nothing to be heard. Nothing to be done. I sit myself down on the chest in the hall, my mind properly numb. I'm woken by the French clock chiming midnight, and the sound of Sir William's sobbing.

I wait till the house is sound asleep and, pulling my shawl about me, go to her chamber. The door creaks something terrible and for a moment I stand stock-still, feared to be discovered. Then I move quiet to her bed. There are candles lit everywhere, casting a good light on her pale face and beautiful hair, all spread on the pillow. I'm thinking she looks like a young woman again. All the anxiousness of these last weeks forgot. I should like to stroke her hand but remembering my place, pull back. I'm glad, though, to have these few quiet moments to gaze upon her one last time.

There are several coaches. The Frenchwomen have one to themselves. No one's keen to journey with them. We're in the last one; me, Bridget and Hetty and Mr Swift. None of us talking. Hetty weeps. She's a soft-hearted girl. I wish I could weep. It's as if everything's dried up inside me.

The Abbey at Westminster is cold and dismal. My lady never liked it. It was Sir William sought permission for Nan to rest here.

Now they're opening up the stone so's my lady can lay alongside her. It's surely what she would have wanted. The Frenchwomen are weeping. I think of poor Jack, wishing he were here aside his mother and sister. It's only a moment afore the stone is wedged in again. Sealed up. Everyone makes to leave. I hang back a bit, just to say my farewells. "You're together now," I tell her. "Safe with Nan and God." I should like to rest my cheek against the stone. That's when I finally feel the tears prick.

Sir William won't talk to no one. He's taken to his chamber. He don't even care to have Hetty with him. Sitting with her in the kitchens, she asks, "Do you think things will ever again be the same, Jane?"

I can't lie to her. "No, Hetty dear. With Lady Dorothy gone, things can never be the same." We're still there when the new in-between maid comes in. She's only about twelve and almost topples trying to do a good bob.

"Lady Giffard waits on you in the withdrawing room, Jane," she says.

Miss Martha's playing on her virginals. She don't stop. I feel properly awkward standing here, so I say, "That's sad music indeed, Miss – your ladyship."

She don't answer and it's a good long moment afore she finally stops her playing. She don't get up, or invite me to sit. She just comes straight to it. "With Lady Dorothy gone, we shall no longer have need of your services, Jane." For a moment, I'm not sure what she means.

"Will you be wanting me to go back to Pall Mall, Miss Martha?"

"I should think you might want to return to Guernsey and your family," she says.

I've known moments like this before, when you feel like you're watching yourself from somewhere else. I'm still aware of my head throbbing, though – and my heart dancing about. "I've got none left in Guernsey, Miss Martha." I blurt it out, pride forgot. "If I might just speak to Sir William."

Her voice is cold. "Sir William is in deep mourning. He can see no one." Then she softens a bit. "If you're set on remaining nearby, there is surely a woman in the town who will welcome a paying guest." She don't look at me when she says this. She's busy studying her music score. "Sir William shall of course provide for you."

My mantle is packed and ready in the hall. There's a splash of sunlight through the house. Rare to see that of a February. Hetty and Mr Swift are in the driveway. "Let me find a groom to bring the carriage."

I decline Mr Swift's kind offer. "My mantle is light as a feather," I tells him. I'm determined to leave in dignified fashion.

Hetty says, "But Jane, where will you go? How will you live?" I show her the note. '*Mrs Grey, over the butcher's shop, next to the Pig and Whistle*'.

"Come and visit me, Hetty."

Walking down the driveway, I feel in the pocket of my cloak and my fingers close around my treasure, safe and sound. My own small miniature: an image of a sweet young girl with deep, sad eyes.

EPILOGUE

SIR WILLIAM TEMPLE, diplomat and essayist, died on 27th January 1669. At his request, his heart was placed in a little silver dish and buried under the sundial in the gardens of his home at Moor Park, Surrey. His body was interred in the nave of Westminster Abbey by the side of his wife, DOROTHY OSBORNE, and his daughter, DIANA. In 1722, the tomb was opened and his sister, MARTHA GIFFARD, joined the little group.

JONATHAN SWIFT returned to Dublin where in 1713 he became Dean of St Patrick's Cathedral. In 1726, he wrote his satirical masterpiece, GULLIVER'S TRAVELS.

ESTHER JOHNSON followed Swift to Ireland. The two never married but maintained a close relationship until Esther's death in 1728. Swift immortalised her in his work: A JOURNAL TO STELLA.

WILLIAM III (WILLIAM OF ORANGE) reigned until his death in 1702. He never remarried.

With thanks to the staff of the British Library Reading Rooms for their unfailing help and advice during research for this book.